Titles by Robin D. Owens

HEARTMATE
HEART THIEF
HEART DUEL
HEART CHOICE
HEART QUEST
HEART DANCE
HEART FATE
HEART CHANGE
HEART JOURNEY
HEART SEARCH
HEART SECRET
HEART FORTUNE

GHOST SEER
GHOST LAYER

Anthologies

WHAT DREAMS MAY COME
(with Sherrilyn Kenyon and Rebecca York)

HEARTS AND SWORD

GHOST LAYER

ROBIN D. OWENS

BERKLEY SENSATION, NEW YORK

THE BERKLEY PUBLISHING GROUP
Published by the Penguin Group
Penguin Group (USA) LLC
375 Hudson Street, New York, New York 10014

USA • Canada • UK • Ireland • Australia • New Zealand • India • South Africa • China

penguin.com

A Penguin Random House Company

GHOST LAYER

A Berkley Sensation Book / published by arrangement with the author

Berkley Sensation Books are published by The Berkley Publishing Group.
BERKLEY SENSATION® is a registered trademark of Penguin Group (USA) LLC.
The "B" design is a trademark of Penguin Group (USA) LLC.

For information, address: The Berkley Publishing Group,
a division of Penguin Group (USA) LLC,
375 Hudson Street, New York, New York 10014.

ISBN: 978-0-425-26891-9

PUBLISHING HISTORY
Berkley Sensation mass-market edition / September 2014

PRINTED IN THE UNITED STATES OF AMERICA

10 9 8 7 6 5 4 3 2 1

Cover art by Tony Mauro.
Cover design by George Long.
Interior text design by Kelly Lipovich.

*To my longtime friends, critique partners,
brainstormers, and all around great writers:
Cassie Miles (Kay Bergstrom) and Sharon Mignerey.
I couldn't have done this without you.*

COUNTING CROWS RHYME

One for sorrow,
Two for luck;
Three for a wedding,
Four for death;
Five for silver,
Six for gold;
Seven for a secret,
Not to be told;
Eight for heaven,
Nine for [hell];
And ten for the devil's own sell [self].

ONE

ZACH SLADE'S NEW cane had been delivered when he was gone. It was a necessity, but also a better weapon. The hook handle could snag and yank a leg. The box the cane had come in leaned against the gray rough-cut stone of the mansion where he rented the housekeeper's suite. Sticking both old and new canes as well as the box under his left arm, he unlocked the side doors to the great house. Since he'd been shot below the knee, which severed a nerve, and his left ankle and foot didn't flex, he lifted his knee high simply to walk into his apartment.

Yeah, he was disabled. Had foot drop. His career as an active peace officer, his most recent job as a deputy sheriff, was over at thirty-four.

He and his partner had pulled over a drunk driver, an ex-cop his partner had known. His partner had treated him friendly and hadn't searched him for weapons, and Zach hadn't corrected her mistake. The drunk had pulled a gun, and in a scuffle, Zach had been shot just below the knee, which shattered the bone and severed his peroneal nerve.

Instead of wallowing in anger, he had to move on to damned acceptance. He wouldn't slip back into denial again. He'd finally gotten beyond that. Maybe.

The heavy security door slammed behind him. Cool air flowed over him and he realized how sticky he was from the long two-day drive from Montana. At least his clothes fit better. He'd finally packed on more muscle after his weight loss due to the shooting.

He tossed the box and his old cane on the empty surface of the long coffee table in front of the big, brown leather couch in the living room. Then he slashed the new wooden cane through the air in fighting moves. He was learning bartitsu, the Victorian mixed-martial art that featured cane fighting.

There'd been no bartitsu studio in Montana, where he'd been called back to testify against the parole of a serial killer he'd put away a year and a half ago. He'd been gone for six days . . . had only had a single easy day before that with his new lover, Clare.

Very new lover, along with his new life—moving from Montana in the first place, finding a job and an apartment . . . and Clare.

While gone, he'd thought often enough of her to keep track of the days. They'd met only two weeks ago tomorrow, so about thirteen full days.

If he wanted to do the calculations of twelve days, twenty-some hours, and minutes and so on, he could do that. But he'd leave that up to Clare, the ex-accountant good with numbers.

Still, of the thirteen days since they'd met, he'd just been gone six. Not a good average.

He held the cane in both hands, tested it . . . yeah, he could snap it if he wanted; his upper body strength had increased what with being on crutches for three months.

The peace of his apartment wrapped around him. It had come furnished for a man, except for the small twenty-inch TV screen. He liked the couch he could sleep—or make love—on. A couple of deep chairs, the sturdy coffee table, and a thick old rug with faded colors that must have been expensive at one time.

A floral scent teased his nose and he saw a colorful bouquet of fresh flowers on the dark granite counter of the breakfast bar separating the Pullman kitchen from his living space. He didn't need flowers in his apartment, but guessed that both the old ladies—the housekeeper, Mrs. McGee, and the wealthy owner of the mansion, Mrs. Flinton—thought he did.

He'd pushed the drive because he'd wanted to see Clare, even though those seven days with her had been the weirdest in his life . . . what with Clare learning to see ghosts and help them move on and all.

During that week, Clare'd had to accept that she *wasn't* going crazy, but that she had an unexpected and unwanted psychic gift. That if she refused to believe in the gift, she'd go mad. And if she denied the psychic powers she'd inherited through her gypsy blood, she'd die.

Zach'd had to decide whether he could accept a woman with such a psychic gift, and him being able to see ghosts when he touched her . . . and that he'd work with her to send that gunfighter spook on to whatever came next.

Yes, the week with Clare had been weirder than when he'd gotten shot a few months ago. That had just been stupid and devastating.

Right now all he wanted to do was sluice off the travel grime and rest a little so he'd be in prime shape for Clare.

After a quick rap on the door between his apartment and the rest of the mansion, Zach's elderly landlady, Mrs. Flinton, opened the door and glided through it with her walker. He'd met her the same day as he'd met Clare. Mrs. Flinton had taken him under her wing when he'd arrived in Denver and insisted on renting him this place at a nominal fee.

"Zach, it's so good you're back," Mrs. Flinton said.

He grunted, then realized he wasn't among his former cop colleagues anymore and had to actually respond. "Good to see you, too. Good to be back in Denver." And the hell of it was, that was the truth. He'd left his job and the scene of the shooting in low-populated Plainsview City, Cottonwood County, Montana, and traded it for big-city Denver, and remained okay.

Mrs. Flinton stopped close and tilted her creased cheek as if for a kiss, so he gave her a peck. She smelled better than the flower bouquet, her perfume fresh and perky. "Have you called Clare yet?" she asked.

He leaned against the back of the couch. "Not yet. I just got in ten minutes ago."

Scowling at him, Mrs. Flinton poked his chest with a manicured, pale pink fingernail. "Did you two talk while you were gone?"

"We texted," he mumbled. Then he rubbed the back of his neck. His hair had grown longer than he'd ever kept it as a deputy sheriff. But his neck, and his fingers, and the whole rest of his body recalled intimately Clare's fiddling with that hair, how she liked it shaggy.

"The week with Clare before I left was pretty extreme," Zach told the older woman. Yeah, extreme with events, and incredible sex, too . . . and startling intimacy. His body yearned for Clare.

Mrs. Flinton tsked and shook her head. "You're doing the rubber band thing."

"What?"

"Coming close together, then drawing back."

"It's not only me!"

She sniffed. "Clare needs support during these first weeks of learning her new psychic gift, as I know from my own experience. There aren't many people who can or would help her."

"She's got that damn phantom dog, Enzo, to help her," Zach said.

Another finger poke and a steely gaze. "That's not the same. And you need to talk to someone about your own gift."

"I don't have a—"

"Yes, you do, and don't pretend to *me* you don't." She gave him a stern look. "When was the last time you spoke to anyone about your gift?" she persisted.

He might have thought, once, that he'd shared an extraordinary talent with his older brother. But everything had changed the day Jim had died in a drive-by shooting when Zach was twelve. None of that was Mrs. Flinton's business.

His phone buzzed, and he welcomed it, then paused when he saw Clare was calling. Mrs. Flinton noticed, too. Suppressing a sigh that his first call with Clare after he'd returned to town would be overheard, he answered, "Zach here."

"Hi, Zach." She sounded like the former accountant she was, cool and professional. Her voice still zinged down all the nerves in his body.

"I just received a call from your boss, Tony Rickman . . ." Zach lost the rest of the sentence at the pang that he was now working as a private investigator for money instead of in the public sector to serve and protect.

Mrs. Flinton elbowed him, bringing his attention back to the call.

"Sorry, missed that, say again?" Zach asked.

"Zach, do you know why Mr. Rickman would like to meet with me?"

That made him blink. "No. He didn't say anything to me about that. When did he ask you?" Zach's thumb skimmed over his phone, hovered on the icon for video calling. He wasn't ready to push it and see Clare's face if she was on visual, get slammed with more mixed feelings.

"Rickman called not more than ten minutes ago and wants me there within the hour." Her words were crisp.

"Meet her there," Mrs. Flinton said.

"I'm sorry?" Clare asked. "I didn't hear that."

Now Zach rubbed his forehead. "I just got back from Montana. If you want, I can meet you there at the top of the hour."

"Oh."

"You didn't tell her when you were coming home?" asked Mrs. Flinton.

"Zach?" Clare asked.

"No, Mrs. Flinton," Zach said loudly. "I didn't tell either of you when I'd be in. Wasn't sure of the drive myself. Get over it."

Mrs. Flinton pouted, then angled closer to Zach's phone. "Hello, Clare, you and dear ghostly Enzo-pup need to come over for tea again."

"Oh." Just one small word and Clare sounded confused, wary. Just like Zach. He smiled.

"Do you want me to meet you at Rickman's?" Zach asked.

A small pause. "All right. I've never met the man, and

don't know what he wants. I only did that little accounting job for him." Clare sighed. "The ghosts have been bothering me more lately, especially downtown. I'll call the car service."

"That sounds excellent, dears," Mrs. Flinton said.

"Gotta clean up. Later," Zach said, bending a stern look at Mrs. Flinton. She just smiled and sashayed out of his apartment. He understood why the housekeeper, Mrs. McGee, preferred to live in the carriage house. At the moment, a little space between him and the mansion would be welcome.

Zach rubbed his neck again, limped over to close the door behind his landlady—he only had his orthopedic shoes on for driving, not the light brace—and headed to his bathroom.

A few minutes later when he left his apartment and his ass complained at hitting the seat of his truck again after driving for so long, he just grumbled under his breath. Then he looked up and saw crows sitting on a power line, half a dozen of them, quiet in the heat. His jaw clenched. He hadn't seen any of the damned birds in Montana, but here they were.

As always, the "Counting Crows Rhyme" his maternal grandmother had taught him ran through his mind.

Six.

Six for gold.

He ignored their beady eyes as he exited the circular drive.

Clare Cermak changed clothes just because she'd be seeing Zach—from new designer jeans and a silk blouse to a thin peach-colored sundress. She didn't care what Rickman—whom she'd never met—or anyone else at his business thought of her . . . except Zach, her newish lover.

They'd gotten so close when she'd thought she was going crazy. It turned out that along with her great-aunt Sandra's fortune, Clare had inherited the family "gift" for seeing ghosts and helping them move on to . . . what came next. She still had a shaky grasp on that, particularly since she preferred rationality in her life. Her now exploded past life as an accountant.

Hello, Clare! We are going OUT? Enzo, the ghost Labrador dog, sent mentally. He'd materialized from nothing to sit panting at her feet, gray-white shadows and shades.

"Yes. Zach's boss, Tony Rickman, wants to see us for some reason."

We are seeing Zach? Enzo hopped to his feet and his whole body wiggled front to back.

"Yes, apparently he's back from Montana." She frowned, not knowing exactly how she felt about that. She'd missed him outrageously in bed. No, scratch that thought, she missed him outrageously, period, darn it. She wanted him . . . and she'd forever be grateful that he'd helped her during the time she'd had to deal with her first major ghost. Did that make her dependent on Zach? She didn't think so. They had a lot in common, and he was just plain fabulous in bed . . .

CLARE!

She thought back to what Enzo had asked. "Yes, we are seeing Zach." Grudgingly, she added, "You can come with me." Not that forbidding Enzo would make any difference. He appeared and vanished as he pleased.

I would like to see a new place with new people and maybe some ghosts?

"A high-rise downtown." All right, she admitted she was curious about Zach's place of employment. Frowning, she glanced at the old map of Denver she'd hung on the wall of the tiny bedroom she'd designated as her "ghost laying" office in her new home. "There might have been buildings there in the late eighteen hundreds," she said to Enzo.

The dog itself—himself—had told her that the human mind could only comprehend ghosts from one slice of history. From her experimentation this last week, she'd determined that her period was from 1850 to 1900. She seemed to specialize in Old West phantoms.

A toot in the driveway announced that the car service she now had on retainer had arrived. She couldn't drive in heavily ghost-populated areas anymore—it was too dangerous when apparitions rose before her or pressed around the car, or invaded it.

She locked up, greeted the driver, and sat in the back of the Mercedes, heart pounding at seeing her lover again.

* * *

Zach arrived at Rickman Security and Investigations before Clare, shoved through the heavy glass doors—wouldn't surprise him if they were bulletproof—and into the lobby area. The walls were pale gray, the reception station dark gray stone with a glossy black top, and black computer and phone accessories.

He nodded to the receptionist before heading straight to his boss's door. Zach stood with his hand on the lever until the electronic lock buzzed to let him into the inner office, decorated in gray and cream.

Two men watched him with military assessment as he entered. Tony Rickman, a craggy-looking man in his late forties with buzz-cut salt-and-pepper hair wearing an engraved wedding band, sat behind his dark wooden desk.

The guy standing near the desk, six foot six, two hundred and seventy-five pounds, pale white blond hair in another buzz cut, light brown eyes, had "ex-special-ops" written all over his body and attitude. He wore expensive black trousers with knife-edge creases, dull but not scuffed shoes, a black silk shirt, and a lightweight black jacket.

"Hello, Zach," Rickman said.

Zach nodded and made an effort to keep his walk as smooth as possible, even with his cane and brace, as he headed toward the far left of the four gray leather client chairs. "Hello, Tony."

"Clare Cermak called you?"

"That's right."

"Obviously, you're back from Montana." A note in Rickman's voice told Zach that the man had expected Zach to check in.

"Just arrived a half hour ago." He sat and stretched his jeaned legs out, propping his cane against the chair.

"Make yourself at home," Rickman said.

Zach smiled. "Thanks, I will."

"I don't believe you've met another of my operatives, Harry Rossi. Harry, this is Zach Slade." Rickman gestured to the guy, who scrutinized Zach and his threat level. Zach stood, studying Rossi with his flat cop stare. Something—shadows—in the man's eyes showed he'd had to kill. Zach figured that showed in his own eyes.

After a few seconds, the big man smiled and took a few steps toward Zach. Zach met him halfway and offered his hand.

"Good to meet you," Zach said.

"Likewise," said Rossi. A quick, hard grip and then they retreated at the same time.

"Rossi works mostly as a bodyguard," Tony said. "He's currently placed with a long-term client of mine, Dennis Laurentine."

Zach nodded. "Rossi looks good for bodyguard work."

Rossi gave a quick grin, ostentatiously adjusted his shirt cuffs.

Returning to his chair, Zach said, "I don't think Clare needs a bodyguard . . . yet."

With a bland smile, Rossi said, "Not with you around."

"Looks like we need Clare," Tony said.

"Is that so?" asked Zach.

A quick double buzz came from the door lock as the receptionist opened it.

Clare walked in and Zach had the novel experience of having his heart jump in his chest. Damn, she looked good.

Rickman stood and so did Zach, automatically moving toward her. Just a step or two and he scented the exotic fragrance she wore that reminded him of more than kisses. He fought to control a hard-on. Did the damn multiplication table.

Still, she looked good, better than he'd last seen her the morning he'd crawled out of her bed and headed to Montana. Better than he'd ever seen her.

She'd come into her own and was done with the worry over closing out her great-aunt's estate, moving into her own home, and dealing with a gunfighter ghost. The peach sundress she wore accented her golden skin and hazel eyes. Her brown hair with red tints was rich and glossy. He thought he made a noise in his throat.

She smiled like she was glad to see him and all his irritation at the wearying day vanished.

"Hi, Clare." Moving quickly, he took her hand, kissed her cheek. Oh, man, that perfume and her natural scent did a number on him. He didn't want to be with her here, with two other guys in the room. He wanted to be in her bed, or have her in his.

She brushed a kiss on his lips and relief flooded him. They were still on the same page, goddam good.

"Hi, Zach."

He didn't put his arm around her as he turned to face the men, but kept his body intimately close. "Clare, the guy behind the desk is the head of Rickman Security and Investigations, Tony Rickman. Beside him is Harry Rossi, another of Rickman's men." Zach had no clue how much she observed. As far as he knew, she wouldn't recognize a military man by his stance, his movement, his attitude. Wouldn't know when a guy was armed. She'd once said that she didn't watch crime shows, so she was learning about police officers from him.

"How do you do," she said politely.

Rossi nodded and stood at ease. Rickman came from behind the desk and offered his hand. Clare donned her professional woman manner, gripped it, and shook.

"Please, have a seat," Rickman said. "Would you like some tea?"

She gave him a cool stare. "You've been talking about me with Mrs. Flinton? She's the one who offers me tea."

Rickman's gaze cut to Zach. The guy wanted backup. Zach decided to test his luck, put his hand around her upper arm, and gave the lightest of tugs toward the chairs and stepped toward them himself. She slid her glance to him, and followed, answering Rickman's question. "No tea, thank you. Coffee would be good."

"Fine." Rickman returned to his desk and pressed the intercom. "Coffee, cream, and sugar for Ms. Cermak."

Zach took the last left chair, and Clare sat in the one next to him. He wished it were closer.

"You asked for this meeting?" Clare said.

Rickman lowered into his executive chair, but kept his manner casual. "Thank you for your work on the accounting ledgers in Mrs. Flinton's case. She has spoken highly of you," he said.

Clare inclined her head.

"We have a problem we'd like you to help us with," Tony Rickman said.

Clare stilled beside Zach, wet her lips. "As a forensic accountant?"

A long, thumping pause.

"I'm afraid not. As a ghost banisher," Rickman said.

Clare flinched. Her fingers tightened on a small purse she'd moved from her shoulder to her lap. "I'm not in that business."

"Can you please hear me out? We have a problem," Rickman repeated. "Or rather, one of our clients has a problem." He gestured to Rossi, who treated Clare to a smile that showed male appreciation and twinkling eyes. Zach revised his first good impression of the man.

"I'm the bodyguard to Dennis Laurentine," he said.

"The billionaire," Rickman said.

Clare blinked. "Dennis Laurentine? No. He's not. As of last month, Forbes's website listed his net worth as being valued at approximately nine hundred and sixteen million. That makes him a multimillionaire, but not quite a billionaire."

Rickman looked disconcerted. Rossi's smile widened.

"Never argue with an accountant about money," Zach said, lounging even more in his seat.

Clare sighed. "Well, Mr. Laurentine is very wealthy, and a client my former firm would have loved to have—would love to have. What does that have to do with me?"

"Why don't you, ah, tell the story, Rossi," Rickman said.

"Sure." The bodyguard moved to the front of Rickman's desk, leaned against it, his gaze focused on Clare. "Mr. Laurentine has a ghost problem on his ranch in South Park." The ends of his mouth lifted in a half smile. "Or to be accurate, a bone problem. A dead guy is leaving his bones around."

TWO

❦

CLARE'S EYES WIDENED. A hundred questions already buzzed in Zach's mind. He watched her head tilt in the way that showed she listened closely. "Bones appearing after they've been buried? That doesn't make sense," she said.

Rossi said, "I've seen it happen twice. Mr. Laurentine knows the legend of this ghost guy and his bones—Higgenberry? Humperdink? The story's very famous." Rossi lifted a brow.

Clare shook her head as if she didn't know the story. Hell, Zach didn't either, and he'd been born in Colorado.

Shrugging, Rossi continued, "We opened the guy's grave, no bones, reinterred the skeleton—and the signed poems that he'd left with his bones—at the cemetery near the original site of the town, fifty miles away and up a canyon. We also put observers and rigged cams on the grave. No one dug the skeleton up, but the bones appeared again."

Crossing her arms, Clare shifted her gaze and stared out the window, that showed a panoramic view of the Front Range mountain peaks.

Clare said, "I can only . . . help ghosts of a certain time period." Her gaze flittered to Zach and he smiled, hoping she knew he hadn't backslid about acknowledging she had a gift for ghosts.

And she did. He could see them, too, when he touched her. Rickman sighed. "We are not proceeding in an orderly fashion about this. Ms. Cermak, are you aware that Mr. Laurentine purchased an old ghost town, a mining town, had it disassembled and reconstructed on his ranch?"

Clare's mouth dropped open. Zach's stare went to Rickman, who looked as stern as always, and Rossi, who rolled his eyes.

"The expense—" sputtered Clare before her mouth snapped shut.

"Probably why he's only a multimillionaire," Zach drawled. "That had to cost a pretty penny."

"He gave local labor good jobs," Rickman said.

"Why would he move an entire Western town?" Zach asked.

"Because he's crazy about the Old West, being born in Rhode Island and all," Rossi said sardonically. "He likes the flavor out here. So he says."

A crack of laughter escaped Zach. "So when he moved the town, the ghosts came right along with it."

"Seems so," Rossi said.

"What were the dates of this town?" Clare asked prissily, obviously trying to wiggle out of the request she could see looming. As far as Zach knew, she had no intention of hanging out a shingle as a psychic, and probably resented being here. He'd sure rather be with her somewhere else, too. This meeting was a waste of time.

"The dates of the town," Rossi repeated. The bodyguard and Rickman shared a glance. Rickman shrugged. Rossi turned his head back to look at Clare, then lines around his eyes tightened as if he was thinking back. "It was booming in the eighteen seventies maybe?"

Clare sniffed.

"Mr. Laurentine will be joining us shortly," Rickman said. "You can get specific information from him."

"I'm not a medium," Clare stated.

Everyone just looked at her.

She endured the silence with tight mouth and body for a

good full minute before Rossi cleared his throat and said, "Ma'am, the bones appear in the beds of real nice women."

Now all eyes focused on Rossi.

"This happens mostly when Mr. Laurentine is entertaining, has a whole houseful of people. It scares his guests, especially when we take the bones out, rebury them with respect, and they show up again." Rossi shook his head. "Laurentine's losing local people who don't want to work for him, and they're losing paychecks."

Every guy in the room seemed to know Clare's soft spot.

"He needs help," Rickman said, then more quietly, "and you'll be paid well."

Clare's gaze lasered from Rickman to Rossi, fixed on Zach. "Evidently my gift is common knowledge."

Zach matched her glare with his cop one. "I told no one." Then he thought he heard barking, which meant Enzo the ghost dog was probably here and talking to Clare. Zach watched the other two men. Rickman appeared too casual— did he hear the dog, too? And what did that mean? Rossi was the original stone face and Zach couldn't tell what he might hear, see, or know.

At that moment the door buzzed again, no warning before the door opened. Rickman scowled. If Zach was to guess, Rickman would be having a chat with his receptionist before the day was done.

The man who walked in was the shortest of them all, five-seven, blocky build, shoulder-length sandy hair and pale green eyes, probably in his fifties. He wore designer jeans, a tailored polo shirt that matched his eyes, and a lot of power.

Nodding toward Rickman, he took the far right chair as if he owned the room, hell, as if he owned the building and all of downtown Denver. He glanced at Clare, his gaze dismissing Zach sitting beyond her. Rossi moved between the guy and the door.

"Mr. Laurentine," Rickman said. "I'm glad you could join us."

Laurentine sighed. "I suppose this is a matter that I must handle myself, since you haven't wrapped up the deal within the time frame I thought you would."

Rickman ignored that, went straight to the meat of the matter. "We need information about your town."

"Curly Wolf?" The man rubbed his hands, his eyes lit with the gleam of an obsessive collector. "Fabulous place. A real jewel, I have some extremely historic buildings." His face set. "I've been criticized for taking the town, moving it to my own personal and private property. But the buildings would have fallen apart and been lost to the future if I hadn't saved them. Park County already has one ghost town for historic purposes, and there was no funding to take care of Curly Wolf."

"What time period was the town active?" Clare asked.

The rich guy turned to face her, brows up. "You haven't heard of Curly Wolf?"

"No."

"Or its ghosts? Ghosts well known during the time? Such as the people who died in the smallpox epidemic of 1861, or the apparition now plaguing me?"

"No." Clare wanted to squirm and suppressed the urge. Why was she being questioned? She was here to listen to a proposition for her to help; instead it felt like she was being attacked. Granted, Mr. Laurentine had eight hundred and ninety-six million dollars more than she, but she had enough so she could walk away.

Laurentine grunted. "Not well educated on this matter, are you? You get rid of ghosts? Prove it."

Clare stood. "I'm sorry, Mr. Laurentine," she said in a chill tone. "You mistake me for someone available to hire to handle . . . an unusual problem for you. I am not in that business." Turning on her heel, she made it only a step before Enzo barked.

Wait, Enzo yelled in her mind, then, in a deeper tone Clare dreaded because it wasn't the ghost dog but that spirit she called the Other who spoke through the dog, said, *Watch!*

Stomach lurching, she did. A figure in prospector's garb materialized no more than a pace in front of her. She'd have to walk through him to the door. He wore heavy pants, a light-colored shirt, a vest, and had a trimmed beard. He stretched out a hand. *Help me!*

Not again.

What do you want? Clare directed her mental thought to the ghost.

"Ms. Cermak?" asked Rickman.

Without looking at him, she cut off his words with a gesture. Freezing air wafting from the spirit passed around Clare and into the room.

They said that I died of accidental causes. The phantom wore a sad expression on his youngish face. *That I fell from the mountain while picking wildflowers.*

Clare sighed. *They were wrong?*

He nodded. *Yes. I was murdered.*

"Of course you were," she murmured.

"What's going on?" asked Laurentine. He strode to her, curved his hand around her upper arm.

"Take your hand off her," said Zach in a low, dangerous tone. She heard him rise from his chair. He moved into her peripheral vision, and the millionaire's blocky fingers fell from her arm.

Rossi, the bodyguard, circled around her from the opposite direction and went right into the ghost. Rossi's eyes widened and he grunted, pivoted in an athletic motion, and stepped out of the miner.

THANK YOU! shouted the ghost toward Rossi, but that man was saying to Laurentine, "You should sit, sir."

"I don't think so," said Laurentine. Now he moved into the specter . . . who hissed.

Scowling, Laurentine faced Clare. "You're acting odd."

She shrugged, watched as the prospector stepped aside from the live man with an expression of distaste. *He has no poetry in his soul.*

Is that so? she asked the phantom mentally.

The apparition spread long, artistic-looking pale gray fingers over his heart and inclined his torso. *It is very so, my sweet.* He winked.

Uh-oh.

"You're all acting odd," complained Laurentine.

"Maybe you should take your business somewhere else," Zach rumbled.

Rickman, the boss, sighed.

With narrowed eyes, Laurentine studied Clare. "I do have

a problem. A very nasty problem that seems . . . supernatural." He made a disgusted sound. "As much as I can figure that. I handled the bones myself, watched them buried." He stomped away and she heard leather rustle as he sat.

The miner's wraith shuddered. *They ARE my bones.*

Enzo, can you tell me anything about this gentleman? Clare asked.

The ghost dog sniffed all around the phantom. *I like his smell, Clare,* Enzo, not the Other, said. Enzo's tongue lolled. *He is the one we need to help now.*

What's your name? she asked the specter mentally, now flushing and very aware that everyone stared at her.

A dark bowler hat appeared on the apparition's head, just in time for him to doff it with a bow to Clare. *J. Dawson Hidgepath, at your service, miss.*

His name meant nothing to her.

Enzo, can you show Mr. Hidgepath to the carriage house I use for consulting?

You're going to open that space for consulting? Hooray! Enzo hopped around. *I told you that you needed to do that, and that it would be a very good space.*

I'm using it to consult with . . . She glanced at Hidgepath. *Those who've passed on. I prefer to see them there.*

Again the apparition winked. *I prefer ladies' bedrooms.*

That sounded just great. Clare sincerely hoped to see no bones in her bed, no phantom, again, at the foot of her bed. She let herself relax as the wraith followed Enzo through the door. The cold dissipated.

She stood with her back to the others for only an instant then turned around and, keeping her expression bland, met Laurentine's gaze and said, "Tell me about J. Dawson Hidgepath."

The bodyguard, who'd stationed himself behind the millionaire, seemed to shake himself, rather like her ghost dog.

She remained the focus of all eyes. Zach took her arm and began to lead her back to her seat.

By the time she sank into the plush gray leather of the barrel chair, and Zach took his own chair, Enzo galloped back into the room, tongue lolling.

Hi, Zach! Enzo sent to her mind as his muzzle opened and

he barked. He trotted around the room, sniffing the living men, then came back and licked Zach's hand. Zach stiffened. Her lover had admitted he could see ghosts when he touched her, and believed it was due to her psychic gift and talent. She thought otherwise but hadn't said anything about it yet.

She angled to look at Mr. Laurentine, two seats over to her right. Enzo leapt into the chair between her and the multimillionaire.

Mr. Laurentine glowered at her, tapping an index finder on the arm of his chair. "So now you suddenly know about J. Dawson Hidgepath."

"I know the name. He was a prospector?"

"His bones have been legendary for over a century, though they seemed to have stopped appearing near the turn of the twentieth century," Mr. Laurentine said, then waved a hand. "But, of course, I didn't move the cemetery of Curly Wolf when I bought the rest of the town. I only moved the buildings. I would not disturb the dead."

"I see," Clare said. Unfortunately she saw way too much . . . like ghosts.

"But the bones have begun to appear again," Zach put in.

"How are you involved in this?" Mr. Laurentine asked.

"He's one of my operatives," Rickman said.

"He's a friend of mine," Clare said.

"He doesn't look ex-military," Mr. Laurentine said.

"I'm not," Zach said, and his body and his eyes changed in that way he had.

"Cop," Mr. Laurentine said, glanced at Zach's cane. "Ex-cop."

Zach shrugged.

The multimillionaire shifted more toward Clare. "And you're Clare Cermak."

"That's right."

"And you can lay ghosts."

Yes, she can! Enzo shouted, though his confirmation didn't seem to have been heard by anyone else.

"You vouch for her?" Mr. Laurentine asked Rickman.

"Yes, enough that I'm willing to negotiate a fee for her as a consultant."

Clare shrugged, not interested in that right now, but figured like most executives he'd take it for assent. "Mr. Hidge-path told me that his death wasn't accidental. He said he was murdered."

The word electrified the men.

Zach sat up straight, reached for his cane, and ran his hand over the curve. She noted it was a new cane with a hooked handle and looked more old-fashioned than his other one.

Rickman scowled. The bodyguard . . . shifted or some-thing, and looked about ten times more dangerous.

Mr. Laurentine's eyes popped a little. He blinked, then an-swered her with suppressed excitement. "I'm an expert on Curly Wolf and its history and I've never heard this. His death was ruled an accidental fall from a trail to his mine near Mount Bross."

"Sounds suspicious to me," Zach said—and *he* sounded as if he were just being contrary. "And I think I'm the only one here who's ever investigated a murder."

Everyone shifted their attention to him and she was glad. For a minute she'd felt like a pinned butterfly.

"*Tcha!*" Laurentine made a disgusted noise. "As if you could find out what happened nearly a hundred and fifty years ago about a man whose whole life doesn't amount to more than a few paragraphs on the Internet."

Rossi, the bodyguard, gave a little cough. "That's true enough. Most of what we know about him concerns his bones."

Mr. Laurentine scowled. "His bones. Those damned bones. I wish they'd remained legendary." He ran a hand through his shoulder-length hair. Clare studied him. His hair-style didn't look quite modern, more like something she'd seen in the many antique photographs in her books on the Old West.

"J. Dawson Hidgepath?" she prompted.

"If he was murdered, maybe Clare can't send him into the great beyond until we find out the truth," Zach added.

"J. Dawson was a ladies' man, and considered himself a poet." The multimillionaire leaned back in his chair, like a storyteller. Clare didn't think he'd be a good one.

"Just the facts," Zach said.

"As I said, there seems to be a dearth of facts. But if you

wish a quick and dirty summary, the prospector 'courted' several ladies, a saloon girl, a teacher—any new woman showing up in Curly Wolf would get a bouquet and a poem. When he *fell off the mountain*, he was no sooner buried than his decomposing body appeared in the saloon girl's bed."

"*Eeewww*," Clare said.

"They reburied him in the Curly Wolf Cemetery and a few nights later he showed up in the schoolmarm's bed, even more disgusting, along with a poem. Again they buried him, this time at an unknown location with the ministers from all the churches from all the towns around taking part in the service . . . and yet he continued to rise throughout the end of the century. When we buried him, we went back to his first grave."

"It was a localized haunting, then?" Clare asked. Of the three ghosts she'd actually sent on, two had seemed to be local, staying in the same place as their death.

Enzo said, *Ghosts stay where they feel they need to be, but they can move around lots if they think they have to.* He yipped cheerfully. *It all depends.*

How wonderful, still no darn solid rules. Clare's fingers went to tug at her hair—a new bad habit that she hadn't had as an accountant—but she stopped the gesture and turned it into a roll of her hand for Mr. Laurentine to go on. The man shrugged. "That's all I know."

"Until now," Zach said. "He's back."

Another frown from the multimillionaire. "So we believe. My last two house parties were spoilt; the two ladies whose beds he showed up in were extremely unhappy and left in the middle of the night. They won't return despite my persuasions." He scowled, flushing with anger. "I lost other guests, too. Worse, I've lost some of my housekeeping staff and a couple of caretakers, carpenters, of Curly Wolf itself. I don't want a ghost that will cause me problems or a haunted house." His jaw set and he appeared once more a formidable man, accustomed to wheeling and dealing in millions of dollars.

Then his pointed stare fixed on Clare. "If I hire you, I'll expect you to produce results."

She met his gaze calmly. "If I accept the consultation, I will do so to help Mr. Hidgepath."

Mr. Laurentine stood, reached into his pocket, and pulled out a gold card case, took the top card, and held it out to her. "This is the address of my ranch in South Park. I'm heading straight up after this meeting. I'll tell my people to expect you in no later than forty-eight hours."

Only the image of J. Dawson kept Clare from saying something snippy. She stood and Zach and Rickman followed. She stared at Mr. Laurentine's card. She really didn't want to do this.

This is your next ghost to help move on! Enzo ran around her in a circle, seeming happy as usual. *He is waiting for you at your carriage house.*

As long as it wasn't her bedroom.

Come ON, Clare! Enzo shouted.

She looked down at the doggy spirit, slid her gaze toward the arrogant Mr. Dennis Laurentine with all his expectations and no belief in ghosts or her. Perhaps she could show him something.

With a gesture, she asked Enzo to sit and shake. He sat and offered his paw and she took his icy paw in hers, gave it a good squeeze. When she initiated contact with ghosts, and she always had to do that to help them, she experienced their frigid selves with cold sleeting through nerves and muscles to settle in her bones. The experience was always worse than if the ghost touched her.

She let go of Enzo's paw and saw Mr. Laurentine and Zach watching her, the other two men, Rickman and Rossi, ostentatiously looking elsewhere.

Chin high, she strode over to Mr. Laurentine, and began to take the card, making sure her cold, cold fingers brushed his. His hand jerked and the card fell.

And Enzo *lifted* it to her fingers.

"I didn't see that," Rickman muttered.

"I didn't either," Rossi said.

"What are you talking about?" asked Mr. Laurentine.

Zach laughed.

"I'll be in touch, Mr. Laurentine," she said, and strolled toward the door, putting a little extra sway in her hips for Zach. He'd been gone six days.

The electronic door lock released with a click, probably

from Rickman's desk, and she opened it and sauntered out, hearing Rickman say, "Let's talk provisional terms, Laurentine. Zach, please stay on Clare's behalf."

"Oh, very well," Mr. Laurentine said. "And I suppose you want me to hire the ex-cop to look into a more than century-old death by accident."

"We'll negotiate," Rickman said smoothly. "But first, Ms. Cermak's services . . ." The rest of his words were cut off by the door shutting, and the sass in Clare leaked out of her like air from a deflating balloon.

Whatever Rickman charged Mr. Laurentine would be both too much and too little. Too much because she *had* to help ghosts pass on to whatever awaited them, or go crazy. Too little because money, no matter how much, didn't make up for her life being totally screwed up now.

THREE

A HALF HOUR later, after a ride home during which she hadn't wasted any time checking out Curly Wolf and J. Dawson Hidgepath and the cemetery on her tablet, Clare went through the iron gate next to her large new-to-her home into the backyard. She walked down the red flagstone path set in thyme to her carriage house or, since her house had been built in the twenties, an early garage. She hadn't visited the smaller building since the day she'd toured the property with her realtor, eleven days ago, and hadn't paid much attention to the one-story-and-a-loft building.

During the last week she'd been occupied in the main house, arranging her portion of Great-Aunt Sandra's furniture, setting up a home office for accounting and perhaps tax preparation services, and a tinier office for her "ghost layer" psychic gift.

Learning the rules for helping apparitions move on had not been going well. Enzo would sit next to her as she read books written by mediums and other psychics and shake his big head mournfully, saying, *It is not like that with us.* He'd been her great-aunt Sandra's dog and was now Clare's, to help her.

She thought she'd rather have a cat.

Great-Aunt Sandra's jumbled journals didn't help much either, assuming Clare knew items or procedures that she didn't, talking about ghost laying in Sandra's own personal terms, which made Clare's brain hurt.

But Great-Aunt Sandra *had* made another fortune for the family . . . as had Sandra's predecessor, Great-Great-Uncle Amos. Sandra had compiled money both as a psychic consultant and, as she had told Clare in a video, because "the universe supports our efforts."

Clare had found that out from experience. At the end of her first case, she and Zach had found a gold coin that was so rare it was currently sitting in a New York City auction house valued at four million dollars. That still staggered her. Four. Million. Dollars. For one "case," as Zach would call it. She still didn't know how that worked.

Unlike her great-aunt, Clare hadn't intended to make the psychic thing a business, and yet here she'd been dragged into a paying job. Rickman had probably already negotiated her fee from Mr. Laurentine.

Come ON, Clare! Enzo popped out of the oak wood door of the small brick building.

The Labrador was always cheerleading and she was always dragging her feet. That wouldn't happen with any cat, real or ghost.

She used key and keypad to open the door and walked in, and the sunny cream-yellow walls made her smile. Pretty light from high horizontal windows and the huge skylight in the roof of the nonloft part of the room illuminated the space. The shabby floral pastel furniture from her great-aunt Sandra's secondary sunroom had been temporarily placed here by the movers. Clare recalled now that this team was also the one that had done the kitchen, and had been led by a woman. She'd done a good job, setting up a cozy conversational area near the small kitchen area, revealed by an angled lacquered floral screen of a pale blue. And *that's* where Great-Aunt Sandra's copper teapot had gone, along with a new coffeemaker. Clare approved.

Miss. The ghost of J. Dawson Hidgepath bowed before her, his bowler in his hand. He wore a new and elegant suit.

Clare offered her hand. He took it and kissed her knuckles. She felt nothing but chill, no icy drops of spit or anything.

"So, J. Dawson, what is your first name?"

He smiled slyly. *It could be John. Or James. Perhaps Joseph or even Jedidiah.* He winked.

Great, he wasn't going to be forthcoming. Clare let loose a sigh, perched on the seat of a wing chair. "What do you need from me, J. Dawson?"

He scowled, hovering close, but appearing distracted as he looked around the room. *This place is only as big as a cabin, and too fussy. I'm better outdoors. That's why I left my family back East.*

"I'm not consorting with ghosts in my backyard," Clare stated. The brick walls around her place were twelve feet high, but her neighbors' homes were also two to three stories, with balconies in the back.

Struggling for more courtesy so she could get this done fast, she said, "Ah, J. Dawson, tell me why you began leaving your bones around again, and at Mr. Laurentine's."

Another sly smile. *He has pretty ladies at his house.*

"I'm sure he does."

Now the apparition looked serious. *And in the grayness of my existence, I . . . felt . . . the movement of Curly Wolf, how it bloomed again.* He placed a hand over his heart. *It stirred me.*

Mr. Laurentine would not want to hear that, and it was time to get to the bottom line. "You were murdered, J. Dawson?"

He stopped floating around, clenched his fists. *Yes, someone pushed me off the trail!*

"I'm so sorry," Clare said. And she was.

Enzo whined and rubbed against J. Dawson, and that reminded her that if she wasn't helping J. Dawson, she'd be struggling with some other ghost. She'd just hoped that the next big test of her very puny skills and limited understanding would have come later . . . maybe even a month later rather than a week.

Gently, Clare said, *Your murderer must also be . . . gone by now.*

I want the truth! His next words came with a fierceness that had ghostly spittle flying from his mouth. *I am a phantom, stuck in gray space, stuck in NOWHERE, mind being*

nibbled away by time until I am only shreds on the wind UN-
TIL YOU FIND ME THE TRUTH.

Clare felt herself paling. "I *am* sorry, J. Dawson. I will do my best to help you, uh, pass on."

If she'd gone whiter, his aspect had gained a darker shade—embarrassment, she thought. His bowler appeared and he pulled it low over his head rather than tilting it at a jaunty angle. *My deepest apologies. I should not have raised my voice to you. I am ill-mannered and have behaved like a cad.* He made a jerky gesture of distress, then vanished.

Clare tugged a strand of her hair. "That didn't go well." She wasn't pleased with herself either. She stood. "I have so much to learn."

Enzo licked her hand, a cold swipe along her skin. *You did okay, Clare. I will help you!*

"Thank you, Enzo."

And this is a very nice space.

"Yes." She smiled. "But I can't see Mr. Laurentine here, and I'm not inviting that man into my home. Home is for sanctuary." She sensed she'd need every smidgeon of peace she could find while dealing with her gift for the rest of her life.

Clare let out a huge breath as she entered her wonderful and huge home by the modern kitchen . . . and went straight to the bar. She assembled a pitcher of margaritas, poured herself one, and wandered to the living room and the multipaned bay window, which curved out over the front yard.

She was hoping Zach would drop by. It was evident that he wasn't quite sure of their relationship, of bonds forged between them in danger and weirdness. Well, neither was she.

Then his large, dusty black truck pulled into her wide driveway, and she set her drink aside and sighed in relief.

Zach's here! Enzo said, running to the old-fashioned boxed radiators built in around the bottom of the window and sticking his head *through* the glass. A pause. *He's just sitting there. Why isn't he coming in?*

She couldn't prevent herself. "Why don't you go ask him?"

Yes! I will. Someday he will hear more than just my barks. Maybe today! The dog galloped out.

Clare went to the kitchen, and pulled out one of the Tivoli beers she stocked for Zach. Denver was a microbrew center and she'd gotten other beers the person at the wine store said someone would like if they liked Tivoli. Trying to lure the man to spend more time with her? Absolutely. She didn't know what they had, but felt deeply in her bones . . . wait, not a good phrase right now . . . Felt their sex and sharing and intimacy could lead to a solid, true, and lasting relationship. Not that she'd tell him that.

Enzo zoomed into the kitchen, stopped abruptly, and skidded on the tile clear across the room, like a real dog might, a look of astonishment on his face.

Clare laughed.

He grinned back at her, complete with wide mouth and draping tongue. *You need to laugh more often.*

"I've always been a serious person," Clare said, but smiled.

He heard me bark, I'm sure of it. But he didn't hear anything else.

"Oh."

And he's still in his truck.

"Ah." Clare stared at the bottle of beer in her hands. Her cell phone played a rock tune that reminded her of Zach, so she'd programmed it for his calls—hot, edgy, nearly losing control, but never going quite that far.

She plucked her smart phone from her pocket and answered. "Yes, Zach?"

There was quiet.

"Zach?"

"Clare, you know that thing I asked you about before I left last week?"

Her mind scrambled; they'd had only one full day together and that had been a workday for Zach. "I'm not sure."

He cleared his throat. "When I drove in today, I stopped in Boulder to see my mother."

Memory kicked in. "Of course I'll go with you to visit your mother." Mrs. Slade was a resident of a mental health facility in the college town where Zach's family came from . . . though Zach's father was career military and Zach had grown up all over the States.

"Mama was having a good day and recognized me. She asked about, uh, girlfriends, and I told her about you and how you'd visit with me."

"Okay," Clare said.

"I got a call from the facility just as I left Rickman's. Apparently Mama thought I'd just gone out to get you and is waiting for us. She's . . . agitated."

"I'll be glad to visit your mother with you right now."

"Good." She heard him exhale. "That's good." A note of amusement entered his voice. "Clare, I don't dare come into that house or we won't make it up to Boulder tonight."

"Ohhh." She flushed, with pleasure, with yearning. "I'll be right out. Keep your hands on the wheel, mister."

"I'll do that."

"Do you want some bottled water?"

"That would be great. I didn't drink anything at Rickman's, and I've been on the road since early this morning and a lot of yesterday."

"Sandwich?"

"The least I can do is treat you to dinner in Boulder."

"Sold. Be right there."

"You don't need to freshen up. You're gorgeous as is."

"Thank you."

I'm coming, too! Enzo said.

For the first time, Clare hesitated. She didn't know Boulder, where the historic places were, where she could expect to see ghosts. Maybe even in the residential facility itself.

Zach said, "Clare, the place is on ten acres with a view of the Flatirons and was built just after World War One."

Bless him for sensing what she was thinking. "Thank you." She glanced down at the ghost Labrador. "I think Enzo is coming, too."

"If he must, he must. Get a move on, Clare."

"Be right there!" She clicked off, dumped her drink in the sink and rinsed the glass, stuck the beer back in the fridge . . . and smoothed her sundress with a twinge of disappointment that Zach and she wouldn't be making fast, frantic love on the couch, or in the tiny elevator, or in her new California king bed.

She set the alarm, exited by the side door next to the driveway, and saw that Zach wasn't even watching her, which was a little deflating. He sagged over the wheel.

He is tired, Enzo said.

With her new sandal heels clicking on the concrete, she crossed to the driver's door of the truck and opened it and tugged on his arm. "Come on. I'm driving."

Zach gave her crooked smile. "Damn, the sexual buzz has crashed. I'm blocking your car in the garage."

"No you aren't. I got a new one." She gestured to a black luxury sedan of a modest size. Like most guys hearing the words *new car*, Zach perked up a little.

"You can be my first passenger."

Enzo barked.

"Other than Enzo."

Zach looked at the ghost dog. "Hope you didn't leave any nasty residue, guy." The man hesitated.

"I know you prefer to drive, Zach, and like being in control, but I'm fresh and you aren't. Give the macho thing a break."

A spurt of laughter came from him as he shook his head and stepped from the cab, pulling his cane after him.

He aimed a kiss for her lips but she turned her cheek, having no doubt at all that those sexual urges in him could easily revive. He *was* the sexiest, most macho man she'd ever been with. One of a type she'd never have considered.

He was extremely competent when faced with danger—or a woman seeming to go crazy. Yes, the feelings he aroused in her—not only lusty ones—made her brain whisper that she'd like to keep him as long as possible.

But he moved close, his left arm with the cane went around her back, and she was pressed against his hard body. She looked up at him, riveted by the hungry look in his eyes, one that caused her own desire to flare high. She thought his need—and her own—was more than lust, sliding into an emotional connection.

His touch had her whole body clenching.

Then his head bent, and his lips were brushing hers, and she *had* to have a taste . . . Zach and that hint of sage and other spices.

God, he felt good, and his tongue sweeping through her mouth, and the simple large *shape* of his body. She put her arms around his neck and flattened herself against him.

Clare! Zach! Are we going for a ride?

Chill zoomed through her. Zach flinched, too, and let her go. She stepped back with wobbly knees to see Enzo circling them, grinning.

Zach cleared his throat. "We gotta go."

"Yes." She kept to his left side and his bad leg, and placed her hand lightly on his left upper arm, the arm he used for his cane, keeping his right hand free for his gun. When they reached the car parked on the street, she pulled out the fob and held it close to the door, then realized that she didn't need to insert a key because there was no key. She pressed the button, feeling a little embarrassed. *Everyone* knew about fobs, and most people had a newer car than she. But she'd maintained the one she'd bought fourth-hand in college and had seen no need for such an expense when the old one ran fine.

With a slight smile, Zach said, "You could have done that from the driveway."

She chuckled at herself. "Yes, I'm not used to it yet. I've been mostly walking around the neighborhood. I'm getting a bike, too." She opened the door with a flourish. "You can give me the coordinates for the GPS, then nap on the way. I know you won't want to fight traffic."

"Got that right." Just before he sank into the seat, he handed her some folded papers that he took from his jacket pocket. "Rickman said he'd e-mail you these, too, but here's the contract Laurentine signed, and an agreement to consult for Rickman Security and Investigations."

"All right." She stuck them in her purse, setting it in a cubby between the seats. "I'll look at them later."

"You'll scrutinize every word later."

"That's true. Settle in, Zach."

He grunted and strapped in and tilted back the seat, then reeled off the address in Boulder for his mother's facility, and seemed to fall asleep before she'd programmed the GPS.

Clare glanced over at him. She hadn't often gotten to see him asleep. The few nights they'd slept together, he'd awakened before her.

He still appeared dangerous, and tingles jumped inside her. Her very own bad-boy-slash-good-man. Bad because she sensed that edge in him, and she'd been around a few times when he'd acted violently—defeated thieves and a kidnapper and had gotten the job done. A good man, because he controlled his aggression and used it, and he was grieving at the loss of his career in the public sector. He'd taken that "serve and protect" peace officer motto to heart.

She thought of how, if she signed the contract, she'd be working for or with Tony Rickman. She got the idea that man had maneuvered Zach into consulting with him, too. Zach had made his disdain for private investigators plain, yet here he was, a valued member of Team Rickman.

The changes in her life were altogether odd, but this job consultation thing was the least of it.

She remained a private, introverted person. Mostly in revolt against her extremely casual upbringing by parents who had no problems with drama, outrageous scenes, and an open marriage.

Clare hadn't seen her parents in two years. They hadn't bothered to come to Great-Aunt Sandra's funeral, didn't even send flowers or a card, and Clare and her brother had had to arrange with their attorney where the older Cermaks' share of Great-Aunt Sandra's furniture would be warehoused.

Clare swallowed. Most of her feelings for her parents were irritation and pain with traces of love. She understood now that their priorities were themselves and having a good time, and as much as she told herself not to judge, that was difficult.

But for *her* to be fulfilled, she had to contribute to society, do work she felt was meaningful. Before her gift, it was helping people understand their finances as an accountant. Now, she didn't know, but at least she had a significant amount of money to donate to charities . . .

Zach grunted in his sleep. He'd miss his work, too. He said he'd gotten disability and retirement benefits from the county where he'd been shot in the line of duty, enough so he could retire. Of course, she hadn't pressed about the figure, but he'd made it clear he hadn't wanted to retire at thirty-five.

She knew his father was in the military. Two of the things they had in common were living a lot of places as children, and a need to make their own way.

As for his mother . . . Clare felt he loved his mother deeply, but pain and frustration were wrapped in with that love. A woman he intended to visit weekly because of that love and despite the pain.

But his family had been torn apart by the drive-by killing of Zach's beloved sixteen-year-old brother when Zach had been twelve.

Clare ran into traffic and concentrated on her driving for the rest of the way.

When she pulled into the parking lot of a three-story building with lovely landscaping and stopped, Zach woke up and stretched, then rubbed his face with his hands.

"God, too much time in a damn vehicle." He opened the door and stepped out, and Clare noticed he used his brace as well as his orthopedic shoes. Still, he hauled out his cane.

When she locked the car and came around it, he twirled the cane.

She smiled. "I noticed the new one."

"Better for bartitsu."

"Ah."

"I've signed up for regular classes at the studio in Denver."

"What mixture of martial arts is it again?"

"Cane fighting, boxing, and jujitsu."

"Okay."

"I think I'll put my own spin on it."

"Naturally."

"We'll see how the teacher-owner handles that." Zach sounded pleased with the challenge. Again he stretched and Clare looked at the residential mental health facility where his mother lived.

Even after the hottest August in Colorado, the lawn and bushes were green. Banks of multicolored roses flanked the concrete walk up to the front entrance. The blond-beige brick and red-roofed building with a hint of "Southwest" style was common for institutions built around the turn of the twentieth century.

"Enzo?" she asked. The ghost Labrador had disappeared from the backseat of the car, and she didn't know whether he'd traveled with them that way or by supernatural means.

No ghosts from your time period, Clare! Only Indians who don't want to talk to you! Enzo projected.

"That's fine with me."

"What?" Zach asked.

She smiled at him. "No ghosts who want to speak with me here."

"Sounds good."

It was her turn to stretch discreetly. They began to walk up the concrete ramp with metal side rails. "What should I call your mother?"

"Call her Geneva."

"All right."

"Uh, something you should know before we go in."

Probably a lot of things, issues piled upon issues, that Clare couldn't even guess. "Yes?"

FOUR

ZACH SAID, "MY mother and I don't. . . and nobody on the staff . . . talks about Jim."

"I won't bring up Jim."

Zach cleared his throat. "She knows I'm grown but still thinks Jim's alive . . . and sixteen. It doesn't make sense, but that's how it is. Jim's always just stepped out of the room, or gone to get her something, flowers or a present maybe."

Clare stopped on the wide porch, a couple of yards from the first set of double glass doors. "Should we have gotten her flowers?"

"I brought some earlier today," Zach said. "White roses, her favorite." In an exaggerated gesture, he bent down and sniffed her neck. "Nothing like this perfume you wear. Exotic, sexy."

She swept a look at him from under her lashes, then her half smile faded with memory. "It was Great-Aunt Sandra's. It smelled different on her." Clare bit her lip and blinked back tears. "The perfume is outrageously expensive, and since the fragrance was discontinued, she stocked up before it was gone. She had five huge unopened bottles of it."

Zach turned her face so she looked him in the eye, and a

sizzle zipped through her. "You tough and frugal lady," he teased. "You can't tell me you don't miss her. Or that you don't like the scent yourself. It mixes with your own smell really well." His brows went up and down and she had to smile.

Clare let her shoulders sag. "I do miss her." She swallowed to keep the tears from leaking. "I avoided her. I wanted to live a rational life." She didn't like the plaint in her voice, so she removed it. Curling her fingers around his hand, which stroked her cheek, she said, "It's good that you're doing this, that you come and visit your mother, no matter what. I wish—" She shook her head, made a gesture of futility. "I regret what I did in the past. You should always keep visiting. It's the right thing to do, even if it is hard on you, and yes, I can see that it is."

He looked away and his hand dropped, but the side of his mouth rose in a half smile. "Fierce lady. I like that."

"You haven't seen anything yet," she said, though she hadn't been fierce in her old life, had never let the strain of gypsy blood, of gypsy music, run free in her. But now that the "gift" had come through that blood and destroyed her normal life, she might explore that side of her nature.

Just before they stepped through the doors, Zach said, "And don't mention the General, well, she thinks of him as the Colonel. It distresses her. Not as much as trying to convince her that Jim is dead, which will shred her sanity, but if you mention my father, she will expect him to walk through the door and that will destroy her serenity. He hasn't visited her in years, won't have her living with him, and she doesn't want to live with me and cramp my style. She gets confused and stressed on her own and doesn't make good decisions." Zach puffed out a breath. "So many topics to dance around."

She squeezed his upper arm. "Rules," she said firmly. "Rules of courtesy to interact with your mother. I'm much better knowing the rules."

"Yeah, you are, and you don't challenge 'em much, and for that, in this instance, I am grateful."

Tossing her head and letting her hair whirl felt good. "I'll show you fierceness, Jackson Zachary Slade. Tonight."

"I'll hold you to that."

Once they were inside, one of the nurses behind the main desk came around to greet them. "Thank you for coming, Mr. Slade. Your mother's been fretting, waiting for you." The nurse nodded to Clare. "And your girlfriend."

At the door, the nurse knocked, then stepped aside and let Zach and Clare go into a medium-sized room painted a rich cream that had a few antique pieces, several paintings, and a small sitting area facing a wide window.

The hominess of the place allowed Clare to relax. It appeared more like an apartment than an institutional room. Proof, had she needed it, that Zach cared for his mother. That warmed Clare's heart, though jitters skidded along her nerves. Would Geneva like her?

An elegant woman sat in an old-fashioned rounded and soft armchair with a white blanket over her knees, a book on her lap, perfectly groomed. She turned her head and her melancholy expression became hesitant. "Zach?"

"Yes, Mama."

With a smile, she put the book and blanket aside and stood, not quite as tall as Clare herself, and almost painfully thin. Her hair was silver and styled in short, soft waves around a face several shades paler than Zach's. She opened her arms. "So good to see you."

Zach limped the few steps to her, and Geneva's gaze skittered away from the cane and his bad foot and fixed on his face.

Clare flinched. Zach's mother didn't seem to see that he limped. She wasn't ignoring it like Clare did, but put it out of her mind the moment she noticed.

Maybe "bad" things, particularly bad things that happened to her son, didn't make it past the shell she'd encased herself in to deal with the world.

When he neared her, he set his cane against the large round arm of the chair and embraced her. He was careful, as if her long, thin bones might break. When he rocked with her, Clare's throat closed at the love expressed between them.

After Geneva let go, Zach reached for his cane and stepped back. Enzo, who'd been sniffing around, sat and stared, head tilted, ears lifted slightly, at Geneva Slade. *She is a pretty and nice and sad lady.*

Clare thought she saw a tiny flinch from Geneva and the woman's body angled away from the spectral dog—could she sense Enzo?—as she faced Clare. The older woman's smile bloomed and Clare relaxed. At least Zach's mother liked what she saw. Maybe Clare would get through this meeting all right.

Geneva held out both hands. "Look at you, so lovely!" She smiled at Zach, too, including him in her delight. "Introduce us."

"Clare, this is my mother, Geneva Warren Slade. Mama, this is Clare Cermak."

Clare took the woman's hands, soft in her own. "I'm very pleased to meet you."

"Oh, I'm so pleased also." Geneva sent a teasing glance at Zach. "He hasn't brought a young lady to meet me in ages."

"Mama," Zach protested.

"Then I'm doubly happy," Clare said. "That I'm meeting you and that he likes me enough to bring me to see you." That was only the truth.

Geneva squeezed Clare's hands with a light grip then released them and gestured to the four chairs grouped around a low, square table of dark wood with fancy legs and carving around the edge. Atop it stood a beautiful china vase of pastel pink containing long-stemmed white roses. "Let's sit and visit. Zach, you just missed Jim. He went out to play basketball."

Zach tensed.

"But he brought me these beautiful roses." Geneva sniffed at them before she sat.

It was easy for Clare to feel the emotional pain radiating from Zach. He'd given his mother those roses and she'd forgotten that, preferring to think that they'd come from his dead brother, who still lived in her mind. Preferring that child over this man.

Clare moved close to him and put her arm through his.

Enzo nudged Clare. *Give her this.* Something solid was in his mouth—although Clare still didn't understand how that could be—and she took it and flinched at the cold metal. It felt like a trinket box. She moved to bump her hand against Zach's, murmured so only he could hear, "A gift for your mother." He took the little box in a smooth move that seemed more criminal-like than cop-like, betraying nothing on his face or body, and offered it to his mother. "I have something for you, Mama."

"Oh?" Geneva looked quizzical, shook her head. "Don't think you have to bring me something every time you come."

He went over and opened his hand in front of her, and both of them jolted. Tears welled in Geneva's eyes and trickled down her cheeks. She raised her hands to her mouth. "Oh. Oh," she said from behind her fingers.

Zach stared down at the little box on his palm, gold-toned with a china top that had a painted classical pastoral scene. His head slowly turned to Clare, surprise in his eyes.

Geneva took the trinket, swallowed hard, and Clare drew some tissues from a container on an end table and hurried over.

The older woman turned the box over in her hands, opened it, and Clare saw hairpins.

"Oh! I lost this when—at a bad time in my life. It was my grandmother's!" She put it down and used the tissues. "Zach, you are so clever to have found it."

"Sure," Zach said, his voice creaky.

Clare touched his wrist so he could hear Enzo, and sent a thought to the ghost dog. *Where did you find that?*

Enzo tilted his head in the other direction. *It slipped in-between. Stuff sometimes falls in-between.* His tongue lolled. *Like the pocket watch and the gold coin that I got from in-between and put on your bureau.*

Oh. Another thing to figure out when she had time. Though the very idea sent a shivery snake down her spine. She didn't know if her mind could handle it.

Zach pulled away and moved a chair closer to his mother's. "I didn't want to make you sad. I can take it away if you—"

Geneva snatched at the little box, held it close to her bosom. "No. I truly want it, Zach. It's too lovely to be sitting in the drawer of a bachelor's desk or dresser." She smiled now, lowered her hand, and stared at the treasure. "And don't tell me you'd keep it out to look at, because you wouldn't. Not a female thing like this."

Clare took a seat at right angles to Zach. "You know your son well."

"I know both my sons well." She paused, murmured, "My very special sons."

"Not that special, Mama," he replied as softly as she. His gaze slid to Clare, then away, and his jaw flexed.

An awkward pause ensued.

Geneva said, "So, Clare, are you a Colorado native like my sons?"

Clare cleared her throat. "No, I was born in Chicago, where most of my family is from, though my parents traveled quite a bit and my brother and I grew up all over the States."

Geneva's face stiffened. "You don't look like a military child."

Clare didn't know what that meant, but answered, "No, my mother was lucky enough to inherit a sizable trust fund when she was twenty-one, and she and my father prefer to travel. They took us with them."

"Ah." A faint line of disapproval showed in Geneva's forehead. "I understand about trust funds." She made a graceful gesture. "But my family and I believe we are custodians of the money for the future." She shrugged. "To each their own."

"I agree with you about fiscal responsibility," Clare said, leaning toward Geneva. She'd already invested most of her inheritance and made a will in favor of her niece . . . the next victim of the curse of ghost seeing if Enzo was right. Clare smiled. "I'm an accountant." And she *was*; she just wasn't with a large firm anymore, because someone else needed the job more than she.

"Oh." Geneva smiled. "You don't look at all like my accountants. They are the typical stuffy old men."

Zach reached out and clasped Clare's hand. "She's also a gypsy."

Now Geneva's expression cleared and she chuckled. "Oh, how intriguing! That would explain the need to travel."

Clare nodded. "It could. And my father is from a Romani family, too, though I don't think my parents, or even my grandparents, were an essential part of their clans. I believe the connection was lost when my family emigrated."

"Ah. And I think my family tends to hold on to its roots too much." Geneva shrugged. "It's in how we were raised, even in our blood, I think."

Enzo barked as if in agreement, went over, and put his head on Geneva's knee. *Good blood, good family.*

Geneva turned pale and began gasping, her hands twisting together.

Enzo, Clare sent a mental rebuke, *I think you should leave. You are bothering her.*

But, Clare! She smells really, really good. Not as good as you or Mrs. Flinton or Zach, but gooood. He gave her the big puppy dog eyes.

Zach had gotten up and drawn his mother into his embrace, frowning at Clare.

Enzo, go! Surely there are some ghost squirrels to chase . . . or real ones for that matter.

Squirrels! Enzo squealed, hopping to his feet and looking at the window, zooming through it without a word.

Geneva rested on her son, then said, "I'm sorry, I seem very tired now." She looked up at Zach and smiled. "Thank you for visiting, and bringing Clare." The older woman held out a hand and Clare was glad to see it didn't tremble. Clare wrapped her fingers around Geneva's, thinking that something in addition to cherishing family roots traveled through the woman's blood. This was where Zach got his sensitivity—which he wasn't forced to acknowledge as she had had to do—or which he didn't admit to her.

They said their good-byes and left, Zach limping heavier than he had going in.

He studied her car. "I'd like to drive—do you mind?" It was nearly an order.

"All right." Clare handed over the fob, glanced around for Enzo, who was nowhere to be seen.

Once in the car, Zach flexed his fingers on the wheel. "Do you think my brother's ghost haunts my mother?"

FIVE

HER BREATH GASPED on the intake so she couldn't answer as casually as she'd hoped. Scrambling for all she knew
about ghosts so far, she said, "Your brother sounded as if he
was a well-adjusted person. I'm not sure that he'd . . . remain,
let alone bother your mother."

Zach's fingers flexed again on the wheel. She saw a movement of his left foot, as if he'd been used to a clutch and standard transmission. His left foot didn't flex on its own, how
hard for him!

"Yeah, Jim was very well adjusted, but his murder was
never solved." Zach gazed at her. "And he might feel like he'd
left things undone." One side of Zach's mouth twitched up.
"Like looking after his younger brother." More quietly he
said, "Or the rest of his devastated family. God knows, he was
the one we all loved best. Isn't that always the way. The key-
stone of the family, lost."

Clare cleared her throat. Neither she nor her brother was
very important to her parents, and though she loved her
brother, of course, they weren't very close. She loved her
niece, Dora . . . as did her brother and his wife . . . Dora,
who'd inherit the ghost seeing talent if Clare died.

They lived in Williamsburg, Virginia, and Dora loved colonial history. Clare winged a prayer to The Powers That Be that Dora would be spared the insanity Clare had gone through for several weeks. She'd make sure to talk to Dora about the talent somehow.

Now she flipped the original question back on Zach. "Do you think your mother sees your brother's ghost?"

His shoulders went tense. "I don't know."

So he wasn't going to talk about how Geneva might have seen Enzo. And she didn't want to bring anything up that might have them at odds when she wanted to get her hands on him.

"I don't want to go to dinner." He sucked in a breath. "And I'd like to ask some follow-up questions of you."

Of course he would. "Eating at my place is fine."

He stared straight ahead. "You can't see ghosts of the present?"

"No."

He cleared his throat. "Would Enzo know if my brother's ghost haunted my mother?"

Clare blinked. "I don't know. I can ask." It only took a mental thought to have the spectral dog appearing on her lap and licking her face.

Hello, Clare! I love you Clare! His breath was . . . indescribable. What kind of strangeness was that?

He burped. *Ghost prairie dog energies are de-li-cious.*

Well, that answered her first question but, as always, brought up a slew more.

Zach might have felt the chill, because he wrapped his large fingers around the nape of her neck, blessedly warm, prompting Clare to ask, "Ah, Enzo, would you know if Zach's brother is haunting his mother?"

Another freezing swipe of tongue on her nose. *Maybe, Clare!* He looked at Zach and barked. *Maybe, Zach!* Turning back to Clare, Enzo said, *But I am tuned to you now, Clare, and you are tuned to Old West ghosts.* He yipped and Clare thought she heard the answering wails of wraiths. She shivered.

Still not looking at Clare or Enzo, Zach said, "Would that other spirit who sometimes comes through Enzo know?"

Clare froze. Had she spoken of the Other to Zach? She couldn't recall. Bracing herself, she waited for the being/ whatever to make its appearance. This was important to Zach so she wouldn't fuss, would endure any scrutiny the entity gave her. She always felt insignificant to the Other, as if she were an ant marching in an army while it watched the pattern.

Enzo got heavier on her lap, the atmosphere in the car crystallized—thin and cold. Zach shifted his fingers on her neck, lovely heat.

The phantom dog's eyes went from dark to milky white with split irises of smoky gray with fog moving in them.

Yes, Clare? The low reverberation of the Other's mental voice rasped her nerves. She'd avoided it as much as possible, praying it would leave soon. Not this time. Zach's thumb stilled on her neck, so they were linked enough for him to hear the Other.

Clare dampened her lips automatically, even though she'd be speaking telepathically. *Does any ghost haunt Zach's mother, Geneva Slade?*

Zach slid his hand down to hers and linked their fingers, squeezed. The Other swung Enzo's head to contemplate Zach. Clare was glad not to be under its scrutiny, and thought Zach's heartbeat pulsed faster.

The Other turned its stare back to her and spoke into her mind. *I understand why you would ask such a thing. The answer you would comprehend is that Geneva Slade occasionally attracts the energy of her mother and that energy only. Not her older son.*

With an almost audible *pop*, it was gone and Enzo leapt off Clare's lap and through the roof. *Gotta run, Clare! Gotta run and run and run! See you at home!*

Clare realized she was stiff and quivering a little.

"Sorry about that," Zach said. "I shouldn't have asked. You don't need to reveal all your secrets to me."

"That's all right," she gasped. "The Other says Jim doesn't haunt your mother."

"No. It isn't all right, but it's done now." Both his hands closed around her waist, and he lifted her with pure strength from her seat to his lap.

She ended up sideways on his lap, not cramped as much as

she expected. There were reasons to buy a luxury car. And once she felt his thighs under her, his chest against her shoulder, she shifted to get even closer, so she could hear his heart. All her tension drained, leaving her limp. Her breath sighed out, and she listened to the thumpity-thump of Zach's heart.

"Uh, Clare?" Zach said in a strained voice.

"Uh-huh," she replied, discreetly sniffing the scent of him through his fine linen shirt—Zach, a trace of his aftershave, and a faint whiff of sweat. September continued to be hotter than normal.

"Clare. We've got to leave. Now."

She became abruptly aware of one extremely hard muscle. The best muscle on his body, despite her appreciation of his shoulders and his butt. Sexual warmth and need filtered through her, warming her from her core and sensitizing her skin.

"Nice as it is, this car isn't good for getting it on."

Clare choked on a laugh.

"I want you in a damn bed and under me soon."

Her brain seemed to fizz away, tangled with passion. "Me, too."

He moved her back into her seat. "Hold on, I'll be pushing the speed limit."

"Sure."

And he peeled out of the parking lot. She snuck a glance at him, tall in the seat next to her. Her height was five feet seven inches, but he was six-four with broad shoulders and a muscular body.

Studying him, she noted he was still a little too lean, and lines of weariness and pain etched in his face showed in the harsh afternoon light. His black hair, shaggy around his collar, showed no hints of another color. Her own body thrummed with the memory of sifting her fingers through that hair as she strove to reach climax with him. Holding him close for deep kisses, to feel his body pressed atop hers, linked by mouth and sex.

The sunlight also brought out a hint of gorgeous bronze in his skin. He'd told her that he had some Native American blood, and it certainly added to his attractiveness.

And she recalled his comment about secrets. She was

learning his body, but thought he still shielded vulnerabilities from her.

As she did from him.

Zach set his teeth as he turned down Clare's street. He'd howl soon if he didn't get his hands on her. His dick pushed against his jeans, hard and throbbing and ready to plunge inside her.

She murmured words he didn't hear, but liked the intimate tone of.

But he knew he wasn't going to make it up the stairs with Clare to her bedroom before he pounced. Need for her consumed him, fire blazing through his veins.

SIX

BY THE TIME he pulled into Clare's driveway, Zach's movements weren't as smooth as usual. If he lifted his hands from the wheel, they'd shake. He didn't bother with the garage. Didn't want to take Clare on concrete. She deserved much better . . . like the polished hardwood of her entryway. He eyed the alcove holding the deep-set front door; too bad he'd installed a nice bright light above.

But he'd had no idea he'd want her this much. Hadn't thought he'd ever want a woman this much. It was her scent. Had to be. Or maybe the timbre of her voice.

Something. He didn't know what. But his mind had taken a hike. He didn't think Clare had noticed.

Or maybe she had. She'd stopped speaking and her breathing had turned ragged. Her skin seemed to gleam a little— sweat? He hoped she was hot. And wet. A hot and wet Clare . . . his seat belt trapped him in the car as he flung open the door.

He stumbled as he got out of the car, forgetting his foot and leg didn't work right, and flushed with embarrassment, but by the time he got his cane from the back and slammed the door, he saw the wisp of Clare's floaty sundress skirt disappearing into the alcove. She seemed to be in a hurry, too. He heard her swearing—the endearing mild curses she used—at the alarm system.

Grinning, he picked up his pace, leaning on his cane. Right now the fact that his foot didn't flex didn't matter. What mattered was that his favorite muscle was about to be satisfied.

He caught her in the doorway just as the alarm light turned green. She pressed the iron latch and he used his cane to shove the heavy oak door open, then let his cane clatter to the floor. He found her waist easily in the dark, as if he'd always know exactly where his woman was, slipped his arm hard around her, and lifted her for the two long steps to the wall. He moved until he could feel his whole body against hers and, most of all, his needy dick. His mouth found hers, and his heart did that jump thing again when he discovered her lips were open.

He slid his tongue into her wet depths and groaned as his hips angled into her, holding her against the wall with his weight . . . and his arm behind her hurt and there were damn better things for his fingers to be doing, like sliding under her skirt to find if she was just as wet—or more—down below.

If she craved him as much as he did her.

He drew his arm from behind her, and they fit even better so he groaned again. He thought Clare was whimpering, but blood rushed around in his head, thundering in his ears, before dropping straight to his engorged erection.

Her thigh felt so smooth to his palm. And warm. Her dress got caught on his hand because he was sweaty or his skin was rough, damn it! But he found the smoothness of her panties, registering that they felt like silk just before he ripped them off her.

His fingers found her. Warmer than he'd imagined and, yeah, wet!

She cried out, then lifted her leg and hitched it on his hip, and he knew she was open to him and he had to get inside her now. He yanked at his jeans and felt the hook rip, moaned as his fingers brushed his dick under the cotton, swore, prayed, he'd get inside her, where he needed to be, before he came. Found the split in his boxers, freed himself, and plunged into Clare.

She was hot, slick, and she smelled like Clare and sex, and he thrust and thrust and thrust, tried to hang on to a sliver of control to make the ecstasy last but she ground against him and whispered his name and then she clenched around him and it was all over and pure pleasure exploded.

A couple of minutes later they slid down the wall, onto her wood floor. He pulled her over him, so he could feel her, still needing her close. Words fell out of his mouth. "God, Clare. I was away too damn long."

She sniffed.

"Shoulda made them hurry up the damn hearing, not stayed awhile to bullshit with Billings cops, or dropped by to see my old boss. I coulda been back earlier if I'd driven straight through."

She chuckled. "I missed you, too, a great deal."

That should make alarm bells go off in his head and his heart. Going too fast, going too deep into a relationship with Clare too soon.

He heard nothing but their unsteady breathing, and his arms tightened around her.

"I'll get up in a minute," she murmured. Her fingers had slipped through a gap between the buttons of his shirt and she petted his chest. Wonderful.

"I may be up again shortly," he said.

She laughed and rubbed her head against him. As her other hand danced across his hip and began to wedge between them, he grabbed it and stopped it. "I'd like to wait until we're on a bed next time, and with added protection."

He met her eyes as she lifted her head. Her pupils were large in the dim light, and he couldn't tell what color, brown or green, the hazel shaded to.

Snuggling close, she seemed to relax atop him. He closed his eyes, then jolted as he felt a lick on his ear, her teeth close gently on his lobe. *Oh, God.* Now his dick was really interested again. Gently he rolled until she slid from the top of him to her side, her teeth white in a grin in the dim light. Again his heart lurched. He liked seeing her happy.

He stood and stepped from his jeans, then hauled her up next to him, leaving her pretty panties on the floor. With her smile still wide, he figured she wasn't thinking of her tidy nature. Was that an innate characteristic or something she'd learned in order to cope with the chaos of her family life during childhood? Something he'd have to hang around to find out.

"Let's hit the shower," he said. The master bathroom had one of those major deals with multiple showerheads that laid down crisscrossing streams of water.

Taking her hand, he led her to the tiny elevator. He wanted to get to the second floor faster and have sex with his woman instead of slowly mounting the stairs. He tensed a moment, not sure where his cane had gone to, then shrugged and decided to leave it. She had a selection of canes in a fancy Chinese umbrella stand next to "his" dresser.

Yeah, they'd moved fast. So fast, so intimate. So intense that he couldn't turn away from this generous, caring woman.

Sexy as hell woman. Too bad her skirt covered her lower body as they walked.

A few minutes later, all soft and slippery, they'd shouted their satisfaction together once more and were sliding down the corner of the shower, hot water still pumping, nearly too much for his senses to stand. Fantastic.

Clare recovered first and let some steam out as she left the enclosure. The only regret he had right now was that he was damn sure he wouldn't be making love to her in her new bed. Exhaustion hovered like a thunderstorm ready to hit.

Until he heard her scream.

Fear pumped through him. He slammed from the shower, ran with his lurching gait.

When he got to the bedroom, Clare appeared more angry than frightened and gestured with a quivering hand at the bed, covers turned down. Zach blinked. "What?" Then he got closer and saw.

"It's a finger. A whole skeletal finger. All the bones. That *ghost*, that *J. Dawson Hidgepath*, left them. Here. For me." She crossed her arms in a defensive pose, pulling the plush robe around her.

Zach's breathing slowed. Man, he was out of shape, out of practice at handling emergencies. Or maybe it was that his lover had been threatened . . . anyway, he was dealing with a massive surge of adrenaline. He stared down at the four bones, not seeing anything threading them together as if they'd been a model.

The scare and his humor got the best of him. "I've seen enough bones to tell you that it's his index finger and not the middle one he left you."

She glared at him and he coughed to cover his laugh. When she gave him a dirty look, he grabbed her discarded towel and wrapped it around him, then slipped an arm around her waist.

"J. Dawson Hidgepath!" she yelled, with enough volume and a high pitch that made Zach's ears ring. "You get here *now!*"

What is it? What is it? Enzo materialized at the end of the California king bed and sniffed at the bones. *Ooooh. Ooooh. Nice, smelly, BONES FROM A GHOSTMAN!*

Zach heard barking, but since he was touching Clare, he got the full visual and telepathic audio. Clare's arm had gone around Zach's waist, too. She smelled fabulous, fancy peach soap, a hint of roses from the shampoo, and Clare.

The ghost of a man walked through the bedroom French doors to the balcony. The second-story French doors. As always, it was difficult to judge the height of a floating man with . . . no feet . . . more than a regular human.

Zach judged this guy to be five foot eight and with a light frame, on the scrawny side, 138 pounds or so.

The apparition stopped at the end of the bed and doffed his bowler hat, then put it over his heart. *I see you've found the token of my affection.* He gestured and light seemed to sparkle on a rose and a piece of paper under the finger.

"I don't like it," Clare said.

You haven't even LOOKED at my poem! The ghost sounded hurt.

Enzo yipped and began licking the bones.

The ghost yelped, *Stop that!*

Sluurrp. The spook dog ignored the man haunt.

"Enzo!" exclaimed Clare.

"Enzo," said Zach.

Awww, so tasty.

"With what? Ectoplasmic goo?" Zach asked.

Hidgepath scowled at Zach as if noticing him for the first time. "Who is he?"

Zach smiled. "The law."

Too-pointy-to-be-manly chin jutting, Hidgepath said, *You can't do anything to me.*

"Sure I can," Zach said easily. "I can stop Clare from sending you on, let you stay in this half life forever." From what the gunfighter ghost they'd dealt with had said, that was not something anyone wanted to stay stuck in.

Clare stiffened. Zach winked at her then stared into the dark and glittery holes that were the apparition's "eyes." "And who do you think is investigating your murder?"

The ghost literally brightened, becoming better defined shadows. He wore dark pants and a vest, a nice shirt. His hat had disappeared. Hope shone on his face. *You? You'll be looking into my death?* The words resonated deeper in Zach's head.

"That's what I do." Just before Zach had left, Rickman had said something about getting more cases from criminal defense attorneys now that Zach was on staff, maybe even hiring more ex-cops, building that side of his business.

J. Dawson Hidgepath bowed.

"Take the bones and go," Clare said.

The entire body of the ghost slumped as if depressed his offerings hadn't been accepted, but what did the guy expect?

Clare's voice softened. "Where do you *want* to be buried, J. Dawson? I can gather and keep your bones and arrange for a burial in a place of your choosing."

She lied. Zach knew damn well who'd be picking up those bones and storing them for safekeeping. It wasn't Clare.

Scratching his chin, the wraith projected, *I would like to be buried in the Fairplay Cemetery. It was close to Curly Wolf and is a good name for a town, a good omen for me, and it is still being used so I won't be lonely. Though, hopefully, you will find out who pushed me off that trail to my death, and I will rest easier.*

Then the damn ghost winked at Clare. *Or you can find me a pretty little female ghost who is as stuck as I am.* He grinned, cocked a hip. *Everything is better for being shared.*

Clare smiled and made pushing motions with her hand. "Go on with you. Know that we're working to help you. And please, no more bones in my bed. Stick to the consulting room in the carriage house."

"Does the consulting room have a couch?" Zach asked.

She sent him a repressive look. "A love seat."

He could hide his bones in the love seat and I could find them! Fun, fun, fun! Enzo barked and leapt off the bed to land near the ghost, doing one of those long nose-run-up-the-leg deals and inhaling lustily.

The shade of J. Dawson Hidgepath flinched. He tipped his hat—again on his head—to Zach, then a leer and a deeper pull on the brim of his bowler for Clare. *Later, fair lady.*

As he began to fade, a last, echoing sentence came. *I'll see you in South Park.*

"Uh-oh," Clare said. "I think we're not the only ones who'll be gifted with bones." She looked with distaste at the four resting in her bed.

SEVEN

ENZO TILTED HIS head. *I will follow him and see where he goes! He DOES smell soooo good.*

"Good idea," Zach said and watched the Labrador bullet out of the same second-story French doors J. Dawson had entered by.

Clare shifted from foot to foot as if uncertain.

"Go ahead and change the sheets," Zach said.

With a smile, she flung her arms around him, pressed her body against his briefly as she kissed his cheek, pleasing him with the casual intimacy. "I'll help you," he said. He picked up the bones and began to put them on the side table.

"Wait! That's *my* bedside table." She hurried away and came back with a large, fancily painted chest of about two feet wide with a domed top that she carried easily. Zach hadn't begun to take off the sheets, he'd have to move the pillows first, and he knew exactly what would happen if he touched the cases with hands that had held old bones. The pillowcases would have to be stripped and washed, too.

"Let me help you with that." He started forward. Stopped after one step when his left foot dragged along the floor, cringed. He'd forgotten. Despair surged through him. How long would it be before he wouldn't forget his disability?

"It's all right," Clare said cheerfully and he couldn't tell whether she'd seen his emotional pain. "The box is papier-mâché." She looked at it, and her mouth turned down. "I don't like the pattern."

Now he noticed the tiny dancing skeletons in various colors on a black background. His lips twitched. "Something you inherited from your great-aunt Sandra?"

"Yes." She looked at the thing with distaste. "And my brother *knew* I didn't want it. But the thing is, he didn't want it either."

"And he packed up your great-aunt Sandra's house."

"Yes. And here it is," Clare said.

"I'm sure J. Dawson will approve of it."

She frowned at him. "You're just saying that to be polite."

"Yeah, but the box is appropriate." He jiggled the bones in his own hands.

Clare flinched at the clacking sound. "That's just icky." She pulled out the little latch at the front of the box. "Brace yourself, Great-Aunt Sandra kept incense in it."

As Clare opened the rounded top, heavy, pungent smells assaulted his nose. "You think we should put J. Dawson in here?" Zach asked. "Won't his bones pick up residue or oil?"

Clare hesitated. "We'll wrap him up first." She put the box on the bed, hustled to a closet, and pulled out a velvet shawl of vibrant purple.

"I'm guessing that's from your great-aunt Sandra, too," Zach said. When it got nearer, his body tightened . . . Clare used the same scent . . . he liked that scent, mysterious, intriguing, and his dick sure remembered kissing her, making love to her, when all she wore was that fragrance.

"Yes," Clare said, tucking the cloth inside and arranging it. She slid a glance at him. "Do you think this will hold a full skeleton?"

Zach grimaced as he recalled autopsies he'd witnessed. "Nope. But hopefully *we* won't be getting all of the bones. Let Laurentine arrange for his own box."

"All right." She gestured for him to put the phalanges in the box.

"Great," he said, then stuck the bones in it and put it on the floor near his side of the bed. "You want me to take the rose and the poem, too?"

"For sure!"

He reached down, but the moment he touched the rose, it fell apart, the same with the paper.

Clare literally growled and crossed her arms tightly again. "Why are the bones strong and solid and not the rose and paper?" She stomped in place, one foot, then the other. A pang went through Zach at the thought he'd never be able to do that.

"Bones *are* denser. Surely there are still mummy bones around, right?"

"But the paper?"

"Dunno."

"Rules. There seem to be no rules to this stuff!" She glared at him. "Or I can't find any easily in Great-Aunt Sandra's journals."

"Clare," he soothed.

She blinked at him and dropped her arms, breathed deeply enough he caught a hit of cleavage of her full breasts. "Let the questions go for now. We'll sleep on everything," he said.

Her head tilted. "You're the peace officer, the investigator—can you put problems out of your head that easily?"

His lips formed into a half smile. "I've learned, and sleeping on problems can bring solutions." He held out his hands to her.

Laughing and shaking her head, she said, "Go wash up. I'll take care of the sheets."

He wasn't quite sure whether she'd throw them away or not. Her frugality no doubt battled the ick factor.

"I have pizza and beer downstairs. Come down when you're ready."

"Great." He walked to the master bath and scrubbed up. While he did, she stripped the bed and put the contaminated sheets in the hamper, took others from a closet that would fit the bed she'd installed when he was gone. A California king. Yeah, the woman was special.

* * *

Clashing swords yanked Clare from the top of the battlements in her dream to groggily hear a husky man's voice say, "Slade."

Just the one word cleared her mind, made her nerves thrill. Zach was back! And in her bed, and the sex had remained incredible: in her entryway, in the shower, and in the bed.

It still looked like night. She blinked, accepted the fact she was in her new bedroom and her new bed—with Zach!— and this house, like her last, faced west and the sun was nowhere around. Slowly she sat up. The medieval times dream had been a relief; she'd been living so much lately in the Old West.

"It's for you," Zach said, handing her a cell phone that sort of looked like her smart phone but wasn't. She fumbled for it, dropped it. Zach caught it and curved her fingers around it.

"It isn't even dawn!" she protested.

Zach grunted. "We're lucky Rickman waited until six a.m."

"Rickman!"

"Here," said the voice from the phone. He sounded wide awake, just like Zach . . . well, she supposed she could understand that. They'd both been in dangerous professions.

"What do you want?" she asked.

"A few million bucks would do," Rickman said, "but at the moment I'm calling to tell you that an angry Dennis Laurentine contacted me a few minutes ago and wants you, Clare, up at his spread today. Apparently J. Dawson Hidgepath struck again, leaving bones in a bed."

"And they discovered that this morning?"

A pause. "I didn't ask."

Zach laughed. "Some lady was on her way *back* to her bed?"

"Go to the DL Ranch today?" Clare asked.

"That's right," Rickman said.

"And stay until J. Dawson Hidgepath moves on."

"Yes."

She put her hand on Zach's thigh, tried not to notice the hard and interesting shape of him under the sheet. Steadying her voice, she said coolly, "I wanted to spend a little more time with Zach." There, she'd admitted that aloud during a business discussion. If either man thought it was inappropriate, too darn bad. This was her new life, her new "business," and she'd make her own rules.

"I'm sorry that isn't an option for you now," Rickman said neutrally.

Clare sighed, hopped from bed, and drew on her plush robe, that hung from a coat stand.

So far she wasn't working for the man, but she was accustomed to having a superior to answer to. And she'd told J. Dawson that she'd help him. She might as well get paid for it.

Holding the phone, she went to the windows to stare out at the street. "How much time do I have to decide?"

"I told Laurentine I'd call back by six thirty."

"Doable," said Zach.

"Zach will be investigating J. Dawson's death," Rickman said.

"I definitely need to start out with the resources here in Denver. I'd imagine many materials made it here after Curly Wolf dried up," Zach said.

"Or are in the Park County Archives," Clare said. She wanted to delay, but there was no reason to, and Enzo appeared on her chaise lounge near the balcony doors as if to remind her of that.

"I'll take the job and be up there before noon," she said to Rickman. "I'll sign the contract, scan it, and e-mail a copy. Zach can bring you the original."

"Right," Rickman said. "Later, Clare." He sounded as if he moved on to the next item on his list . . . his next case.

"C'mere," Zach said, patting the bed beside him.

Just his glance made her hot, hot, hot, and giddiness swept through her.

She studied him, let her appreciation of him show in the dawning light. He stacked his hands behind his head and let a smile linger on his lips as she strolled toward him. The ruby-colored sheet over his lower body rose a trifle and heat slipped hotter through her veins.

She ran her hands down her sides, letting the plush of her expensive robe tingle her palms, ratchet up her sensuality another notch. Her fingers stopped at the belt and slipped open the knot, let the belt hang and her robe open.

Zach's chest went up and down faster with his breathing. That pleased her. She was always surprised that she excited a man like him. At the foot of the bed, she slid the robe off and laid it down, then circled the footboard to his side and stood before him, nude. Reaching down, she flipped off the sheet and scrutinized him head to foot, slowly. His eyes dilated as he stared at her, and she made sure that he noted her gaze lingered on his scarred leg, especially under his left knee. He had to know that she found him sexy just as he was.

Then, of course, her gaze focused on his shaft, so strong, so vital. Her knees loosened. He put a hand on her upper thigh and her brain went to mush and she didn't care. She moved onto the bed and over him, caressed his erection briefly, closed her eyes at his moan, before she took him inside her.

For a moment they stayed there, quiet, connected, neither of them moving. Then he brushed her nipples with his fingertips and her lashes flew open, her gaze latched on his dark, fierce one. His hands cupped her breasts and he angled up to taste her. She gasped at the dual sensation of his kisses and movement inside her.

She closed her eyes and set her hands on his chest, felt the crinkles of his light hair against her sensitized palms. She heard her own breathing, louder than the pounding of her pulse in her temples.

Slowly she lifted until she could barely feel him, then plunged down. A sound ripped from him, and his hands went to her hips. She leaned back, batted them away, and took control of the lovemaking. She set the pace, slow and tortuous so she could feel him slide all the way in and out of her, experience how he thickened more to fill her.

His hips rose and she matched his thrusts, hurried the beat of bodies moving together until the dizzying peak was close, closer, *there!* She cried out, felt him pulsing within her, then she subsided on atop him.

His hands fell from her. "We haven't talked about protection lately."

   She stiffened and propped herself up on his chest to stare at him sternly. "Since twelve days ago?" Her words came out clipped and she didn't mind. "Did you sleep with anyone else?" She leaned to roll away and his arms clamped her to him.

EIGHT

"NO, CLARE. I didn't sleep with anyone else. Yes, I can still give you my latest health records if you like. I saw my doctor in Montana. I'm clean. So did you sleep with anyone while I was gone?" His big hand stroked her head, played with her hair.

"No. I had no urge to sleep with anyone else."

"Ghosts keep you busy?"

She relaxed on him. "Not so much. This house did."

"Uh-huh."

"I can give you my latest blood work, too."

"Not necessary."

"And I remain on birth control."

He kissed the top of her head. "Good."

"Yes. I am so not ready to have children. Though, unlike many women, I have enough financial resources to be a single mother easily. I wouldn't ask for any support, Zach."

He yanked her hair. "Get this. If something happens and we make a baby together, I want to be part of the kid's life."

She shivered at the thought that she might have a child she'd pass her gift on to. That certainly gave her pause.

"Clare?"

"I like you, Zach. I think you're a good man. Of course I would let you share any mythical child's life."

"'Kay. We got the topic covered?"

"I think so, yes."

"Let's hit the showers. Separately this time or we'll never get out of here."

"Yes."

But he rolled over so she was under him, fully aware of his body. His mouth touched hers, his tongue demanded entrance, and she let him in, joined with him that way. Let sexual attraction sweep her away again.

He broke the kiss, and angled up so their glances met. A smile hovered on his lips. "I'm not nearly done with you, Clare Cermak. Just started, in fact."

She nodded, mind still fuzzy.

His eyes gleamed with satisfaction. "Good." He rolled off her, and off the bed, made a wide gesture for her to head into the master bath. He didn't want her to see him walk, then. She swallowed a sigh and got off the bed with less grace. She stopped in front of him and pulled his head down for a quick, claiming kiss, her blood stirring. Then she sashayed away.

After showering and dressing in a pair of new jeans and a long-sleeved silk blouse, Clare read and signed the short contract with Rickman to be an independent consultant for one job only. The terms with him were fair. The minimum fee and the hourly rate sent a balm to her accountant's heart.

It wasn't the fee that her great-aunt Sandra could have commanded, but it was more than respectable for the trip and stay and stopping J. Dawson Hidgepath from doing more damage.

The cost of sending the apparition on to his next destination couldn't be calculated. Those horrible moments when she had to initiate contact, sink into him, see whatever he—or the universe—needed her to see, then free him with whatever words came to her chilled mind and frozen lips.

She shook off the memory of helping her first major ghost, and e-mailed the contract to Rickman, then left her "ghost business" office to pack a bag, and looked around her home.

Zach had dressed and kissed her jawline, then turned her and slid his mouth on hers, darted his tongue inside so she tasted him. One last glorious pressure of lips on lips and he stepped away. "I like your new digs, Clare."

She sighed. "Yes, I love this house."

"And it looks good on you, wealth," Zach said.

She shrugged and his hands came up to curve around her upper arms. "You won't waste it like your parents. You'll shepherd it."

"Absolutely."

"But you'll enjoy it, too, like your great-aunt Sandra did."

"I suppose."

"I'm staying here in Denver to hit the library and the History Colorado Center for whatever they might have," he said reluctantly. "Shouldn't take more than a day, do you think? You're the historical research expert."

She grimaced. "I'm getting there, aren't I? But I've got a feeling Mr. Laurentine was right. We won't find any solid, original source material on J. Dawson, especially down here in Denver. I think most everything will be in Park County."

"Good." He kissed her. "I'll be up in a day or two."

When she finished packing a large bag, Zach said, "Don't forget J. Dawson's box."

"You think I'll need it before you come up?" She hoped she wouldn't.

"Oh, yeah."

She fixed breakfast and they ate. Then she gave Zach her resource list for Western history in Denver, and had no more reason to linger. As it was, she'd be leaving during rush hour. She double-checked her route to avoid ghosts lingering around the car and obscuring her vision. She was getting better at ignoring the stray one or two while driving.

After a last, sizzling kiss with Zach, she departed. Enzo popped up in her passenger seat before she got down the block.

He panted cheerfully. As usual, strings of ghostly drool hung down from his muzzle. *Whee! WE ARE GOING TO THE MOUNTAINS!*

"I know. I'm driving."

I have never been TO THE MOUNTAINS!

"I guess not. You'll find it cooler." Would he notice? "It's coming up on autumn, though I don't think the aspen leaves will quite have turned gold yet."

There will be MOUNTAIN GHOSTS.

"Yes, a lot of them." She wondered if she dared visit some of the towns. They'd be as thronged with ghosts as downtown Denver. "Many people lived in the mountains during the time period I'm sensitive to. Miners, prospectors, and everyone who could make money off of them."

This will be FUN! Enzo stared out the windshield.

"It will be business." She hesitated. "Did Great-Aunt Sandra enjoy her business?"

Mostly. Enzo turned his head. *Sometimes helping ghosts is sad.*

"I'd imagine so. Thank you for coming with me, Enzo."

You are welcome. I am your companion helper.

"Uh-huh."

With traffic, there was no fun to be had until they hit Turkey Creek Canyon and the sun was at her back.

Enzo stuck his head out the window. *WHEEEEEE! Thank you for taking me to the mountains! You are THE BEST!* He didn't just stick his head out; he put his paws on the sill and stuck his body out. Not a hair on him moved, but he appeared to feel the wind and his expression was pure bliss.

The winding trip was lovely, and Enzo commented on the tall walls of the canyon, the steep grade, the rock faces, and the stream. Clare didn't stop until she reached the scenic overlook atop the hill before descending into South Park.

Enzo shot through the door and past the paved parking lot through the wire fence to the scrubby bushes near the edge of the drop-off. Since he lifted his leg, and *something* seemed to come out of his nonexistent bladder, she stared. This was the first time he'd done *that*.

She left him to whatever strange ghostly business he might have and took in the view. As always, the huge open space of the geological basin that had once been an inland sea made her catch her breath with its beauty. It was early September, and the green from the summer afternoon rains had transformed into dry yellow, which would stay until the deep snows.

Standing and breathing the lovely air, she welcomed the soft rays of the sun in the thinner atmosphere. For a moment she toyed with the small notion of buying a place here . . . but there were so many gorgeous places in Colorado . . . and she'd just bought an expensive home . . . and . . . maybe . . . someday . . . she and Zach . . . She was afraid she wanted too much from him, too quickly. She *didn't* want to be dependent on him. That was no way for a relationship to work . . . being more dependent on a man than he was on you.

She glanced at her wristwatch. She was ahead of schedule, but anything could happen between here and the DL Ranch. The main road was paved and two-lane, but went up and down over hilly ridges, and she had no idea what the road to Mr. Laurentine's estate was like. Her navigation system showed him atop a low rise on the outskirts of a mountain, neighboring a state wilderness area.

With a mental call to Enzo, she did a last stretch and got back into her car.

Clare, it WAZZZ WONNERFFUL! Enzo hopped onto the seat.

She glanced at him sharply. He sounded odd, almost if he were a person, drunk. The dark mist of his eyes swirled and showed more glitters than usual. Starting up the car, she said, "Enzo, are you all right?"

New place, Clare! New sights and smells and ENER-GIEEEZ all around. Animalzzz I don' know, old, old spiritzz who don' wanna talk.

Clare figured those would be Native Americans. She thought the Mountain Utes had used South Park as a summer hunting ground.

"All right," she said. "The GPS says we should be at the DL Ranch in under a half hour. You know that Curly Wolf will be there, just down the hill from the main house."

If possible, he perked up even more, ears lifting. *Hooray! More ghosts like J. Dawson!*

"Hooray," Clare said unenthusiastically. She listened to classical music as she wended her way through South Park.

She passed Fairplay and the road up to the original site of Curly Wolf, then drove another thirty miles or so to a county road. There she turned onto the private drive leading to the DL Ranch over a cattle guard—a steel grid over a ditch with bars too far apart for animals to walk over.

Tall iron gates with fence posts strung with barbed wire on either side stopped her progress. The gates showed the fancy encircled DL initials at the top and a little brick guardhouse just beyond. Slowly they opened and she drove through and across another cattle guard.

We are here! Enzo stood with paws propped on the dash, phantom tail whisking back and forth. He turned his head and his eyes appeared almost natural. *This is very nice! Better than the lake with Sandra!*

As always, the thought of how she'd ignored her great-aunt stabbed through Clare. She forced a smile so she wouldn't dim the dog's enthusiasm and waved a hand. "Go, explore. Chase all the ghost and real wildlife you want." She hesitated. "You might check out the property for ghosts of my time period." The uprooted town of Curly Wolf would sure hold some.

Enzo leapt up to the dash, his claws scrabbling at the narrow ledge, and through the windshield.

She gave her name and handed her ID to the uniformed security guard. Something in his eyes or the way he looked at her reminded her of Zach, and she thought the guard might be an ex–deputy sheriff like her lover.

"Thank you," she said.

He nodded and gave back her driver's license, "Have a good time, Ms. Cermak. The house is just past the town of Curly Wolf, up on the hillside."

"So he can look down on his treasures," she murmured, but obviously not softly enough because the man pokered up.

She wiggled her shoulders, trying to release some of the tension that had settled in her back. "I don't have to drive through Curly Wolf, do I?"

"No, ma'am. Just follow this road."

"Thank you." She drove on the asphalt road just under the posted speed limit of fifteen miles an hour, knowing the guard's eyes were on her since she'd be the only threat around.

There was a turnoff leading to a historic-type gravel and dirt road to Curly Wolf, then the main road climbed and finally ended in a parking area at the west side of the mansion.

She'd never seen anything like the luxury Western-style log house . . . or maybe she had at one of the National Parks . . . Yellowstone or the Grand Canyon or Glacier. The appealing dark honey-colored wood seemed to radiate comfort and welcome. A house . . . home . . . that contradicted its cool and calculating owner. In any event, the sprawling building appeared to be a modern rustic style and hopefully held no other ghosts besides J. Dawson Hidgepath.

The A-line front indicated a two- or maybe three-story great room with a lot of glass that even thermally treated would be an energy sink in the winter, though she could see Dennis Laurentine being arrogant enough to put a lot of glass in a high mountain house just to impress. He might only spend a few days here in the winter anyway, for winter sports.

As she exited her car, a man paused by the door of his own high-riding dusty black pickup. Then he crossed to her. He wore a cowboy hat, weathered jeans, a plaid shirt, and a bolo tie with a small silver disk slider. He looked like the real deal, an actual rancher, or maybe the manager of this ranch.

She went around to her trunk and again fumbled with the fob close to the lock, then jumped as a beep sounded from another car in the lot.

Opening the trunk, she grabbed the handles of her suitcase when stronger, older hands nudged hers aside. "Let me take that, ma'am," the man drawled.

"Sure. Thank you." Clare stepped aside, watching as he easily lifted the bag. It contained clothes, a couple of reference books, and her laptop and tablet computers. She was a sucker for backup. The cowboy stood a few inches taller than she at about six feet, and was lean with a creased and tanned face and hands that showed he spent a lot of time outdoors.

She judged him to be in his mid-sixties, older than Mr. Laurentine.

Putting out her hand, she said, "I'm Clare Cermak, from Denver, working on a project for Mr. Laurentine."

He shook her hand with the one that wasn't firmly holding the handle of her suitcase. "Baxter Hawburton, Bax." His smile showed deep lines around his eyes. "I'm a neighbor, was just consultin' with Dennis myself."

Clare studied him. "I think I recognize your surname from, ah, the Curly Wolf Cemetery."

Now he grinned. "Probably. My family has been here for a while." He jerked his head toward Curly Wolf. "One of the buildings down there held my great-great-grandpa's store. Pleased to see it restored."

"You don't look as if you followed the family business."

He chuckled. "Nope. We diversified. Used the money from the store to buy land and started ranching." He winked. "Like a lot of folks, did a little gold panning and placer mining on the side in the early days."

"Ah." She saw Enzo in the distance, felt a gentle tug from him for her to head down to the ghost town, but she'd postpone that as long as possible. Still, she stopped and looked at the view of Curly Wolf.

"Are you a historian?" he asked as he gestured toward the house and began walking, carrying, not rolling, her suitcase.

"I do a lot of historical research," Clare said, which was all too true. It was a good thing she'd always loved Western history.

"You've got a lot in common with Dennis, then."

"Some." She fought to keep the cool note from her voice, stuck in some warmth and self-deprecation. "Of course, I don't have the money to be a serious collector."

Baxter grunted. "Not many do."

And not that she'd need to collect anything. If life continued as it had, Enzo or the Other would be dropping off rare items as "payment from the universe" every time she helped a ghost pass . . . to wherever.

They approached the large double doors, and Clare hurried

to open one for Baxter. He just slanted her a look and pulled open the other and they went through together.

A tall woman with a straight spine and pale blond and silver hair in a braided coronet came forward. She wore nice black slacks and a navy shirt. Her expression was stern. She nodded to Baxter. "Thanks for helping out." Then she gestured and a tall and gangly young man came and took Clare's suitcase. "Tyler, take that to the jade guest room," said the woman.

"Will do," Tyler said.

"Good meeting you, Clare," said Baxter. "You'll probably see me around." With a last nod he loped from the building.

"You must be Clare Cermak," the woman said. "I'm Patrice Schangler, the housekeeper." She didn't offer her hand.

"Yes, I'm Clare."

"We were not told how long you might stay," Patrice said.

Clare eyed Patrice. The Schangler name was mentioned in the cemetery records, so she was probably hired locally . . . though Clare couldn't know whether Schangler was the woman's maiden or married name. But it was easy to sense the distrust since it showed in her stance and her attitude.

Mr. Laurentine had said that J. Dawson's bones appearing had spooked some of the locals and cost them jobs. So would Patrice Schangler welcome Clare more if she knew Clare was trying to get rid of the bones-appearing phenomena?

Perhaps because she wasn't an accountant at a prestigious firm anymore and her gypsy blood might be welling through her a bit, Clare wanted to see this woman's reaction to the truth. "I'll be here until I help J. Dawson Hidgepath move on." She paused. "And ensure he stops leaving his bones in women's beds."

The housekeeper looked startled and a hint of something else appeared in her eyes. Fear? Discomfort? Wariness? Clare couldn't gauge the flash of emotion.

"Ah," the woman said, and looked her up and down. Clare got the impression the housekeeper hadn't expected her to be so up front about her task.

"I imagine you want the bones," Ms. Schangler said.

Clare flinched. "Yes."

The corners of the woman's mouth curved in a tiny smirk.

"Yes," Clare repeated to remind herself this was now part of her life and she should darn well get accustomed to it. "Yes." She took a quick breath. "What kind of bones are they?"

NINE

"THERE'S A COMPLETE foot," Ms. Schangler said.

"Oh." Clare wet her lips. "Were there any flowers or a poem?"

The woman stopped smiling, sent Clare a sidelong look. "I wasn't told." Reluctantly, she added, "There was a heap of dust on the sheets." Ms. Schangler sniffed. "Missy Legrand insisted that the sheets be changed early this morning. Such a fuss!"

Well, of course. "The actress?" Clare asked.

"That's what she calls herself, though she hasn't been 'working' all summer long. She's been here."

With a quiet breath, Clare glanced around the huge great room as she followed Ms. Schangler across the area.

Naturally, the room showed Mr. Laurentine had spared no expense. Several sitting areas were delineated by Native American patterned rugs and grouped brass-studded leather furniture in earth tones. The polished floor was hardwood; the rounded log walls gleamed. So did the three-person-wide wooden staircase that led to the second floor. At the top of the steps was an equally wide corridor open to the room below with another carved balustrade.

They went through a door that seemed reserved for staff, and the area beyond looked less like a movie set and more like a workplace.

"I put the bones in the second pantry," Ms. Schangler said.

Clare became diverted by thoughts of antique bones being close to food she might be eating and, worse, how she was going to carry the bones to her room, and the fact that she'd left J. Dawson's chest with the other bones in the trunk of her car. She stiffened her spine.

The second pantry looked to be mostly for storage of canned goods—both store-bought and homemade. Clare was impressed by the amount and variety of the food, enough for several people to eat if they were snowed in for a couple of weeks.

Sturdy built-in shelves painted beige and some cabinets ranged every wall, getting the maximum amount of space usage.

Ms. Schangler pulled out a drawer and lifted up the first worn thing Clare had seen in the house, a stained tea towel, probably used as a rag. Clare heard the scratchy clatter she was afraid she'd become familiar with. The housekeeper placed the bundle atop the counter and briskly unfolded the cloth before Clare could brace herself. She swallowed hard, staring down at the bones, which appeared a lot like the finger she'd seen the night before—colors of white and ivory and brown areas that, presumably, dirt had marked.

The housekeeper stood quietly but Clare thought the woman sensed Clare's discomfort and was amused.

"A foot?" Clare asked faintly.

"Yes." Ms. Schangler lifted her brows. "Do you want me to arrange them for you?"

"No need. So the bones don't bother you? And them appearing in beds doesn't bother you?"

The woman shrugged. "The *bother* is the screaming and carrying on over a lot of old bones and the disruption of my household."

"I understand," Clare said. "You live here, manage this lovely house year round?"

"That's right."

So Ms. Schangler would think of the house as more hers

than Mr. Laurentine's, Clare bet. "You don't wonder where the bones came from?"

Ms. Schangler shrugged again. "J. Dawson Hidgepath's legend is old and comfortable around here, along with Silver Heels and other ghosts of South Park. Mr. Laurentine likes the stories of Curly Wolf and Fairplay and South Park City and the rest, so we all know them."

"You think J. Dawson is back?"

The housekeeper laughed. "No. I think some very alive human put the bones there."

"You don't believe in ghosts?"

She sniffed, stared with more than a little contempt at Clare. "And I don't believe in fakes who pretend to talk to them, 'help them move on.' Charge an arm and a leg"—she glanced at the jumbled bones—"and a foot, for some scam."

"Ah." Clare considered calling Enzo for backup, but who was she to rock someone's world with proof that ghosts were real? She hadn't believed in them herself a month ago. Ms. Schangler might not be susceptible to feeling ghosts anyway.

And if Tony Rickman in Denver continued to find Clare consulting jobs, she'd better become accustomed to attitudes of contempt, like a lot of other new things in her life that came with the gift to see ghosts.

"What do you want to do with these?" Ms. Schangler poked the small pile of bones. Her elegant, live, and healthy finger contrasted sadly with the bare and brittle sticks. A delicate diamond and platinum watch flashed on her wrist. Clare figured she must be working in a supervisory capacity if she wore such a thing.

"Ah, um," Clare said. "Do you have a sack?"

After lifting her eyes upward, the housekeeper opened a tall door and removed a canvas bag, the type Clare used for grocery shopping. "Thank you. I'll bring it back."

"See that you do." With a gesture, she indicated that Clare should precede her back toward the main portion of the house. Just before they got to the staff door, Enzo charged in, followed by J. Dawson.

The ghost dog barreled straight through Ms. Schangler and Clare. *Sorry, sorry, Clare! Did you call me?*

"Not really," she muttered, keeping an eye on the housekeeper. Talking to herself—and Enzo—in public made her wary. But the housekeeper's attitude had dropped away. She appeared shaken.

J. Dawson doffed his hat at them. He stepped around Ms. Schangler, but she still shrank away from the chill. The hallway was definitely a few degrees cooler than a minute before.

Excuse me, good woman, said J. Dawson. *Good morning, Clare.* He beamed and nodded to the bag. *I see you have my foot.*

Reflexively, Clare glanced down at the apparition's feet, both encased in tough work boots.

Good morning, J. Dawson, she sent mentally.

I can't hear you, Clare, the phantom said roguishly with a side glance at the housekeeper, who'd paled.

Clare stopped a sigh. "Good morning, J. Dawson," she said aloud. "I thought we agreed that you wouldn't leave your bones as a gift anymore."

He smiled, tilted his head. *I do not recalling agreeing to that.*

"It would make it easier—" Clare began.

GOOD MORNING, CLARE! GOOD MORNING, LADY! Enzo shouted as he pranced around them both. *I FOUND J. DAWSON DOWN AT CURLY WOLF!*

Ms. Schangler didn't actually bolt, but she hurried through the door without a backward look. Since the woman had left Clare in the housekeeper's domain, Clare was pretty sure she'd felt *something.*

Enzo sniffed. *I like the smell of her.*

"You always say that of people who can sense you."

Because it is true.

"I'm going to put away your foot, J. Dawson," Clare said, trying not to hear the impossibility of her own words. She cleared her throat. "I brought a box to hold the bones."

It is a good box! Enzo wagged his tail. *I will show you!* He darted out.

J. Dawson lifted his bowler an instant, then put it back on his head. *My thanks, Clare.* He sauntered after Enzo.

Clare held the canvas bag gingerly as she walked. She found Ms. Schangler, stiff-backed, awaiting her near the main staircase.

The housekeeper nodded, then pivoted toward the stairs. "I'll show you to your room." Her posture remained inflexible, and Clare decided the woman was trying her hardest not to believe in ghosts.

Clare'd been there, done that, and failed.

Once up the stairs, they turned left. Enzo materialized at the end of the corridor. *Hi, again, Clare! Hi, lady! We're staying here?*

This time Patrice Schangler gasped and hopped back, bumping into Clare, who had to steady her. They both fetched up against the wall by the door to her room. Ms. Schangler was made of strong stuff, however, and pushed away from Clare immediately, her spine a ramrod. From a pocket she took a key and slipped it in the brass door lock, then swung the door open and gestured for Clare to enter.

Enzo slipped through the wall. *It's beautiful! Though it doesn't have a dog bed. Do you think we could get a dog bed, Clare?*

Ms. Schangler flinched.

I have one in the backseat of the car, remember? Enzo had decided last week that he'd wanted a bed or two. *I'll bring it in.*

Yay!

Though it had to be one of the simplest guest rooms, the chamber was spacious and beautifully furnished. The walls were a delicate green. "Ah, the jade room."

The housekeeper's lips tightened. "All the rooms are named after minerals or jewels." Her eyes shifted as if she watched Enzo barrel through emerald-colored curtains.

Clare supposed that Mr. Laurentine had a gold or diamond suite. She said, "It's beautiful. Thank you for your help, and thank Mr. Laurentine for his hospitality."

With a curt inclination of her head, the woman said, "We are serving lunch now. It is a buffet in the breakfast solarium and served from eleven thirty a.m. to one p.m. Dinner is at six thirty and dress is business casual. Breakfast is from six a.m. to nine a.m. Pajamas are not allowed." She turned on her heel and left.

Enzo's head popped through a curtain. *There is a balcony, Clare! Can I have my bed on the balcony?*

"Let me see." She opened the heavy curtains to see translucent shams of a light gold, pulled those back to reveal the sliding glass door. After opening the door and the screen, she stepped out onto the balcony.

There was a sharp dip to a small, deserted valley below her, but filling her vision, up and up, were a couple of rough-hewn mountain peaks, all bare granite at this time of year. The air, though, was fabulous, warm and pure. Above the mountains showed the bright blue and cloudless sky.

We should go down and see Curly Wolf, Enzo said.

"Not yet." She'd put that off as long as she could. "I'm hungry." She checked her watch. "And I have a meeting at one p.m. with Mr. Laurentine."

Enzo whined and lifted a paw. *Zach didn't come.*

"I miss him, too." There, she'd admitted it aloud. "I'd like him to be here." She wanted to call him, tell him that she'd arrived safely, but he hadn't asked her to and he was probably at work. She had an ironclad rule that she wouldn't text or call anyone who might be working. But her fingers stroked her phone, itching.

Rustling noises came. Clare whirled, scanned the room. "Did you hear that?" she asked Enzo. "Is it a ghost?"

Someone suppressed a chuckle . . . from the closet on her immediate left. This guest room was set up more like a hotel room than anything else, definitely not how she'd have done it. "Come on out," she said, her voice calm. "If I open the closet door and you pop out at me, I won't be pleased."

The door slid open and a blond-haired, blue-eyed teenage girl stepped out, looking guilty and highly anxious. Her gaze darted around the room, didn't quite meet Clare's. "Please, please, ma'am, don't tell on me. I'm not supposed to be here."

"What are you doing here, Miss—"

Now the teen tried a winsome smile, showing deep dimples and beautiful teeth, but her fingers twined together and she shifted foot-to-foot. "Visiting my boyfriend."

"The young man who brought up my luggage?"

The girl gave a short nod. "Ms. Schangler's nephew, Tyler Jorgen."

Clare studied the bed.

"Not making love! Not here! We wouldn't do that! But Ms.

Schangler said I distracted Tyler and I couldn't come any-more. But I *had* to see him."

Enzo barked and sniffed around her. *She has a young smell.*

She IS young. Clare sent this to the phantom dog's mind, glad she'd recalled to do so before speaking aloud. Since Enzo didn't *looove* her scent, the girl must have little psychic power . . . or whatever he sensed most with his nose. And being young, her emotions drove her more.

The door opened behind Clare, catching her in the shoulder. "Ouch!"

"Ohmygod. Ohmygod," said Tyler Jorgen. "I'm so sorry! God!"

Clare rolled her shoulder. "It isn't bad. Don't worry about it." She moved from the hallway that held the bathroom and the closet to the medium-sized bedroom.

Slanting a glance at the girl, Clare said, "Though you'd better leave. And don't come back. At least to this room." They hesitated.

"I won't speak to anyone here about this," she said. She waved a hand. "Just go."

"Right, right." Tyler nodded quickly. His Adam's apple bobbed as he swallowed. He stepped into the room, snatched the girl's hand, and tugged. "Emily, the coast is clear, we can take the stairway down and be out the east side door without anyone seeing." Just before the door shut, his eyes met Clare's. "Thanks a lot, Ms. Cermak, for not telling on us."

"Thanks!" echoed Emily.

The door shut quietly but firmly, the latch catching. Since this was second from the last room and opposite the east set of stairs, it was no wonder the couple met here. Clare did a quick survey of the bed and bathroom, but they didn't look used. The young people had been endearing . . . though if Mr. Laurentine and Ms. Schangler had impressed Clare as being of a generous bent, she might have said something about the two she'd surprised. She shrugged and began to unpack, and took her phone from her purse and put it on the table. Maybe Zach would call her.

*   *   *

Zach reluctantly prepared to leave Clare's amazing house . . .
not that he didn't have a nice apartment, because he did. But it
sure didn't come with a hot lover who could cook in and out
of bed. Nope, more like two old ladies, one really wealthy
Mrs. Flinton, who cheerfully intruded on his business and
personal affairs, and one Mrs. McGee, who gave him good
food and occasional trenchant advice.

He wanted to *be* with Clare. Missed her the minute she
walked out the door to head to the mountains . . . while he
was stuck in Denver.

Mrs. Flinton was right, though—it had been a mistake to
pull back from her the six days he'd been away. He'd only
texted Clare a couple of times, hadn't taken time to call and
talk. Just . . . everything had been too intense.

For Clare, too, he suspected. Somehow they needed to
catch their balance in this . . . relationship. Figure out where
they were going, or wanted things to go.

He was too deep into this affair, the more-than-an-affair
already, in just two weeks.

They'd had a day together before he'd had to leave for
Montana. He wanted more. There was just something about
Clare that resonated . . . filled . . . the hell with specifics. He
just wasn't done with her yet.

She presented a puzzle he had to study, to untangle, to
plumb.

The thing of it was, he was sure she thought of herself as
simple to understand, but beneath that logical accountant was
a gypsy heart—and man, did he want to learn about *that*
woman. Who she might be.

A small tingle slithered along his spine at the thought that
they wouldn't have met, that he wouldn't have noticed those
depths in her eyes, if he hadn't been shot.

Washing his coffee mug in the kitchen, he deliberately
took the stairs to the second level and the master bedroom.
He wore the loathed brace as well as the orthopedic shoes,
had his cane.

On impulse, he went into the walk-in closet and looked at
the shelves that held Clare's perfume . . . two scents, one light
and citrusy that a professional woman would wear, the other
rich and exotic, the one that accented her own womanly

fragrance. The bottles she'd inherited from her great-aunt Sandra.

In front of the various bottles, lined up by size, was a tiny sample-size deal. Zach removed the bitty stopper, sniffed. His senses clenched at the remembrance of Clare in bed, this smell mixed with her own, though there didn't seem to be any liquid in the thick glass container. With Clare gone, he had to have it, so he'd make damn sure to give Clare a gift or two to keep with her to remind her of him. She'd reciprocate and he wouldn't be sneaking into her closet and sniffing her perfume.

Back in the bedroom, he took pen and pad from the side table with the landline telephone and scrawled a message on it, just in case she got back before him and noticed the bottle gone.

Missing you. Took your little bottle. A kiss will get it back. He grinned as he signed his name. Then he stopped and stretched long and completely, feeling his muscles, and let his smile linger. Yeah, he was in good shape. He felt fine, better than fine emotionally. For the first time since the shooting, he accepted easily that his old life was gone without swearing, without regret.

Clare had helped him, just like he'd helped her. They'd each met the right person at the right time. Where they went from here, he didn't know, but he hoped it would be together.

As he walked to his new truck, that now had plenty of miles on it, he heard a crow caw and hunched his shoulders. The heat of the late morning, which hadn't bothered him, now sent a trickle of sweat down his spine. Despite himself, he had to look, and found two beady black eyes staring at him from the top of Clare's wall.

One crow. One for sorrow.

His teeth clenched. Damnation.

TEN

DRESSED IN HER most expensive business suit, Clare walked into Mr. Laurentine's home office and blinked. It was about three times the size of her room upstairs, and held a massive wooden desk with marble inlays. The wall behind him consisted of tall bookshelves, nicely filled, and a wide sliding glass door that led to a terrace. The other walls had pale brown wallpaper with a raised design that looked like tooled leather.

Mr. Laurentine lounged behind his desk in an antique wooden swivel chair. Knowing him, the thing probably belonged to some famous Old Western banker.

Everything about his attitude showed that he liked his wealth and position. As an accountant, she'd had a few clients like him and had treated them with the deference they expected even if they didn't deserve it—after all, she represented her firm.

When he gestured a lazy hand at one of the leather-with-brass-tacks chairs, she took it.

"I asked around and got a few reports on you," Mr. Laurentine said as he studied her. "Folks seem to think you're the real deal, a psychic who can communicate with ghosts and make them go away."

Heat painted the back of her neck and cheeks. "I prefer to think that I just have a gift for helping apparitions move on."

He swiveled slightly. "I looked you up . . . and your great-aunt Sandra. I'm willing to have you help me with the bones. I signed the contract for a week with an optional additional week." His mouth pursed and tightened before he continued, "God knows, I don't want to lose any more staff, and I don't feel right about entertaining when I have this fucking problem." He sulked for a few heartbeats. "The leaves have started turning and Curly Wolf is completely rehabbed and ready to show off. I'd planned a huge party for the fall equinox in a little over two weeks." He scowled at her and drummed his fingers on the desk, his manicured nails clicking on the marble. "I really want him out in that first week, no later than two. Can you get him gone by then?"

Pressure seemed to compact the atmosphere around her. She'd been accustomed to deadlines in her old job, but didn't know so much about this one.

Clearing her throat, she said, "I don't know." She lifted her chin. "If you spoke to Tony Rickman about me, you know that I have just come into my gift. I don't have a lot of experience." A thought struck her. "You might want to, ah, consult with someone better, more well known than I."

He shrugged a shoulder, pointed his right index finger at her. "You're not off the hook. Rickman negotiated a high fee for your services. I expect you to deliver. And I expect you to be available whenever I have a question."

Clare's teeth clicked together. She shouldn't have left this negotiation in Rickman's hands. Now she knew better. "Then let's get to business. Speaking of questions, I'd like to ask you a few. You only have a minimum of guests now?"

"That's right."

"Do you have any female guests who might be targeted by J. Dawson?"

"The only one I have who's sleeping alone is you." He smirked. "Since Missy Legrand was targeted last night, she's now staying in my suite."

Clare had heard of that actress, though now Clare questioned her taste. "When did you start having problems with J. Dawson?"

Mr. Laurentine frowned. "Mid-August, last month."

Clare continued, "And he's left bones three times, as follows: once a full skeleton, which you interred and which then vanished from the coffin; a second time a full skeleton, which again vanished after burial. And last night, the foot."

"That's correct," Mr. Laurentine growled.

"Any poems or flowers?"

He stared. "Once, the second time. How did you know? I didn't tell Rossi."

She kept a pleasant smile on her face. "I received a few tokens last night myself."

A crack of laughter escaped the multimillionaire, then he shook his head. "At Denver and the DL Ranch. Hidgepath was a busy man—ghost—last night."

Clare wasn't about to tell Mr. Laurentine that she had no idea how ghosts transported themselves. "I have a box up in my room with the bones I received last night. I checked on the . . . uh . . . foot you got and the bones certainly look a lot alike." She straightened her shoulders. "Would you like me to return the foot to you?"

"Fuck no," Mr. Laurentine said. He gestured to a burlap sack. "That's where I'm keeping the bones." He scowled. "I paid for a gorgeous coffin for the guy that he apparently doesn't like, so now he gets a sack."

"All right. I think that's all I need to know right now." She stood. "I'll see you later." She inhaled discreetly and decided not to hide anything from this man she liked less and less. "Enzo?" she called her ghost dog companion. Since Mr. Laurentine seemed to want results, she might as well give him a little sample of how she worked, no matter how it might appear to him.

Her dog loped through the wall and bookcases behind Mr. Laurentine, rushed up to her, and rubbed his chilly self on the fronts and the backs of her calves. *Hi, Clare, hi! I was back in the town.*

"Did you see J. Dawson Hidgepath?"

The dog shook his head. *No, but he might not be here. He likes the night. And this isn't the place where the real town was.*

"Maybe I should go to the old cemetery, then."

Road trip! yelled Enzo and galloped through the wall in the direction of the parking lot and Clare's car.

She lifted her gaze from where the dog had been to Mr. Laurentine. He studied her like she was some strange bug.

"I'm going to check out the original cemetery of Curly Wolf."

Mr. Laurentine shrugged negligently. "You do that. I don't have a man there anymore, but you'll notice the cameras in the trees and on the fence near J. Dawson's *new* grave." Mr. Laurentine's smile was wintry. "No one has bothered to steal the cameras, though I think everyone in South Park knows of . . . the situation."

"I understand," Clare said.

"Do you?" He slapped his desk. "I sure the fuck don't. What I want, Ms. Cermak, is results."

She straightened her shoulders. "That's what I intend to provide." She let her own lips form a cool smile. "For J. Dawson and you." She turned on her heel and went back up to her room to dress in jeans and hiking boots more suited to walking around an abandoned graveyard.

ELEVEN

ZACH DROVE TO the History Colorado Center and went to its library. He began digging into Curly Wolf and the untimely death, *murder,* of a guy called J. Dawson Hidgepath.

When he sauntered out of the building, he knew he'd gotten as good a handle on the conditions surrounding the prospector's death as Zach thought could be found in Denver.

He'd contacted the Park County Archives and had discovered that they had an old journal of the sheriff's from the time. As far as Zach was concerned, that was pure gold. Unfortunately the pages were use-gloves-delicate and hadn't been scanned, nor had the full content been transcribed.

Zach had corresponded with the archivist and gotten an e-mail with the few pages that *were* available. From what he read, the man sounded like he'd been a good sheriff, factual and no nonsense, and as far as Zach knew, this guy had been the one to handle the "accidental" death of J. Dawson.

Since the archives were open only upon request and for a few hours on Friday, which happened to be tomorrow, Zach had made an appointment for the next day. He already knew he wanted to be where Clare was.

* * *

Later that night, sitting on the terrace, Clare watched the shadows deepen from evening to night as the sun sank over the mountains.

Missy Legrand had Mr. Laurentine to keep her warm. They cuddled together in a large reclining lounge chair near the outdoor fireplace.

At dinner there'd been Clare, Ms. Legrand, Mr. Laurentine, the rancher Baxter Hawburton, and a couple of other men who were business acquaintances of Mr. Laurentine.

The dinner itself featured gourmet French food. As soon as the meal was done, the businessmen had excused themselves to walk down to Curly Wolf, along with one of Mr. Laurentine's men as a local guide. Clare got the idea they were there for the night only. Mr. Hawburton had left.

Clare had gravitated with the others to the terrace, not wanting to visit the ghost town, especially in twilight. She'd had enough exercise that day pushing through tangles of bushes and climbing up and down the hill of the old Curly Wolf graveyard. She'd found no ghosts except Enzo and let the serenity of the place infuse her.

It had rained, and when she'd returned to the ranch, two huge delivery trucks had taken up most of the parking lot. She'd arrived at the door with a wet umbrella and muddy shoes. Ms. Schangler had met her, told her the mudroom was at the back, and stated that if Clare wanted her car moved, to give her the keys or car fob. Clare had, and was informed that her fob would be on a hook in the second pantry. She should really retrieve it.

When another ripple of low laughter came from the couple, she wished Zach were there . . . that she shared a fire with him. Her lovely new house had an outdoor fireplace, but the weather had been too warm to use it.

Something to look forward to. Despite the fabulous night before and this morning, despite their conversations, doubts about their relationship had seeped in with the dusk.

They hadn't contacted each other more than once or twice when he was on his trip to Montana, and that was both their faults. She'd remained a little shell-shocked from accepting her gift and laying—sending on—her first major, powerful ghost. It had taken more than a few days to process those experiences. And mixed up with those events was the sex and rocketing relationship with Zach. So when he'd been gone, he'd pulled back, and she'd let him, and pulled back herself.

She didn't want the same thing to happen with this trip. She'd call him.

Standing, she didn't bother to excuse herself to the couple entwined on the lounge and went up to her bedroom.

Enzo materialized in his dog bed and lifted his head. *I am out here, Clare, looking at the stars and smelling all the night smells!*

"Good for you." She smiled.

I will stay out here and guard you tonight.

That gave her pause. "Are there . . . inimical ghosts out there?"

He stood and a doggie shrug rippled down him. *There is a bad ghost but not one you could help, too fresh.*

Clare shivered. She had *no* experience with "bad ghosts." She'd barely heard of them and only knew they held more negative energy than regular ghosts.

"Too fresh a ghost?"

A little older than you. Enzo barked loudly enough for Clare to cover her ears. *See, he is afraid of me. He goes away!*

"Good job." She retreated to the bed and flicked on the table lamp. Soft light flowed through the green Tiffany-style shade. She took her phone from the charger, gave it her password, then pressed Zach's number.

He answered immediately. "Hey, Clare."

Everything in her warmed. "Hello, Zach."

"You doing okay?"

"I'm here." She paused.

"What?"

"I'm wondering if it's whining to say that the housekeeper doesn't like me and Dennis Laurentine is a jerk."

Zach chuckled. "It was obvious in Rickman's office that Laurentine is an asshole," Zach said.

She found herself smiling.

"Who was the lady whose bed J. Dawson violated? And who was she sleeping with?" Zach asked. She could hear him moving around, and sounds like dishes. Since she hadn't been to his apartment, Clare couldn't visualize him, and that was a pity.

"Missy Legrand."

A long whistle came over the phone. "That so?"

"Yes, very so. She's sleeping with Mr. Laurentine."

"Not surprising."

"No. How was your day?"

"Easy. I just did research on J. Dawson. Everyone lists his death as accidental."

"That's it?"

"Yes, but . . . you're interested in my day."

"I am interested in you and your day . . . and your cases."

"Huh."

"What?"

"I've never talked to anyone, any woman I've been with, about my work before. Even in this PI business, it's not going to be all roses."

"Roses with thorns," she said. "And this isn't the first case we've discussed, you know."

"Mrs. Flinton's was hardly a case at all."

She continued, "And you listened plenty when I was going through the ghost stuff."

"That was fascinating."

Laughing, and feeling lighter just talking to him, she said, "I'm glad you think so."

"You're okay?" he pressed.

"I'm fine. Let me tell you about this place; it's gorgeous."

They talked another half hour, and when they hung up, a sweet warmth suffused her. They *were* developing a relationship, more than sex, with solid respect and friendship.

She changed and slipped into bed and began to read a history about mining camps. It didn't mention Curly Wolf or J. Dawson, but it did go into the everyday life of boomtowns based on the extraction of silver and gold.

Sometime later, her telephone pulsed with the tone she'd assigned to Dennis Laurentine and she jerked awake. "Hello?" she asked groggily.

"Meet me now," the man said.

"Now? In your office?" But she was talking to air. Grumbling, she dressed fast in jeans and a sweater and stuck her feet in her new loafers.

When she exited her room, she noted that the lights in the house had been turned down, and it felt as if she had the huge place to herself.

Clare paused in the upstairs hallway looking over the great room, leaning for an instant against the polished and sturdy walnut balustrade. She didn't see Mr. Laurentine and wondered about his urgent call. Had J. Dawson left his bones in *Mr. Laurentine's* bed? She shivered.

These weren't the business hours she was accustomed to, and she disapproved. If they had to adjust her fee so he didn't feel free to call her around midnight, they certainly would.

Or did he think that because she communicated with ghosts, she did most of her "work" at night?

Clare gave a hollow laugh. If only the spirits who visited her would restrict themselves to set hours instead of drifting in at any old time, she'd be much happier. Always thinking that if she turned around a new specter would be behind her, expecting help, spooked her nerves.

Again her phone buzzed. Without looking at it, she straightened from the rail and turned toward the staircase and hurried down, the carved pinecone newel post like silk under her testing fingers. She'd—

Her foot slipped on something oily.

She fell. The first thump knocked the breath from her. Then she tumbled down the stairs, covering her head with her arms.

TWELVE

SHE LANDED AT the bottom of the stairs, gasping, shuddering with fear and adrenaline pumping through her, huddled on her side in a nearly fetal position.

Clare! Enzo was there, staring down at her with a deeply concerned doggy expression. She turned her head, relief flooding her that her neck worked.

Then Enzo's muzzle shut and depthless eyes surveyed her, the Other spirit.

Panting, spots swirling before her eyes, she tried to rip her gaze from the entity's, and couldn't.

Clare Milena Cermak, the bass tone rumbled through her brain, and her eyes widened more than she'd ever thought they could go. She wanted to wet her lips but couldn't even move her tongue and her mouth was dry, dry, dry.

It is not your time to die. We have much for you to do.

A tiny niggle at the back of her mind wondered what this "we" business was. Her thoughts coalesced enough for her to shoot him a question. *Not my time?*

No. A slow and stately nod of the ghost dog's head that Enzo could never manage. *One of the conditions of the pact we made with your ancestress when we asked you to help was*

*that we would advise you when your death was imminent, as
we did with Sandra. Do you wish this?*

Yes, she replied without thinking . . . not that she was doing much thinking, her vision was going dark. She couldn't
move, couldn't even flop around like a fish, and she needed
air!

BREATHE! the Other commanded. The ghostly Labrador's
mouth opened and touched her own. Warm, sweet-meadow-
summer-flowers air pushed into her: throat, chest, lungs, bringing with them a serenity she'd never felt before, such a lovely
feeling that tears welled from under her shut lashes.

Breathe, Clare, BREATHE! It was Enzo again, licking at
her with a cold, cold tongue. She sucked in cool air, then the
harsh dry stuff of the great room, tinged with wood and
fire . . . and the scent of furniture polish. She shuddered, began to straighten her legs inch by inch. When she had enough
breath, she screamed.

In less than a minute the lights of the great room brightened, making her blink. Then a crowd gathered around her,
most talking, questioning her. She saved her breath to inhale
and exhale, steady herself, put aside the Other's revelations
until later.

"What's going on!" demanded Mr. Laurentine.

The crowd of people—six? ten?—moved aside for him
and Rossi, who followed, scanning the area. Clare choked.
Mr. Laurentine wore an old-fashioned nightshirt. It looked
like the finest ivory linen, and draped over his knees. His hair
had a case of the frizz. She coughed and this time her tears
were amusement.

Then she realized he probably hadn't contacted her to discuss something.

"Not an accident," she gasped. "I was set up."

"That so?" asked Rossi. Now he held a gun in one hand
and he gestured to someone else to investigate.

"Oily spot, top of the stairs," Clare said.

"This is Dr. Burns. Move aside."

Again people parted. She noted most were in nightwear,
pajamas or nightgowns. Missy Legrand wore a slinky red
sliplike "gown."

"A doctor?" Clare squeaked.

"Of course I have a doctor on hand; the closest hospital is in Leadville or Frisco. Not bad if it's summer, but tough when it's winter," Mr. Laurentine snapped.

"Move your toes for me, please," Dr. Burns insisted.

She flexed her feet, both feet, thinking of Zach, who couldn't do that with his left foot, and swallowed tears. She *needed* him, someone she could trust absolutely.

"Good," Dr. Burns said. "Where does it hurt?"

"All over." She put her hand to her ribs. She'd had a cracked one before and knew the pain.

"How's your neck?"

"Okay, I think."

"All right, we're moving you."

"Uh-huh." She concentrated on Mr. Laurentine's cool blue eyes as a focal point when hands clasped her ankles, went to hip and shoulder. and rolled her to her back. "I guess you didn't call me to discuss my consulting contract with you?"

His groomed brows winged up. "At this time of night?" Missy moved close to Laurentine and snugged her arm through his.

"I don't know your schedule," Clare bit out with a hiss of air and put both hands to her right side. "Oh, man." She winced. "Cracked ribs for sure."

"Found the oily spot up here," someone said from above her.

"An accident . . . or not?" Mr. Laurentine said thoughtfully, still staring down at her. "Interesting."

"It appears as if someone doesn't want her here," Rossi said.

"And someone doesn't care if anyone else might take a bad fall," Dr. Burns snapped. He was feeling her limbs, didn't poke at her rib cage, for which she was deeply grateful. "We can move her on a stretcher. I can examine you in my office, but if you'd like to be taken to the Leadville hospital, about forty minutes away, or Frisco, over an hour—"

She stared at the doctor and did her own internal survey. She didn't seem to have any broken bones, except the bruised or cracked ribs. Her head hadn't hit anything hard . . . and Leadville and Frisco, both mining towns, would swarm with ghosts. She thought Leadville was especially haunted. "I'll stay."

As soon as she was placed on the stretcher, Mr. Laurentine said, "So has this scared you away, Cermak?"

"I'll have to think on it," she managed.

J. Dawson Hidgepath materialized near her head, overlapping into a burly guy Clare didn't know and who didn't seem to notice the apparition. The shade's expression was mournful and he held stems of drooping, ghostly daisies. *Now you know what it feels like*, he murmured in her mind, shaking his head. *But you were lucky. Please don't go, Clare. I need you to help me.* The spirit looked around, the flowers in his hands disappearing as he took his bowler off and held it against his chest. *And it seems to me that my death casts a long shadow, might somehow be affecting your present events.*

Do you think so? she asked.

Why else would someone hurt you?

But why?

I don't know.

Mr. Laurentine snorted. "You're going to let someone drive you away from fulfilling your job?"

Clare's lips thinned. "I don't consider this a job for you."

He laughed with disgust, a man accustomed to buying anything or anyone he wanted. "What do you consider it?"

The words *a higher calling* sat on her tongue, especially since Enzo whined near her and J. Dawson walked along as she was carried to the doctor's suite. She closed her eyes, tried to relax all her tension-tight, fall-stiff muscles, surely making every ache worse. Her lips curved. "Your bodyguard might get hazard pay, but I don't. And furthermore, I don't need your job or your money or this house or even the town of Curly Wolf for access to J. Dawson Hidgepath." She opened her eyelids to see Mr. Laurentine's eyes blazing with anger. Whoops.

She shrugged and hissed in a breath at the pain in her ribs. "I'll think on this situation *in the morning.*"

Probably a real mistake to dismiss the multimillionaire, but truly, what could he do? Smear her name in his social circles? She didn't travel in those. Denigrate her as a psychic?

She didn't want that business either. As far as she was concerned, he needed her more than she needed him.

She wondered how many times the man had been told no.

Zach sat in the back garden of Mrs. Flinton's house, tired but unable to sleep. He'd had dinner with the elderly ladies and had told them of his progress on the old murder of J. Dawson Hidgepath. Mrs. Flinton considered herself so close to her godson, Tony Rickman, that she was an honorary member of the business.

She wasn't . . . though she'd sure blabbed about Clare to the guy.

Now it was midnight and he couldn't sleep. He'd tried. But he'd seen the damn crow behind his eyelids, even had one of those stupid flashbacks to the shooting that had crippled him.

And another flashback. Gone *way* back to the worst day of his life, when he was twelve. His parents had promised him that he could leave the base alone next time they moved. That was before his father got an early promotion. When they'd hit the new base, he'd wanted to explore the city outside and was shut down. He'd taken off anyway.

Though pissed, Zach *had* stayed inside the gates. Unfortunately his brother Jim hadn't known that and had left the base, searching for Zach.

And gotten killed in a drive-by shooting.

Horrible. Zach pressed his hands to his head. Yeah, that was when he'd stopped believing in that little gift he thought he and Jim had shared.

Because Jim shouldn't have been looking for Zach off base. Jim *should have known* where Zach was. But he hadn't, so whatever extra sense Zach had thought he and his brother shared had been wrong.

So he didn't have a special gift, and Jim hadn't either. Because Jim had died.

But Zach had been seeing crows. Since Clare.

No, since he'd been shot.

Couldn't trust anything like that.

Around and around his thoughts went, and the image of the crow loomed large.

So he pulled on pajama bottoms, made a few cups of the despised decaf coffee, and wandered, then sank into the lounge chair. The evening cool was turning into a cold night that he welcomed after the hot day.

His phone rang and his gut twitched. Late-night calls never brought good news. Whatever happened had happened, but fear twisted his nerves and sweat popped out on his face, his neck, his chest.

Clare. He stared at the phone as it pinged a standard tone. No number. Shrugging, he answered and said, "Say it fast."

"Clare had a fall. She has two cracked ribs. The Park County sheriff is on the way," came the measured words of Rossi.

"She's okay?"

"Laurentine's doctor has checked her out. Only bruises otherwise."

"What kind of fall?"

"Slip and fall down the main staircase."

Not outside on a mountain trail like J. Dawson Hidgepath.

"Looks like some furniture oil had pooled on the wooden stairs," Rossi continued.

Why anyone would want a wooden staircase without carpet, Zach didn't get. Furniture oil. Clare had said the housekeeper didn't like her. "Why's the sheriff coming?" Zach asked.

"A little suspicious. Laurentine is bandying around the words *attempted murder*."

Zach snorted. "Damn stupid way to kill someone."

"Slade, it's pretty evident Clare was targeted by a phone call." Rossi ran through the whole thing for him, in detail, then ended with, "The deputies took her cell."

"I'm on my way."

"Figured."

"I want to talk to her."

"She's being seen by the in-house doctor."

"Gimme Clare."

"Hang on a minute, I'll take the phone to her."

Zach paced, heard Rossi shout orders to a couple of guys to watch Laurentine until he relieved them. Noises came of opening and closing doors, a pedantic tone that might be from a doctor.

"Zach?" Clare sounded a little breathless, was all.

"You okay?"

"Pretty much. I have a couple of cracked ribs."

"Why aren't you at a hospital?"

"I'd rather not be transported . . . and the choice was Leadville or Frisco."

"I'm coming up. Now."

"You don't have—"

"I'm coming."

A sigh. "All right. I'll wait up for you."

"Stay with people, Clare."

"I'd rather go to bed."

"Stay with people."

"All right." A pause. "Thank you, Zach."

"No problem." He cut the call, hustled into his apartment, dressed fast, and threw clothes and extra ammo in his duffel, trying to keep his mind from running on a hamster wheel.

Clare was hurting. He needed to ease her pain.

Clare was a target. He needed to protect her.

Clare was too damn far away. He needed to be with her.

Glancing around the room, he saw the tiny sample perfume bottle he'd taken from her closet sitting on his dresser. Two strides and he closed his hand around it, felt the glass, the edges of the bottle hard against his palm. He lifted his hand and caught a whiff of the scent, Clare's fragrance. The fear lessened and anger was burning under that, but he couldn't afford to let that out now.

He tucked the perfume bottle into an inside pocket of his bag, swept his gaze around his bedroom. Nothing more he needed. His other weapons were in the gun safe.

After he switched off the lights, he strode into the living room, stepped near the small passage to the open kitchen, and flicked on the night-light stuck in a wall socket. For some reason the ladies liked it on when he was gone. Even after so short a time living with them, he had begun using it as a signal that he'd be away during the night or, like now, several days. Hell, he supposed he should leave them a note.

At the dinner they'd insisted he share, he'd told them he'd be going up to Park County to do some research and might stay with Clare. He'd just say he *would* stay with Clare. If Laurentine wouldn't accept him as a guest at the DL Ranch, Zach would take Clare the hell out of there . . . maybe he should anyway, though he usually liked keeping an enemy close . . . and he didn't know what Clare wanted. Yet.

Given the nature of her gift, Zach suspected this wouldn't be the last time people might threaten her. Should he help her become accustomed to that? Instinctively, he wanted to protect her, take her away from any danger, make her problems go away.

Clare was a strong woman, a woman redefining herself as Zach had been forced to realign his own life, which was part of the reason they clicked. His mouth flattened as he realized he'd have to let her decide how much danger to have in her life.

So he concentrated on the puzzle of her "accident." Through his work he knew the past could hold secrets that affected the present.

Clicking through scenarios, he liked the one of a prospector being murdered near his mine. A mine he hadn't heard being worked by anyone else. An unregistered mine that might now be on federal land. The mountains of Colorado were honeycombed with mines, some old with poisonous gas and most unstable. Hard to find just one without knowing exactly where it was.

With the economy being what it is, a secret cache of gold might come in handy.

Looking at his watch, Zach headed out. How long would the sheriff question Clare? If it had been him, and he had a wounded victim, maybe only forty-five minutes or so for a simple fall, but that couldn't be it because Rossi said Clare had been targeted and Laurentine seemed to think the fall wasn't accidental. Even pressing the speed limit, it would take Zach two and a half hours to get there.

THIRTEEN

WHEN HE GOT into South Park, zoomed past Fairplay, and left it behind, he could see a big house on a ridge with lights blazing. His gut clutched. Everyone was up because of the incident with Clare. She'd better damn well be all right or he'd . . . speak to her strongly about leaving this job. And his mind had done the hamster wheel thing after all.

At a set of iron gates, the guard came out of his hutch bundled in a coat. From the way he walked, Zach knew he'd been on the job as a policeman . . . probably a deputy sheriff as Zach had been. At least he appeared alert and on the ball.

Zach rolled down the window and passed over his ID: driver's license and the card that said, RICKMAN SECURITY AND INVESTIGATIONS. The man scrutinized him. "PI," he sneered.

"Ex-cop, just like you," Zach shot back. He jerked his head toward the house. "Sheriff still up there?"

"Nope." Dark eyes scrutinized and craggy face set. "What county did you work?"

Shrugging a shoulder, Zach said, "Cottonwood in Montana was the latest."

The guard grunted.

"How many guards does Laurentine employ?" Zach asked.

After eyeing him another few seconds, the guy answered, "Round the clock here at the gate, so three. He has that big bruiser as a body guard." The man's mouth turned sour. "From now on, he'll probably have some of his hands patrolling that old ghost town of his to keep it safe." The guard finally handed Zach back his license and card. "What are you up here for?"

"I don't take kindly to having my lady hurt."

Thick, dark brows rose. "You're screwi—you're interested in the ghost chic—woman?"

"Ghost seer," Zach corrected smoothly. He leaned out the window companionably, though the cold was more than nippy. "Anyone come up here tonight before the incident that shouldn't have?"

Another shrug. "Laurentine likes having guests, will even accept some of the wealthy locals if they want to brownnose with him. Charlie, the guy on before me, said he saw some lights moving through Curly Wolf after dinner, but Laurentine has businessmen over tonight and usually shows them around."

"Dinner's when?" Zach asked.

"Seven p.m."

"Near dark."

"That's right."

"So you talked to the guy on before you and know what he and the sheriff discussed?" Zach asked.

"That's right. We're friends and the assault is the most stir we've had in a while. At least of a threatening sort. Charlie was called up to the house, and when they were done with him, he passed a coupla minutes with me."

"No one came through the gates on his shift?" Zach asked.

"Two people came and went for dinner, nobody after that. And nobody on my shift except for the sheriff. I came on at eleven p.m."

"You didn't see anything—any lights—up by the house near the time of the incident?"

"I can't see anything near the house." The guard stepped back. "The estate's big. If someone wanted to sneak in, there wouldn't be a problem. More likely the person who hurt your woman was inside the house, though."

"Uh-huh," Zach said.

As soon as he entered the house, a woman came toward him, waiting for him. She radiated disapproval. She was tall, a good five-nine, slender build, and had her pale blond-gray hair done in a braid around her head. "Mr. Slade?" she asked in cool tones.

"That's right."

"Mr. Laurentine is expecting you. Ms. Cermak is with him and Ms. Legrand in Mr. Laurentine's office." Now that he was closer, he saw the lines framing the downward curve of her mouth. She turned, expecting him to follow her, and he did, through a luxuriously furnished great room. His cane made soft taps on the wood, the sound disappearing when he reached rugs. All the lights were on, here and in the upper corridor. She walked quickly and he only had time to glance at the stairs—wider than he'd imagined and glossy with polish—before she led him through a wide hall and down to a door that Rossi stood outside of.

"Hey, Rossi."

"Slade." He jerked a head at the large, also polished, walnut door. "The man wanted me out here." Skin tightened around his eyes, and Zach figured there was plenty of access to the room through windows or other doors. He gave Rossi a nod that he'd be alert to any danger, and the fine tension in the guard's body eased. Zach wasn't lying. He'd be sharp to field threats to Clare, to himself. Then he'd take care of Laurentine. That guy might be Rossi's priority, but he wasn't Zach's.

The housekeeper—Clare had told him her name was Patrice Schangler—opened the door, gestured for him to precede her, then followed and closed the door behind her.

Zach's gaze went straight to Clare, who huddled in the corner of a love seat, her skin pale beneath the tan of her skin, smudges under her eyes. He strode over to her, took her hands. They seemed too cool between his.

The housekeeper said, "If that is all for now, Mr. Laurentine?"

Laurentine, dressed in custom jeans and a tailored denim

shirt, waved a hand. "Of course. I'll see you at breakfast," Laurentine said.

Without another word, the woman left.

"How are you?" Zach asked Clare.

She smiled. "Pretty well."

"I'm fine," Laurentine said. For an instant, Zach caught a flash of slyness in Laurentine's eyes. Was he just maliciously amused? Or was he involved in the accident? He sat on a couch with his arm around the beautiful Missy Legrand, who leaned against him. From the subtle body cues, neither of the two was more emotionally involved than hot sex and posturing for others.

"Good to know." Zach's gaze met Laurentine's for a fleeting instant as he checked out the rest of the room. Heavy, floor-length curtains probably masked tall windows or sliding doors. The rest of the room was decked out as an office, with an impressive desk that screamed look-at-me-I'm-a-big-shot and loaded bookcases. Since some of the volumes appeared well read, Laurentine's character rose a bit in Zach's estimation.

He released Clare's hands after chafing them to warmth and he stared at Laurentine. "So do you want to tell me what the sheriff found out?"

Laurentine arched his brows. "You'll get Clare's story later."

"They took my phone," Clare said. She straightened her back until she sat ramrod stiff, mouth flat, staring at Laurentine. "Mr. Laurentine made it clear when I spoke to him yesterday afternoon that I was to consider myself on call. So when I received a phone call from him near midnight, I, of course, came down to see him."

"You work from eight a.m. to eight p.m. from now on," Zach said. "No earlier and no later. Rickman will adjust the bill, if necessary."

Clare turned a chill look on him. Uh-oh.

"I will take your advice under consideration," she said.

"Right. My advice."

"I don't mind paying for Ms. Cermak's time." Laurentine's smile showed an edge of teeth. He seemed to want to aggravate the situation. Because he liked trouble making, didn't like Zach, didn't like Clare, or didn't like them both.

"That was not the impression I received from you yesterday," Clare said. "I will discuss any hours with you, and confirm such with Tony Rickman tomorrow."

"If we stay," Zach said, reached for her fingers and squeezed them, then sent her a tender and lopsided smile he hoped would soften her.

She glanced sideways at him. "If we stay. I don't need to speak with J. Dawson here." A tiny sigh escaped her. "I suspect he'll follow me until we find his murderer."

Missy Legrand's eyes widened. Maybe Laurentine had kept her in the dark about the situation.

Clare waved a hand. "To continue, I hurried down the stairs and slipped on some furniture polish on the third or fourth step." She grimaced and her fingers tightened on his.

"The sheriff found more than what is used to polish the stairs," Laurentine said. "Nearly a pool, and it wouldn't be easily seen, since apparently it blends in with the wood." Laurentine flicked his fingers. Of course he wouldn't know about furniture polish. "Naturally the lights are low in the corridor and the great room at night."

"A lot of furniture polish is almost clear," Clare said.

Zach grunted. "Anything else?" He'd take her through everything once they got back to her room, then talk to the sheriff in the morning.

Laurentine said, "The sheriff found an outside door unlocked." The multimillionaire scowled. "I pay people to do a security check, and I have a system."

"Who checks?"

"Ms. Schangler and her nephew see to the windows and doors. Of course, they state that they'd checked everything, and all was fine."

"I'll take a look at the door shortly, if you don't mind."

"It's late," Laurentine said.

"It's assault," Zach stated. He stood and went to the curtains, separated them enough to see they did cover a door to a terrace. A door with standard locks. Pitiful. Zach'd ask Rossi for a floor plan. The guy would have one and was easier to work with than Laurentine.

He saw nothing in the dark beyond the doors, but didn't

plan on giving his eyes time to adjust. "Why didn't you want Rossi here with you?"

Missy Legrand rose with a sensual movement and said, "I asked Dennis to have him stay out there when the sheriff and his two deputies came in. So many men in law enforcement." She scanned Zach, and, like Clare, ignored his cane. Point for her.

"I get tired of having Rossi with us all the time. Are you done, Mr. . . . Slade?"

Zach offered his hand. "Zach Slade, I'm with Rickman Security and Investigations."

"You were wounded by an armed drunk driver in Montana six months ago." Missy took his hand, gave him a soft grip. The touch of her skin had no effect on him; her scent was pleasant but not interesting. He stiffened at her words.

"I'm a bit of a news junky," the actress said. "I recognized you."

Zach let her fingers go. "Ms. Legrand."

Clare stood slowly, as if her body pained her. He moved to her side.

Looking at Laurentine, she said, "I'm off the clock until eight a.m. tomorrow morning." She paused, then ruined the moment by saying, "Unless J. Dawson visits me."

"Come on, Clare," Zach said.

"I assume you intend to stay with Clare," Laurentine said.

Zach shrugged. "If you have a problem with that, we'll leave." Again he met Laurentine's eyes. "Feel free to fire us."

Clare stiffened beside him, no doubt her frugal soul flinching at the thought of doing work for no money. Or at him making decisions for her again.

"That reminds me." Now Laurentine stood. "How are you doing at solving J. Dawson's murder?"

Smiling with teeth, Zach said, "Pretty well. We can talk later."

Since Clare was moving slowly and steadily toward the door, he didn't taunt Laurentine any further. Zach reached the door first and opened it for Clare.

"I'm on the second floor," she said.

"Is there an elevator?" Zach asked, tapping his cane louder than necessary in the hallway.

Clare didn't even glance at him, lifted her chin. "It's best I get accustomed to taking the stairs. I can't ignore staircases the rest of my life."

"We'll be careful," Zach said. She wasn't moving with her usual suppleness.

"Absolutely," she said. "Especially since I have some pain meds in me."

He wanted to take a good look at the scene, too. Unlike Laurentine, he knew what furniture polish looked like.

They walked slowly side by side to the stairs and went up. There were fancy gold velvet cords attached to posts blocking off the top three stairs, which left only enough room for a person to pass on the right, next to the wall. Ropes like the kind that were used in a museum. Like what Laurentine might have in the ghost town of Curly Wolf.

"I wasn't running," Clare said with only a small hitch in her voice. "Even though he'd—or I thought it was Mr. Laurentine—called twice."

Zach smiled. "The irritation and rebellion factor."

"Yes." She wet her lips. "I'm not . . . not sure how much worse it might have been if I'd been going faster."

"Hard to say. Did the voice sound like Laurentine's?"

"That's a good question. The number showed up as his. As a house phone."

"Interesting." And not too surprising that a place in the mountains would have a landline as well as a satellite.

"I suppose. To be honest, I don't know if the voice was Mr. Laurentine's, the words were so short."

"Yeah?"

"'Meet me now.' Like I said, the sheriff took my phone to check the logs or do tests on it or something."

"Uh-huh." They turned left and walked down the hall that was open to the great room. She stopped at the second to the last door on the right, which would face toward the back. No view of Curly Wolf.

Once inside they turned to each other. Zach put his arms around her carefully as she held him tight, burrowed into him.

"Clare." His own voice caught. Here she was, close, so he could feel her, her curves against him, the fullness of her in his arms, the *life* of her. And her scent washed through him and she was near and safe. "Clare."

"Oh, Zach." Her voice came muffled and her back trembled as he stroked her. "I don't trust anyone here except Rossi."

"Good choice."

"But he's not you."

He touched her side under her robe. "Cracked ribs?"

"Yes, two cracked ribs and multiple bruises." She pulled away from him before he was ready. Her eyes were damp but no tear tracks showed. Tough lady.

She dropped her robe, standing in panties only, and let him circle her, see the darkening of the skin on shoulder and arms and hip.

"Just how far did you fall?"

"Most of the way down." She lifted her hands, wincing, and sifted them through her hair. "Thankfully, I didn't hit my head."

Zach thought he heard barking, and that usually meant Enzo was around. He felt a chill around his legs, a touch near his groin. "Will you tell him not to do that?"

Clare laughed and it was the most wonderful sound he'd heard in hours. He glanced at the bed. "Queen, huh?"

She lifted her nose. "This is the jade guest room. I don't think it's one of the premiere rooms in the house." She smiled, petted an invisible Labrador.

"Where was Enzo when this was happening?" asked Zach. "What's the use of having a ghostly companion if he doesn't help out?"

Clare tensed.

"What?" Zach asked.

"Um, Enzo says there's a bad ghost out in back."

"A bad ghost?"

"It's not of my time period, so I don't need to deal with it, but Enzo seems to think it could harm me somehow. Ah . . ." She turned pale, stumbled to the bed, and sank onto it as if her knees had given out.

Zach picked up her robe and bundled it around her though the room was warm, then sat next to her.

"Ah, what?"

She leaned against him and he put his arm around her, keeping his clasp loose since his arm caught her near her bad ribs. "Right after the fall, I had a conversation with Enzo and the Other about, ah, life and death."

He tensed. "Do I want to hear this?"

"I don't know. I'm not sure I want to talk about it."

"All right then." He lowered them down backward, his hand going naturally to her full breast, covering it, feeling the steady beat under his palm, and his own body gave one atavistic shudder. She was all right. Not hurt too bad. And he was with her and she was safe with him.

He rolled onto his left side, felt the strain on his leg brace, ignored it. Nothing mattered but Clare. He'd like to feel her surround him in the best way possible, but not when she was hurt.

A sharp bark, then eerie silence. Enzo was gone. Fine with him.

Carefully, making sure he wouldn't jostle her, he took Clare's mouth, felt the softness of her lips, the warm tangle of her tongue.

FOURTEEN

HER SCENT ENVELOPED him, stirred him, let him *know* she was all right. Especially when he moved his lips to the pulse in her neck, and felt the throb of her blood under his mouth. He molded her breast, and her nipple hardened in his palm.

God, all he wanted to do was tuck her under him, be inside her. But he had work to do . . . to protect her . . . and she was hurt.

He let out a long sigh and relaxed, rolled from his side to his back, ignoring his erection. His hand fell away from her breast, but he reached for, found, and twined her fingers with his. "Despite what we said to Laurentine, you don't want to move somewhere else?"

"I think we—I—need to stay here in South Park until I"— she made a futile gesture—"get a feel for the place. Fairplay's the closest town. I'm sure that town wouldn't be good for me because there'd be too many ghosts."

"You're determined to help J. Dawson."

Clare squeezed his hand and turned her head to meet his eyes. "So far, it seems that I've been *assigned* ghosts to help. Helping my first major ghost move on was tough, but he wasn't too scary, and neither is J. Dawson. Perhaps The Powers That Be or the mechanics of my gift are easing me into this . . . new vocation." She waved her free hand. "It's better that they choose, than I go fumbling around finding ghosts myself."

"All right. We'll stay for now. I think most of my research into the murder will have to be here." He found himself smiling. "At least Laurentine didn't kick me out of the house. I'm here with you."

"I'm glad you are."

"Good." He glanced at her old travel alarm clock, which she'd set on the bedside table. "We need to get some sleep to function well tomorrow . . . later today. I have an appointment with the Park County archivist late in the morning, but I'll want to interrog—talk to some of the staff before then. And whoever's handling this in the sheriff's office."

"Breakfast is from six a.m. to nine a.m." As always, she knew the rules.

He grunted. "All right. I'll set the clock for eight." He got up, limped to the table, and reset it from 6:45 a.m. to eight. "This will give us time to wash and dress before we eat. Still too short on sleep, though." Especially since he still needed to check the door that had been found unlocked, and he had a very full morning planned.

He waited until she fell asleep, then with a kiss on her temple, he picked up his cane and trod softly to the door. He slipped from the room, walked to the staircase in full light, and wasn't surprised when the bodyguard at the bottom of the stairs whirled around with a gun.

Rossi grunted, slipped his weapon back into his shoulder holster. Ms. Schangler and a man who looked more like a handyman than indoor staff had faded back down to the bottom of the stairs, along with the poles and ropes. The housekeeper's eyes flashed with anger. "We got the all-clear from the sheriff to remove these," she said stiffly.

Zach nodded to her. "I'm glad you're still up. I'd like to speak to you."

Her lips thinned, then pursed. "I've already discussed everything with the sheriff. Neither I nor my housekeeping staff was responsible for leaving a puddle of furniture polish on the stairs." She sniffed.

"Of course not," Zach said. "Do you know whether it was your furniture polish that was used? Or did the culprit bring his or her own?"

"Huh," Rossi said.

Awareness dawned in Ms. Schangler's eyes. "I hadn't thought of that." In and out, her lips puckered, relaxed. "The sheriff didn't ask. But they took *all* my polish."

"Which step was the liquid on?"

"Mostly the third, some on the fourth," Rossi said. "And some down the stairs, smeared, maybe, as Clare fell."

Zach's gut tightened at the thought of her plummeting. He nodded. Addressing Ms. Schangler, he said, "Do you know if the furniture polish smelled the same? Looked the same as the product you use?"

She hesitated, then nodded reluctantly. "Yes. I think I would have noticed if it had been a different brand."

"All right, then." Zach made a memo in his phone. "I'll talk to the sheriff about the—cans?"

"Bottles."

He nodded. "Bottles and any fingerprints that might be on them."

"Can I take these things back to the storage area in Curly Wolf?" asked the man.

Ms. Schangler looked at Zach and he nodded. The guy left.

Proceeding down the stairs, Zach said, "Did you check the locks tonight?"

He glanced at Rossi, who grimaced and answered, "Laurentine knows what I think about his locks, and I always give him a hard time when I check them, so he doesn't want me doing it." The bodyguard shrugged his heavy shoulders. "This is a quiet location." His lip curled as he slanted a stare at Ms. Schangler. "They don't even turn on the alarm most of the time. And they have some house cameras but they weren't on either. Used mostly for big parties. We had them on when the bones first appeared and saw nothing about how they came. Laurentine didn't like that. I think it weirded him out wondering how they showed up, so he turned the cams off again when the entertaining was done. This isn't Denver. The staff isn't used to being always observed and people don't like it."

"Someone knew the cameras were off," Zach said.

The housekeeper's shoulders sagged a little. "My nephew, Tyler, checked the doors and windows before he left at eleven p.m. He would have told me or Rossi if anything was amiss. And no, the alarm was not on tonight." Her chin lifted. "Though if it had been, the *intruder* was probably smart enough to get around it."

"Who has the codes?" Zach asked. He kept his voice conversational and slowly took the stairs one foot at a time. It would make him appear less dangerous.

Rossi opened his mouth, and Zach shot him a look to keep quiet.

"I have the code, of course, as does Mr. Laurentine," Ms. Schangler said. "So does the foreman of the ranch, the manager of Curly Wolf, Rossi, my nephew, the chief maid."

"When was the last time the code was changed?" Zach asked. He was now close to her and decided to move a little more rapidly so he wouldn't tower over her.

"I believe it was changed three months ago."

"We didn't handle the house alarm system," Rossi stated. "Security sucks."

Ms. Schangler clicked her tongue in disgust.

"Do you know if the sheriff or his deputies spoke with your nephew?" Zach asked Ms. Schangler. He put his back to the wall and leaned against it.

She nodded. "Yes. Tyler called me. He was upset. He did his job."

"I'm sure. Can I speak with him, too?"

"He doesn't remain onsite. He'll be back on tomorrow at three. He has flexible hours, comes in when I need him."

"All right," Zach said. "Thank you for your insights."

With a last sniff, the woman turned and marched down a corridor to her left, her quarters, Zach figured.

"Show me the door," Zach said to Rossi.

"It's one of the two in the back, the southernmost one." Rossi shook his head. "Lock is just pitiful."

"Was it broken?"

"Forced, not broken. And I doubt Laurentine will upgrade his security here, despite this incident. He's more interested in Curly Wolf, and he doesn't keep his most important treasures in this house."

"Uh-huh."

Zach looked at the lock, agreed with Rossi about the security, got the floor plan, and made an appointment to speak with the sheriff later that morning. He scrutinized the stairs as he took them back up to Clare's and his bedroom. Nothing to see, some scuffs maybe, where Clare had landed. No blood, thank God.

By the time he'd reached their room, the adrenaline keeping him sharp had drained and he was glad to shuck his clothes and stick them on a chair and curl around Clare, absolutely wonderful in his arms.

Waking up with Zach was lovely, but Clare knew from the various aches of her body that rolling away from him and just sitting up in bed would be bad. But her bladder insisted and she'd been given some pain pills that Zach had put in the bathroom medicine cabinet. Which was another incentive to move.

With her teeth set, she slowly pulled herself from Zach's arms and rolled. Ouch, that hurt! She felt every one of the bruises she'd gotten as she'd tumbled down the stairs. She stood, and kept as straight as possible.

She wanted to shower, but figured that might be beyond her. As soon as she'd flushed the toilet, washed her hands, and was angled stiffly over the sink to brush her teeth, Zach swaggered in and gave her a narrow-eyed stare.

"Your bruises are darkening."

Clare made a gargling noise of agreement, rinsed, and left the small room. "Be right back."

"Sure. You can count on me to help you with your shower."

Zach made good on his promise.

They went down to breakfast, hand in hand, at eight thirty. As they descended each step of the large stairway, she looked out at the huge Alpine-style windows, rectangular at the bottom and coming to a pointed A at the top—at the magnificent view of hills with evergreens and grasses, and deciduous trees turning shades of yellow or gold. South Park spread out in a shallow basin below.

She stopped Zach, and they stood for a moment taking in the panorama. They sighed together.

"Hard to top Colorado for sheer beauty," he said.

Clare smiled. "Montana has it."

"Yeah, but it's not home." Zach squeezed her hand.

Studying his face, which looked as serene as she'd ever seen him, she said, "Even though you grew up all over the world, you consider Colorado home?"

"Yeah. At one time I thought I'd stay in Montana . . ." Before he'd been shot, when he'd had a career he loved, she understood. "But it would have been a mistake." He made a noise in his throat. "I even like weird-ass Boulder, where the family house is."

"You couldn't ever sell it."

"Nope."

"Colorado is my home, too. I made it my home when I came here for college."

"You have one nice place in Denver, that's for sure."

"Yes." Her gaze lit on the landscape. "The trees have started to turn." She took a breath. "Mr. Laurentine has an autumnal equinox party he doesn't want to cancel because of J. Dawson. He—Mr. Laurentine—was firm about that." She grimaced. "I'll have to move faster somehow."

"We'll get it done," Zach said, proceeding down the stairway. "I don't want to be here any longer than we have to." He paused at the bottom of the steps. "It's still warm enough to camp out, plenty of places up here."

"I don't camp out."

"No? We could get a really sweet RV . . ."

She lifted her nose. "I know when I'm being teased."

"I'm sure Rickman and Rossi and his men know where to bivouac around here. Wouldn't surprise me if he has additional eyes on this place."

The housekeeper, Ms. Schangler, strode toward them, expression austere. "We will be clearing the breakfast table in half an hour."

"Understood," Zach said.

The breakfast room held only three people; Mr. Laurentine's business associates who'd been at dinner had apparently left. Mr. Laurentine and Missy Legrand flirted with each other and the multimillionaire ignored Zach through breakfast. Patrice Schangler was more tight-mouthed than ever when introducing Zach to the servers—one male and one female—who looked at him with appreciation and wariness.

Clare introduced Zach to the neighbor rancher, Baxter Hawburton, who grinned and shook Zach's hand. With twinkling eyes, he said Mr. Laurentine had invited him to have his second breakfast with them.

No one mentioned the assault on Clare. When Zach said casually that he was going to Bailey to review the Park County Archives, the talk turned to history. Mr. Laurentine became more animated as he talked of Curly Wolf, and eyed Clare consideringly in a way that made her lose her appetite as her stomach tightened.

A clock bonged nine and the two servers came in and whisked the plates away. Zach's was clean and he looked amused. Clare hadn't been able to finish her waffle.

Zach rose and tugged Clare up, smiled genially at the other three, though Clare had noted he'd observed each person with that flat stare of his during breakfast. "See you later. Clare will be doing computer research in her room until I get back."

That was the first time she'd heard about that, and she gave him a narrow-eyed sideways look.

"I think Laurentine is just about ready to nab you for a tour of Curly Wolf, and whatever you can tell him about the ghosts who haunt his precious town," Zach murmured in her ear.

She said courteous good-byes and walked with him back upstairs. Since the morning was heating up, Clare went to the sliding door and opened it, letting brisk fresh air into the room as she stood out on the balcony.

"Don't lean against the rail until you check it," Zach said.

She'd been about to do that, and flinched.

"You told people at breakfast that I was staying in my room this morning. You're pushing me, Zach."

"You're in danger and staying in your room is reasonable."

She stared at him. "Perhaps, but you don't make my decisions for me."

"I'm here to help you."

"Thanks for that, but I don't want you taking over." She paused and revealed a fear. "And I don't want to become dependent on you."

"You can trust me, Clare."

"That's not the point. I'm used to making my own decisions, but you muddy my mind, Zach."

He came to her and put his arms around her, held her in the sun, and the whole moment condensed to one she'd recall forever. Murmuring in her ear, he said, "I'm glad I muddy your mind, because you do the same."

"You're trying to get around me."

"Maybe, but it's the truth. And I believe you're in danger *and* hurting and should stay in. Just for the morning, lover."

She sighed. "I happen to agree."

"Good, and we're going to get you a little insurance."

That piqued her interest and she let him draw her back through the sliding glass door. He sat in the large chair facing the view of the mountains in back and drew her into his lap, so gently she didn't bend wrong and hurt her ribs. Then he settled her as he wanted, wrapping his arms around her. She ignored that her bottom rubbed across his groin and he hardened, since he seemed to do the same.

"What insurance?" she asked.

Zach raised his voice. "Enzo."

FIFTEEN

THE GHOST LABRADOR leapt onto the balcony, solidi-
fying atop the rail, then hopped down and ran through the
glass doors.

*Hello, Zach! You called me, Zach! I am happy to SEE you.
You're holding Clare so you can see me easier, too!*

Zach's arms had tightened around her when the dog had
materialized. Now he cleared his throat and said, "Yes, I can
see you, Enzo."

Clare wondered just how much he could see the ghost.
Enzo was pretty gray-and-shadows solid to her. His tongue
draped outside his muzzle as he gave them a doggie grin. He
tilted his head. *What do you want, my friend Zach?*

After a little cough, Zach said, "Twice in the last few
weeks Clare has been hurt and you haven't been . . . ah . . .
available."

Enzo's good cheer evaporated. He lowered himself to his
belly and his ears lost their perkiness, his tail drooped. The
darkness that was his eyes seemed to dull. He whined. *I am
sorry, sorry, sorry, sorry, sor—*

"I understand," Zach said calmly. "You were with the

ghost Clare was helping a week and a half ago, and last night Clare said you were guarding her from a bad spirit?"

Yes. Sometimes it is only one bad spirit, a bad man or woman who stays, sometimes it is the evil a person leaves behind and it becomes sticky and other bad stuff and spirits paste to it and—

"We don't need to know that now," Zach said. "Was it that ghost that hurt Clare on the stairs?"

No, it was a human! Enzo rolled eyes that now had their regular little spark in them as Zach asked questions and didn't accuse him of anything. He still stayed low. *My nose for real smells is not as good now.*

"All right." Zach flicked his fingers. "What about this evil spirit outside?"

Enzo sat up and raised his muzzle. *I watched and then I made it go away!* His eyes slid aside. *Maybe the Other made it go away. For now. Clare is too new to handle it, and it is out of her time.*

"Okay, then back to the human who hurt Clare. Is there any way you can help her?"

I would not have smelled the stuff on the stairs. His ears raised slightly. *If I saw someone put stuff on the stairs, I could tell her.*

"Uh-huh. Could you attack a person if you saw them hurting Clare?"

Drooping again, Enzo said, *No. I am a spirit companion and guide for Clare. I can't hurt a human. Even a bad human. Then I would turn into a bad ghost, too, and mean and evil and Clare would have to kill me.*

"I couldn't!" Clare cried.

He inched closer to them and put his chin on her knee. *I know, Clare. But it would not be me.* The chill of him soaked through the thin layer of her sundress. He turned and licked her hand and she felt cold ghost drool.

"I've seen you lift and move objects. Could you throw something at them?" Zach asked.

But Enzo was shaking his head, a cold caress across her leg.

"Hmm," Zach said, still sounding contemplative. He rubbed his head on her hair and she sighed.

"Could you scare people? That sounds easy for a ghost," Zach offered.

Maybe. But they would have to really believe I could hurt them. Most bad people don't.

"I see." Zach's thighs tensed under her. His chest rose with a quiet, deep breath, "Could you come and tell me if something has happened?"

Enzo barked. *I could! I could! I can run fast!* He zoomed around the room until he blurred, then disappeared. An instant later he sat in front of them again, looking more chipper.

"All right," Zach said. His chest stilled a second as if he suppressed a sigh.

Later! said Enzo and vanished.

"He didn't give a reason for leaving," Clare muttered. "He usually does." She shifted on Zach's lap.

Zach stroked her hair. "I asked him to go."

Her brows went up as she leaned back to look at him. "Oh, did you?"

"Yes." Zach's gaze shifted. "Telepathically."

"And I didn't hear that."

"Guess not. Said I wanted private time with my lady."

She lifted her arms and set her hands behind his neck and stroked him there . . . and noticed his erection growing, and that had her body reacting. Her breasts felt heavier and more sensitive, and her nipples peaked. Her lips plumped and her mouth needed the taste of him. She wanted to kiss him with closed eyes so she could savor his flavor . . . right there on the side of his jaw.

"Clare," he said, low and grumbly, and his voice ruffled her nerves in the very best way. "We're getting really close."

She chuckled in her throat. "Not close enough."

But he didn't laugh with her, so she met his gaze again. His eyes were all too serious. She stiffened. "I was speaking physically, but you were talking about . . . emotionally. You don't want to be close?"

"I don't know what I want. I don't want to feel the fear for you that I did for three damn hours last night."

She frowned. "I told you I was okay."

"Yeah, but that didn't help much. I wanted to be here, to protect you." He paused. "And I don't *ever* want to arrive too late."

That had her gulping, but she said one of the truths she'd come to learn and live. She put her hands on either side of his face. "I know you have this protector gene, Zach, but this is my new life. There will be dangers in it that I can't anticipate, that you can't anticipate. Enzo can warn me about a bad ghost. The best we—I—can do is, um, do my job, cope with my gift, and do my best. It's like regular life, Zach; there's unexpected danger around every corner. Car accidents, muggers, avalanches, snake bites. I'm not a fatalist, but there's stuff I—and you—can never foresee."

His mouth flattened, then he put his hands over hers and said, "There's something about this whole setup that bugs me."

Her brows rose. "About J. Dawson?"

"No, not the woo-woo stuff. Your assault, the people you're involved with here."

"I barely know anyone. I just arrived yesterday!"

"Doesn't mean they don't know more about you than they let on, especially Laurentine."

"You didn't like him from the get-go."

"That's true."

His phone beeped an alarm. "I gotta go, but first—" He took her chin and she stared into his dilating pupils, which edged out his beautiful blue-green eyes. Then his mouth was on hers and his tongue was tasting hers and dueling with hers in her mouth and his taste exploded into her, coffee, Zach, mint, Zach . . . clear through her. She could've melted . . . or caught fire.

But the nasty alarm was insistent and wouldn't let her relax, so she pulled away, let her head sag against his shoulder. "I guess I can stay in and do a little more research."

Zach grunted and lifted her off his lap and onto her feet with ease. Her knees wobbled, then locked. He stood and he was too close or not close enough. This time he kissed her nose. "Later."

"Yeah," she managed.

"One last thing." He got the notepad from the desk and handed it to her. "Authorize me to pick up your phone from the sheriff's department, if they're done with it."

"Oh, yes!" She wrote a short note, signed it, and gave it to Zach.

"You know, you could catch up on your sleep."

That had her eyes opening wide. "Nap! In the middle of the morning?"

"You're injured, and didn't get enough sleep. Leave the damn computer off and crawl back into bed."

The bed they had already made. "I don't think—"

"Nope, don't think. Do it." He grinned. "I want you frisky in the afternoon."

She laughed and her ribs told her that a nap might be good. "Maybe."

He strode out of the room, whirling his cane more than using it.

As pure tiredness fell on her like a smothering blanket, she understood she didn't know her own limitations in this new life. Or what demands—mental, physical, emotional—her changed circumstances might put on her.

She glanced around the pretty room, out toward the balcony, and the view beyond. The bed was ready for her to collapse in, or if she wanted, her computer was ready and waiting.

She looked at the alarm clock and wondered whether to set it for lunch . . . and when Zach might be back since she was supposed to wait for him. He hadn't given her even an estimate of how long he might be, and she wanted to know. She headed down the hall to see if she could catch him. When she reached the open rail above the great room, she saw him already heading out, moving faster than she'd anticipated. Yes, he managed the physical part of his life very well.

A hint of chill, a whiff of dying flowers, drifted over her and had her spinning, putting her hand to her ribs. The air in the hallway morphed and wavered.

SIXTEEN

CLARE CAUGHT HER breath, set her shoulders, and strode back. The corridor was cooler than just a few seconds ago, and in front of her door, she saw a small pile of bones and flinched. They might be toes.

Enzo hopped around tumbled bones like he was a real dog scenting roadkill, sniffing lustily. *Oooh, oooh, oooh. It IS J. Dawson. Two toes.* Sniff. Snort. Enzo sat and looked up at her. *J. Dawson left you a present.*

"He doesn't have to leave his bones around to get my attention," Clare grumbled. She stared at the toes. She'd have to take care of them herself, and the idea had her stomach pitching. So much for a good breakfast; she'd be lucky if she didn't upchuck.

She pulled a tissue from her sundress pocket and dropped it over the old and twiggy-looking metatarsals.

Bending, she quickly grasped the small bundle and glanced down. She'd gotten everything . . . but the thin tissue sure let her know what she was holding. She should have continued to carry her bandanna, a thicker piece of cloth.

She unlocked the door, kicked it open, and hurried to the upper shelf in the closet, where she stored the box with the dancing skeletons. She flicked that clasp up—thankfully it didn't stick—and dropped the bundle, tissue and all, into the box. It fell and hit the other bones with a nasty clatter.

A long black envelope with a piece of tape on the back fell from the inner top of the box onto the bones. Snatching it up, Clare let the box shut and retreated from the closet and closed the door.

You got it! The thing you didn't find before and we wanted you to see. Yiiipppyyy! Enzo raced around the room. He sounded as happy as if she'd won the lottery . . . which she'd rarely played, the odds of winning were so poor.

When she turned the envelope over, she saw carefully pretty cursive writing in silver, surrounded by silver stars and a scattering of glitter, and read, "Auntie Clare!"

Only one child would address her that way, her brother's daughter, Dora. Dora, who was slated to become the next ghost seer in the family if anything happened to Clare. Dora, whom Clare was determined to protect . . . from the "gift" and . . . the Other.

Dora and her father had packed up Great-Aunt Sandra's house, and now Clare knew who'd included the box in her portion of the furniture.

With a smile, Clare went to the small desk and took the letter opener from a pottery mug of utensils and sliced open the top of the dramatic envelope. Inside she found a tri-folded piece of pastel paper, and she flicked it open to see: "Great-Aunt Sandra left a note about this box! She said to send it to you and that you'd find it within a couple of weeks when the 'time was right.' I thought it'd be cool to include my own note! Use SeeAndTalk to call ME! *XXXXX00000000, DORA!*"

Rolling her eyes, Clare stared at the computer, where she could do some work on Curly Wolf . . . then at the bed . . . then at Enzo. "You think I should call Dora?" she asked.

Yes, yes, yes! he yipped.

Clare wasn't so sure. She could use her tablet—since she didn't have her top-of-the-line new phone—and leave a message on Dora's cell in good conscience that she'd tried to reach her niece . . . Clare had a niggling suspicion that she might not want to hear what Dora had to say.

Still, she sat down and logged into SeeAndTalk and pinged

Dora's number but her niece didn't answer. It was two hours later in Williamsburg, Virginia, and a school day. Enzo appeared disappointed.

Clare sent a brief report to Rickman Security and Investigations regarding her conversations with J. Dawson Hidgepath and Dennis Laurentine.

When she continued to check her uninspiring e-mail, the phantom Lab bounded through the sliding glass door, off the balcony, and into the air, where his grays faded and he matched the blue of the sky and disappeared.

He was gone, and she was finally alone. Her shoulders relaxed from a high line of tension, and she closed her e-mail and left the desk.

Stiffly removing her clothes, she slipped into a nightshirt, and left the drapes open so she could see the sun and the sky and the wisping clouds. She snuggled into bed and plunged into sleep.

The first thing Zach did was check out the ground around the door that had been left unlocked.

The terrace showed the marks of a lot of traffic. Where the terrace ended, there were signs of trampling around, but he noted a rough path to the edge of the hillside then around to the left of the house—east. He followed it to the woods, eyes sharp for disturbed pine needles, until he found the break in the barbed wire fence where a thin person could squeeze through.

Checking, he saw that it wasn't electrified, and muscled through the opening. Parallel to the fence were ruts in the grass and dirt. It had rained yesterday, and he squatted and stared at the wide tire tracks that belonged to a big and heavy truck. One of the tires had picked up a nail or a screw, something that had damaged the tread. Plenty of trucks in ranch and farm country. A tingle at the top of his spine told him he should pay attention to this.

As he stood, he saw that the truck tracks overlaid a line of narrower ones both before and beyond the wide tires. These came from a smaller car, and left less of an impression.

He took pictures of both sets with his phone, though he was

sure the sheriff's department had already done that. Didn't look like they'd taken any casts.

With a shake of his head, he went back through the fence, called Rossi to tell the ranch manager it needed to be fixed, and headed out.

Zach drove to the Park County Sheriff's Department in Fairplay, where he met with the man himself, a white-haired, lean, and tough guy who appeared to be near the end of his career. Zach introduced himself, gave the man his card from Rickman Security and Investigations—suppressing his wince as he did so—and took the chair the sheriff indicated.

Zach talked the talk and limped the walk, dropped names of people he knew: his old boss in Montana, Wyoming peace officers, and Denver policemen. None of these seemed to overly impress the guy and Zach liked him for that . . . though the sheriff had one of his deputies take note of the names to check them out.

Even with his most persuasive manner, Zach didn't get all the notes regarding the case. He did get the opinion that the sheriff thought the best thing for Clare and him to do would be to leave the DL Ranch and return to Denver—advice he'd have given if he'd been in the sheriff's seat. The general idea was that the "trap" set for Clare was to scare her away.

Zach couldn't shake the feeling that it was more . . . or that Clare might be a threat because someone believed she could contact J. Dawson, and something from the past was carrying over to the present.

The sheriff himself had advised Laurentine to up his security, probably in a smoother manner than Zach or Rossi, because the man lived near the multimillionaire and was a public servant.

It occurred to Zach that he'd been more abrasive now that he wasn't a deputy, and that was a change he liked—to be able to speak and act more the way he wanted than was politic. Even now the sheriff was speaking to *him* because it was polite to do so, not that he wanted to.

Definitely a check in the plus column of going private.

When the deputy walked back in after having made the calls to his references, she appeared impressed in spite of herself and told the sheriff, "He's good."

That opened the man up enough to have him reveal the list of the witnesses they'd talked to—everyone Zach had, though a deputy had awakened and gotten a foggy nothing of interest from Tyler Jorgen, whom Zach hadn't spoken with yet.

He offered Clare's authorization to retrieve her phone and her signature was compared to the one when they'd confiscated it. They were through with any investigation regarding her telephone.

They'd found that the calls had been placed from the DL Ranch landline and the one Clare had answered had lasted under a minute. They'd gotten the exact time of the call, short minutes from when Rossi reported they'd heard Clare scream and discovered her.

Zach put the phone in the satchel he carried his tablet computer in, stood, and made a comment that he was headed to the Park County Archives to read a former sheriff's diary. That sparked a good discussion, and Zach casually mentioned J. Dawson and the probability he might have been murdered, which had everyone talking and throwing out opinions.

When he left, he thought he'd made himself welcome and was happy he'd formed some new connections.

The trip to the archives in Bailey and the reading of the sheriff's journal, which the volunteer archivist had marked for Zach, went smoothly.

The fact that the sheriff put down that he had a gut feeling about J. Dawson's death hadn't surprised Zach. But the lawman had nothing to go on, even after he sniffed around. J. Dawson had fallen and been found quickly, dead, and some flowers drifted down with him. The pair of prospector brothers who'd heard his last cry figured he'd been picking flowers for one of the recently arrived women in town.

There were only a couple of notes. After his death, no one filed a claim on J. Dawson's mine. The sheriff had visited the mine and it hadn't looked like much. Nothing had shown on the narrow, rocky trail that might have indicated foul play.

Skimming the rest of the entries, Zach got the impression that there was so much going on in Curly Wolf that even a conscientious sheriff would have to move on pretty damn fast to other, more significant, matters.

The guy couldn't take time from his job just because of a

gut feeling that something was wrong with the accidental death of a lightweight, and J. Dawson had been considered a lightweight. A dreamer.

A romantic.

Zach understood constraints of time and money and man-power and the press of other cases for damn sure, but it always hurt to let a case go when you *knew* there was something hinky about it.

He didn't have to do that anymore. He could almost taste the sweetness of that thought on his tongue. He had enough money from his disability pension and his savings, from the consulting job, that if something crossed his path that felt just plain *wrong*, he didn't have to walk away from the case because of practical realities.

His mind spun with that knowledge. He wouldn't ever have to walk away from a case.

True, he didn't have the badge to force people to talk to him . . . and he might have to smooth out his manner now and again . . . and he didn't have authority to go where he might need to be, but a cop needed a search warrant.

Still, there could be a workaround to that, too. If there was enough reason for it. He'd have to make sure he wouldn't turn righteous vigilante, which was a damn slippery slope.

Clare would help keep him honest, and honorable.

He looked at the general information on Curly Wolf that the archivist had printed out, studied it for a few minutes, absorbing the facts.

"Are you done?" the archivist asked.

Zach blinked. He probably hadn't moved in the last few minutes. "Yeah. Can I take pictures of Sheriff Benson's journal entries with my phone?"

She frowned. "No flash."

He nodded. "All right." He tried a smile. "I'll be out of your hair in a minute. Thanks for setting aside this time for me. You've been a great help."

"You're welcome."

The insistent chirping of a baby bird, along with the cold sweep of a ghostly tongue across her face, woke Clare.

It's Dora! Enzo's drool might vanish before it hit any floor or rug, but it dripped on Clare's face like thawing ice just fine.

She jerked up.

Dora wants to talk to you! Enzo said.

Yes, the chirping bird was Dora's call signal on SeeAnd-Talk. Clare lunged from the bed for her tablet on the desk, accepted the call. "Just a minute, Dora."

"Okay, Auntie Clare. I'm walking out of school to the commons courtyard, so I'll get you better. You sound a little fuzzy."

Not just because service was iffy in the mountains, even with the big satellite dish that Dennis Laurentine surely had. Clare had been *gone* in sleep. And—three hours!—had passed.

She hurriedly dressed again, put on her light sundress in yellow and peach hues—the house was warm and the outside temp was mid-seventies.

To clear her head a bit, Clare took her tablet to the balcony and looked around. With a deep breath, and standing outside in the mountains on a weekday morning, she knew she was blessed that she never had to work again. Even the thought that she had a gift that wouldn't let her rest seemed tolerable . . . Perhaps, just perhaps, in this moment, she could identify with a little with her parents. They'd spent their whole lives doing nothing but living on a trust fund and enjoying moving from pleasurable moment to pleasurable moment.

"Hello, Auntie Clare!" Dora said.

Clare jerked, tore her gaze from the thin white clouds ribboning the blue sky, and said, "Dora? Aren't classes going on?" But Clare smiled at Dora's round and cheerful face, surrounded by the straight and dense dark brown hair that Clare envied her. Their complexions were the same, a natural tan due to their heritage.

Enzo yipped. *Hello, Dora!*

"It's free period and I'm outside and I can turn my phone on . . . and you're an approved adult anyway," Dora said. "So Dad and Mom didn't block your number during the day."

"Uh-huh," Clare said.

"You're my auntie and an emergency contact."

Clare winced. Of course she'd drop everything and head

for Virginia if Dora needed her, but just like any adult, she didn't like the idea that Dora might have to call her in an emergency.

Dora grinned. "I guess you looked in the box. Isn't it a-*mazing!* I made sure it got to you."

"I'm not too fond of dancing skeletons, Dor-ee."

Girlish laughter rolled from the phone. "Maybe you can send it back to me, then."

"Maybe I can. You wanted to speak with me?"

The girl's eyes rounded, her glance slid away, then back. "Auntie Clare, you sent me—us—a video that GG-Auntie Sandra left for us."

Clare sat. "Yes, I did."

Dora hesitated, then said, "You didn't send all of the videos, did you?"

Clare's spine stiffened. Great-Aunt Sandra had left a multitude of videos, for various circumstances: to her brother and his wife if Clare went crazy, to Clare's brother and his wife if Clare had reached the point of no return as her health deteriorated from not accepting her gift and she died.

There had been four videos for Dora—doomed to receive the ghost seer gift after Clare, as it stood now. The thought of a special daughter or son wisped through Clare's mind.

She answered Dora. "No. I didn't send all the videos." She'd only sent the ones that had applied to the situation.

Dora wriggled. "I want to see the ones addressed to me."

Clare opened her mouth, then changed the negative that immediately came to mind. "I haven't viewed them, and *if* I view them, I will talk to your parents about whether to send them to you or not."

Brows down and her lower lip out, Dora stared at Clare. "I want to see them. GG-Auntie Sandra was talking to me about the Cermak Gift, and ghosts." Dora's square chin angled up. "She wasn't talking to *you* about them 'cause you wouldn't listen." Dora narrowed her eyes. "But *I* want to learn. I need to know."

SEVENTEEN

"I'M NOT SURE of that." Clare's insides trembled. She still thought of her psychic power as more of a curse than a boon and wouldn't inflict it on anyone, let alone her beloved niece.

"Auntie Clare—"

The landline house phone rang and Clare guessed it might be Dennis Laurentine. Enzo flickered, then faded away, obviously not interested in listening to the multimillionaire.

Clare said, "I have a client. I have to go, penyaki—niece. We'll talk later, latcho drom."

Dora ducked her head with a serious expression. "Latcho drom, Bibio Clare," she replied with the standard "good journey." Her app closed.

With a sigh, Clare answered the phone, glad she didn't have to look at Mr. Laurentine. She moved to the desk and noted down the time as on the job.

"This is Dennis Laurentine."

"Hmm," Clare said, though unlike last night, she thought she recognized his voice. She looked at the readout on the phone. "This is also the same number someone called me from last night." She couldn't prevent a smile, but kept it from her tone. "Perhaps we need a password."

A hiss came over the speaker. Yes, she'd heard that frustrated hiss before from Mr. Laurentine. "I'm paying you six hundred dollars an hour," he snapped. "You think I'd tell anyone how much you're hosing me for?"

"I'm not," Clare said primly. "You signed a contract with Tony Rickman for my services. You're paying him." Though she was getting more of the fee than was usual for contract workers. She cleared her throat. "You may tell me to leave at any time." She paused. "I have bones from a hand, a foot, as well as several toes that I will be glad to leave with you and your men for interment."

This time the man literally growled. Clare waited. There was a heavy sigh, then Mr. Laurentine said, "Ms. Cermak, would you please meet me in the great hall? Would you like me to send someone to escort you?"

"My pleasure, Mr. Laurentine, and I can find my way there," she said. "I'll watch the other doors along the corridor so no one pops out at me"—no one alive at least—"and you're expecting me and it's your house so you know how long it takes to get from the jade room to the great room. I'll be there in just a moment, sir." And she'd had no idea how being near the end of the hall still rankled.

"At least you're respectful on the surface," he grumbled. "See you shortly."

Like last night, she didn't hurry, but this time she watched her step extremely carefully on the stairs—and under the eyes of those gathered below—Dennis Laurentine, Missy Legrand, and Patrice Schangler.

Mr. Laurentine posed against the back of a chair near the fireplace, in a space not quite big enough for two. Missy Legrand sat on the high hearth with crossed legs and a tight skirt sliding up to just below her crotch. Patrice Schangler stood near the big double doors.

As Clare walked up to him, Mr. Laurentine said, "You found more bones?" His smile was false, his eyes laser-like.

Clare nodded. "Do you have cameras in the house?"

He gave her a wintry smile. "Of course, but I don't have them on except during large house parties. I suggest you leave the investigation of your accident to the sheriff and Slade. And did the ghost of J. Dawson accompany his bones?"

"I haven't seen him since last night."

"You saw him last night. What did he say about his hauntings?"

"We didn't speak about that. We spoke of death and transition. Would you like a report of the conversation?"

Mr. Laurentine flinched. "That's not necessary."

Clare inclined her head. She didn't want to lower herself to the chair and jar her ribs so she sat on the rounded leather arm of a chair that faced the double doors.

"Shall we adjourn to your office to speak about my fee? I've started an itemized spreadsheet of my hours on and off the job—"

He jerked his head in a negative. "Fee's set. I called you down to meet someone, a new guest." He smiled with real pleasure. Missy Legrand stiffened and turned her head slowly to stare at him. "She's on her way up from the guardhouse."

Patrice Schangler shifted in place near the door, ready to open it when needed. But she missed her cue. The doors were flung open and one of the most stunning women Clare had ever seen strode in. She wore tight, faded denim jeans, a long-sleeved red top with inset white lace against gorgeous café au lait skin, and high-heeled boots of dark brown leather that came up to her knees.

Her face showed the beauty of mixed races, with long and slightly tilted deep brown eyes, arched black brows, and long black hair with hints of mink brown.

In general, Clare liked her body, thought of herself as womanly, soft with full breasts, a narrower waist, curvy hips. This woman was leaner, with defined muscles, and an air of complete competence. Clare suddenly wanted to have a body like the new guest's, though it looked like it would take a lot of work.

"Hello, Laurentine." The newcomer inclined her head toward the multimillionaire. She turned to look at the housekeeper, who nearly vibrated with intense emotion. "Hello, Patrice. Can you have my duffel taken upstairs, please?"

The moment and the atmosphere turned into one of those crystal-clear stage-like scenes for Clare . . . knowledge screeched along her nerves that the three other women here had slept with Laurentine.

She hoped her face revealed none of the shock or distaste, but she did fade back a step, drawing the new arrival's attention. The unknown lady flashed Clare a smile full of fun that nonetheless showed perfect white teeth.

Missy Legrand had stiffened and strolled over to Mr. Laurentine, threading her arm through his the instant he pushed away from the chair. He disengaged and sauntered a few paces to embrace the striking woman.

Clare was not surprised to see how easily the newcomer evaded him, but managed a kiss on his cheek, and caught his hands with her own.

"It's good to see you, Desiree," Mr. Laurentine said. "What brings you here?"

Of course she'd be named Desiree.

"Why, Dennis, you always said I could drop in on you anytime. I needed a break from the city."

Clare blinked. Desiree's voice was higher than Clare had expected; she'd thought she'd hear low and husky. Clare wondered which city she needed a break from, Los Angeles . . . New York . . . Paris. The woman had a slight accent Clare couldn't place.

With a smooth move like dancing or martial arts, Desiree turned and slid away from Mr. Laurentine and slipped one of his arms around Missy's waist, then stepped out of the man's reach. Desiree winked at the actress.

Missy's brows rose and her lips twitched upward.

"Like I said, I needed a break," Desiree said with a smile at Missy, then gave the same smile to Clare, who blinked.

"And to keep an eye on things," Desiree ended.

A disdainful sniff came from Patrice Schangler, who was fiddling with her diamond watch, and jolted Clare into recalling the woman was there.

"I'm not paying you, am I, Desiree, as a security consultant?" asked Mr. Laurentine with an edge of suspicion in his tone.

The woman laughed. "Not this time." Her brown eyes sparkled, and with a lilt of glee, she said to Clare, "I'll bet no one's shown you the highest lookout point on the ridge, have they? Come on, let's take a walk."

Clare blinked as she realized that "keeping an eye on

things" might refer to the assault on her last night. "You're correct. I haven't explored any of Mr. Laurentine's estate." She didn't move.

Another laugh from Desiree, with head tilted back and beautiful throat shown, though Clare sensed the woman still observed everything from under her lashes. When she finished the rippling laugh, Desiree held out a long, fine-boned hand to Clare. "I'm Desiree Rickman. Tony is my husband." The laughter in her voice smoothed into a proud smile.

Clare finally noticed a thin, engraved gold band on Desiree's left ring finger. "Oh."

"Let's walk and talk," Desiree said, exuding charisma. Clare felt like she was sinking into a vat of effervescent syrup for the third time and going under. In no way would she be able to keep up with this woman.

"All right," Clare said, but glanced down at her frothy sundress and sandals. "I need to change clothes and shoes."

"I'll wait." Desiree put her hands on her hips, pivoted on one of her high heels, which Clare had no doubt the woman could stride up any hiking path in existence in.

Turning slowly and studying the room, Desiree Rickman said, "Dennis, your house looks great. I didn't visualize this when I saw the plans five years ago. *Very well done.*"

Mr. Laurentine beamed. "Thank you. Let me, uh, us, show you around. Patrice?"

"I have work to do. I'll get your bag." The housekeeper slipped from the room. Mr. Laurentine shrugged, made a sweeping gesture. "Take a good look, Desiree."

"I'll be right back," Clare murmured. Yesterday, she'd have taken the stairs fast. Now she scrutinized each step before she set her foot on it.

When Clare returned to the great room, Desiree Rickman was talking to Rossi and the man who Clare recognized as the main caretaker of Curly Wolf, and a security guard. Clare was sure Desiree drew a small crowd of men—anyone— within her range. She had that kind of charisma, and seemed a sociable sort.

Desiree nodded to Clare. "Let's go. You'll love the view." With a smile for her admirers, she strode out the door and Clare trailed after her dubiously.

Once they were away from the house, Clare felt Desiree's scrutiny but said nothing as they walked up the hill. The path wasn't too arduous an incline and was wide enough for two. Most of the way had a rising hillside to her left and a steep drop-off to her right. Desiree took the outside.

Fifteen minutes later, they'd hiked up and along the ridge to a craggy point that was only slightly taller than the house. There Clare found a bench had been set in concrete atop a rock outcropping. The seat was wood, the arms and back were curlicued iron, showing the initials DL in the top. Any small trees and brush that would have blocked the view of South Park basin had been cleared. The wide mountain valley rolled out in front of them, showcasing the north fork of the South Platte River, which wandered through the yellow-grassed landscape.

"Quite a view, isn't it?" asked Desiree.

"Yes."

To the right, and below them, she could see the peaked roofs and false fronts of Curly Wolf, then the winding and manicured drive from the DL Ranch into the valley, then South Park itself.

Desiree said, "I wanted to introduce myself to you and welcome you to the Rickman Security and Investigations family." She met Clare's eyes. "And let you know you can trust me, in every way."

Desiree sat first, and Clare looked out at the view and soaked in the quiet before taking a seat. If she couldn't trust Tony Rickman's wife, whom could she trust? But not in every way.

Enzo? she asked. The dog appeared and zipped around the woman sniffing. *I like her, Clare!*

Clare wasn't sure that was any recommendation.

She smells good! Enzo barked, then laid his chill body on Clare's feet.

To Clare, despite Desiree's beauty, the woman smelled slightly astringent. Clare brushed her hair back from her face so she could get a whiff of her own perfume, the one that called to her gypsy heart and made her feel sexy.

As she studied Desiree with a sidelong glance, which the woman knew about and seemed fine with, Clare figured that

Desiree was the type Zach would usually choose: muscular, able to handle herself in any situation, thought fast and well on her feet . . . Most of those qualities Clare lacked.

Desiree stretched out her legs, seemingly casual, though she felt alert next to Clare as Zach so often was. Clare let the fresh air, the warmth of the sunlight, slip serenely through her, aware of Desiree but letting silence spin between them. A few more breaths and a meditative state began to envelope—

Desiree's feet twitched. "Wow," she said, turning her head to meet Clare's eyes. "You do that pretty well." She continued to consider Clare. "There's a lot under that uptight accountant look of yours, isn't there?" Another smile showing perfect teeth.

Clare responded with a stingy smile of her own. "Meditation is a new process for me. Due to circumstances." She ignored the slur. Somehow, even in jeans and a silk shirt—well, all right, it was a button-down shirt with a collar she'd had forever and was soft and . . . but the collar *was* buttoned down. Yes, her image hadn't changed as much as she'd thought, especially as much as she *felt* she'd changed. She slid more into a slouch. Desiree laughed.

Words escaped Clare's lips. "So you're Tony Rickman's wife."

"Oh, *yeah*," Desiree said, returning her stare to the view. Her smile moved into a grin. "He's gorgeous, isn't he?"

"I didn't notice," Clare said politely. She hadn't paid much attention to the man, and her main impression was big, tough, older than she, and authoritative.

Another ripple of laughter from Desiree. She nudged Clare with her elbow. "Good." And with a sigh, the woman's manner became quieter, not so much look-at-me! Did she reel in the charisma somehow?

"Tony's aura is so complex and intense, layered with deep colors," Desiree said.

EIGHTEEN

CLARE JERKED, STILLED. She should have guessed. Everyone she knew who was associated with Tony Rickman had shown herself or himself to be a little odd. "Aura?" Clare asked.

Another nudge from the woman.

"You don't believe in someone who can see auras, Ms. Ghost Seer?" Desiree asked, then continued. "Tony's like the sun, pulling interesting people into his gravitational field. But then, he has help with that from his godmother, Barbara. She introduces people to Tony. She has a pretty aura, too. All blues and pastels with a hint of sparkle."

"Barbara?" Clare asked.

"Barbara Flinton." Desiree's lips curved. "She has a smattering of several psychic gifts. Nosy old lady," she added with great affection.

Enzo shifted on Clare's feet then leapt right onto Desiree's lap, nearly taller than she. She showed no indication she noticed him.

He thumped over to Clare, swiped his cold tongue along Clare's cheek, and hopped back down to her feet. This time he sat, looking up at her, and his tongue came out to flick his nose. *This female smells good. But she doesn't have our magic. Our gift. Her gift is for the living only.*

A pang went through Clare, and envy nipped at her with little sharp bites. This woman, so full of life, had a gift that embraced life. Clare was stuck with ghosts. What did that say about her?

Enzo barked. *It says you can see more! That you are a Rom, a Cermak. Like Sandra and all the others!*

This time Clare felt the weight of the quiet between her and Desiree, and that it had lasted a little too long. Clare said, "Barbara Flinton being Tony Rickman's godmother explains a couple of things." Like how Tony knew all about Clare. She and Barbara Flinton had met and been to tea before she and Rickman had met.

"I'm sure it does." Now Desiree had angled to scrutinize Clare again, perhaps looking at her aura.

"Clare, may I call you Clare? Please call me Desiree. And if I could make a personal comment, Clare?" Desiree said.

Clare was surprised she even asked. Shrugging, Clare said, "Sure, call me Clare. As for personal comments, why stop now?"

Desiree chuckled. "Your aura is a little thin around the edges."

"Is it? What does that mean?"

With a sober expression, Desiree said, "It means you're coming into your gift. You still have layers and layers to go. But it's very beautiful." This time her smile was sincere in the face of Clare's gaze. "And someday, all those gypsy colors— the scarlet, the gold, the purple, the gleaming copper—will be radiant around you, nearly blinding to the inner eye. I'll need sunglasses."

"Uh-huh," Clare said skeptically.

A movement caught Clare's eye and she turned to see Zach striding up the path, using his cane and with a fierce expression on his face.

When he saw her, he seemed to ease . . . though his gaze had gone to Desiree first—because she was a newcomer, or a threat, or because she was stunning?

"*Hrmph.*" Desiree scowled, a little line twisting between

her eyebrows. "I suppose that's your Zach Slade? Jackson Zachary Slade?"

"Yes." Clare knew that even that one word lilted with affection, perhaps more, for the man.

Desiree looked irritated. "Rossi would have told him you were safe with me." She squinted as if checking out Zach's aura. Then her tone changed. "Hmmm. I understand what you see in him. Nice colors. Darker than my Tony's. More pain, both old and recent." She stared at Clare, then Zach again. Desiree's lips quirked and a brow rose. "I can also see that you complement each other." There she really caught Clare's attention, enough that she wanted to probe deeper into the topic.

Desiree frowned as she continued to appraise Zach. "He has some sort of gift, too. Not surprising, but . . . hmmm. What is it?" She shook her head. "I can't tell, because he's suppressing it."

"Don't tell him that," Clare muttered.

Desiree switched topics. "Nice body."

Clare tensed. "Yes."

"Go to him," Desiree said with a small urgency. "He'd like that."

Sitting straighter, Clare asked, "Really?"

"Yeah, really." Desiree hit her with a shoulder nudge.

Clare stood and ran the few yards toward Zach, who'd reached the flat area. He stopped and braced himself, but she didn't fling her weight at him, just moved in easily, hugging him, brushing a kiss on his lips.

For an instant his arms tightened nearly painfully and she thought another piece of uptight Clare crumbled.

She didn't know exactly who she was becoming, this ghost seer, Clare; Zach's lover, Clare. Fear of change still zoomed a whirlpool inside her. But she might be able to like the person she was becoming. She did enjoy the feel of his strong, hard, rangy body against hers, and how her own, softer parts cradled against his.

She hooked her arms around him and swept her tongue across his lips . . . but his taste and that of coffee and maybe a hint of chocolate tempted her and she tested his mouth with her tongue. He opened his lips, and she delved in for more than a taste.

"Yo!" called Desiree, far too soon, and Clare leaned back to look into Zach's darkened blue-green eyes.

"Glad to see me?" he asked with a pleased smile at her.

"Yes."

"Good." He stepped back from her and began walking toward Desiree. Clare wanted to take his arm, but couldn't. Disabling his gun hand wouldn't endear her to him.

Desiree watched them approach with a smile. When they were a couple of yards away, she said, "You know how to use that cane as a weapon."

They stopped and Zach scanned Desiree with his cop stare. "Yeah. I know how to use the cane as a weapon." He twirled it, a side of his mouth lifted and he winked at Clare.

To Desiree, he said, "You're Rickman's wife? Pleased to meet you."

"Tony's my husband," Desiree said, coming to them and offering her hand. "Call me Desiree."

Zach shook it briefly. "You and Tony are quite a pair, aren't you?"

"Yes, we are." She rolled a shoulder and continued. "How'd your discussion with the sheriff go?" Desiree asked, just as Clare said, "What did you find out at the Park County Archives about J. Dawson's death?"

"We'll talk later." He glanced at the view, said, "Pretty," then jutted his chin back toward the path.

"You want to leave already?" Clare asked. She swept a hand to the bench. "It's lovely up here."

Zach grunted. "We're on the job." He glanced at Desiree then back to Clare. "At least you and I are."

Clare shook her head. "No, I consider this personal time." She suppressed a sigh. "And you have new information."

"Not exactly new, but important."

"All right."

Zach gestured for Desiree to go first.

She lifted her chin. "I'm taking care of Clare."

"Clare can take care of herself," Clare said. Neither of the two deigned to reply since they were caught in a stare-off and didn't want to give an inch, so Clare started down the trail herself.

"Dammit, Clare!" Zach called. "Stay close."

Desiree's rippling laugh followed Clare as she strode down the path.

There was a shot, and the next thing Clare knew, she was on the ground with a body atop her and the pain in her ribs stopped her breath and had black spots dancing before her eyes. Her cheek had hit a rock, but she didn't think it was broken.

The body—Desiree, who wasn't as tall as Clare but whose muscles were sure enough harder—removed herself and dusted herself off.

"Wha—" Clare blinked as the sun hit her eyes, dazzling her.

Zach dropped his cane, reached down, and hauled her up, one handed with his left hand. His right fingers curled around the grip of his weapon. Nausea swam in her stomach, crawled up her throat, and she dropped her head and concentrated on breathing through it.

"Wow," Desiree said. "You really hit your cheek. Gonna have a bruise."

"Rifle shot, Desiree," Zach said. From the corner of her eyes Clare could see him scanning the area.

"I don't think it was aimed at her, Zach. I didn't *see* anything," Desiree said. "Maybe the shot wasn't even here on Dennis's ranch. Sound carries."

"I don't like it," Zach snapped, but he holstered his weapon under his jacket. He bent down and picked up his cane, went around to the valley side of the path, and crowded Clare nearly into the hillside. He took her arm. The better to throw her down again, she figured. "Though there's bound to be some sort of hunting going on now."

"Stop it, Zach," Clare managed.

"What?" he asked, not looking at her, his gaze continuing to rove from the hillside to the path to the valley. Desiree walked behind them.

"Stop marching me down the darn path. I need to go slower—my ribs and cheek hurt."

"I don't want you out in the open," he muttered.

She sucked in a breath between her teeth. "Ease up. I'm feeling queasy." She yanked on her arm and he let her go.

"All right, but call Enzo."

"What?"

"*Enzo!*" Zach yelled.

"Who's Enzo?" Desiree asked. She didn't sound out of breath at all, darn it.

Enzo popped up right in front of them, so close that their next steps took them right through him. Clare shivered.

HI, ZACH! I HEARD YOU CALL! Hi, Clare! Enzo ran along the side of the path near the drop-off, mostly on thin air.

Zach's fingers curved over her shoulder again, squeezed slightly. "I need to see Enzo."

"Uh-huh, he's here." Still feeling sick and not caring how she appeared, she turned her head—and her neck twinged!—toward Desiree. "Enzo is a ghost dog."

"Cool," Desiree said, and Clare caught the woman's brief nod before she concentrated on the path.

"I need you to scout, Enzo. Check all along the trail below us for any human with a gun. Look through the estate, too."

I WILL, ZACH! Enzo shouted, curved around, and ran back down the path.

"I can hear him just fine if I'm connected to you," Zach said. Clare thought he'd be able to hear and see Enzo if he just wanted to.

"He came and went?" Desiree asked. "I didn't hear or see him at all. What kind of a dog?"

"Labrador," Clare and Zach said in unison.

"All right," Desiree said. "He's scouting?"

"Yes, he can do that. Can't affect humans much otherwise," Zach said. "Dr. Burns will need to look at Clare when we get back."

Clare let out a little moan.

Zach glanced at her. "That cheek needs icing."

"Sorry," Desiree said, not sounding like it, and Clare got the impression she was scoping the area just like Zach.

"I will remind both of you that my 'accident' took place in the house," Clare said.

"Yeah, but we can limit access to you in the house, and not much chance that a rifle will be aimed at you in a fake hunting accident inside."

"Oh." She kept her mouth shut and her feet going.

When they reached the house, the door opened and Ms. Schangler and Mr. Laurentine stared at them.

"Fall off the path, Ms. Cermak?" Mr. Laurentine raised his brows.

Without thought, words came out of her mouth. "I'll be glad to give you J. Dawson Hidgepath's bones for you to handle and I can leave—"

"Clare." Zach's tone was a warning. "We need to talk. Later."

"Yes, we do," she replied.

Zach glanced at Mr. Laurentine. "Clare should see Dr. Burns now about her ribs and face."

"He's at lunch," Mr. Laurentine said.

"Ms. Schangler, can you have him come to his office? Desiree, can you accompany Clare there?" Zach asked.

"Zach—" Clare started.

"What's being hunted now?" Zach asked Mr. Laurentine.

His forehead lined. "Early September? Big game? Only bear."

"Bear," Clare repeated faintly.

Desiree gripped her elbow and moved them to the right to the corridor that held the doctor's suite.

"You have rifles?" Zach asked.

"Of course."

"I want to check them. All of them."

Mr. Laurentine sighed. "All right. Did someone shoot at Clare?"

"There was a rifle shot," Zach said.

Shrugging, Mr. Laurentine said, "Rifle shots and other gunshots aren't uncommon around here, Slade." He turned and tromped away, his cowboy boots clacking on the floor, Zach followed . . . and her lover didn't even give her another glance, which just added insult to injury.

Desiree walked her to the doctor's office but didn't come in. Clare got the idea that the woman was either standing outside the door or arranging for someone else to do so.

A few minutes later, her ribs had been examined and she'd been given an ice pack for her cheek. She'd figured out that Dr. Burns worked for Mr. Laurentine instead of a clinic because the physician had no bedside manner whatsoever.

Walking a little stiffly, she opened the doctor's door.

Enzo was guarding it.

Hi, Clare! Desiree and Zach told me to sit here and warn them of any negative humans. But I didn't FEEL anyone, so let's go back to our room, 'cuz Zach says you need to rest.

"Negative humans?" she asked. She glanced around but no one lingered in the corridor that led to the great room. No one was there to see her talking to the ghost dog, or was any threat.

Hopping to his feet and with a full body wag, Enzo began trotting down the hallway.

Yes. Desiree asked Zach if I might be able to feel, um, ill-intent or threat to you, or negativity, and I said YES! Enzo turned his head back to look at her and it didn't matter that he dipped in and out of the walls as he ran.

"I thought we'd figured that out this morning," she muttered.

And I can move fast and look all around the yard and all the paths and Curly Wolf and—

"I get it," she said.

She walked into the great room and paused at the bunch of people in the conversation area before the main fireplace. Mr. Laurentine sat in the most prominent wing-backed chair, Rossi standing near him and scanning the area. Missy Legrand sat in a chair next to Mr. Laurentine's and their fingers were intertwined.

Desiree Rickman sat on the hearthstone in front of the unlit fireplace. Zach lounged against the stone column of the chimney.

Clare hesitated too long and was seen, by Desiree first, then Zach straightened and walked toward her. He didn't hold out his hand to her, and Clare didn't know whether that was because he was keeping it free for his weapon or another reason.

Mr. Laurentine turned and studied her as she and Zach walked toward the others.

"You are definitely looking the worse for wear, Ms. Cermak." There seemed to be a note almost like gloating in his voice.

She hadn't taken the time to think things through before she'd signed the contract. All right, she'd wanted to be paid for doing something she'd have to do anyway. And she felt that if she was being paid, she was doing a real job. Maybe that was wrong. "I can return J. Dawson's bones to you, if you like, and leave, cancel our contract," Clare offered.

His eyes narrowed. He glanced at Zach. "You're safe here. For your information, Slade checked *all* the weapons in the house and none of them have been fired recently."

"I—" she began, and Zach's hand went around her upper arm. "Please excuse us. I think Clare'd like to change," he said and squeezed.

The way he kept interrupting her, Clare was starting to think Zach wanted her to stay at the ranch for some reason. Putting the ice pack back on her face and allowing herself a grumble, she kept pace with him to the elevator and up, her back stiff.

He unlocked and shoved open the door and she went in first. "Zach, I don't like—"

His voice rode right over hers. "What's going on, Clare?"

NINETEEN

"WHAT DO YOU mean?"

"You're not wholeheartedly committed to this job," Zach pointed out.

She took the chair at the table, kept the ice pack on her cheek. "I'm committed to helping J. Dawson Hidgepath."

He leaned against the wall and stared at her. "I don't get the difference. Tell me what the problem is."

She wanted to hunch over, hide somehow. "I don't want to be a psychic detective!"

"And I don't want to be a private investigator."

They stared at each other for a long throbbing moment. She popped up from the chair and flung herself at him. He caught her and held her, so solid when she was on shaky ground.

Letting the sob in her voice come through, she said, "I'm a square peg in a round hole."

His laugh was short. With his free hand he stroked her hair. "So am I, Clare."

Tears leaked from her eyes and caught on her lashes so she had to blink twice to see him clearly. Then she saw the downturn of his mouth, and lines deepening there, the shadow of pain in his eyes. But his was physical and emotional pain due to the change that had occurred in his life.

Their gazes locked and she said, "I don't think being a private eye is as poor a fit as ghost seeing." She winced, held on tighter. "That didn't come out right." She took a breath and tried again. "Law enforcement . . . and your brand of it, isn't as far from private investigation as you think," she stated, sure of that, at least. He'd like the puzzles more than the rules. And he'd like helping people more than enforcing laws. As far as she could tell, he'd moved from police forces in busy cities to sheriff's departments in less-populated states, which might mean more personal leeway in handling people and laws. He'd said more than once that he wanted justice. Even a solid rule follower like her knew that justice and laws weren't the same thing.

He grunted like he didn't really agree and drew her over to the bed. Then he sat, and propped his cane beside him. She sat on his other side and he slipped his arm around her waist. She leaned against him.

Zach said, "Neither of us want to be doing the jobs we're doing, so what do we need to decide about this?"

She rubbed her head against his side. "I don't know. I hate saying I'm a psychic."

"From what I've seen, you've liked making people uncomfortable here by talking to ghosts."

"Only if they can feel something but deny it." She stopped. Sighing, she admitted, "All right, I'm still angry at The Powers That Be for pushing this gift on me and I'm taking it out on others?"

He squeezed her. "Maybe. But it doesn't help that they are assholes."

"It always sounds so weird if I say something like: 'I can see ghosts and they tell me things and they want me to help them move on to . . . whatever's next.'" She squirmed. "I *didn't* believe Great-Aunt Sandra when she said that."

"I think you did, deep down. You just didn't want to admit it." He paused. "It was just a part of the weirdness of your childhood lifestyle."

"You're probably right. I wanted—want—a nice normal life."

Another squeeze from him, a pat on her hip. "You wanted a nice square hole."

Her turn to think in silence for two seconds. "And I made my life a nice square hole."

"You're a round peg now, Clare." He turned and kissed her hair.

"I thought I was doing better at this than I am," she said in a small voice.

"Yeah, I know that feeling." He paused. "We have to speed up our learning curve, Clare."

She sniffled. She'd need a tissue soon but didn't want to leave him to get one. "You mean me."

"Maybe," he repeated cautiously.

"You think we should stay not only in South Park, but here at the ranch."

"It's better that we're here in South Park for J. Dawson. Easier for hands-on research. Also simpler to smoke out the damn villain here. I've got a feeling he or she isn't going to quit."

"A feeling," Clare said carefully, watching him from under her lashes. "A cop feeling, or . . . something more?"

His jaw flexed. "I don't want to talk about anything more than, yeah, my cop hunch right now."

"I hear you." Just hearing him admit that he might have more than just intuition was a big step.

He said, "What are our options other than staying? Ghosts litter the old mining towns in this area. You don't want to camp. Denver's two and a half hours away, going back and forth isn't feasible. Bottom line for this situation is that you have to help J. Dawson move on."

After a puff of breath, she said, "Yes. He is my next major project."

"You're getting paid a good fee."

"The fee is the least of it. You know that," she shot back. "You've said more than once that working for people who can pay a detective isn't the same as working in the public sector, where you can help people who are in trouble and can't pay."

A sound rumbled in his chest.

She continued, "And not only am I getting paid a big

amount, like you said, but I'm getting paid by people who don't respect me because I'm weird."

"So there's the matter of respect."

"Yes." She lifted her chin and squeezed her eyes shut against more tears. "People don't respect me or my . . . my gift, and that hurts."

"No way you can force people to respect you, Clare. Best you can do is a good job and fulfill your contract. If you want such a contract. So decide."

"You've made your point . . . points," she said stiffly. "I'll swallow my pride and do the job and be more courteous to my employers."

His arm tightened around her.

"I'm sorry this continues to hurt you, Clare."

"I am, too, and I need to just get over it." She took a couple of steady breaths. "Thank you for your help."

"Always."

He fell back on the bed, taking her with him, then he pulled her over him. They lay there together, more tender than lusty.

Stroking her hair, Zach said, "Meanwhile we need to know more and talk more seriously with J. Dawson Hidgepath."

"Easier said than done," Clare murmured. "He only shows up when *he* wants to."

ZACH, CAN I COME IN NOW? Enzo shouted.

Clare smiled, though she didn't think Zach could feel it, and that was fine. "Been talking telepathically to my dog, Zach?"

"Maybe," he said.

"You wanted to talk to me about my issues without him?" She began to feel a little sleepy.

"Enzo is *part* of your issue, Clare."

"I s'pose."

"Come on in, Enzo," Zach said without raising his voice.

Desiree wants to come in, too. Can Desiree come in, too, Zach? Can Desiree come in, too, Clare?

Irritation washed through Clare. *Is she there?*

Yes, she is about to knock, Enzo said.

Sure enough, a rapping came at the door.

Zach didn't move. "Tell her to go away. I don't want to talk to her." His hands went to Clare's butt and his shaft hardened beneath her stomach. "In fact, everything else can wait," he ended.

She propped herself on her elbows and their lower bodies rubbed together. "Desiree seems more your type."

His hands fell away and his half-closed eyelids rose and he stared at her. "You've got to be kidding."

"Why?"

He jerked a shoulder irritably. "I've seen her type before. Yeah, she's riveting and fiery, but she's a loose cannon, quirky. Can't tell which way she'll jump, except that where and when she does, she'll cause you trouble."

His gaze locked on Clare and his face softened and his lips curved. He lifted his hand and feathered his fingertips down her cheek. "Not like you, lover. You're the real deal, solid."

Clare was torn between pleasure at the comment and thinking that she was stuffy.

He smiled. "Perfect for me. I can count on you."

She sniffed. "I'm *not* perfect."

Laughing, he said, "No. But . . . we fit . . . a lot. You've made mistakes and they show. You doubt yourself, and I can see that and want to be there for you."

Clare grimaced. "I'd rather be fiery and riveting like Desiree." But warmth suffused Clare's body. She leaned down and nibbled his lips. She angled her mouth and slid the tip of her tongue into his mouth, moving her body slowly against his, giving them both pleasure by rubbing her breasts against his hard chest, her sex against his erection.

His brows went up and down and his hand trailed from her cheek down her neck, along her collarbone to drop and curve over her breast. "You've got that gypsy in you, and that gypsy magic." He grinned. "You'll get there, and I'll have a helluva great time watching you."

"Oh."

Another, harder, knocking.

Zach turned his head and raised his voice, "Go away, Desiree."

"Laurentine wants to see you now. Both of you." She sounded amused.

His whole body stiffening under hers, Zach drilled Clare with an intense gaze that tinted his eyes more toward blue. "Decision time, Clare. Do you want to get paid for helping J. Dawson transition?" Zach asked. His gaze didn't waver.

"I don't know," she said, even as the frugal part of her shuddered with the thought of working hard—and sending major ghosts on was hard work—and not getting paid.

"In this particular instance," Zach said, "Laurentine has more resources than we do. And since you're going to be helping J. Dawson anyway, we should use them."

"That's logical."

Still watching her, he lifted his head and brushed her lips with his own. "But feelings aren't logical and you're used to suppressing your feelings."

"Yes, and it's poor timing on their part to start becoming so unruly."

He laughed.

"Clare, Slade, our client is impatient," Desiree Rickman stated.

"He's got an agenda." Zach sat up and set Clare on her feet, then stood himself. His face hardened. "Do we pack or not?"

With a small sigh, Clare shook her head. "Not."

Zach gave her that ironic half smile. "You'll have to suck it up, Clare, the lack of respect."

"I know."

"We're coming," Zach said loudly, then hauled Clare in for a quick, hard kiss. "And you and I will return to this activity later."

Her exhalation was shaky. "Oh-kay." She liked the taste of him, wanted to stay and saturate her senses with him, but duty, the duty she'd just truly accepted, called.

"Here." He reached into his jacket pocket and took out her phone. "The sheriff's department is done with this."

"Oh! Thanks." She crossed to her purse in the closet and put the phone in its pocket.

No more than three minutes later, she and Zach were downstairs in the great room. Desiree had excused herself.

Mr. Laurentine aimed a false and cheery smile at Clare. Rossi stood beside him.

Rubbing his hands, Mr. Laurentine said, "I think it's time you see Curly Wolf." His smile widened. "It's completely in your area of interest, isn't it? Both historically and ghostwise? If you haven't been leading me on."

So he hadn't liked her previous barbs. Well, she didn't like his continuing superior and patronizing manner. She stiffened, almost, almost ready to walk away again.

Zach caught her fingers in his. "I'm sure Clare can handle the place. I spent some of the morning at the archives, and the historical reports only have three ghosts in Curly Wolf, not including J. Dawson Hidgepath. And that's when it stood on its native ground. Who knows whether they came along or not?"

Chin jutting, Mr. Laurentine said, "We still have a great atmosphere, with or without ghosts, but I'm sure what was in Curly Wolf when I bought it and moved it remains."

"You're probably right. All the buildings belonged to the town. It's complete. It's not as if Curly Wolf is Buckskin Joe," Zach said.

Clare had vaguely heard of Buckskin Joe. "Wasn't that a theme park?"

Zach nodded. "But it wasn't a full, original town like Curly Wolf. Buckskin Joe had buildings brought in from other towns, and one was cobbled together from a barn and a couple of other structures. That barn had been the scene of hangings."

Clare shuddered. "No, I couldn't go there."

With a not-nice smile, Zach said, "Documented restless ghosts in that town." He lifted a shoulder in an uber-casual shrug. "But the *billionaire* who bought and moved Buckskin Joe in southern Colorado didn't seem to care. He's probably not having ghosts bothering him up in his home. They stay tidily down in the town."

Mr. Laurentine flushed; his breath came out in a hiss. Zach had insinuated he was a copycat. And Clare knew she'd just lost any chance of avoiding the stroll down Main Street Curly Wolf.

Before they stepped out the front door, Zach murmured, "Enzo?"

The ghost Labrador appeared, as cheerful as ever. *I am here, Zach and Clare!*

"Take a look around the area, as far as you can, and see if you can sense any danger from live humans to Clare," Zach said in a quiet tone.

Yes, Zach! Yes, Clare. I love you, Clare. He slurped an icy tongue along her free hand and she rubbed it on her jeans to warm it, as she replied automatically, from her mind to the dog's, *I love you, too, Enzo.*

Zach kept his hand holding hers as the four of them walked down the drive to the reconstructed town, his pace faster than her own lagging steps. She insisted on coming to a stop about ten yards outside the transferred town. It looked pretty, painted in good, solid colors, and the old buildings of unpainted wood had been weather treated. A couple of men were working.

Mr. Laurentine had done well by Curly Wolf. But the place seethed with energy she could all too easily sense; an oppressive atmosphere wafted to her like a cold and stinging wind waiting to wrap around her like a smothering ice blanket. She braced herself.

TWENTY

ZACH TOOK HER arm and ordered Rossi with a gesture to walk on her other side. The bodyguard raised his brows and glanced at Laurentine. Zach frowned. Rossi shrugged. Clare thought she actually figured out the little byplay—Rossi was hired to take care of Laurentine—but nothing so far that she'd seen had shown he was in danger.

Unless her accident was only an opening move in a game that would escalate to harming the multimillionaire.

Clare took a step past the edge of the first building, and her chest constricted as the air became harder to breathe. She kept on.

Rossi walked with her and Zach, the three of them following the owner of Curly Wolf. The bodyguard had sharpened his observation. She also figured that Rossi should have refused Zach's request to stay by her side . . . but both of the men thought *she* was the real target? She didn't know the inner workings of men's thoughts, let alone military or cop types, but she supposed she would learn if she stuck around them long enough.

Zach angled his head and spoke in her ear. "It's all right. I don't think any of the ghosts are on this end of town."

Perhaps that was true, but the town was saturated with the past, nearly vibrating.

"Comin' up behind you," a man called and Rossi whirled, a gun appearing in his hand. Zach had yanked Clare around, too, then dropped her hand and pulled a gun from the small of his back.

He kept his gun beside his leg, out of sight.

Baxter Hawburton loped toward them, a smile creasing his weather-beaten face, with a rifle in his hand. He noticed Rossi's gun but didn't react.

"What about bartitsu?" Clare asked Zach under her breath. "Your cane is a weapon, too."

He didn't even look at her. "Not a projectile weapon. Hard to fight a damn bullet with a cane."

"But you can use a cane to disarm a man with a gun," she said. "You've proven that."

His smile lifted a side of his mouth. "Those were urban street toughs and amateurs. Not a man with a hunting rifle that has a range of a couple of hundred to several hundred yards. An excellent sniper can make eight hundred yards."

She did the calculations in her head and felt the blood drain from her face. "That's twenty-four hundred feet."

"That's right." His expression hardened. "Can I check out your rifle?" Zach asked Mr. Hawburton. Zach's own gun had been replaced in his holster.

The rancher frowned, then shrugged. "If you gotta."

"Please," Zach said but it was more of a demand. He handed her his cane, then did something to the rifle that was too fast to follow and handed it back to Mr. Hawburton. Zach's nostrils flared. "This weapon has been cleaned recently."

"Well, sure," the rancher said, keeping the barrel pointed at the ground. "No use carrying a dirty weapon. Elk season is coming up in a couple of weeks." He shrugged. "There are mountain lions around here, too."

"Right here and right now?" Zach asked dryly. "Is that why you're carrying a weapon?"

"Hereabouts," Baxter said. "And I have the rifle because it's an H-S—"

"Precision 2000 PHL customized weapon," Zach said. "Guarantees a half-inch minute of angle."

"That's right. You know your rifles." Mr. Hawburton's forehead creased as he looked at Zach, the sports coat he was wearing, unlike the plaid shirts that Mr. Hawburton himself and Mr. Laurentine wore. Zach did have more of a city look.

"I wouldn't have taken you for a hunter," the rancher said.

"I hunt." Zach's smile showed an edge, and Clare suppressed a shiver. He hunted men . . . people . . . and puzzles, too, but mostly people who didn't think laws and justice were for them, she guessed.

"The FBI sometimes uses H-S rifles," Zach said.

Rossi grunted agreement. Oh, yes, he hunted people, too.

She didn't quite hunt ghosts, not yet, but from what Enzo and the Other intimated, she might in the future. That was not her idea of a good deal.

Mr. Laurentine walked up. "What did you think of the H-S PHL, Baxter?"

"Very nice. Thanks for letting me try it out." He handed the gun to Mr. Laurentine.

"You're welcome. You can put your weapon away, Rossi," Mr. Laurentine said. Reluctantly, the bodyguard did so.

"Did you fire the H-S this morning?" Zach asked.

"Nope." Mr. Hawburton barely spared him a glance as he studied the main street of Curly Wolf before him. He smiled at Mr. Laurentine and then Clare. "Mind if I walk along? Been a coupla seasons since I saw the old store. You were going to paint it white with blue trim?"

"Since that's what your records say the original colors were."

"Not my records, Dennis. We don't have detailed records like that, but that's the family lore. Great-great-granddad hated red."

"That's right," Mr. Laurentine said easily, turning and beginning to saunter back into the town. "It's Patrice Schangler's folks who wrote down such particulars in their journals."

"Don't you need to put that . . . probably very expensive gun away?" Clare asked. "Give it to one of your men to take to the house?"

Mr. Laurentine grinned. "Not right now." He patted the part that Clare thought looked like wood—the stock? "I like this rifle, and I know how to use it. Rossi can continue to guard you," he ended on a slightly mocking note.

Clare's lips compressed but neither Zach nor Rossi showed any emotion. Mr. Laurentine began a steady stride, and once again she had to put one foot in front of the other on the hard-packed dirt road that ran straight between the Old West buildings.

Gesturing, Mr. Laurentine said, "Maybe you should try the boardwalks. They're in fine repair, I assure you."

"No, thank you," she responded. She wasn't going close to the buildings if she didn't have to.

Rossi had heightened his vigilance again. Zach only carried his cane as a visible weapon, though since he used it for balance, maybe Mr. Laurentine and Mr. Hawburton didn't think of the stick as a threat.

They passed a drugstore on the left and the newspaper office—*The Howl*—on the right, then walked by the house of a prominent person. Shadows and lingering pressure from the past tingled against Clare's skin, but she sensed no strong and coalesced ghostly presences.

Enzo? she whispered in her mind, surprised he hadn't returned before now. How far had he roamed? The dog appeared, running flat out toward her.

Glad you're here, Clare. Hi, Zach! I didn't find anyone hating at Clare around the ranch.

Good to know, I guess, Clare aimed her telepathy at both Zach and Enzo.

Yes! Enzo nodded and trotted next to Zach.

Zach nodded, too, so he must have heard Enzo's and her conversation.

At that moment, Rossi relaxed infinitesimally, his steps became less sharp, even slightly louder in the dirt, and Clare noticed that Desiree Rickman had separated from the shadows near the saloon doors and walked out to join Mr. Laurentine. No doubt Rossi considered her able to protect his—their—client.

You are doing fine, Clare. Enzo's mental voice took on a cheerleading quality.

"Three," she murmured.

"What?" Zach asked.

"From my research there are only supposed to be three ghosts haunting Curly Wolf."

"But J. Dawson isn't included," Zach said.

J. Dawson ROAMS, Enzo said.

After filling her lungs with as big a breath as she could take, Clare repeated, "J. Dawson roams." She winced. Who knew how many other unknown ghosts she might encounter?

"Right," Zach said, and his steel-like right arm came around her waist. That settled her. He usually kept his right hand free for his weapon.

"This appears to be wearing on you," Mr. Laurentine said to Clare. He raised a hand and waved at a man standing in the doorway of the general store to the right. The guy nodded and went inside, came back with a small crate that contained gleaming metallic multicolored sports bottles, all with the logo of the DL Ranch.

Mr. Laurentine beamed. "I have souvenirs for all my guests."

The man held out the tray. Mr. Laurentine picked out a pink metal bottle—the only pink bottle in a nice lot of darker colors—and held it out to Clare.

"Is something in it? If so, what?" Zach asked suspiciously.

"Water from our own well," Mr. Laurentine said. "Have one?"

Zach took a black one. He looked at Rossi. "You've drunk from these bottles?"

"Yeah," Rossi said. "Often."

Zach promptly opened the top, poured out some on the dirt, sniffed the bottle, and took a glug. Then he took Clare's, smelled it, and did the same. Two little wet patches showed on the hard-packed road. He handed Clare back her bottle.

Mr. Laurentine rolled his eyes. "It's water." He wiggled the bottle at Clare. She wasn't too fond of pink, and rather resented the fact that Dennis Laurentine apparently considered her a woman who would prefer pink. But she realized that her mouth *was* dry.

She pulled open the top and took several gulps of cool, refreshing water.

Meanwhile Zach was drinking. After he stopped, he

wiped his mouth on his hand and attached the bottle to a belt loop of his pants with the hook. Mr. Laurentine gave Desiree Rickman a maroon-colored bottle. She licked her lips and the men focused on her mouth, then she opened the thing and drank. The multimillionaire snagged one of the bottles diagonally striped in "his" colors—dark brown and white—and drank, too.

Baxter Hawburton took a red one and chugged some down.

"Good enough," Zach said.

With a nod, Mr. Laurentine dismissed the man with the bottles back to the general store. They all waited while Clare continued to sip, delaying until Mr. Laurentine swept his arm in a wide gesture, and with a smirk, said, "Shall we?"

As a last delay, Clare turned to Mr. Hawburton, and asked, "Was that your forebear's store?"

He smiled and shook his head. "No. There wasn't any shortage of stores in a mining camp. My great-great-granddad had plenty of competition. But his wares were the best quality." Mr. Hawburton winked at her and pointed to a white building with blue trim in the middle of the block to the left. "That was Hawburton Emporium." Clare gritted her teeth. Of course, he'd said the building was white and blue, just minutes ago, and she'd forgotten! An indication of how rattled she was about this whole business.

It occurred to her that if she moved faster, she could get this over with sooner. She began to jog, saw Zach looking grim as he kept up, so she slowed to a walk that would stretch her legs but not bother her lover.

"You were saying about the ghosts, Clare?" Zach asked, catching her fingers in his.

She answered, "Most historic records place J. Dawson at the Curly Wolf Cemetery and agree that there are only three ghosts in the town. The first is the little boy who peeks through the second-story hotel window."

Zach nodded to one of the largest buildings on the right-hand side four structures down. "There's the hotel." He grinned. "And I read about the moaning and vomiting drunk in the old saloon." The dance hall and saloon was just this side of the hotel painted a gaudy red. Neither the hotel nor the saloon had false fronts like some of the others, to make the buildings look taller and more elegant.

"I'm not going inside *anything*," Clare said, her mouth flattening at the words. She didn't see any ghosts exactly, but there were shades and shadows that weren't caused by the sun . . .

Enzo, who'd been sniffing at the others, with various reactions and nonreactions, then running in and out of each building, trotted to her side. *Hi, Clare! Hi, Zach. Clare, you are here! I knew you would come and I told my new friends so! I have been here many times and talked to them!*

"Yes," Clare hissed between her teeth as quietly as she could.

There is a ghost who needs your help!

Her lips formed no, but she didn't say the word. Instead she sighed, and found that her breath flowed warm over her cold lips. She gestured to a moving patch of gray. "Those aren't complete ghosts. What are they?"

Enzo huffed. *Just leftovers of ghosts that have passed on, the very last of their energy that got stuck in buildings or something. They are NOT bad composites. Maybe fading emotions.* His head wrinkled. *That one is worried.*

"Nothing to be worried about, he's dead and gone," Zach said.

Rossi slanted them a glance but said nothing. Mr. Laurentine and Desiree sauntered a couple of yards in front of Zach and Rossi and Clare and apparently didn't hear the byplay.

SHE, Enzo said. *She is gone.* He snorted and looked straight at Clare. *Too many people worry TOO MUCH!*

"Yeah, yeah," Zach said. "We'll teach Clare not to do that." He looked at Rossi, who was staring straight ahead. "Not to worry too much."

Yes! said Enzo. He shot down the street to the end, then back in a streaky smear of gray.

CLARE, A GHOST NEEDS YOUR HELP NOW, HURRY! Enzo danced in front of them, then raced through them; she felt the freeze through her jeaned legs and hiking boots. Zach grimaced. Rossi flinched.

"If a ghost needs Clare's help, he's already been here a long time and can wait a little longer," Zach said.

She! Enzo corrected again. *At the train station at the end of the street!*

Clare's gaze met Zach's. "The third documented ghost of Curly Wolf, the brunette lady—"

"In black silk," Zach ended.

With another good breath—she could breathe easier now she'd become more accustomed to the heavy atmospheric pressure in the town—Clare said, "Let's go then." She started walking a little more quickly. The dirt road was smooth, with no fake wagon ruts . . . or tufts of grass that might grow in a real abandoned town. Mr. Laurentine kept the street grated.

"Are the ghosts here a threat to Clare?" Zach stared at the trotting Enzo.

The ghost dog whirled, then loped back toward them, his eyes serious. *It IS safe. None of the shades or ghosts will bother Clare. They are old and familiar with this place and fine with being here and not grumpy or scary . . . but the lady is very, very sad. She cries and cries. You need to help her, Clare.*

"Uh-huh," Clare said, wondering how much "need to help her" would cost her in terms of strength, energy, and respect. *I'll help,* she said mentally to Enzo. She'd been told that if she didn't accept her gift, she'd die. Well, she'd accepted it.

If she didn't use her gift, help ghosts, she'd go mad. And she believed that, too. It wasn't as if any of them—including Enzo and the Other—would go away if she ignored them. More likely they'd turn into incessant screaming banshees in her mind. Even so, the more she got to know the people the ghosts had been, the more she felt she was helping them in her new vocation. That was important, and would comfort her.

Enzo stopped abruptly, sat and tilted his furrowed head, then shook it. *You need to talk to the little boy first,* Enzo said. *Her son.*

"The boy in the hotel is the son of the lady in black silk?" Clare asked.

An exclamation came from Mr. Laurentine. "That makes sense. And now we have another nugget of information that we can use for research for my town." From the corner of her eyes, Clare could see him beaming and rubbing his hands.

Everyone clumped around her. Even Rossi and Desiree seemed a little distracted from their jobs.

Clare looked up at the window of the hotel. Sure enough, a solemn boy stared at her. She waved, and his face lit with joy and he waved back and jumped up and down.

Now he knows that you can help him. He hopes you can take him to his mother. He's waiting for his mother, Enzo said.

"He's waiting for his mother," Clare repeated aloud. "And she's waiting for him."

"Sad," murmured Desiree.

Heading toward the hotel, Clare thought she could hear an excited child's noises, perhaps words.

Zach said, "The little boy in the hotel and the lady in black silk are child and mother. The boy's ghost can't leave the hotel to find his mother, just down the street at the narrow gauge train station?"

His father was very strict, Enzo said. *She can't move,* Enzo said. *She promised her husband she would not move.* The dog snorted. *He is long gone. He left them.*

Clare repeated the information aloud.

Enzo lifted dark and depthless eyes to Clare, with more than a hint of the Other looking out, and his mental voice deepened as that being spoke to Clare. *You have already learned that some apparitions are limited to a special location and some roam free. The mother is also trapped, but she will be easier to free than the child. It would be best if you brought her here after you speak with the boy.*

She gulped and nodded, and the ankle of her hiking boot hit the edge of the boardwalk and she understood she'd lost track of reality, which was so not good. Her vision had faded to grays and white and black with a hint of sepia.

But she sensed Zach on her right and Rossi on her left, both watchful. Clare shifted her weight to her back leg, moved the other foot forward to feel the height of the walk . . . not too tall here, four inches. She blinked as the colorful blur of Desiree smoothly slid in front of her and opened one of the double doors of the hotel and went in first. Clare and Zach followed.

Zach stopped Clare with a hand on her arm at the bottom of the narrow stairs. "The building is sound?" he asked Mr. Laurentine. "And the steps?"

"Everything has been restored," the man affirmed.

With concentration, Clare cleared her sight enough that her gaze met Zach's serious green-blue eyes. He nodded at her, scanned the area again, then fixed on her. "Go on up," he said.

Soft footsteps indicated that Desiree had preceded Clare once again.

With only a quick glance around at the polished wooden floor, an old patterned carpet still with plenty of use left in it, and paint a color of green that might be appropriate to the period but that Clare wouldn't have in her own house, she moved to the stairway and put her hand on the simply carved wooden rail.

From above, Desiree called, "I looked at the steps. They're a little dusty, haven't been polished lately, but you're safe. I don't know what room the ghost is in."

Yet Clare could already feel the chill of the child's shade. She climbed the steps and met Desiree in the upper corridor.

As with most buildings, the hallway was small. People were smaller then, and materials were at a premium. Desiree stood with hands on her hips and looked down the hall at all the open doors on each side. "It's a hotel," she said, frowning. "The doors should be shut for privacy."

"It's a display piece," Clare reminded her.

"Which room?"

The little boy came to the first door on the left, his expression hopeful. He wore pants with suspenders, a linen shirt, and a small billed cap. The style of his clothes placed him in the late 1880s.

Enzo materialized next to the child and the boy petted him.

I am stuck, the boy said.

TWENTY-ONE

CLARE RESPONDED TELEPATHICALLY to the ghost. *I can see that. Your mother is the lady in black silk?* she asked.

The boy worried his lower lip. *She wears pretty clothes. I can hear her crying, but I can't go to her and she won't come to me! I'm stuck. WE'RE stuck.*

Enzo licked the boy's hand. Clare took a sip of water. *I can . . . get you unstuck.*

He said you could. The child petted Enzo.

"Are you talking to them?" Mr. Laurentine asked. "Not much to watch, is she?" he muttered.

Clare jumped. "Can you please not distract me?"

"What's his name?" asked Mr. Laurentine.

That was a good question.

My name is Samuel Graw. The child apparition made a little bow.

"Samuel Graw," Clare repeated.

"Make a note of that, Clare," Mr. Laurentine ordered.

If she sent Samuel and his mother on, Clare would experience a few of their memories, certainly know their names, and wouldn't forget. She took a deep breath and sloughed off the irritation of Dennis Laurentine's comment. Bracing herself, she walked forward and offered her hand to Samuel. "I am Clare Cermak."

He put his small and frigid hand in hers and she felt his fingers and emotions rush from him to her . . . and she understood that this was not just a remnant of a person, but a fully trapped spirit. She shuddered and he dropped her hand, but she still felt the sorrow, a deep yearning, and patience beyond what she'd ever experienced. The being who'd been Samuel had grown after his death.

Do other ghosts visit you? Clare asked. Maybe the boy would have information on J. Dawson, though the prospector had died about two decades before Samuel.

No. I see people and spirits but no one has come except for the doggie.

I will be back with your mother shortly, she promised.

His eyes shone with a glimmer of dampness and unearthly light.

It is hard to wait. The small voice was back. *But I can.*

"You are a strong and determined spirit. I won't be long," Clare said aloud, praising him for all to hear.

"Huh," said Rossi.

Zach put his hand on her shoulder, squeezed a bit, and stared at the ghost, no doubt seeing the boy due to her connection. "Cute kid," he said.

The boy grinned and ducked his head. *I'll watch at the window. Soon my mother will come. Now I knowww,* and that sound seemed to echo in the room. Rossi shivered.

Enzo barked and ran into the room near the window. *I will wait with you, so you are not alone, and can't fear you'll be left behind again. It is very hard to be left behind. Go get his mama, Clare.*

"We're off to the train station and the lady in black silk, then," Zach stated to all the others who'd stayed in the hallway.

"What happened in there?" asked Baxter Hawburton. The rancher was the closest to the top of the stairs.

"I met Samuel," Clare said and hurried past him and down the steps. "As I said before, he is the son of the lady in black silk at the train station."

"Samuel. What was the kid's last name again?" Mr. Hawburton followed her down the stairs, then she heard Zach and his cane and, later, Mr. Laurentine. Rossi's and Desiree's steps were too light for her ears to catch.

Clare reminded herself that Mr. Hawburton was local. "Graw. Samuel Graw."

Nodding, Mr. Hawburton opened the door for her, took her elbow as they left the boardwalk for the middle of the street. "I think there're a couple of Graws buried in the Curly Wolf Cemetery."

When they went outside, from the cool shadows into the sun, a touch of nausea whirled in her stomach and her breath came raggedly, and Clare was glad of the rancher's steady hand.

She swallowed hard. She had a job to do.

The train station was across the street at the far end of the town, across from the stables. Again Clare went to the middle of the street. There she stopped and looked up at the hotel. Sam grinned and waved to her, his other arm draped around Enzo, who panted cheerfully with his tongue out.

Zach caught her hand and set a pace that was faster than she'd anticipated from him, and in a couple of minutes they were all in the station. A shadowy woman in a beautiful watered silk dress and bonnet rose from a bench holding out her hands in a pleading gesture. *Help me. The dog spirit said you could. You could see me and feel me AND HELP ME FIND MY SON!*

"That's right," Clare said, answering aloud. Rossi and Desiree had kept up, and Zach, of course, was staring at the phantom. She added silently, *Mrs. Graw?*

Yes, yes, I am Mrs. Graw! Silvery, insubstantial tears ran down her face. She wrung her hands. *I have forgotten so, so much.* She lifted her face imploringly. *But I haven't forgotten that I cannot pass on before I have my son, my Sammy.*

Clare stepped away from Zach, nodded to him, then met the gazes of Rossi and Desiree in turn. "I'm going to hold Mrs. Graw's hand and run as fast as I can to the hotel." It would be better if the spirit took her hands. If Clare initiated contact with a ghost, the chill of the connection became freezing, at least twice as bad as when a ghost touched her.

And she *had* to walk into them, or take them into her for them to transition. That process was one of the costs of her gift.

After getting a nod from Rossi and Desiree and a frown from Zach, Clare offered her hand to the nearly transparent Mrs. Graw. *Take my hand and hold on tight. I will lead you to your son.*

More tears. *I've tried and tried to leave this benighted place. I haven't been able to move past the door. And I know my Sammy needs me!*

"You can leave with me," Clare said out loud to give the words more force, the force of a prayer, the force of a woman who called on her gift and it *would* help her do what needed to be done, rules or no rules.

THANK YOU! The apparition grabbed Clare's fingers tightly in a frost-cold grip. "We're going fast," Clare said to the living. Mentally she projected, *Look at me, Mrs. Graw. Focus on me. You are coming with me and nothing will stop you. Nothing CAN stop you.*

Nothing can stop me. I am going to my son. You are taking me to my Sammy!

That's right, and we are running. Run with me. Clare sucked in a couple of deep breaths and took off, shooting to the door and . . . snagging. *Look at me.* She stared at the spirit woman, who gazed back. Clare grabbed the woman's other hand and knew that was right. Her fingers went numb immediately, but she *yanked*, and she and Mrs. Graw were through whatever barrier had stopped the woman before. Clare dropped the hand she'd clasped, and ran. It was more like a jog than running flat out, the way she'd imagined, and she didn't question how the ghost kept up with her, running or floating or what.

Clare's footsteps pounded on the boardwalk now, the sound reassuring her that the bright yellow of the sun that had disappeared in a world of gray shadows was just beyond, in real life. The sun was out there somewhere, ready to beam on her with warmth when she finished what she had to do.

She, they, ran. Slower than she wanted. They passed the store that had once been Mr. Hawburton's ancestor's. It looked light gray with dark gray trim. Clare's teeth began to chatter and she pressed on . . . A blur shot by and she saw

Desiree holding the door to the hotel open. Clare's fingers tightened—she hoped—on Mrs. Graw's hand. They shot in, and panting, Clare ran up the stairs. She knew she wasn't alone because the ghost impinged on her right side, the cold of the once-woman freezing even through Clare's clothes.

Sending the mother and son on would test Clare. She'd never been so cold to start with. She clenched her jaw. She *would* do this.

At the top of the steps, Clare heard Sammy shriek, *MAMA!* The cold presence slipped from her hand and from along her side.

Samuel! My Sammy boy! the woman cried.

Clare stepped slowly to the door, which beamed white light, gathering her irregular breath and her strength, trying to focus on the visible dimensions—contemporary and the gray ghost dimension. She'd had a little practice and no doubt would become an expert eventually, but for now it was still tricky.

Desiree moved from the top of the stairs into the narrow hall, a quizzical look on her face. Her shoulders wiggled a bit and she frowned. "There are vibrations here, and energy, but I can't see or hear anything. Very disconcerting."

"I'm staying down here," Rossi said from the landing halfway up the stairs. "If you go in the room, Clare, stay away from the windows."

She blinked. There wasn't a tall enough building opposite the hotel for a person to shoot from . . . then she recalled Zach and his twenty-four hundred feet. Mr. Laurentine's house was above the town, and parallel to it, and perhaps you could see the second-story hotel window from the house or even the grounds.

Or the rifle shot that morning could have been completely unrelated to her, could have been a hunter or a rancher scaring away something . . . or due to any of a half-dozen things Clare couldn't imagine.

"Clare? Stay away from the window." Rossi sounded impatient, and pulled her back to the moment.

"I will."

Enzo gamboled around her, saying, *Clare, you are back,*

and with the mother's ghost! The Other didn't know if you were strong enough to do that! Yay, yay, yay!

"So it was a test?"

I knew you could do it, Enzo said smugly as he chased his tail just beyond the threshold of the open room door.

Thank you.

Enzo sat. *You have to help them now, Clare. They have been here too long and are too used to this existence. They were good people.*

Clare swallowed hard.

Mrs. Cermak, we are ready! a female voice trilled in Clare's mind. She paused a little, then figured out that to Mrs. Graw, a woman of Clare's age was likely married.

She took another couple of steps toward the door, saw the woman holding the boy . . . who was probably too big for her to carry, but neither of them minded that, and they were, after all, insubstantial.

The boy was grinning, the woman crying. Clare thought this time she wept with joy and smiled herself until she felt the nudge in the backside from a cold and pointy muzzle. *Come ON, Clare, it's time to move them on. The quicker the better,* Enzo said.

She stood stubbornly. *You're always dropping hints like that and never explaining them. Why is it better?*

It just IS. Every minute a ghost stays, there is a chance for it to turn bad.

Bad?

Enzo goosed her again and she gave a little yelp and moved into the hotel room, sidled back into a far corner away from the window.

Desiree moved into the room and the opposite corner. She said, "Are you going to do your ghost laying thing now? Can I watch?"

Clare sighed. "Yes, I'm going to send Mrs. Graw and Sammy on. Yes, you can watch, but I don't know that you'll see anything." Zach hadn't told her what he'd seen when she'd helped her first major client transition.

Looking at Mrs. Graw, she said, *One thing first. Do you know a man, or a ghost, called J. Dawson Hidgepath?*

Mrs. Graw shook her head and said, *No.*

So Clare straightened her shoulders and considered logistics. Both apparitions wore expectant expressions, and Clare didn't think she should send one on, then the other. That didn't seem right according to some inner sense. And now that she thought about it, there *did* seem to be an inner pressure building within her that these two needed to go—wherever they went. Discovering where the ghosts went was absolutely the last of Clare's priorities. Discovering how to make their transition easier on them, and her, was the first.

She shook out her body and loosened her muscles, aware Desiree scrutinized her. Clare took another swallow of water from the despised pink bottle, a bright, modern color that seemed so wrong in these surroundings. She shrugged the thought off, hooked the bottle to her belt loop again, and said, "I think you should put Sammy down, Mrs. Graw, and just hold his hand," Clare stated so Desiree could listen.

You won't separate me from him again!

"No. I won't separate you," Clare said, just as Sammy wrapped his arms around his mother's legs and said, *No, the nice lady won't make us go on alone.*

That had to be a factor as to why both ghosts had stayed. Some people didn't want to die alone, Clare knew, and perhaps the reverse was true. Some people liked to die and transition alone. Were there ghosts around because they'd died with a mass of people? Clare didn't like thinking of mass deaths . . . and the ghosts a horrific event could throw.

But now the Graws stood closely side by side, Sammy leaning against his mother, and her hand around his shoulder and gripping it. No, the woman wouldn't let go of her son easily, nor the son his mother. Clare wondered briefly about the husband in the equation, if he had found himself out of the circle of their love, or if they loved each other more because he'd pushed them out of his affections.

She might find out, since she had to merge with them.

"All right," she said. "Mrs. Graw, I know that timing matters in when a ghost can go on. What is the timing here?" She had to get some solid rules to go by.

I manifest every day, the woman said simply. *Every day I want my Sammy, and as the sun reaches the zenith of the sky,*

I stop listening to him whimper in the dark and come to try and find him in the light. Her ghostly bosom shivered with a sigh. *But there is no good light, only dimness.*

"There's light now," Clare said.

The phantoms nodded.

Clare shot a look at the windows and said, "Can you please come to me for your transition? I'll hug both of you," Clare said.

They smiled, their features hauntingly alike, and glided to within inches of her.

Clare tried to still her mind; instead it seemed like she'd just dropped a blanket on top of a bed of worries that wriggled under it like frantic puppies. She ignored incipient fear.

She held out her arms; the ghosts surged toward her like flames in a draft. Like the other spirits she'd helped, these wanted to leave, which was all to the good.

Trying not to tense, Clare stepped into them, wrapped her arms around them, both shorter than she. Emotions flashed through her, fear of dying, fear of being alone, loneliness of being lost, then knowing the other survived . . . somewhere . . . and being trapped and prevented from going to son, to mother.

Heart-wrenching longing infused Clare. Body-wrenching cold, cold beyond freezing, cold to stop her blood from flowing, ice forming around her heart to stop it from *pumping*, encased Clare.

She saw the hotel room as it had been, colorful, then everything tinted sepia.

In memory, Sammy's mother and father leaned over him, worried, sad. She felt the heat of the fever scourging the boy and his determination to stay with the parents he loved and life slipping beyond his grasp. The scene changed to the train station and sitting in the midst of people but alone with heavy grief. Her child was dead. Her husband had dropped a wall between them, and love was gone, gone, gone. Along with the man who had once loved her and whom she had once loved. People milled around her but didn't speak to her and then pain speared her and she was gone, too . . . and lost.

Clare shuddered from the cold, her arms frozen in position. Summoning all her thoughts, the last of her warmth, she said, "You . . . are . . . to-gether. Go! Go!"

Mrs. Graw gasped and pointed behind Clare, or upward. *Look, look, Sammy! He's there waiting for us, your papa!*

Papa! yelled the boy ghost and vanished into a swirl of rainbow sparkles that tugged on the woman in the black watered silk dress, who turned into a shower of fireworks and disappeared.

Clare fell over.

TWENTY-TWO

"WOW," DESIREE SAID, moving toward Clare along the wall and staring at her. "I didn't see much, but it sure felt like fireworks in here."

You did it, Clare, you did it, you did it! Enzo licked the side of her head. *I am going to tell Zach. Maybe he will hear me! I am going to tell the last ghost. Maybe he will want to transition, too!* The dog ran straight out the second-story window.

Groaning, Clare managed to roll over. She hadn't landed on her hurt cheekbone, but her ribs had felt the shock and throbbed.

Desiree offered her hand, Clare took it, and the smaller woman drew her up easily. Clare had already decided Rickman's wife was stronger than she looked.

"Thanks," Clare said, gingerly dusting herself off. The hotel room wasn't as clean as it had been in her vision in the past. She glanced around. "You know, I think I like the way this room was decorated in the 1880s better."

"Is that so?" Mr. Laurentine's voice rose from downstairs. He sounded the tiniest bit threatening.

"Everything okay, Clare?" asked Zach, coming through

the door and along the wall. There, just there, finally. He slid his arm gently around her and she let her hand—which had been holding her ribs—drop to her side.

A big sigh echoed up the stairwell, and Clare realized it had come from Rossi. "Yeah, they're gone. This place, this whole damn town, feels better."

"What! Two of *my* ghosts are gone?" Mr. Laurentine demanded. "Two items that are special to Curly Wolf and make the town what it is?" He stomped upstairs. "And they've left already without me here to watch you? I didn't think you could—" He stopped.

"Yes." Clare met his eyes. "Little Samuel Graw and his mother had someplace to be and had stayed long enough."

Zach snorted and met the man's eyes. "Yeah, now you're only left with a sick, drunk guy. If you ask me, he was the most colorful of the three anyway. A lost mother and child couldn't be too interesting for most of your guests."

The multimillionaire continued to grumble, his face set in a scowl aimed at Clare. "You're going to move J. Dawson Hidgepath on next. He's colorful, but he is a pain in the ass."

She jutted her chin. "Yes, I will help him leave."

Mr. Laurentine's lower lip curled. "And before my party for the beginning of autumn and hunting season."

"Mr. Laurentine, believe me when I tell you that I have no wish to spend any time here seeing people shoot and kill and bring dead animals back to your house."

He made a disgusted noise.

"Pity that J. Dawson is such a recalcitrant ghost," Zach said. "And won't stay down here in Curly Wolf with his bones. *He* would give you back the character you think you lost when the pitiful mother and son ghosts moved on."

Pivoting, Mr. Laurentine stomped back down the stairs, obviously put out because two of his tamer ghosts that stayed properly in Curly Wolf were now gone.

He threw back over his shoulder, "I think we need to discuss J. Dawson Hidgepath more."

"I e-mailed you my complete report of what I found out at the Park County Archives this morning," Zach said flatly, his arm still circling her waist as they negotiated the stairs carefully, walking around Rossi, who stood guard on the landing, ready to defend from threats above and below.

Clare glanced at Zach from the corners of her eyes. He was lying about including all he knew in a report. She didn't know how she knew, but she did . . . a slight alteration of the line of his shoulders? Discreetly, she checked out Desiree, Rossi, and Mr. Laurentine. All of them appeared to take Zach's statement at face value.

Mr. Laurentine crossed the hotel lobby, threw open a door, and strode outside. "I haven't heard an update from Ms. Cermak," he snapped.

"On J. Dawson or the Graws?" she asked.

Pausing on the boardwalk, one thumb tucked in his belt, the other still holding the gun, muzzle pointed down, Mr. Laurentine said, "You know more about the Graws?" His lips tightened. "At least we can have them written up in the town's lore."

"Frances and her husband—"

"Frances, that is, was, her name?" Mr. Laurentine demanded.

"Yes."

"And her husband's name?" he asked.

Clare shifted her feet, scrolling back through her experience, and the fragmented memories she'd sensed from Frances. Frowning, Clare finally said, "Xavier. Frances and Xavier Graw and Samuel. He was eight when he died. Frances was—"

Mr. Laurentine made a cutting motion. "That should be sufficient to track them for now. I expect you to submit a detailed written report to me with regard to this matter."

Clare nodded austerely. "Of course. Do you want to know what happened to them or not?"

"I'd like to hear the story." Oddly enough, that came from Rossi.

"Absolutely, continue," Mr. Laurentine said.

Blinking, Clare ordered her thoughts, hoped saying the data that she'd garnered—more like sensed during Frances's and Sam's transitions—would fix the facts in her mind. Though now that the experience was over, all the vague extraneous stuff associated with Frances began to fade, like the details of a dream when one awoke.

"The Graws' son had died of influenza and been buried here, and Mr. Graw insisted that Frances and he leave," she said. Everyone seemed riveted by her straightforward and sad story. "Frances, of course, was grieving, and the train was late pulling into this last spur of the line. They'd reached the station, and she realized she didn't have her son's favorite hat; she'd left it in the hotel. She began to leave the station and return to the hotel to get it, but she was tired and sick herself, moving slowly. Her husband said he'd fetch the cap."

Sammy had been wearing that hat when Clare had first, and last, seen him.

"Xavier was impatient with her, and he made her promise not to leave the station. They were respectable people, not riffraff, and she should stay off the streets. He hurried away. The last thing she recalls seeing is watching him stride down the boardwalk toward the hotel. Then she collapsed and died."

"Huh," said Rossi, descending the stairs after Desiree.

"Go on," said Desiree with a gleam in her eyes.

"Frances had promised Xavier that she wouldn't leave the train station, and she didn't, though she continued to mourn her son, knew he, um, lingered as a ghost, too, but was unable to go to him, and unable to help him."

"Very sad," said Mr. Laurentine.

"Yes," Desiree nodded. "Until Clare came along and set them both free." She lifted one beautifully shaped and arched brow at Mr. Laurentine. Apparently he recalled he'd lost a couple of ghosts that added to the atmosphere of his Old West town and he frowned again.

"What happened to Xavier Graw?" asked Rossi.

Clare shrugged. "I don't know. Neither Frances nor Samuel knew what became of him after he left Curly Wolf." She gave a little cough, hard because her face felt numb. "Xavier didn't stay any longer than a day after she was buried."

"Nice guy," said Desiree.

Clare shared a look with her, then frowned. "I don't think he could bear to be here."

"Oh?"

"He was there for Frances and Sammy," Clare said.

"Where?" asked Desiree.

Shrugging, Clare said, "In the light."

"In the light," Rossi repeated. His shoulders rolled. "In the light. Good to know. You hear things, but . . . good to know."

"You think they're both, mother and son, buried at the Curly Wolf Cemetery?" Mr. Laurentine asked.

"They were," Clare said.

"I recall that, too," Baxter Hawburton said.

Mr. Laurentine glanced around as if needing a flunky, then said, "I have a list of the graves, I can check if they're noted." His eyes narrowed. "You have any idea whether Mr. Graw would have sprung for expensive headstones?"

"I don't know," Clare said. Weariness began to creep through her veins sluggishly, slowing her down, and her stomach didn't feel so good. Her breathing hitched now and then.

"In the light," Mr. Laurentine snorted and looked toward his bodyguard, who stood next to Clare. Rossi appeared imperturbable.

Clare said, "Let's go. As I said, I liked the previous wallpaper better up there and in here. This is . . . uninspired." All right, she wasn't above continuing to take potshots at Mr. Laurentine.

Mr. Laurentine stepped back into the hotel lobby from the boardwalk, put his free hand on her arm. "Wait, wait, what did the hotel really look like?"

She smiled. "I've made mental notes. I'll put them in my report later." She passed him and clumped out onto the wooden walk, smiling at Zach, who had his expressionless face on and matched her step for step.

He twined his arm through hers, bent his head close. "Everything go all right with the transition?"

"Fine."

"You still look a little washed out."

"Thanks a bunch."

His smile was brief. "Sorry, I just remember how you handled the gunfighter. Wiped you out."

"Washed out is better than wiped out, for sure," she said lightly.

He glanced around, pulled her into an embrace, and kissed her, and she swirled into a dark, heated place, so different from where ghosts dwelled. She tasted him, let his tongue sweep into her mouth and make her knees weak, her whole body weak so she clung to him and cherished his warmth.

His hands went to her hips, turned her toward him so they were heart to heart, pressed against each other. He was her solid set point in a tornado, the man who offered heat to offset the cold that was now her life. And for all the darkness and sadness the ghosts infused in her when she helped them pass on, Zach gave her earthly vitality.

She slid her arms around his neck, steadied them both. Yes, she needed this man, more than she cared to admit.

"Hey, you two, break it up," Desiree said, and Clare actually heard her stomping down the boardwalk. Someone snickered and Clare thought it might be Mr. Laurentine, and she, at least, was on the job. She'd banished two ghosts for him.

Reluctantly, she drew away, staring into Zach's deep green-blue eyes, the ones that had the shadows in them that seemed to match her own. More, she'd seen those shadows of pain, physical and emotional, but she'd also seen the knowledge of how to deal with those shadows and overcome them. She'd needed that.

She leaned down and picked up the cane, which she hadn't heard fall to the ground, and handed it to him, her breathing a little rough, then let her appreciation of him show in her smile, her look that told him they'd make love later. "Thank you."

His return smile was slow, caressing. "You're welcome."

She wanted to ask him always to be there after she'd dealt with apparitions, but that was too close to true intimacy, to admitting she might need him more than he needed her and insert an inequality to their relationship.

Her own smile was a little difficult, her face a little numb, perhaps from the lingering cold of sending the ghosts on, though she'd thought her blood had pulsed fast and hot . . . from the kiss.

They all walked toward the train station. Once again Clare preferred to stay in the middle of the street and Zach accompanied her on one side and Rossi the other. She'd almost gotten used to seeing Mr. Laurentine carry the rifle since this little stroll was turning into such a production, but it made her a bit twitchy. Of all the men there, she'd trust Dennis Laurentine the least with a gun.

TWENTY-THREE

MR. HAWBURTON WALKED with Mr. Laurentine only
a yard ahead of them, then paused once more near Hawburton
Emporium. The rancher glanced back at her and made a
sweeping gesture. Clare looked at it. Unlike many of the others, it had a false front to appear more imposing. Just beyond
it was a rough, wooden planked building showing the steeply
angled roof that would be needed here.

"Jorgen Brothers, Carpenters."

"The Jorgens ran it," Mr. Hawburton said.

"I can see that," Clare said.

"Patrice Schangler's family," Mr. Laurentine added with a
note of smugness. "Her maiden name was Jorgen."

Baxter Hawburton shrugged. "A lot of the old families are
still here." He pointed across the street to the stables and continued, "Patrice married Jerry Schangler, the last of the folks
who owned the livery. He's gone now, poor guy, six years. Car
accident in Denver."

"Oh," Clare said.

"So do you feel anything of J. Dawson Hidgepath here?"
Mr. Hawburton asked.

"No."

"But you spoke to him last night."

Mr. Laurentine's question distracted her, and that was good. Her stomach had begun to swish with the acid of anxiety . . . aftermath of sending the ghosts on, or having to make this walk that she'd never wanted. She swallowed hard. "That's right. He asked me how it felt to take a fall, like he did."

Desiree winced. "Not too sensitive, is he?"

"He wants to know the name of the person who murdered him."

"Murder? I thought he fell picking wildflowers for the ladies," Mr. Hawburton said.

Clare flushed, knowing that respect she prized would be chipped away some more when she answered.

"According to Ms. Cermak, J. Dawson Hidgepath's ghost says he was murdered. She can communicate with them. Told you that, Baxter," Dennis Laurentine said.

"Oh. Right." A false smile curved Mr. Hawburton's lips. "Well, he was a womanizer. Maybe a jealous husband did him in."

"He was a romantic," Zach said dryly.

"I didn't talk to J. Dawson today, but I did receive another token of his affection," Clare said dryly.

Desiree slanted Clare a glance. "That would be bones?"

"Yes. He left me four phalanges, apparently from two toes."

Desiree's eyes sparkled and her lips rounded. "Ohhh."

Mr. Laurentine seemed to shiver a little at the sound. Missy Legrand would not have been pleased.

"Real, physical bones?" Desiree asked.

Clare shared a look with Zach. Rossi appeared inscrutable. Rossi knew of the bones, and Desiree didn't. So just how involved was Desiree in this case? Had Rickman sent her, or had she come on her own?

"Clare?" Desiree prompted.

"Yes, real, physical bones," Clare said. "At least they sure seem to be, to me. I must admit I am not an expert." Yet. She could have tagged that on. The way her cases were going, she'd be very familiar with all sorts of body parts she'd rather not know about in detail.

"Hmm. Dennis, did you have Dr. Burns look at them?" Desiree asked.

"The first time the bones appeared, the full skeleton, of course. Most of the larger bones were broken—arms, legs, pelvis, caved-in skull. Was a real puzzle to put together . . . and makes leaving his bones even easier," Mr. Laurentine said sourly. "Dr. Burns also handled the bones the second time the full set appeared. Now J. Dawson, uh, seems to be spreading himself out." His lip held a slight curl. "To Ms. Cermak."

"And Ms. Legrand," Clare added.

"Yes," Mr. Laurentine said.

"All right!" Desiree's smile was blinding. "Maybe I'll be blessed, too."

As they passed Jorgen Brothers, Mr. Laurentine said, "So you've apparently banished two ghosts today and you've been a ghost seer for how long?" he asked.

"You are the first client Mr. Rickman convinced me to consult for," she said, feeling prickly at his question. Her lovely, staid life had disappeared just weeks ago. She began stalking at a quicker pace toward the church at the end of the street. It was only a third of the size of the saloon.

Zach accompanied her, as did Rossi, the other three lagging behind, which was fine with her. She wanted this done. A couple of yards past a schoolhouse painted red and white and with a tiny bell steeple, Zach's steps slowed. "Crows," he muttered. He tilted his head as he looked at the ridgepole of the train station coming up on their left. "Damn cawing." He dropped his arm from her waist to rub at his ear. Clare followed his gaze, craned to look at all the buildings in sight. She saw and heard no crows, no birds at all.

"Three." Zach sighed, putting his arm around her again. "Three for a wedding."

"What are you talk—" Clare began.

Enzo appeared. *Hello, Zach. Don't worry, Zach. Everything's A-OK. Hello, Clare, you did good, Clare. Xavier and Francis and Sammy are all where they should be. They went on, their ghosts are laid to rest.* He licked her hand, and she knew from the chill that her skin had finally warmed to normal again.

Did you notice, Clare, some of the shadowy shade-ghost remnants have gone away, too! Just from you walking down the street! And some left when Francis and Sammy transitioned! The lower part of his jaw opened in his grin. *And I HELPED.*

"I can't deny that," she said. "You helped."

He pranced along the street with her.

Zach's shoulders shifted. "There don't seem to be as many shadows lingering near the doors of the buildings."

"Town does feel different," Rossi said, but his eyes remained sharp and continued to scan the area. "Easier to see, too, without as many shadows." Then he seemed to understand what he was saying and snapped his mouth shut.

Once they reached a bench to one side of the church, which was identical to the one on the ridge, Clare was glad to see another road up to the house.

"I'm not going back through the town," she stated. Everyone except herself looked cool and calm and unruffled. Even though she'd been chilled to the bone helping the boy and his mother walk into the light, that coolness had vanished and a sheen of sweat covered her. Or perhaps, it was the melting of the ice that had coated her, turning into perspiration. Her clothes were nastily sticking to her. Her face was probably too flushed. Not to mention her hair, which felt like each curly strand had slipped out of her band and sprung around her head in an aura of frizz.

"I really think—" Mr. Laurentine said.

"No," she said.

His lips pursed in something close to a pout, and he turned on his colorful snakeskin cowboy boot stacked heel and stared back in town. "Pity two ghosts are gone."

She held back the irritation inside from lacing her voice. "It was. A very great pity for them to have to linger in an abandoned town, alone and yearning for each other, for a hundred and twenty years." Not being able to stand the heat and a trickle escaping from her hairline to dribble down the side of her face, she searched her jeans pocket for a handkerchief, didn't find one, and wiped her face with the long sleeve of her shirt. She should have brought a hat.

"Clare?" asked Zach.

"Are you hot?" she asked.

He angled his head. "No. Not hot."

"I need to get out of here," she said.

"Take it easy, Clare," Desiree said.

"When I say so," Mr. Laurentine said.

With a chuff of her breath, she swung away from the group, too irritated—and too darn sensitive to that irritation—to be with them. They sure couldn't understand what she'd just gone through! Couldn't appreciate it. . . . and she was back to the issue of respect.

She needed respect. She wanted it for her work, as she'd gotten it in the past for her accounting career.

But it was becoming all too obvious that she wouldn't be getting it for her vocation in the future, or for her gift, which people didn't understand or sneered at. That hurt her on a deep level.

It didn't help that if she hadn't had this gift, she'd have done the same.

She realized her vision was impaired by her swelling cheek, and that was just great. Her ribs throbbed and she couldn't even relax into a tiny slump because of the ache that would come.

With a quick pivot on her heel, she headed off toward the road carved out of the hill.

"Clare!" Zach yelled, and she heard anger. She didn't care.

"Clare, please wait." That came from Desiree Rickman.

Neither Zach nor Desiree had scorned her for her gift or patronized her, but in the moment, that didn't seem to matter.

Clare, said Enzo, moving through her legs, cooling that part of her down, at least.

She reached down and patted his head and found herself looking into the depthless fog that passed as the Other spirit's eyes.

"Oh."

Clare, you are not progressing as quickly or as well as you should be, the being, the thing, reprimanded her, and right in her very own mind!

Tears rose behind her eyes, pressed painfully against her sinuses. *I don't care.*

You should. Try harder. Read Sandra's journals daily.

Then it, and Enzo, flicked out like someone had turned on the burning sun and banished their shadows.

"Clare, are you all right?" Now Zach sounded a little worried.

Her lips were too dry to answer him aloud.

"No, I can see you aren't. Infection or altitude sickness or heatstroke or something."

TWENTY-FOUR

ZACH SET HIS arm at her back and bent, and she knew that he meant to pick her up and carry her.

She pushed at him, shook her head so the buzzing inside it didn't distract her. "Don't lift me, Zach. I want to walk on my own two feet."

"We need to get you back to the house ASAP. And checked out with Dr. Burns. Again."

"I don't—" but a huge wave of nausea gripped her and she only had time to turn and vomit into the road.

Desiree came and put a strong arm around Clare, steadying her, and she grunted as her ribs twinged when she tried to hunch.

Zach's hand slid along her waist, and she felt him unclip the nasty pink bottle, heard him say, "Laurentine, have someone bring that case of water bottles up to the doctor's office. Ms. Rickman, can you please confiscate everyone else's?"

"Sure," Desiree said. She whipped out a folded bag from a pocket, whisked it open. Rossi was the first to drop his bottle in it, then the rest did, including Zach.

"What! You think something was in the water?" the multimillionaire asked after calling and telling the guy in the general store to bring up the crate.

"Lean on me," Zach murmured to Clare, then replied to Laurentine, "I'd feel better if I collected all of them, just in case. We need a ride for Clare *now*," he snapped.

Yes, since she seemed to be swaying. He *was* solid.

"On that," Rossi said. "I'll alert Dr. Burns."

"What's with the water and the bottles?" Zach demanded of Mr. Laurentine.

"I have the souvenirs delivered to the house, Patrice fills the sports bottles from our well, sends them down to the general store."

Zach grunted. "They aren't tamperproof?"

"They're regular bottles."

Clare hadn't wanted the damn bottle in the first place. If she ever saw another one, it would be too darn soon. Her skin had gone clammy with cold sweat. Slowly she straightened, inhaled deeply through her nostrils—and smelled the dust of the town and the past.

"The vehicle's in sight," Desiree said.

Frowning, Zach looked up the road, at Clare, and then at Mr. Laurentine.

"Let me help Clare while you discuss this matter with Dennis," Desiree said.

His frown deepening into a scowl, Zach muttered under his breath. Clare straightened and stepped away from her lover and began putting one foot in front of the other to slog up the road. Desiree slipped a sturdy arm around Clare's waist.

Zach shot out questions, "Where are the bottles kept up at the house? Who has access to them? How does Schangler prepare the water? Why did you give Clare the pink bottle?"

Clare knew the answer to the last one. "Mr. Laurentine thinks I'm a girly girl," she said, but didn't know if the others had heard it.

"Come on, Laurentine, answer my questions," Zach snapped.

"Clare's right. She wears pink."

"I wear peach or coral," she enunciated. "Because the

colors flatter me. Does not mean I want a damn pink bottle."
Shudders ran up and down her nerves just under her skin.

"Sure," Desiree soothed. "That color range looks great
against your skin." She muttered under her breath, "Men."

"Here's the case of bottles," the man from the general
store huffed as he jogged to them.

Zach's voice was cold as a ghost. "You didn't answer me,
Laurentine. Where are the bottles kept up at the house? Who
has access to them? How does Schangler prepare the water?"

"Fuck it, Slade!" Mr. Laurentine said. "How the fuck
should I—"

"Answer the man, Dennis," Desiree tossed over her shoulder. They hadn't gotten very far up the road. Clare needed to
take bigger steps. In a minute. She paused to catch her breath.

Desiree continued, "Don't you know what happens in your
house?"

"Boxes of empty bottles are kept in a storage room. A
dozen are on the shelves of the back pantry. I could have
drunk out of any of those." He jerked his chin toward the
crate.

"You gave Clare the pink one," Zach said. "Would you
have drunk out of the pink one?"

"No. Would you have?"

Zach didn't answer.

"Go on, Dennis," Desiree prompted.

"We use well water. We have an excellent well, and the
water is filtered."

"I've seen a cooler of water with citrus fruit, lemons,
limes, and orange slices in the dining room," Zach said.
"Would that mixture have been in the bottles?"

"I don't know. Maybe." Mr. Laurentine sounded increas-
ingly irritated.

"Clare, what did the water taste like?" Zach asked.

Her tongue just curled up and she swallowed down another
upsurge of bile. "I don't recall. Metallic, maybe."

"You tasted hers yourself," Mr. Laurentine said.

"She'll be fine with Burns," Rossi said. "Give some of
Clare's water to Dr. Burns to test as well as the cops. He's a
better researcher than a people doctor, has a little lab." Rossi
looked thoughtful.

A two-seater Jeep motored into her range and the driver stopped. Clare had plenty of help getting into the passenger seat. Zach unclipped the bottle from his belt, curved her fingers around it. It felt cool but a little slippery from the sweat on her palms. "Give that to Burns. I want to ask more questions."

She nodded.

He took her phone, thumbed on SeeAndTalk, opened the same on his phone so they were connected.

"Look at this until you're in the doctor's office. I'm monitoring you."

She nodded, saw his grim face on her phone.

He kissed her cheek, then the vehicle took off, zooming along up to the house.

Zach's heart thudded hard in his chest as he watched the Jeep speed Clare to the doctor. He wanted to go with her but thought he'd better strike with questions here when people were more off guard.

"A deputy's coming out from the sheriff's department," Rossi said.

Zach wanted to squeeze every drop of information out of Laurentine. He also wanted to be with Clare. "That's good."

The Jeep disappeared on a switchback behind tall pines.

"I can't believe this," Laurentine said.

Zach turned back to look at him. Guy wasn't happy he wasn't the center of attention. Zach scanned the rest. Rossi, solid, helpful. Hawburton the rancher, faded a little to the background . . . separating himself from mostly city folks? The man with the crate appearing uncomfortable and stoic. Desiree Rickman, holding her bag with the bottles still enough that no clinks came, watchful but with a half smile on her lips. Woman liked excitement.

In the far distance a siren wailed, rising from the wide valley up the mountains. The sheriff, maybe an ambulance. He hoped not.

"We had an outbreak of pesticide poisoning—animals— about a month ago," Rossi said. "Killed a bunch."

That riveted Zach's attention.

"Pesticide outbreak," he said with an edge of savagery in his voice.

"Real old stuff lying around."

"Might have given someone a bad idea," Zach said. His jaw felt tight from clenching his teeth. "As for Burns, is he from a local family, too?"

"No," Laurentine said. "He's from Boston. A good man. Like Rossi said, he prefers to do research. My demands upon him are rarely onerous." Laurentine sent a sideways glance to Zach. "Until Clare arrived."

The man's attitude stank. Zach didn't have a badge, but he had his own attitude. He stared at the guy as if he might arrest him the next minute and make his life hell in an interrogation room for long hours.

Laurentine stepped back until he joined the rancher. So did the guy who still held the box.

Rossi looked impassive. Desiree Rickman . . . almost perky, an odd expression on a stunning woman.

"About Dr. Burns," Zach continued to the bodyguard. "Did you check him out?"

"Tony checked everyone out before we took this job when Mr. Laurentine approached us three years ago to guard him in Colorado. Tony updated the info before I was assigned this summer." Rossi nodded respectfully toward the multimillionaire, who eased a bit. Desiree blinked and went to the man, took his arm.

"Come on, Dennis, let's walk up to the house. Or do you want to go back through your fascinating town?"

Laurentine angled his body so he could see the town, and his shoulders lowered as he saw proof of his worth . . . and Zach had to admit that the man had done well in saving the town. Better if he hadn't moved it and made it his personal property, but too many Western towns were nothing but a few planks or logs, some nails.

"Mr. Laurentine, why *do* you have a bodyguard?" Zach asked.

The man grimaced. "I have a crazy ex-wife and a restraining order against her, but that means nothing to Maria."

"No incidents since I've been on the job," Rossi said. Then added without expression, "Except these against Clare. But we think they're about her and not Mr. Laurentine. She was the one set up for the fall. She's the one who got sick."

"Understood. I want everything Rickman has on all the players, immediately. Nothing held back. Got it?"

"Got it." Rossi sent a message on his phone.

Patrice Schangler opened the house door, her eyes stormy in a masked expression. "Ms. Cermak, exactly what did you say about my water or the water bottles?"

"Nothing."

"The sheriff is coming to get the bottles I sent down this morning to be tested for contaminants. There is absolutely nothing wrong with that water." The woman snatched the pink bottle from Clare's hand, her mouth curving down in distaste at the color, flicked the top open and brought it to her mouth, then hesitated.

"Go ahead," Clare said tiredly. "Prove your point and drink it. *I* don't care. Just step aside so I can get to Dr. Burns's office. I'm sick."

"Give me the bottle, Patrice." The Jeep driver had dropped his hold on Clare and held out his hand. "Let's not make all of this worse."

"What now?" Dr. Burns bustled up, his eyebrows lowered.

"I vomited," Clare said. "It might have been the water in one of the DL Ranch bottles."

"I was never in favor of those bottles and well water. Better to have clear bottles and use custom water," the doctor grumbled. "Did anyone save me a sample I can analyze?" His gaze fixed on the bottle and the housekeeper reluctantly handed it over. He stuck it in his lab coat pocket and put his arm around Clare's waist, took some of her weight, and started moving them at a near jog.

"You have a lab here?" Clare puffed out with a breath.

"I'm more of a researcher in microbiology, and the lab is well equipped. One of the staff sometimes helps me out if I need it," Dr. Burns said. "You're pale and sweating and have some caked vomit near your mouth that I might be able to analyze, too."

Ick.

He took a wipe from his coat pocket and scrubbed at her mouth, then moved away toward his office, saying, "Excellent. I'll contact one of the Curly Wolf caretakers to get a good sample of your vomit."

"Wonderful," she said as she tottered after him. When she went through his door, she sank into a comfortable chair instead of proceeding into the inner examination room and onto the dratted table. She saw the doctor hand off the bottle to one of the female staff and told her to prepare a sample for him. He gave her the wipe, too, and mentioned test strips.

Then Dr. Burns returned and made her go back into the exam room. "Symptoms?" He took his stethoscope from the counter.

"Um, hot? But it's a hot day walking in the sun."

The doctor nodded shortly.

"Nausea," she said.

"Still feel sick?"

"Not so much."

"Open your mouth."

She did and he scrutinized her throat. Her face twitched and she trembled.

"Does your face feel numb?"

"A little."

He studied her eyes, her ears, checked her heart and her breathing. He had her go through the whole scenario of what she drank and what it tasted like going down and coming back up.

"How much of that did you drink?" he asked.

Clare usually monitored her liquid intake to ensure she was hydrated. She'd always had a bottle of water at her desk at her job and kept it filled. Since she was no longer with the accounting firm, she hadn't been doing as well. She'd had some sips and some gulps . . . but no prolonged glugging; she'd been too busy for that.

The telephone on his desk in the outer office rang and he picked it up. "You think so?" he barked after a few seconds. "The thought had occurred to me, too. For pesticide the best thing to do is treat her symptoms as they come along, alleviate them. No stomach pumping. I haven't looked at the solution yet."

When he came back, he asked, "Got any idea how much you had?"

"I guess not more than four ounces." She shrugged. Her nerves seemed to have subsided.

He shook his head. "We'll watch you closely. I'll check the solution and I'll compare the liquid remaining in the bottle you drank from to that of a full one in the pantry."

She nodded.

"Did you have any auditory hallucinations?"

Clare stared at him. She saw and talked to ghosts. How would she know? "No," she finally said.

"Fine." He treated her bruised cheek and checked her ribs.

His assistant came in. "It's pesticide. I'm not sure what kind, though."

TWENTY-FIVE

CLARE GASPED. "PESTICIDE doesn't sound good."

"It's not. You stay right there while I check this out. Lie down." He strode from the exam room.

Clare slid down onto the table, contemplated the beamed ceiling, and took stock of herself. Her heartbeat felt fine and steady; her breathing was regular. She didn't feel terrible. Alternating between the freezing chill of helping ghosts transition and walking in the direct sun in the heat of the day at high altitude hadn't helped whatever had ailed her.

Or had it? Who knew exactly what physical harm—or good—ghost laying could do her? Great-Aunt Sandra had died at ninety. Clare visualized the family tree. Great-Great-Uncle Amos had died in his mid-nineties, too.

The sheriff's car picked up Zach along with the crate of bottles and Desiree Rickman's sack. Hawburton excused himself to get back to his ranch, Laurentine decided to stroll back through Curly Wolf and up the regular paved drive, and Rossi accompanied him. Laurentine and Rossi would meet the deputy at the house.

Zach was fine with that—it gave him time to fully brief the deputy sheriff, a woman he'd met before, on the bottles and the walk, Clare's sickness. He told her everything he could remember. She recalled the pesticide incident.

At the house, she secured her vehicle with the evidence and went in to speak with a hovering and pale Patrice Schangler.

He headed toward the doctor's office, heart thumping hard. Poisons were tricky things. He'd had one case when he was a city cop, studied up on some of them. Knew about drugs, both legal and illegal, and they messed with your head and your body.

The outer office held a desk, a laptop computer, old-fashioned file cabinets, and a couple of client chairs. Beyond the desk were a wall and a closed door. He strode over and opened it . . . saw Clare looking . . . all right. Okay. He let out a big but quiet breath. She still wore her clothes, though they looked loosened. She smiled at him, a smile he'd seen her give no other person. God, he cared for her. A lot.

"Does she need a hospital?" he asked.

The doctor whirled, scowled, but didn't reprimand him and said, "I don't believe so. They can't do any more for Ms. Cermak there than I can do here. I'm perfectly competent to handle this case."

"Okay."

"I would prefer for her to stay here in the house to rest, and for me to observe. If there is any bodily twitching, tremors, or convulsions, call me at once." He pulled out a card and wrote a number on it. "This is my private cellular telephone."

Zach took the card, entered the number into his own phone, and stuck the card in his jacket pocket.

"So was it a pesticide like the previous incident?"

"That's right. Based on the tests I've done so far on the water, the pesticide in Ms. Cermak's bottle was in powder form, old and a relatively small amount," Dr. Burns said.

"Your best opinion," Zach said. "Was this a fatal dose or not?"

Dr. Burns shrugged. "If she'd drunk the whole bottle, and quickly . . . it could have been very bad. Very bad."

Clare stared at them wide-eyed.

"As it is . . ." He shook his head. "I think if we watch you closely for any symptoms . . ." Once again he moved close to Clare, stuck his stethoscope on her skin, and listened. "No irregular breathing or heartbeat." He checked her reflexes. "Your muscles seem all right, no extraordinary twitching. How does your face feel?"

"No longer numb."

"Fine." He looked at Zach. "We'll treat the symptoms." He disappeared a minute, came back with a needle, and gave her a shot. "This will help."

"I want to take her up to bed," Zach said.

Clare smiled; the doctor scowled. Zach raised his hands. "To rest." To be in an easily protected room.

The doctor hunched a shoulder. "Go. I'm continuing my tests." He scowled at Clare. "You were lucky."

She nodded.

Zach put his arm around her and said to Burns, "The deputies will want to speak with you and take the bottle."

The doctor grimaced. "If they must."

"Yes, they certainly must. Please copy me with any report you do on the solution." Zach took his old card, which stated he was a deputy of Cottonwood County, State of Montana, out of his jacket pocket, scratched out his title—which was becoming a little easier to do—and added his personal e-mail.

"I suppose," the doctor grumbled.

"There's no one who wants to get to the bottom of this matter and out of your hair more than I do, Doctor," Zach said.

The man stared at him, nodded, then took his card.

Zach *ached* to pick Clare up, hold her, and carry her up to their room. Couldn't. Even with his good shoes and braces, he limped a bit.

"That grinding isn't good for your jaw or teeth," Dr. Burns said to him.

"I know it. Clare, honey, can you walk?"

She looked at him, all soft expression, beautiful clear and unwavering eyes, mass of curly hair that she didn't suppress anymore, making her downright beautiful.

"Sure," she said. She slipped from the table and walked slowly toward him.

"How do you feel?"

"All right."

"Can she eat as usual? I don't think she had lunch."

The doctor nodded. "I'll have someone bring up a light omelette."

"Thank you," Clare said. She held out her hand to the doctor. "Thank you for all the care you've given me, Dr. Burns."

His face eased from deep lines. He took Clare's hand. "You're welcome. Take care of yourself."

"I will."

He shot a look at Zach from under lowered brows. "You take care of her, too."

"I will." He linked fingers with Clare. God, her palm in his felt good! They walked without speaking to the outer office; Clare opened the door to the corridor. After they went through, he glanced both ways. No one else was in the hallway, though there seemed to be a little commotion down to their left in the great room at the end of the hall.

"We need to discuss J. Dawson, maybe speak with him, too. You up for that?"

Her hand tensed in his, then relaxed. "Yes. I don't want to touch him, though."

"Where's Enzo?"

"I don't know. He took off when the Other appeared and scolded me for not learning fast enough, not reading Great-Aunt Sandra's diaries enough."

"Bullshit," Zach said. "You're moving fast enough in the ghost seer stuff."

Clare looked up at him with surprise. "You don't use language like that." There was a question in her voice. Since they were moving slowly and still some paces away from the great room, he gave her the truth. "One of the last things I promised my older brother was not to curse. You only cuss mildly, too."

Her smile was ironic. "Because every other word out of my parents' mouth is foul. They are *not* Rom in that."

And her parents had hurt her with their selfishness. He squeezed her hand and she squeezed back.

"Something else we have in common," she said, as if she needed to total up something in a "Shared Qualities" column. He wondered if she had a "Too Different" column for them, and he didn't like the thought of that.

They reached the great room and found much of the staff, Laurentine, Missy Legrand, and Desiree Rickman gathered around a happy teenage couple, a boy and a girl.

"Do you know them?" Zach asked.

"Yes. The boy is Ms. Schangler's nephew, Tyler Jorgen."

Zach glanced at his watch. "He's early for work."

She tilted her head. "Is he?"

"Yeah, he's the only one of the staff who was working at the time of your fall that I haven't spoken to. I need to talk to him now. Who's the girl?"

"His girlfriend, Emily Johnson." Clare paused, a little frown line twisting between her eyebrows. "I didn't tell you about meeting them, did I?"

"No. You can do that later." They'd taken several paces to the gathering when it struck Zach—he recalled the crows he'd seen. "Crap. Wedding," he muttered.

"They're too young to get married," Clare said.

But Zach got this terrible feeling in his gut that the crows—and he—were right. What a wedding had to do with him and Clare, he didn't know.

When they walked up, Tyler met Clare's glance a little defiantly. "We're getting married."

Zach had the idea that the only reason Clare didn't blurt out something negative was because she'd had a few seconds' warning. She smiled, but it wasn't one of her best. "Congratulations." Then she said, "You're lovely together."

The young man's brows wiggled at the word *lovely*, but the girl beamed. "Thanks, Ms. Cermak." She nudged the boy with her elbow.

"Thanks, Ms. Cermak," he echoed.

"Congratulations," Zach said.

The couple nodded. Zach saw that the only person who seemed less than pleased was his aunt, Patrice Schangler. Families. Still, something about the subtle way the couple interacted struck Zach as a good match now . . . and that they might be able to grow and stay together.

Shifting from foot to foot, Tyler stared at the multimillionaire. "Emily and I want to get married next June. Would you . . . would you let us say our vows in that nice little meadow off to the east of the house? The one surrounded by pines? We're not going to have a big ceremony."

Mr. Laurentine grinned and puffed up, taking on the aspect of a benevolent uncle. "Of course, of course."

"Oh my God!" squealed Emily. "Thank you *so much*, Mr. Laurentine." She flung herself at him and hugged him, kissed his cheek. "This is so amazing!"

"Congratulations again," Zach said, then continued, "Mr. Jorgen." The young man flushed as if he wasn't usually called that. "I'd like to speak with you regarding the night Clare fell."

Tyler frowned. "Sorry about that, Ms. Cermak, anything I can do—"

Laurentine moved close to the youngster and laid a heavy arm around his shoulders. The kid tensed. "Nonsense, Slade. What we need to do now is talk about the wedding. Isn't that right, Tyler?"

He flushed. "Yeah, sure."

The girl looked thrilled. "Oh. Oh. Oh! How wonderful." She gazed at the teen with tears filling her eyes. Young Jorgen stood tall.

"Please come and see me in Clare's room after you're done, Mr. Jorgen."

The young man met Zach's eyes, his own a clear blue. "Yeah, sure."

"We'll discuss the wedding in my office, where we won't be disturbed," Laurentine said, moving in that direction and keeping his arm around Tyler.

Zach projected his voice. "Mr. Jorgen is the only one I haven't spoken with about Clare's fall."

"You don't need to talk to him now, Slade," Laurentine said, his jovial manner replaced by irritation. The girl looked back at Zach nervously as if he might wreck her wedding plans. So he kept quiet. Tyler had slowed his steps, though.

"Besides, a deputy sheriff already talked to Tyler, didn't he?"

Tyler perked up. "That's right. They woke us—me up at two a.m."

No, Zach couldn't barge in right now. And he didn't feel like hovering around Laurentine's door to nab the kids when the couple came out . . . if they didn't leave by way of the terrace. Dammit! He wanted, needed, to spend time with Clare, and figure out more about her accident. And J. Dawson's death that might be the wellspring of the current problems. Clare could talk to ghosts, find out more from J. Dawson about his murder. Murder could echo through the years, smearing names and reputations.

"Zach?" Clare asked.

He needed to make sure she was fine physically and emotionally. In private, just the two of them.

"It can wait," he said, hoping that was true. There was no one for him to depend on in this investigation, no backup except Clare, and she was injured. Rossi had his own job and wasn't an investigator. Nor was Desiree Rickman. "Come on, Clare. Your food will be waiting."

"I am hungry," she said.

"Let's talk about Hidgepath, I'm sure all the present troubles link back to his murder," Zach said. "Nothing happened until you were on the scene and folks knew you could talk with ghosts."

Desiree Rickman detached herself from the group. "I'll go with you." She smiled at Zach. "I'm a good bodyguard, too."

"You just think most of the action here is with Clare and me." Zach gave her a hard-eyed look . . . and it actually seemed to affect her . . . for five seconds.

Then she smiled and said, "Sure." She came close and lowered her voice. "And you two are more my people than anyone else here except Rossi."

They'd reached the steps, and he took the stair rail side and reluctantly dropped Clare's hand. Desiree crowded Clare a little as she took the wall side. Zach approved. They wouldn't let Clare fall again.

By the time they reached the door to her room, Clare was tired . . . but as if he'd heard them talking about him, a gray-toned figure stood outside it, dressed in a nice suit and his bowler hat. Beaming at a few small ivory-colored bones at the bottom of the door.

TWENTY-SIX

ADRENALINE SURGED THROUGH Clare as she studied them. "J. Dawson! Really!"

He shrugged.

"What's going on?" asked Desiree Rickman, appearing fascinated.

Zach put his arm around Clare's waist. "J. Dawson Hidgepath is here."

Desiree crossed her arms, her mouth turning down. "And I can't see him."

"Where do you get your bones?" Clare asked.

He shrugged. *They are with me, here.* Then he frowned. *Or perhaps I put them somewhere else in the space around me.*

She recalled what Enzo had said when they'd visited Geneva Slade. "Ah, *in-between*?"

Some may call it that. I've heard the spirits say so. It may also be where I am . . . not life, not death . . . LIMBO! His voice rose to a ghostly shriek.

Clare jerked, put her hand to her ribs, and swallowed. "Please don't do that."

He stopped, stared. *You are hurt! More hurt than you were.*

"An accident," she lied. She didn't want to get into everything with J. Dawson, though irritation throbbed through her in time with the hurt in her cheek.

Desiree squatted on her heels and still looked gorgeous. She stirred the bones with her forefinger. J. Dawson must be running out of small bones and these didn't look like any Clare recognized.

"Ossicles," Desiree said.

"Left ear," Zach added.

Of course they'd know.

"*Eeeep!*" The sound came from a female staff member who stared at the bones. The tray with Clare's omelette tilted, slopping coffee. With a burst of energy she didn't know she had, she lunged forward and caught it, steadied it.

"Sorry, sorry," the woman said, her eyes filling.

Desiree scooped up the bones in her palm, hid them, and gave a bright smile. "All gone from view."

The server bobbed her head.

"Thanks so much for bringing me a bite to eat," Clare said.

The woman drew a shuddering breath, nodded again, turned, and hurried away.

"I hope she stays," Clare said.

"Hard to say. Dennis said he'd been losing staff," Desiree said.

J. Dawson watched with amusement.

Zach slid the key in the door and pushed it open, gesturing for Clare to pass by with her tray. "Eat that while it's hot." Then he blocked the door so Desiree couldn't get through.

"This is private," he said.

"I can help!"

"No."

Desiree said, "Doesn't Clare get a vote?"

"Clare is tired and needs to eat and sleep."

Which sure wasn't what he'd said to her. Clare put the tray on the table and dug in. It was rude to eat when no one else was, but she was starving and the omelette was delicious!

Desiree leaned around him and her voice became louder. "Clare, what you did for the Graws, mother and son, was very impressive."

Clare looked up from her food. "Thank you, but you're still not coming in."

"Don't you think Zach is being high-handed?" Desiree pressed.

"Yes. But that's between him and me. I want to eat and bathe some aches out and sleep."

"Oh, well." The other woman hesitated. "Is J. Dawson Hidgepath still here?"

"No," Zach said at the same time Clare said, "Yes."

"I suppose you want to talk to him alone."

Neither of them answered her.

"But can you point me to where he is? I'd like to see him."

Clare thought Desiree might want to *touch* him, so she said, "J. Dawson, the lady would like to shake your hand."

Zach moved aside so Clare could see the interaction.

J. Dawson bowed, offered his hand. Desiree stared in his general direction. Then he moved forward, *through* her. His shoulders slumped when she gave no indication of his presence.

"You just can't sense ghosts, Desiree, sorry," Zach said. "Come on in, J. Dawson." Then he shut the door.

"What about these ear bones?" Desiree shouted through the door.

Zach opened it a bit and held out his hand. Clare heard the little clicks as the three bones were poured from one hand to the other. "Later, Desiree." He closed the door.

Clare glanced up. "Put the bones on the desk and I'll take care of them later."

"You will?"

"Yes. The bone box is on a shelf in the closet. J. Dawson, make yourself at home."

This is a very nice room. He sounded impressed.

Zach dropped the ear bones on the desk, went to the curtains, and jerked them closed, making the room so dark that Clare turned on the light on the table. She didn't like being away from the natural light, perhaps a holdover from the ghosts. Except for Enzo, she didn't think the ghosts ever saw or existed in natural sunlight, or moonlight, just shades and shadows and tints of grays.

Turning, Zach planted himself between her and the sliding glass doors.

J. Dawson drifted in, though his legs moved as if he thought he was walking. *I was not finished looking at the view*, J. Dawson said.

Clare nodded and watched him float through the curtains and glass and out onto the balcony. Her brief flash of energy was fading. She finished her food and pushed the plate aside, stood stiffly.

"I'm going to change into my nightgown," she said to Zach, wanting the comfort of soft, long flannel. She didn't even feel up to taking a bath or shower . . . She rose stiffly.

Zach's brows rose. "J. Dawson?" he asked.

She gestured to the balcony. "He's out there. Can you help me undress?"

"Oh, yeah."

A chuckle escaped her and the warmth of affection simmered within her, though she didn't think much lust was in her future.

Between them, they got her undressed and into her nightgown, propped against all the pillows of the bed.

"Huh," Zach said.

"What?"

"You didn't protest my hands that had touched bones, touching you."

"I'm getting over that," Clare said. "A good thing, I think." She frowned.

"What?"

"No Enzo," she said, missing him, wondering what he was doing, or if he was still the Other. Whom she never liked seeing.

Zach came and sat beside her, stretching out his legs. He looked at her, then began to unfasten his special shoes and leg brace. She stared in the other direction since he'd gone tense beside her.

"Thank you," he said. "Shall we call J. Dawson back in?"

"Yes, I feel him hovering outside." *J. Dawson?* she sent mentally.

When he emerged from the curtain to stand at the end of the bed, he wore his work outfit.

Zach clasped her hand, turned his gaze in the direction Clare was looking.

"Hi, J. Dawson," he said.

The ghost nodded, then went back to looking at Clare. She sighed, but said, "Time for some questions, J. Dawson, if you can handle them."

Of course. He ran his right hand up and down his suspender.

"What's the last thing you remember in your life?" Zach asked.

The ghost seemed to think, then his expression—all of him—lightened. "The day before, I found a new mine close to my old one. I'd just hit a huge vein of gold! I had a big nugget in my pocket!"

Zach stared at him.

"Uh-oh," the ghost said. "That's why I was murdered?"

"The sheriff's report stated you had nothing in your pockets."

ROBBED as well as murdered! No! He winked out.

"It's all about money, isn't it? Greed and money," Clare said.

"Looks like," Zach said.

Clare stared up into Zach's eyes. She thought she knew what his gift was now—glimpses of the future, how odd and fascinating. He'd known about the wedding before the announcement.

He raised his brows. "What?"

No, she wouldn't speak of his precognition—was that the word? Her mind ticked down to the next topic. "You have more to say than what you just told J. Dawson, or what you told Mr. Laurentine earlier."

"You're getting able to read me," he said noncommitally.

But she lifted her own eyebrows. "Zach, I am usually able to read you." As soon as she said it, she knew the statement to be true, though she tilted her head and made a moue. "Rather, I should say that I can usually read you as long as it doesn't pertain to our relationship."

"Glad I have some secrets," he said.

"Lots." She relaxed a little, sinking back into the pillows, and smiled. "I'm still getting to know you, though I think one of the reasons we, uh, clicked so fast was that we could read each other." She frowned. "I know that we have generally matching worldviews."

He reached out and sifted his fingers through her hair. His touch almost reconciled her to its being so curly.

Tugging at a lock, he said, "Pretty much."

"So what else did you find out about J. Dawson that you haven't said?"

With a grimace, he refocused on her. "His body was a mess."

"Oh." She paused. "Yes, I think Mr. Laurentine said something about that."

"He fell—"

"Was pushed," she corrected.

Zach nodded. "Was pushed off a rocky trail, more like a cliff side. The sheriff said the body was seen because of his pale skin and the puddle of red blood around him."

Clare swallowed.

"Major head trauma, so scalp wounds that bled freely. Quite a few broken bones."

"He was found the same day he died?"

"That's what the sheriff said, though . . ."

"Though?"

"The sheriff was out of town at the time. His deputy took the report of the 'prominent' citizens who found him and brought his body in." Zach's forehead creased. "No other report of the crime scene. And the group was divided about what he was doing, gathering wildflowers for a lady, or prospecting in his mine."

"And no gold was found on him."

Shaking his head, Zach stood and opened the curtains and door, paced the balcony looking at the distant peaks. "No gold was found. And though the sheriff checked out his mine—"

"J. Dawson's old mine. He just said he'd found a new one."

"Right, old or new, the sheriff didn't leave any information as to where it was. Nor is there any record of the exact location of J. Dawson's mine or his claim."

Clare frowned. "He would have made a record, though."

"Yes. Any prospector would have done that, but the records are missing. Not surprising after such a long time. Even the best records have gaps." Zach shifted. "It was July, he was buried immediately that night, before the sheriff returned, so he didn't see the body. Everyone said the fall was accidental."

"But someone knew it wasn't."

"That's right. Since there's no record of his mine or his claim, we don't know if someone continued to work it." He paused. "We don't know if the mine is still producing gold, is still viable today. I looked at new claims but didn't see any filed in the Mount Bross area for several years after."

Clare joined Zach, but craned her neck to look north for Mount Bross, a futile endeavor. "A lot of the land around Mount Bross is national forest. The rest is owned by big mining companies."

"That's right . . . and, say, if someone is operating a secret mine on national land, still getting gold out of it, that could be a strong motive for . . ." Zach rolled a shoulder.

She spoke a dark truth. "If, perhaps, someone thought a ghost might reveal the location of a secret mine to, say, me, they might want to prevent that."

"That's right."

"That would mean someone believes in ghosts and in me and my gift and in me being able to talk intelligently with J. Dawson Hidgepath."

"Take a breath, Clare."

She did, but tasted a bit of bile again. "Can I have some water, please?"

"Sure." Zach got up, went to the bathroom, and snagged an unopened bottle on the counter, twisted the top, and gave it to her.

Drinking, she considered the new information. "Despite everything, I don't think most people here really believe in my gift. I might have been putting on a really good show in Curly Wolf."

Zach shrugged. "Why take chances? And it may be why the attempts against you have been so half-assed."

"Oh."

"They might have just been trying to scare you off. Or he or she might have wanted your injury and death to look like an accident . . . trip and fall, fatal shooting by a hunter."

"That doesn't explain the poison."

"You think anyone except me would have pressed for tests of that water?"

"I don't know."

At that moment Enzo slunk into the room, tail down, head low.

TWENTY-SEVEN

ENZO! CLARE SAID.

The Lab tilted his head. *You are glad to see me, Clare? If you aren't glad to see me, I have to go away and only the Other will come when it believes you need guidance. It thinks you are too dependent on me. That I am not doing my job right.*

Clare opened her arms and braced for the shock of cold. "I'm glad you're here, Enzo. I don't know what I would do without you." Ooops. "I mean, I'll try harder to work on my, ah, studies, for my gift. I'm not dependent on you, we just have love between us."

YES! YES! YES! That is it! I love you and you love me.

So simple, a dog's love. "Yes."

Chasing his tail, Enzo barked with joy. Clare slid a glance toward Zach. Since he had a hand on her leg, he could see the dog. His half smile was amused.

Then Enzo hopped onto the bed, plowed clear through her, and the headboard and the wall, pulled back, and slathered her whole face with icy ghost doggy licks.

"You're a team," Zach said.

"Yes," Clare said.

Enzo said *YES!* at the same time. *We are ALL a team. Clare and Enzo and Zach. Enzo and Zach and Clare. Clare and Zach and Enzo. Zach and—*

"Got it, dog." Zach reached out to rub the Lab's head, but his hand sank through it.

"I'll get started on learning more right away," Clare said. "Zach, can you hand me the volume of Great-Aunt Sandra's journal I brought with me, please? It's on the desk."

You see! You SEE! Enzo hopped up and down. *It was WRONG. You ARE learning. You brought a journal with you. It didn't think you had. It was WRONG and I will tell IT so!*

"Good dog," Zach said. He circled the bed, then handed her the journal.

Clare scrunched, opened the book to the pages where the leather bookmark was, and began reading the looping handwriting—again, a long and rambling story. She fell asleep.

Zach took the journal from her hands.

His phone rang, but didn't wake Clare. It was the deputy he'd spoken with earlier. She stated that they'd found tire tracks behind the general store in Curly Wolf that looked like the ones near the break in the fence, the same pattern with the nail head. The first tracks he'd seen weren't there anymore because they'd been driven over by another car.

He asked if he could drop by and discuss the matter. The deputy agreed. He checked the locks on the sliding glass doors, put on his shoes and brace, and stroked Clare's head while he looked at Enzo.

Much as it creeped him out to do so, he sent a mental order to Enzo. *You watch her. If any person—good smelling or bad to you—comes here, you run to me FAST.*

The dog gave him big, sad eyes. *She is sick.* He licked her face, and Clare shivered. *I was not there. IT was not there. IT made me go away and Clare got sick.* A halfhearted twitch of his tail.

Some of the simmering anger Zach had reined in at the dog's failure to warn them vanished. This time he spoke aloud. "I guess you didn't sense any bad thoughts toward Clare."

Enzo shook his head. *I didn't.*

"I guess the guy did it cold-bloodedly. Or since he or she

isn't being efficient about this, maybe it was just a dispassionate experiment." He shook his head. "If anyone comes, dog, you run to me right away."

I will. I PROMISE. And IT can't make me break my promises.

"Good job."

Enzo nosed Clare's shoulder. *She will be fine.*

Zach hoped the spirit was right. Clare would be fine. This time. He had to ensure there was no "next time."

On his way out, he asked Desiree to keep an eye on Clare's room and she agreed.

He joined the deputy behind the general store, took more pics with his phone. Yes, the anomalies in the truck tracks behind the general store where the water had been kept were the same as those by the break in the fence. Clearest was the fact that the right rear tire had picked up a nail.

As he walked back to the house, he checked out every truck on the way, and parked in the lot on the west side of the house. No tread matches.

When he reached the house, Mr. Laurentine made a point of telling Zach that one of his ranch hands had shot a coyote that morning when Clare and Desiree were up on the ridge . . . and he'd left a message on Clare's phone.

Zach nabbed a busy Tyler Jorgen briefly and set up an appointment to speak with him the next day.

Once in their room, Zach studied Clare as she slept. Hadn't done that too often in their . . . he counted back mentally . . . sixteen days together. Wow, so short a time, so powerful and profound a relationship.

Yeah, he stared at the beauty of her, and everything in him, gut, heart, cock, tightened at the thought of losing her. He couldn't. Just. No. Not right now . . . maybe when the relationship lightened up, lost its shine and hot passion, whatever, maybe then. But not now.

The red rage he kept battened down—at the loss of his brother years ago to a gang shooting, the loss of his career and his disability a few months ago—surged at the thought of hurt to Clare. He wanted to beat the perp to a pulp until the red block of anger, of vengeance, eased. And that wasn't acceptable cop thinking. But he wasn't a cop . . .

No. Don't go down that road. He believed in the rule of law because it was the closest humans got to justice. Big gaps, sometimes, but he and Clare had spoken of honor, of their own rules. His honor and rules would not let him beat someone bloody for personal reasons, much as he wanted to. He had to make sure he never let that rage inside him blow.

He sat on the bed, slid his fingers through the curls she wasn't taming anymore. He wanted to whisk her back to Denver, stash her in that elegant old house of hers, and protect her, turn it into a fortress against any threat.

His previous reasoning held true. Clare might be easier to kill in Denver. Right now Zach was on the job and close to Clare. In Denver, Rickman might have an urgent case come up that would tear Zach's loyalties. He could always say no, of course, but how long would Rickman put up with that?

A hunch at the top of his spine spreading tension between his shoulders told him if they stayed, the case would break, he'd catch the guy hurting his woman soon. If they left . . . maybe not, even if Zach or Clare discovered who killed J. Dawson and connected that with someone in the present.

Clare awoke and Zach ordered a simple meal to come to their room. They ate, but she remained drowsy, so they didn't talk of anything in depth.

He spent some time looking at tire treads in a database, brushing up on identifying a vehicle using the tires, by figuring the turning radius, the vehicle stance, and the wheel base. He thought he narrowed the heavy-duty truck down to one manufacturer. A brand that Laurentine didn't use for the ranch vehicles. He copied his calculations and his findings to the sheriff's department as the locals were more likely to know who drove such a vehicle, but unless the deputy on duty tonight was interested or bored out of his or her skull, he didn't think his email would be opened.

When he settled down, curving around Clare, he simply let out a long, quiet breath of gratitude that she was safe in his arms before sleep ambushed him.

In the morning, Clare moved even more stiffly than the day before and looked more fragile than Zach had expected or liked. They rose at seven, ate breakfast by themselves in the empty dining room, and then Zach paced as Dr. Burns checked her out. Once again the doctor muttered she'd been very lucky. If she'd drunk more of the solution, or faster . . . He just shook his head.

Zach escorted her back to their room, where he wanted to put her back to bed.

"No." Clare sank into one of the chairs by the table. "I am not going back to bed."

Her eyes showed a hint of rebellion, which he knew would flare into a full-fledged argument shortly. He was braced and ready.

"It doesn't appear that the shot yesterday morning was aimed at me," Clare said.

She was still too pale for Zach's comfort, and he wasn't about to lose this battle with her. He'd failed to protect her from the poisoning, from the fall before.

He scowled at her and she shifted a little, reacting to his cop look. Eventually she wouldn't. She was toughening up fast . . . and he sort of admired that even as he missed the softer aspects of her personality.

"One shot wasn't aimed at you yesterday," Zach stated in a hard tone. "That doesn't mean a shot couldn't be aimed at you today, especially since it looks like our perp did a copycat thing with pesticide poisoning.

"Now I believe J. Dawson Hidgepath was murdered for a large gold nugget he took from his mine, that was not reported being on his body when it was found. I believe the person who killed him kept the mine secret, perhaps hid it, and passed the knowledge down to his or her descendants. And I believe that one of those descendants knows you can speak with J. Dawson and discover the mine. You think that's wrong?"

She was quieter for longer than he liked, stared at the curtains over the sliding glass door that blocked the balcony and the view. Safer for her.

Zach softened his voice but pressed on. "I want you protected. The easiest way, the most logical way, to kill you is in a 'hunting accident.' Especially if he or she is so squeamish that he or she's botching the murder attempts—the fall, the poison."

She went another shade of white beneath her golden skin,

which had picked up more tan in the September sunshine at high altitude.

Then her shoulders straightened. "You're pushing me, Zach."

"I'm doing my job, protecting you."

Her head tilted. "I don't consider that your job."

"I do and you're in danger and I am talking about taking reasonable precautions."

"Staying in bed, in the room, all the time. I'm not sure that's reasonable. Especially when I have a job to do. I can be careful."

"You need a vest."

Clare blinked. "A vest? I don't wear vests."

"Kevlar," he spat out.

She frowned. Even she, who didn't watch crime shows, would know what that meant. "A Kevlar vest!"

Zach went to the side table with unopened water bottles. He wrenched the cap off one, drank it half down, gave it to Clare.

"I'm not budging on this," he said. He needed to do more investigating, talk to the deputies in person in Fairplay, and he had an appointment with Tyler Jorgen to talk to him about Clare's fall before the boy started work later this morning.

She wouldn't want to stay in the room. Also, he figured either J. Dawson or she would wish her to visit his mine. What a mess.

"You should wear body armor. It's the smart thing for you to do."

"Really, Zach—" She scowled back at him, crossed her arms over her middle, her fingers spread instinctively to protect her ribs.

He pulled out his phone. "I can get a vest by tomorrow through Rickman and have it messengered up." Then he slipped his phone back into his pocket, pivoted on his heel, his knuckles tight around his cane. "No. I'll ask Desiree, as a trained operative, if she has one."

"What?" Clare said. "No!"

But he ignored her, went to the door, opened it, and said, "Stay in here." He left, locking the door behind him.

Clare simmered with anger. She wouldn't be stuck in this

room again all day long. How was she supposed to help
J. Dawson move on just sitting in a darn room? So far, she'd
had to be in a place significant for the ghost. Even though
some of them could move around, the time and the place must
be right.

Not for me, J. Dawson said, appearing before her with a
slight smile. *I am different.*

"Different, how?" she asked.

And Enzo was there, too, looking especially doglike today
with no hint of the Other, which was a relief.

I moved my bones around, J. Dawson said proudly.

That makes a difference, Enzo nodded in an exaggerated
manner. *I, we, Sandra and me, never knew anyone who could
move his bones around.* Enzo's tongue came out as he panted.

"Probably never met anyone who wanted to do that," Clare
murmured.

*But I would like to show you . . . and perhaps Mr. Slade,
my mine.*

Zach returned then with Desiree, who carried two vests—
one was light colored and thinner, the other big and black and
looked heavy.

"Hi, Clare. I'm happy to help." Desiree smiled.

Clare studied her. "We are not at all the same size." Desiree was petite; Clare was five foot seven, with a longer torso
and more bust.

"They're standard, not personally tailored to me, so I
haven't worn them too often."

"I called Rickman and bought one for you," Zach said.

Her mouth flattened and she stared at him. "How much?"

"They aren't cheap. But if your gift is going to continue to
stir up controversy in the present, you'll need it."

"Pretty much my last priority for spending my money,"
Clare said.

"So I would imagine," Zach said.

Desiree gestured to Clare to stand up. Zach set aside his
cane, took the large black vest, and dropped it over her shoulders. He adjusted the shoulder tabs and the wide Velcro waist
straps.

"I feel squished." Her breasts smashed down, pressure on
them as well as her ribs now. She scowled, tried moving, and

didn't like it at all. There was also a faint but noticeable smell of Desiree's sweat. Ick.

"It'll do the job. Overt vest . . . goes over your clothes, and should stop a rifle bullet," Desiree said.

"Thanks," Clare said dryly. She hadn't felt so uncomfortable in ages, and she could already feel the heat building up under it. "You might not want this by the time I'm done with it." She wrinkled her nose. "Too sweaty."

"That's all right. I know how to wash it." She began to sit in Zach's chair and he handed the off-white vest to her. "Thanks for your help, Desiree."

With a roll of her eyes, she accepted her dismissal, but at the door she stopped and tossed Clare a serious look. "Use it, Clare."

Desiree left.

Clare began to open the waist straps.

"Was J. Dawson here?" Zach asked.

She paused. "Yes, how did you know?"

He rolled a shoulder. "Standard stuff, a chill to the room. I don't think Enzo cools it down that much."

Enzo barked. Zach tensed.

"Enzo's still here," Clare said.

Zach sat in the other chair at the table and stretched out his legs. "What did J. Dawson have to say for himself?"

"I *might* be able to help him move on anywhere, not just at his mine." She finally got the straps pulled back, and the vest shifted enough to lift it, though her ribs protested.

Then Zach was there, removing it. "He mentioned the mine, then?"

"Yes." She wiggled. "I don't like this."

"I want you to wear this vest every time you're outside this room."

She sent it a disparaging glance. "I don't think so. It sure wouldn't have helped before."

"Might have in the fall down the stairs."

"So you think a 'hunting accident' would be easiest?" She shuddered.

"Yeah. Cop instinct."

She recalled him talking about birds, a wedding, and it

had come to pass. "Nothing a little more solid? No little precognition bit?"

His face went stony. He looked away, back at her again. "This is about protecting you. Not about me. I don't want to talk about me."

"No precognition?" she pressed.

"Logical, cop instincts," Zach bit off. "That's how I'd do it."

Wonderful.

"Promise that you'll use the vest." He moved to stand and wrapped his arms around her, loosely caging her. It should have felt stifling since she was still irritated, but she felt shielded. She didn't want him to shield her.

He continued, "And you are absolutely going to wear it if J. Dawson comes through with the location of his mine and we go to find it." Zach paused. "You think he remembers well enough?"

"I don't know."

"Abandoned mines are extremely dangerous and there are plenty of them around. If he misremembers which damn one was his, you could be in trouble from other sources besides your attacker."

"I know."

All of his body touched hers. His scent drifted to her, the warmth of him heated her from the inside out, and his breath stirred her hair.

"I don't want you going with J. Dawson to his mine alone. Promise me that, Clare. Promise you'll wait for me."

Clare wanted to. Instead, she said, "You know ghosts can be . . . urgent. And this is my primary assignment."

TWENTY-EIGHT

"PROMISE ME, CLARE," Zach demanded.

"I could be in dire straits if I refused to help J. Dawson. It might be that I can only send him on at the location of his mine."

"Or on the damn path he fell from." Zach pressed against her. "You have a right to think of yourself, too. Make sure you put him off until I can go with you. Promise. Don't be stupid."

That had her stopping her words and saying instead, "I beg your pardon?"

"Sorry," he grumbled, not sounding like it. He turned her around in his arms, skimmed a hand from her hair down her shoulder, then her side. "I hate seeing you hurt. Even thinking about you hurt makes me crazy. Use the vest."

That sounded true enough to make her heart pitty-pat with affection . . . until a thought struck her. "Do you have a vest?"

He stilled. "No. It was the department's."

"Then you need one, too."

She saw his jaw flex. He stepped back. "All right. I'll order one—"

"For future cases." She nodded. "And you *will* wear it if you're a target in any case."

"Yeah, yeah."

Lifting her chin, she said, "Do it now, and I promise I'll wear the darn vest."

"And you'll call me before you go out to follow J. Dawson to his old mine and you will meet me before we go there and we will go up together?"

A calculating look came to his eyes and she knew she'd given away too much in this deal. Well, she wasn't sure she'd care to hike a steep mountain path and explore a mine or two on her own anyway. "Fine. And I'm *not* stupid."

"No, you aren't." He picked up the vest and put it on the table, straightening it so it lay flat. "Thank you."

"Order the vest. And I want your word that *if* I need to go to J. Dawson's mine, it's a priority with you, too. You put aside anything else."

He hesitated.

"Okay, agreed." He punched a number. "Rickman, about that vest order, I need one—" Zach stopped, listened. "All right. Later." Zach turned to Clare. "We'll have the vests tomorrow."

"All right."

He cleared his throat. "Yours will primarily be bulletproof. Mine will be body armor, capable of deflecting a knife, too."

"Good."

His phone beeped. "Time for me to talk to Tyler Jorgen."

"Oh, that reminds me," Clare said, then told him about her encounter with Tyler and Emily.

"Interesting. The closest stairs lead to the east side entrance of the house."

Clare grimaced. "Yes. I'm at the opposite end from the parking lot." She arranged the pillows, took off her shoes, and gingerly settled on the bed. "I'll see if I can speak to J. Dawson."

"You don't leave the room without the vest."

She sighed. "I don't leave the room without the vest."

He leaned down and kissed her thoroughly and left her with a warm feeling and the hope that she would be recovered enough for sex that night . . . maybe even that afternoon.

* * *

Zach headed downstairs, stopping to look at the view over South Park, simply so beautiful it hurt his heart. Yes, he was back home in Colorado. He heard the tones of Laurentine pontificating and continued through the great room and the west hallway to the side entrance.

Much as he disliked Laurentine, he didn't think the guy was the one targeting Clare. The man was not local, and he was used to making his money through wheeling and dealing. Zach didn't see him with a pickaxe and dynamite.

Tyler Jorgen was waiting for Zach at the edge of the parking lot, appearing nervous. Zach tried a disarming smile, held out his hand for a shake. The kid took it, and his grip was firm though his palm slightly sweaty.

"Congratulations again on your engagement," Zach said.

Tyler grinned. "Thanks. So, like, what do you want to talk about?"

"Just some follow-up questions about Thursday night. Why don't we walk east a little?"

Some of the cheer of the boy faded. "Walk east?" He glanced at Zach's cane. "You sure?"

"Yes." Zach gestured and began circling around the back of the house. Both front and back walls had a lot of glass, but Zach had noted that the housekeeper tended to keep her eyes on the main door and the great room.

"I usually go in through the west door," Tyler said.

As did most people other than Laurentine. "Humor me."

Shrugging, Tyler said, "Sure."

"So what do you do for Laurentine?" Zach asked.

Another quick smile. "I'm a Tyler-of-all-trades. Whatever small jobs that need to be done that the ranch or Curly Wolf caretakers need help with. Feed the stock, handyman, I'm learning carpentry from my uncle Deke, Aunt Patrice's brother, and I've helped with a little of the restoration. Always something to be done in Curly Wolf . . ."

"I bet," Zach said easily.

"Bellboy," Tyler finished. "I think that Aunt Patrice would like me to go into the hospitality business, but that's her thing, not mine."

"And your hours?" Zach asked.

The boy grimaced. "Whenever I'm needed. Strictly part-time and flexible." His blue eyes met Zach's. "I'm a good worker."

"Sure."

"And I'm saving up for college. Emily's going to CSU in Fort Collins, and I don't want her there alone. *She* got a scholarship, but I don't—didn't—study like her, so now I gotta work harder for the tuition. The family will help, of course, but it's mostly on me, and I've gotta show good faith." He shrugged. "That's life. Mr. Laurentine pays well."

"That he does . . ." Zach gauged his witness. "For an ass— for a guy with specific ideas that don't always make sense. Not always an easy employer." It was a statement.

The boy slid his eyes toward Zach. "I hear you. Aunt Patrice's tough." His eyes widened and he stared at Zach. "But fair. Very fair."

Zach nodded. "I got that from her."

They passed under Clare's balcony but he heard, smelled, sensed nothing. A bird squawked and his shoulders tensed, just a magpie screeching at a chipmunk.

They rounded the corner of the house, and Zach continued on down the faint path toward the breach in the fence, walking on soft dirt and needles beneath tall evergreens. Tyler looked at him uneasily but Zach kept a bland expression.

"So tell me about Thursday. You were here during the day and the evening?"

"Yeah, different times. One of the servers called in sick in the morning, so I helped with breakfast, with taking Ms. Cermak's bag upstairs, and with lunch." He glanced at Zach, who kept his gaze on the barely there trail.

"Yes, Clare told me about meeting you and Emily." Zach shrugged. "No big."

Tyler sighed, nodded at the trees ahead. "That's the clearing where we want to be married. She wasn't supposed to be in the house that morning, but I'd asked her to come. It was a real pretty day and I wanted to propose, but then I got too busy and she came to our meeting place and Ms. Cermac was there and . . ."

All of Zach's senses tingled with the prospect of new information. Vital information.

* * *

Clare sat on the bed, legs stretched out, with one pillow supporting her cracked ribs, the rest of the pillows her back. She sighed, then wished she'd thought to open the door to the balcony and let in some fresh air. Zach didn't like her near the sliding glass door, but the house was built on a ridge with no others in easy distance. If she were the type to parade around in the nude, she could do it . . . though when she recalled the twenty-four hundred feet a rifle bullet could travel, she decided her lover had a point.

Wiggling a little to get completely settled, she breathed in the pattern that Enzo had taught her. Her phone made a drum-whisk sound and she scowled at it. She'd assigned the noise to Mr. Laurentine and was having second thoughts about it . . . but she wouldn't have to put up with it for long.

"Hello, Mr. Laurentine," Clare said.

"I'd like you to walk down to Curly Wolf with me," the multimillionaire said with a lilt in his voice. "I've had a report of a new ghost haunting the morgue."

"From whom?"

Mr. Laurentine chuckled, "From a reliable source. So what do you say?"

"Ah. I say that I'm currently conversing with J. Dawson Hidgepath about moving on, and would you like me to curtail that?" She infused the question with perfect sincerity.

"No. That's fine." Mr. Laurentine cleared his throat. "How long do you think this will take? Perhaps when you're finished? I really don't think you gave Curly Wolf enough of your attention," he said.

She figured that what he meant was that she hadn't enthused enough over his prize. Glancing at the face of her phone, she said, "I believe I'll be done within the half hour."

"Fine. Give me a call when you're ready."

Clare suppressed a sigh. "All right." She wasn't sure whether she'd go or not, but just getting out of the house and into the early fall sunshine sounded good, and she was getting better at tolerating Mr. Laurentine.

"Later," Mr. Laurentine said.

She turned off the phone and placed it on the side table. *J. Dawson?* she called mentally.

At your service, he said, appearing by the bed and bowing.

"Ah, good to see you," she said.

Thank you.

"I'd like to talk to you about moving on and"—she paused, eyeing him—"your, ah, demise," she ended in a whisper.

He nodded.

"Do you need me to go to your mine?" May as well get that concern out, so she'd know whether she needed to call Zach. And she hoped the way was still passable and not too difficult to hike, and that she wouldn't have to break many, or any, laws to get there, like trespassing.

You don't have to come with me physically to a certain place, Clare, J. Dawson said. *I have not been tied to a place, or even one memory, not even the memory of my death.* He smiled sadly. *I have been a roaming ghost. If I was tied to a place, it would have been where my bones were interred.* Now his mouth quirked. *But they couldn't keep me down.*

Clare groaned at the pun but relief sifted through her. With her last case she'd traveled to areas of Colorado and Wyoming.

So, different strokes for different ghosts. It occurred to her that she needed to start a log book with a list of details, then cross-reference it to a complete report she'd write of the case.

Clare? J. Dawson prompted. His expression had turned worried, and his ghost had begun to flicker agitatedly. *You WILL be able to help me, won't you? The distressing manner of my death didn't put you off an association with me, did it?*

"No. Of course I'll help you."

His shy smile returned, and she liked him all the better for the unstudied charm of it. He sat on her bed, leaving no impression. Taking off his bowler hat, he placed it beside him, slicked back his hair. *If we try hard, you can see my memories.* He sighed and Clare felt a chill puff of air. *I am tiring, Clare, and ready to go on . . . but at the same time, I am afraid to let go of what little existence I have.* His eyes were dark and appealing. *I need to find my murderer, and need you to help me go on. It will be easier for me to leave if I am not alone, if you accompany me to the gate.*

"The gate?"

For me, the way to the next world is through a tall, fancy iron gate. I've glimpsed it in the distance now and then. I need you to help me get there, and open it, and . . . and stand and watch while I go through?

"I can do that." She *could*. She *would*. The Other had accused her of not learning quickly enough, so she'd do whatever she had to so she could close a case. She raised her chin.

Good! The word reverberated like a chord of multiple tones; one was Enzo's, one the Other's. The ghost dog had leapt onto the bed to sit beside her, and she didn't look at him to see who or what might be looking out of his eyes.

Instead she kept her gaze on the dead prospector. "You know, J. Dawson, that we think you were killed for your mine."

He nodded . . . and morphed in a silvery wave, then Clare noted he wore work clothes, tough trousers and work shirt, an old vest, and heavy, scuffed work boots. His bowler hat was nowhere in sight.

I can show you my mine, Clare, right now, take you to it with me in this insubstantial state, even show you my memories. I could give the mine to you. Then his dazzling smile faded and his shoulders hunched. *Well, I could have if I'd filed a claim, but I'd just found it, a hidden crack in the mountain. Such a thick streak of gold!*

"Wonderful," Clare said.

The phantom thinned as if with anxiety. *Alas, it was also near the scene of my death, just a few hundred yards along the trail from my other mine.* He became more visible so she saw the dark slashes of his brows lower. *I was on the right track even with my mine. No doubt I could connect the two.*

"Showing me your mine and the scene of your death and your memories could help discover your killer, J. Dawson."

Yes, I will do that. He held out a hand.

Dread squeezed her stomach because she knew the freezing cold that would come next, the strength that would be demanded of her, and the energy that would be drained from her. She swallowed hard and took J. Dawson's hand. This would be a sample of what she needed to do to move his spirit on. But the whole thing could be faster and easier than going physically with Zach.

The phantom's hand felt like solid ice. An instant later the room dissolved and became the dark and rocky innards of a mountain. A lantern sat on the floor, barely illuminating the place, though Clare sensed the space wasn't large. As J. Dawson had said, there was little showing it was an active mine; a couple of wooden braces was all.

He drifted toward the back wall, tugging Clare after him. A gleam showed. *Look at how large the vein is,* his enraptured whisper came to her mind. He put his other hand on it, and the gold streak was nearly as large.

"Impressive," Clare said. She couldn't feel her fingers anymore, and the chill of holding on to the shade crept up her arm.

J. Dawson tapped a hole. *See, this is where I took out my first two nuggets.*

A frisson went down Clare's spine that had nothing to do with connecting with J. Dawson in the spirit world and everything she'd learned about greed as an accountant.

Still smiling, the apparition reached into the watch pocket of his vest and said, *I took one, then the other, out and carried them here.*

"What did you do with them?"

A revelation was coming, Zach knew it. He kept his entire body casual. "So, Tyler, you couldn't propose to Emily on Thursday morning when you asked her to meet you in the clearing."

"No, Ms. Cermak was in the room." His jaw went stubborn. "And who wants to propose in another guy's guest room anyway? And while you're on the job?"

Zach shook his head. "Doesn't sound romantic."

"No, and Emily had to head into town to work."

"So maybe you asked her to meet you late that night in that clearing . . ."

Tyler flushed, hunched his shoulders while he walked. "Those late hours came up unexpectedly. I'd—Emily and me—had plans. But Aunt Patrice discovered that some shelves in the pantry had warped and wanted me to either fix them or find extras in a storage area, or take measurements to replace them. And she wanted it done *right then*." Tyler shook his head.

"Your Aunt Patrice is a formidable woman. Since you mentioned she's interested in the hospitality business, I would have expected her to run her own hotel or bed-and-breakfast."

"Nah. Aunt Patrice doesn't really need to work. She has family money and money from Uncle Jerry's insurance. But she has a thing for beautiful things and houses . . . and Laurentine . . ." He turned red when he said that.

The words the kid said about Schangler's money rang true to Zach's cop sense.

His mind clicked through suspects, considering, eliminating.

Patrice Schangler was local and had family attachments to Curly Wolf, but had enough money and Zach had seen her work, and work hard.

Dennis Laurentine wasn't local, didn't need any money, and liked wheeling and dealing to get that money.

And that left only one suspect, didn't it?

TWENTY-NINE

J. DAWSON'S IMAGE rippled and he wore the very nice suit once more and his bowler hat. *I bought the suit and the shirt and the hat the night before I died. Of the finest quality.*

A notion began to coalesce in the back of Clare's mind. "And you paid for the suit with . . ."

With the first nugget I pried out of my new mine. He rolled the nugget he held in his fingers, a grin on his face. *It was the prettiest gold I'd ever seen. So pure!*

It gleamed yellow, not as ephemeral as J. Dawson. "I hear you," Clare said. "So you hadn't bought items with a nugget like that before."

He shook his head. *No, and I never shopped at the most expensive store either.* His flirtatious manner was back. *Only when I bought a trinket or two for my ladies as gifts, but I couldn't do that very often.*

"I understand. It's a very interesting mine," Clare said, looking around the small cave-like space again, and now that she couldn't feel her arm up to her shoulder, she had to move this along. Clearing her throat, she said, "And could you show me the trail to your mine?"

Her fingers were squeezed hard with searing cold. "You don't have to, if you don't want to," she said.

I kept the new mine secret. His shoulders straightened, his expression turned serious. *I will show you where I was killed. That's what we need to find out before you can lay me.*

Clare choked. "Lay you?"

There are such things as ghost layers. Ghost seers and ghost layers. He winked.

"Uh-huh," Clare said. "I prefer 'ghost seer.'"

J. Dawson's chin jutted. *"Ghost layer" is the proper term in classical literature.*

Enzo piped up, vanishing from the bed to appear and rub against J. Dawson's leg. *Yes, because ghosts float or haunt so they need to be laid to rest. Ghost layers.*

We don't have to rest, J. Dawson said.

Clare kept her imagination absolutely blocked. "The trail, J. Dawson?"

And suddenly they were there, on a steep ledge, and she was falling, and yanked back. "Eeep!" Clare let out a squeak.

You have to be nimble-footed, J. Dawson said. *It's a mountain goat trail.*

"I see that." The place was still gray shaded, but she saw a wide panorama, including other holes—other mines—in the opposite slopes and rocks, and flowers that would bloom in July but not September. "I'm in your time?" she asked.

Yes, in my memories, he said. He gestured behind them, and Clare carefully turned on the trail. He pointed. *See that small dark crack above those trees? That's where my secret mine is.* He pointed farther up along the path. *And that's where my older claim is.* He float-walked toward a slightly wider spot. *This is where I was ambushed and killed and my nugget was stolen, though the killer could not hold on to it. I FELT it in reality and pulled it in here, into this gray nonexistence.* He began to sound sad with an edge of scary, so Clare asked, "You were going home from your mine?"

Yes. I had spent time in my old mine, getting ready to close it up, moving some of my tools to my new mine. And, ah, working around the entrance of the new mine to, ah, camouflage it until I had time to get ore samples and file a claim. His feet shuffled in the path. *I liked looking at the gold vein, and once I began working on it, the loveliness would be gone. I was done hiding the entrance and picking some flowers and had just straightened up when SOMEONE HIT ME ON THE BACK OF THE HEAD AND THREW ME DOWN THE MOUNTAIN!* It came out a roar that shivered and nearly splintered the scene before her.

"So, were you outside Thursday night? Maybe proposing to Emily?" Zach smiled at Tyler Jorgen. They'd reached the clearing, dappled with sunlight and shade, dotted with wild-flowers. "Right here?"

"Yeah. Right here—" Tyler stopped, turned even redder.

"It's pretty now. Thursday night was mild. Must have been nice."

A long sigh from Tyler. "Yeah, yeah, it was." Everything about the young man brightened again. "Big moon, though not full. Soft light. She looked beautiful. I just gave her a little diamond, but she said yes!"

"Good job," Zach said. He continued to walk beyond the clearing toward the break in the fence. Tyler lagged after him. "Did you see a truck near where Emily usually parks?"

"Yeah. Big, red thing."

"Who does it belong to?" Zach was sure he knew, but didn't want to lead the witness.

"Huh?" Tyler scratched his head. "I should know, shouldn't I?"

"I think so."

Tyler gnawed his lip as they came into view of the fence that had been repaired. "Yeah. I know the truck. It's just not the one he usually drives."

"Uh-huh."

A head bob. "Yeah, we know it. Emily was peeved that it was in her spot, both when she pulled up and when I walked her back to her car before leaving myself."

"Who, Tyler?"

The young man stopped and looked at the fence, at Zach, his eyes showing misery, fear. "Baxter Hawburton. He's been behind all this, huh? But why?"

"Nothing I can prove yet. But you're helping—"

"I don't know—"

"He's hurting my woman, Tyler."

Tyler gulped. "Yeah, I guess he is."

"You didn't tell the deputy sheriff about this."

Both of Tyler's hands went through his mop of blond-brown hair. "The deputy woke me up. Woke us up. I forgot. Didn't think about it." He stared at Zach. "Didn't really think about it until now."

"You've had a lot on your mind."

"Yeah." Tyler dropped his hands. "Yeah, I did. Emily and I did."

"No one from the sheriff's department spoke to Emily?"

Tyler pokered up. "She doesn't need to be brought into this."

"Not right now," Zach agreed.

"I don't want Emily hurt either."

"Best if we pick Hawburton up to ask him a few questions then."

"Who's 'we'?"

"The sheriff or his deputies, and me."

Relaxing a little, Tyler said, "That's all right then."

"Trust me, I'm not going to do this on my own. Have you seen Hawburton today?"

Tyler's phone pinged. He flinched, turned back toward the house. "I've gotta get to work."

Zach stood, too, but repeated, "Have you seen Hawburton today?"

The kid looked upset, his mouth set, then he said, "Yeah. I saw his old black truck driving up the road behind the ridge." He hesitated. "That's a circle road, and the only turnoff is the back way up to the ridge lookout." Tyler flicked a hand toward the place Zach had met Clare and Desiree the day before.

Zach's blood froze. Perfect for a sniper.

"Later," Tyler said.

Zach jerked a nod. "Thanks," he said, and slipped the kid a fifty. "For your wedding fund."

The young man appeared surprised and flushed, muttered, "Thank *you*," and took off at a jog back to the house.

Zach couldn't even croak a reply. He tapped Clare's speed-dial. No answer.

* * *

She should wait, keep J. Dawson tethered to reality through her grip, but the cold from her fingers clasped with his was sliding from her shoulders down her chest. Soon it would reach her heart . . . and then what?

"What happened next?" Clare asked.

I died . . . but I stayed. I was so shocked that when the road appeared to the gate, I waited too long and it faded and I missed it.

That's not quite so, said the Other using Enzo's form.

All right! I was angry. I was furious that just when I'd found a good mine with a rich vein of gold, just when I would have enough to buy a house and pretty things for my Annie . . . or Lily . . . or Sarah, someone killed me! I wanted to hunt HIM down and kill him!

And you tried, the Other stated.

Yes. But I was not successful. In life, I could have found him, taken my vengeance, but not in the half life, in the gray-ness. That became despair.

You held on to your anger too long, decades, said the Other. *And to what you found in life . . .*

My nugget, my bones. I also sensed that no one truly missed me. Not one of the ladies I had wooed with flowers and poetry.

"So you visited them and left them your bones," Clare said.

Yes, and I took my bones to others. The iciness took on agitated movement, a wind swirling.

Clare thought of the gate image he'd spoken of. "And then the road to, um, 'going on,' disappeared."

Enzo barked and she believed he was only phantom dog now. Because the Other felt she had a handle on the issue? Whatever, she couldn't stay in this cold space much longer.

"You weren't very good as an evil ghost," Clare said. Mostly he'd been disgusting, but she wouldn't tell him that if he hadn't figured it out.

I loved life, he said mournfully. *I had so much to live for, and I wanted to stay, too. My future was* assured.

"Not anymore."

Another gusty sigh whipped around her, piercing her with ice shards. All right, now she could see the reason for wearing body armor. Or at least thick velvet scarves that kept her warm, like Great-Aunt Sandra had.

No, not anymore. I lost my understanding of living, my verve. I lost my anger at who killed me, and got trapped.

She bottom-lined it. "So you're ready to go on."

His ghost solidified, a determined specter. *Yes. When I know who took my life from me, I am sure the mists will part and I will see the gate again.*

Enzo said, *Yes, you will. For sure!*

"So maybe we can determine who did it," Clare said. And if they figured out who killed J. Dawson, it could lead to who was hurting her. With cold lips, she said slowly. "Can you show me the scene of your death in more detail?"

The focus improved and Clare saw a small gleam, not the same gleam as the gold nugget. Keeping her teeth together so they wouldn't chatter, she asked mentally, *What's that, J. Dawson?*

What? He hovered above the trail, looking down the steep and rocky slope where his body had been pushed.

She pointed a finger trembling with cold. Her body had begun to shudder, but if she let go of J. Dawson's hand, would she be thrown back into her own time without finding out what the gleam was? Or perhaps be trapped here?

J. Dawson squatted. *It's a button.* He scowled. *I know this button.*

Clare did, too. She'd seen one like it before, but not as a button, as a bolo slide.

It's the button of the man who sold me my new clothes. What is it doing here? He wasn't much of a prospector. He kept a SHOP.

Realization came into J. Dawson's eyes as they met Clare's. *I gave him a good gold nugget. He followed me that day, didn't he? He came up behind me and killed me. FOR GOLD,* J. Dawson spat. *For MY gold.*

Hawburton! J. Dawson roared and vanished.

"Hawburton," Clare said at the same time and released his hand and crumbled into the pillows.

Enzo looked down at her, worry in his expression. Then

she pushed upright, keeping her torso stiff so her ribs wouldn't hurt as much. She felt sort of sweaty but not really, more as if she should be sweaty from the effort. And she just knew her hair was a fuzzy mass. She ran her fingers through it and little bits of ice broke off. "Good grief," she croaked, and wondered what her new job would do to her hair. Perhaps she should look into getting conditioner made for especially arctic climes . . . was there a product like that?

Aloud she stated her conclusion. "Hawburton's ancestor killed J. Dawson. I suppose that Hawburton also laid those traps for me." Darn it, she'd liked the guy!

The pillows felt warm under her. "I suppose it was a family secret that the elder, maybe the first, Hawburton here murdered J. Dawson. And Zach is no doubt right. The villain—the current Hawburton—knows about the mine."

Feeling better able to move, she rotated her neck, shook her arms out . . . Enzo licked her cheek and it felt cold, so she knew she was recovering. "Enzo, what is J. Dawson's state of mind?"

Tilting his head, Enzo was silent as she pushed herself to her feet, swayed a little, but remained standing, just to move the blood around in her.

He is angry, but not scattered, and not devolving.

"That's good."

It is very good. People who were murdered and become ghosts have a great chance of deteriorating and becoming very, very, VERY bad.

"I think you said that before."

Enzo nodded. *It is something you MUST remember.*

"Okay."

The spectral dog looked off into the distance. *J. Dawson will be fine. He went to the mine and went to the store in Curly Wolf, but of course Hawburton is not there.*

"Probably lived in peace and prosperity all of his life."

J. Dawson has found THAT Hawburton's grave and is cussing, but his curses mean nothing because the man's soul and spirit are long gone.

"*Grrr,*" Clare said and for an instant had an urge to deface a gravestone. Of course she wouldn't but it didn't seem fair that the guy had gotten away with murder for so long. She asked a philosophical question—one she'd been avoiding asking Enzo or the Other, "Um, Enzo, did he . . . did he pay somehow?"

Eyes more smoke than solid orbs, Enzo nodded, looked as if he might transmute to the Other, then grinned and he was all dog. *And you will tell everyone about the old Hawburton, so everyone will know he was a bad guy. And Zach will tell the person who keeps the history books, and you will both tell people who tell the stories.*

"Yes, we will. But it's time now for me to go tell Zach."

Call him, Enzo said.

"I don't want to do this over the phone." She turned hers on and saw she'd missed a call from him, and pressed the voice mail. "Stay inside! I'll get back to you," Zach barked and cut the message.

Clare sniffed at his order to stay inside the room, looked at the door, the heavy and cumbersome vest. She was still cold so she went to the bathroom and washed her hands, came out. How she wanted the sunshine behind the drapes, the fresh mountain air, the view that would soothe her heart with the colors of autumn.

THIRTY

RIGHT AFTER HE'D called Clare, Zach punched in another number.

"Rossi," the bodyguard answered.

"This is Slade. Keep everyone inside."

"What!"

"I think there's a sniper on the ridge. Hawburton."

Rossi swore, then said, "I've got to stay with Laurentine, then, can't scout it out. Don't trust anyone else."

"I can't raise Clare on her phone. Lock her in or have Desiree sit on her. He set Clare up before and got her where he could hurt her, he's probably done so again. I'm calling the sheriff right now. They might give me a ride up behind Hawburton. I'll try to convince them to take him red-handed."

Rossi grunted and signed off.

Zach phoned the sheriff, got the female deputy he'd spoken with before, Julie Wilson, and laid out his conversation with Tyler Jorgen and his own deductions succinctly. He heard a keyboard tapping. "Yes. The tire pattern would be right for one of the trucks registered to Hawburton's ranch. I'm on my way."

Zach gritted his teeth, spoke through them. "I'd advise coming in soft, cold."

"You want to take a man with a gun rack on every truck he owns, maybe a guy with a rifle, by surprise," the deputy said flatly.

"We know how to do this," Zach pointed out.

A slight sigh. "Wait there, I shouldn't be more than twenty. My partner and I will pick you up. We'll go up the back road, park below the truck Tyler *says* is Hawburton's and is purportedly at that location. Review the situation."

"Right." This time Zach clicked off.

Cold moved through him, and he heard barking. "Enzo, is that you?"

Another series of barks.

"Is Clare okay?"

One bark and a whine. Zach could figure that one out.

"She's in danger from Hawburton—"

A sharp bark that felt like agreement. "Oh, she got to that conclusion, too?"

The bark was repeated. "Good. Tell her to stay safe inside the room."

Yes, Zach, he thought he heard in his head, then the cold went away.

He had to face it again, whatever thing that the crow stuff was, was slopping over to let him hear Enzo without a connection with Clare. He'd think about that later . . . and stonewall any "discussion" until he didn't feel so damn sensitive about it.

Since he wanted to *act* and not wait, Zach took measured steps to the fence, walked beyond the tire tracks on the other side, and with slow and careful movements, he slipped between the barbed wire without any snags. Good job.

The deputies pulled up not long after. Both the man and the woman gave him a hard look, and once Zach was in the backseat . . . which he loathed . . . grilled him on every detail he'd gotten from Tyler, everything else he'd figured out. Then they told him what data they had.

They backtracked off the ruts to a grated dirt road that looped behind the ridge Laurentine's house was built on.

Neither of them looked happy at the prospect of bringing a prominent member of the county in for questioning on an attempted murder.

At the next turnoff, they wound up the ridge. And saw a black truck in the distance. They parked across the road, blocking the way down, but the truck looked to have four-wheel drive and could probably handle the slope . . . with a good driver.

"I'm engaging the camera," the male deputy said, tapping a button. Julie sighed and did the same. Zach figured he could keep his right hand free for his smart phone camera or his weapon. He chose his gun, and wished he had body armor. The other two were wearing covert vests.

"Civilian," the guy said. "Keep behind us and to the side."

That burned him, but he didn't disagree. They walked quietly and stopped when they saw Baxter Hawburton staring down at the house, his rifle in his hands.

"Baxter," said Deputy Wilson.

"Hey, Julie," Hawburton said casually, but his fingers tightened around the stock of his gun. His jaw flexed and his face showed fury before he masked it.

"What are you doing up here with a rifle?"

"What are you implying?"

"I'd like you to come with us for questioning with regard to the attempted murder of Ms. Cermak."

"Rather not."

"Please give me your rifle." She stepped forward and held out her hand for it.

"I don't think so. You have nothing on me."

"I repeat, what are you doing overlooking Dennis Laurentine's house with a rifle?"

A shrug. "Came up for the view, then thought I heard something."

"I'd like the rifle."

He hesitated, his eyes narrowed, his lips thinned, looking grim. Then he met Zach's gaze, said with a sneer, "I see you brought the crippled city boy who's screwing the crazy fake psychic girl."

Both deputies tensed, both faces going expressionless.

"That's an interesting way to characterize a female consultant your friend hired," Julie said. And her tone told Zach, at least, that Hawburton had made a mistake.

"Never thought you could be so stupid, Hawburton, to assault someone."

"You can't prove that."

"I think we can." Zach smiled with an edge.

"Why don't you give me the rifle and you can explain yourself up at the station," Julie said.

It was a basic human need, explaining yourself. One that most cops—investigators—capitalized on.

"This is all a mistake, and you don't have anything on me," Hawburton insisted.

"We have enough to bring you in for questioning," Deputy Wilson said.

"You can't!"

Julie let loose an exasperated sigh. "Yeah, we can. Give me the rifle, Hawburton, and let's move this conversation to headquarters."

It was a stare-down of three to one. Hawburton shoved the rifle at Deputy Wilson. She took it and kept her balance. The other deputy read him his rights and asked if Hawburton understood them. With a snap of his teeth, the guy answered in the affirmative.

"Get in the back of the SUV," ordered Julie.

Another fulminating glare, another three people staring right back. Hawburton stalked to the back of the SUV and got in.

The deputy reported to the department. After a shake of his head, he said, "For God's sake. I have to talk to Laurentine. You take Hawburton in."

Zach moved forward. "Mind if I come along?"

Deputy Wilson gave him the narrow eye, the flat cop stare. Zach stood hard-faced under it. Then she said, "Hawburton doesn't seem to think much of you, and we might be able to use that, so yeah, you can come. Until he asks for a lawyer."

"Maybe I can keep him talking. Make a better case for you."

"Maybe you can. Get in the front."

On the drive to Fairplay, Zach called Clare and listened as

she told him the story of J. Dawson's death. A few minutes later Hawburton was charged with attempted murder and steaming in an interrogation room.

"Would you mind if I took point on questioning him?" Zach asked.

Julie snorted. "Fact is, the sheriff is letting me handle this. He has bigger fish to fry."

"He doesn't want to be associated with the attempted murder of a psychic ghost seer."

"Dennis Laurentine has shine, but he's also a pain in the butt. Right now, I think the sheriff sees more detriments than advantages of being in on this. And you have more experience than me in an attempted murder investigation."

"Some." That was the truth. He'd worked with detectives when he'd been a city cop, then had a few cases as a deputy sheriff in less populated places. "But you know Hawburton."

"Dated his son for a while."

"Sorry," Zach said.

She hunched a shoulder. "Small community." She studied Zach again. "Yeah, maybe we'd make a good team."

"Thanks for letting me participate."

Her brows lowered. "I'll let you run the questioning—"

"Until you won't. I understand, Deputy."

She nodded. "Good."

They went into the room. Hawburton was ruddy, not a good sign. "You don't have anything on me."

Zach shook his head. "You're wrong there. We have tire tracks that match the tires belonging to a red truck registered to you. Those tracks were found at the site of a newly mended breach in Laurentine's fence to the east of the house when you snuck in to pour furniture polish on the stairs, then called Ms. Cermak's room. We have a witness who saw your truck that night."

"Clare's just a stupid, clumsy, crazy woman." Hawburton made a disgusted noise, spat on the floor.

"Hey!" Julie protested.

He smiled at her.

Zach continued. "And we have tracks that match your tires that were found behind the general store that had the bottles with pesticide in them."

"We got your fingerprints from the bottle you used and found them on additional bottles," Julie Wilson put in.

Shaking his head, Zach used the info. "Left your fingerprints on the bottles. Sloppy and half-assed. I'm surprised you managed to run a business. But then you had your own secret gold mine to bail you out when you made a mess of things, didn't you?"

Hawburton half rose from his seat, settled back. "You can't prove that either."

"I think Clare can find the mine," Zach said. "And gold buyers keep good records. If there's a stream of sales coming from you, we'll find them. Check out the composition of the gold—or any you might have . . ." He glanced at Deputy Wilson.

"A warrant's been requested to search his property and is expected to come through shortly."

Zach nodded, saw that sweat began to bead at Hawburton's hairline. "We can cross-check the gold with the mine, with the sales to anyone in Denver."

Hawburton pressed his lips together.

The deputy shook her head mournfully. "This is going to kill your family," she said. "Why on earth would you do such a thing?"

"Deadly family secrets held close enough to spread poison," Zach said. His mouth thinned. "I've seen it before."

Hawburton's expression twisted, then he glared at them and said, "Laurentine said the girl *knew* stuff. I had to protect my secret."

"So you decided to scare her off." Zach leaned close to get in Hawburton's face.

The man shrugged. "Didn't think the girl could see ghosts, but why take the risk?"

"Damn half-assed way to do it," Zach said. "Leaving a puddle of furniture polish on the stairs?" He infused his voice with disgust.

Hawburton jutted his jaw. "Worked, didn't it? Strange woman in a strange house, not paying too much attention? I knew Dennis Laurentine would have given her a lecture on how she should jump when he said jump and come when he calls. Standard for the guy."

"And you knew the house's routine."

"That's right. Rossi would have checked out the doors. I've known the security code for a while, Dennis doesn't change it as often as your boss and Rossi advise. Knew Laurentine himself would be screwing Missy Legrand." Hawburton flicked a rough hand. "I knew everything I needed to about Dennis Laurentine before he moved in."

"And you knew everyone who worked for him."

A shrug. "Sure, from the first. I study and I learn."

"But you don't execute well," Zach said. "Stupid accidents that were too stupidly executed to fly as accidents. Puddle on the stairs and a call to Clare. Poison in a bottle you didn't know Laurentine would give her, didn't know how much she'd take." That made Zach pause as a bitter taste coated his mouth. He sipped some water.

The deputy just shook her head at Hawburton, a sad expression on her face. "Sloppy."

"Stupid."

Hawburton scowled. "The poison should have done the job. Was pretty evident she's crazy enough to know things she shouldn't. I knew Laurentine considered Clare girly, would give her the pink bottle. Thought there was enough in there, even if she did drink slow."

"The poison was just plain stupid," Zach repeated. He'd noted the man had tensed when he'd used the word.

"Should have worked."

Zach shook his head. "You're not a good planner, Hawburton."

The man jerked up straight from his lounging position. "I came pretty damn close."

"Cowardly," the deputy stated, with a disparaging undertone that made Hawburton's face redden.

"I'm not a fucking coward, Julie."

"Yes, you are. There was always something a little off with you that I couldn't put my finger on. You're cowardly and you take shortcuts."

"Just like your great-great-grandfather. His store was failing, wasn't it?" Zach said. "His goods too expensive."

"Because they were high quality. He underestimated the miners' tastes. There weren't enough people who preferred quality over price. Though quality always outlasts cheap." Baxter rubbed his hands on his jeans.

"I have a feeling that J. Dawson liked quality," Zach said softly. "So he came in and paid with a gold nugget and your ancestor recognized it for what it was."

"Pretty damn pure gold was what it was," Hawburton said with a curl to his mouth. "And that *pussy* had found it. Hadn't worked as long or as hard as most of the men in Curly Wolf."

"Luck," Zach said.

"Not as long and as hard as your great-great-granddad did in making a go of Hawburton Emporium," the deputy interjected softly.

"That's the fucking truth. He was losing the store, would have had to close down within a week."

"And the pussy walks in with gold," Zach said.

"Dreams in his eyes, Great-Great-Granddad wrote. Wanted a new suit and a little silver locket for one of the new ladies who'd come to town."

"A gold mine would save your great-great-grandfather's store. He followed J. Dawson, saw the prospector looking at a gold nugget he'd pulled from his mine in the sunshine, and killed him."

"There was a struggle," Hawburton protested. "J. Dawson fell."

"If your great-great-grandfather wrote that, or told that to anyone else, he lied."

Hawburton jumped to his feet, even more flushed, his big hands fisted until his knuckles were white. "My great-great-granddad did *not* lie. He was a good man."

"And brought his sons up right?" Zach mocked. "But you sure went wrong if you targeted a young woman just to keep your dirty little secret that you've been stealing gold from the feds for generations. Your great-great-grandfather killed. He hid and waited until J. Dawson turned to walk down the goat trail then hit him in the head with his shovel and pushed him down the mountain. He set up the scene to make it look as if J. Dawson fell."

"No!"

"Yes. And you set your own little traps and scenes, half-assed accidents that weren't accidents. Slip and fall. Poisoning. Setting up an accidental shooting by a stupid, mythical hunter by aiming at the damn house." Zach stopped a moment to tamp the fury down, keep the red tide of anger from filling his vision.

A deputy came in with a sheaf of papers, looked at Hawburton, and shook his head. "Done for."

Julie riffled through the papers. "We've got not only your confession, but hard evidence, Mr. Hawburton," said Julie. "Tire tracks, fingerprints."

He turned even redder, sucked in a harsh breath, then simply folded. The rancher put his face in his hands. "I'm ruined. My family name is ruined. My reputation."

"Attempted murder," Zach said. "We'll go for attempted murder, along with assault with a deadly weapon, and—" He caught the raised eyebrows of the deputy and realized he wouldn't be doing any charges. Not his job anymore. He was here as a damn courtesy and overstepping the boundaries. He pushed back from the table and walked to the door, changed his direction verbally. "You're done." He shook his head. "And whatever rep your great-great-grandfather had, it's gone, too. He was a thieving, murdering bastard."

"Don't say that! I won't have that said." Hawburton jerked upright again.

"The truth has come out, live with it," Zach said.

"Just a stupid little fake psychic con woman. Who was she to take away my livelihood? To ruin us?" Hawburton snapped. "My family has worked that mine all our lives."

"A secret mine that you didn't bother to register a claim for. Bad all the way down your line."

"Ruined." Hawburton's flushed color had turned grayish, but his hands remained tightly clenched on the table in front of him, and when he met Zach's eyes, his own glittered. "A stupid little fake psychic girl. And the more I spent time with her, the more I didn't like her. Talk about stupid. She doesn't learn either." His chin rose up, nostrils widened. Whatever civilized veneer he'd had peeled off. "I might be done. But my last plan won't fail."

THIRTY-ONE

ZACH FROZE AND cold sweat broke out. "What? What did you say?"

Hawburton leaned back and crossed his arms, lips curled.

"Baxter?" the deputy asked.

A chill having nothing to do with ghosts whipped through Zach. He jerked his phone from his pocket and speed-dialed Clare. His call went directly to voice mail. He called the DL Ranch and it rang and rang.

Yelling in his mind with all his might, he shouted, *ENZO!* The dog did not appear.

Minutes later they wheeled out of the parking lot, sirens blaring, before Zach got his door shut and belt fastened. He punched Clare's number. Nothing. Tried again and again.

He called Rossi's number.

"Rossi," said the bodyguard.

"Where's Clare?" he snapped.

"As far as I know, in her room."

"Find her now!"

"What's going on? Where are you going, Rossi?" demanded Laurentine in the background.

"Emergency," Rossi said. His breathing came a little faster. "Thought you caught the bad guy."

"We did. He laid another trap for Clare somewhere."

"Fuck. Calling the guards. They'll listen to me more than you."

"We're coming in hot," Zach said as the deputy pushed down even harder on the gas pedal. The road was straight and narrow . . . and it was her road.

"Shooting?" asked Rossi.

"With a siren. Make sure the gates are open."

"Will do." Rossi disconnected.

Clare slumped in the desk chair. In a flurry of inspiration, hoping to forget nothing, she'd typed out J. Dawson's story as a report for Mr. Laurentine. She'd revised it and sent it by e-mail. And now her energy had fizzled—as had her triumph at figuring out the person who'd attacked her.

Zach had called and said Hawburton was in custody. It was all over.

It didn't feel over. It *wouldn't* feel over until she looked the man in the eye and confronted him.

Zach wouldn't approve, but she didn't care about that. She'd followed his orders because it had been the smart thing to do. Now she was free! She stood and stretched, and her ribs reminded her of the other price she'd paid for her gift this time around.

She deserved to talk to Hawburton. Weren't victims allowed to see those who'd harmed them? She wanted to, and she would.

After she freshened her makeup, she stared at the bulletproof vest, remembered how tight it fit, squashing her breasts. She hated it.

But she'd promised Zach to wear it if she went out, so even if they'd already caught who they thought was the perpetrator of the assaults on her, she donned it.

A couple of minutes later she strode down the side corridor toward the small parking lot, filled with purpose.

With the help of a ghost, she'd figured out a past murder!

And she knew who'd hurt her. She pressed a hand to her ribs. No, she wouldn't forget that.

J. Dawson materialized to keep pace with her. She glanced at his feet but couldn't see them; still he moved fast.

You have solved my murder. His mind was full of wonder, and if he'd spoken aloud, she thought that his voice might have been thick with emotion. *I . . . feel better, lighter.*

That focused her. *You think you can go on by yourself?* she asked telepathically.

He bobbed close to the ceiling. Now she saw his feet, shod in good work boots. He looked down at her with a wistful expression. *If this had happened sooner, perhaps I could have progressed onward to my destiny alone, but now . . . I don't think so.* The pale grayness of his face showed darker lines across his forehead as he frowned. In a quieter tone, he said, *I think . . . I think . . . the fact that I became so attached to my bones, in keeping them and gifting them to ladies . . . is holding me back.*

Then I will help you transcend, she sent to him mind-to-mind.

His face cleared, his features sharpening to her vision, and he nodded. *I like that word. Yes, I will TRANSCEND.*

They reached the door to the side parking lot, and J. Dawson dropped down before her. Clare hesitated.

Imagine that cad of a shopkeeper killing me for gold! His image began to flush with a thick and sluggish dark color emanating from his chest and his head, his heart, and his mind.

A niggle of danger tweaked Clare's nerves. "Easy, J. Dawson."

Easy, J. Dawson, Enzo said, appearing in the corridor with them. He stared at Clare. *You must keep him calm. You don't want him to be a Ghost Gone Bad.*

Ghost Gone Bad. She reached out and touched the prospector's hand, clasped it, felt the death cold penetrate her palms and pulse to her fingertips, flow past her wrist into her arm.

"J. Dawson," she said softly. "You were a good man. Have been a legendary romantic ghost."

He jerked and the darkness that held his eyes fixed on her.

Slowly, he smiled . . . and the color ebbed from him. *A legendary romantic ghost? Me?*

"Absolutely," she said.

His fingers turned and he held her hand and bent to kiss it with a flourishing bow, then he released it and warmth began to return to her fingers. He straightened and stood tall. *Thank you for reminding me who I was . . . am.*

"You're welcome. And now we'll go tell Zach of our discussion in person. Look at the current Hawburton cad before we lay you to rest for good." Memory tugged. Oh, yes! Reaching into her bag, she found her car fob and pushed the button.

The door shattered inward.

From Fairplay to the DL Ranch wasn't far, but like all times of danger, the seconds took eternity to drop like individual sand granules down the hourglass.

Black birds wheeled and cawed, and Zach tensed even more, but didn't see them, not close enough to count them and didn't know if he was disappointed or not. What if there'd been four? Four for death.

He began mumbling under his breath, "Please God, please God." A quiet whoosh of air came from the deputy and she began reciting the Lord's Prayer in a monotone.

They were at the turnoff to Laurentine's ranch when the sound of an explosion cracked the air . . . and Zach saw flying debris.

The door flung her back and landed on her when she went down. She fell onto her back, her breath thumped from her, saw wood and metal and stone flying, some hit her chest before she ducked, hunched, and covered her head, pulling what she could of the door over her.

She lay, stunned, as screaming and shouting erupted around her.

Then there were hands pulling the door off her, lifting her up. Rossi swung her into his arms and ordered Tyler Jorgen, "Secure the scene. Zach and the sheriff will want to see this."

The young man goggled, his face so pale that freckles she hadn't noticed stood out. "Why would anyone do this? Hurt someone like this?" He glanced at her, then away. "Sorry, Ms. Cermak."

Rossi turned with her before she could do more than give the teen a faint smile. He carried her to the doctor's office just up the hallway. Dr. Burns just looked at her, shook his head, and sighed. Then he opened the door to his examination room, gestured to the table she'd seen all too often.

Zach ran in, his eyes hard and his mouth flat. He stopped abruptly at the sight of her on the table, Rossi standing by.

"What happened?"

"I don't know," Clare said, dazed.

"I saw your car fob on the floor," Rossi said. "Did you use it?"

"Yes. And for once I remembered to do that before I reached the car door."

"Which saved your life. Hawburton wired a bomb in your car to be blown by your fob."

"Must have gotten your car fob and rigged dynamite in your door panel, set the trigger on a switch on the lock solenoid. Not too difficult," Rossi said.

She got the idea he knew how to do that. She also recalled the day she'd arrived, Mr. Hawburton had seen her fumble with her fob.

"Oh." She tried a nod, her neck ached. All of her body ached, pretty much throbbed in time with her ribs. "Yes, he was around when I arrived. He carried my bag in and saw that I wasn't proficient with the fob. Saw me lock it."

The doctor pulled off the body armor and there were more bruises under it and she winced.

"Will you gentlemen please leave?" Dr. Burns snapped.

From the corner of her eyes, she saw Rossi nearly manhandle Zach out the door.

"She's all right, man," Rossi said.

"I'm okay," she said.

"Yes. More bruises but I don't see any broken bones . . . where do you hurt?" Dr. Burns asked.

"Everywhere."

The door closed.

Zach was on the wrong side of the door. He wanted to be in the room with Clare. His blood seemed weak and thin, his insides a little sloshy as if they'd dissolved. He'd been so scared for Clare!

Rossi pulled him from the doctor's office, then his steel-like arm fell away. Zach limped a step or two, then just turned toward the wall, put his good arm up, and leaned. "Good Christ. Good Christ."

"She's okay. She's talking, she's lucid. Any flying shrapnel that hit her didn't make it through the vest," Rossi said. "Do you need to look at the scene?"

Zach just rolled his other shoulder. "The deputy sheriff in Fairplay drove me here. She and her men will take care of it."

"So it was Hawburton?"

"Yes, we arrested him earlier."

Rossi looked surprised. "It really was him?"

"Yeah, I finally interviewed Tyler about Clare's fall. Tyler Jorgen and Emily Johnson saw his truck near the break in the ranch's fence about midnight that night. Hawburton left fingerprints on the bottles from the general store that Laurentine gave us. He's a piss-poor villain."

"Good actor, though. I didn't get any vibe from him. What's the deal?"

"His ancestor killed J. Dawson. J. Dawson had just discovered a rich vein of gold in his mine . . . a mine he kept secret until he shopped at the original Hawburton's store. It was failing, and that Hawburton knew about the gold so he followed J. Dawson to his mine, whacked the guy on his head, and threw him off the mountain. Other prospectors nearby found the body immediately and yelled for help. Hawburton hid in the mine until the rest of them were gone, then obscured the entrance."

"Huh. What does that have to do with our Hawburton?"

Zach pushed against the wall. Stood on his feet. He had his best leg and ankle braces on, so he'd been able to run. Still had been too damn late. He picked up his cane from the floor. Down the hallway, he could hear Laurentine grumbling and the more official-speak of the deputy. They'd do fine without him. He glanced at Dr. Burns's door, still shut.

"She's all right," Rossi repeated patiently. "What does all that antique history have to do with our Hawburton?"

Zach met Rossi's serious and slightly curious brown eyes.

"Apparently the family kept the mine secret—easy enough to do. Mountains in the area are riddled with mines, and no one would find it without knowing where it was. The family used the gold from it when times got bad, didn't file a claim, and the feds made the land it's on part of the national forest."

"Huh, mining gold on federal land. I guess the U.S. government wouldn't approve." Rossi sounded as if he didn't approve either.

"Nope," Zach said. "And along comes Clare, who can talk to ghosts."

"And find out from J. Dawson where his mine is . . . was." Rossi shook his head. "Screwy."

"That's one word for it."

"Dumb."

"And another."

Laurentine marched toward them, features tight. He ignored them and went through the door to the doctor's, then grunted in surprise at the same time Zach heard Clare make a sound of pain.

Rossi straightened. "Jerk ran into Clare. Jerk." He passed through the open door and Zach followed to see a tottery Clare leaning against the doctor's desk.

"I want this over," Laurentine was saying. "It's gone on too long and is a fucking pain in the ass. Hawburton's caught, he's confessed that his great-great-grandfather killed J. Dawson Hidgepath, right?"

"Yes." Clare sounded more solid than she looked, though she stood tall, chin angled. Zach crossed to her and she sent him a stare that told him she wanted to be professional about this. Fat chance. She'd impress not one of the guys in the room.

"So J. Dawson now knows his killer and can pass on, correct?" Laurentine stated.

"Yes," Clare said.

"Then I want him out of here *now*."

THIRTY-TWO

ZACH HEARD LAURENTINE'S other unspoken comment, *I want you out of here now*. The way Clare's eyes flashed, she'd heard it, too. She glanced at her watch on her left wrist. "How about in forty-five minutes?"

Laurentine goggled. "Really?"

Clare shrugged. "I don't see why not."

Zach knew she had no idea. This would be only her second major case, but then her head tilted and he became aware of a draft in the room and he realized she was talking to Enzo.

"Sending ghosts on drains energy from Clare," Zach stated. "She should eat first."

Clare rolled her eyes at him. "No, Zach."

Probably worried she'd puke again.

"I would like to change my clothes, though."

"Fine." Laurentine jerked a nod. "We'll see you in my office. Rossi, with me."

"Yes, sir," Rossi said, and held the door open for the guy to stride out.

Zach stared down at Clare. "So can I put my arm around your waist and help you to the room?"

"As long as you avoid my ribs. Let's take the elevator."

"The sooner we're gone, the better," Zach said.

"I agree."

Clare spent a good half hour making sure her nerves and stomach were settled enough to handle the upcoming ordeal, and she had no doubt it would be an ordeal. Zach helped with her clothes, and even a gentle sponge bath so she felt cleaner and ready to do her job. Not one sexy look did he give her. Instead he got more and more grim, especially when she bit off a moan at the hurt.

"It's a good thing we caught the bastard. I don't like the way this case went, Clare," he said.

"Me either, Zach."

But it is over. No more danger! Now all you have to do is help J. Dawson transition! Enzo sent to her mind as he sat and looked up at her and barked.

"He's ready to go, Enzo?" she asked. Zach's hand was on her shoulder so she knew he heard and saw the dog.

Yes. Let's go! J. Dawson is waiting!

Clare sighed. "Let's go."

Once outside Mr. Laurentine's office, Clare paused.

She untwined her fingers from Zach's before she went into the office. She wasn't sure who all Mr. Laurentine had called to witness her performance of sending J. Dawson on. But she figured she would try to be as professional as circumstances would allow.

After one last big breath, she set her hand on the knob, turned it, and walked in, head high.

As expected, she had an audience. Mr. Laurentine, Missy Legrand, Patrice Schangler, and Harry Rossi. His standard satellites. Baxter Hawburton might have been there, too, if he hadn't been in jail.

Desiree Rickman lounged by herself on a love seat. Patrice Schangler sat upright, hands folded, in a wing chair. Missy Legrand had linked arms with Mr. Laurentine on another love seat. Rossi stood to one side of the open curtains, his gaze making a circuit of the view outside, the terrace, and the room. He nodded to her when she came in, with respect. That eased the tightness in her chest. There were two of them here, just to do their jobs. Time to get on with it.

"You're really going to summon a ghost?" asked Missy.

Clare smiled at her. "Yes, J. Dawson Hidgepath."

The actress gave a little shiver. "I didn't like finding his bones in my bed."

"Who would?" Clare asked.

Zach closed the door behind them with a heavy, final click.

Mr. Laurentine toyed with Missy's fingers; his eyes were hard. "Let's finish this up."

"Dennis isn't too happy that Hawburton deceived him all this time," Desiree added.

"Who would be?" Zach said . . . but there was an edge in his tone that Clare heard, at least, a hint that he'd always known Mr. Laurentine was a man of poor judgment.

Show time. Clare inhaled steadily, tried to quiet her mind. *J. Dawson, it's time for you to move on, come!*

There was an odd breezy whirl around her, but the ghost didn't manifest. She hoped he hadn't changed his mind or, worse, turned into an evil spirit.

J. Dawson, your road and the gate awaits you! She struggled to think of something else to tempt him with. *Your loved ones await you. Won't you see what ladies might be pleased to meet you again?*

That did it. J. Dawson appeared. He bowed and smiled. *Hello, Clare.*

Hello, J. Dawson.

He shifted his feet, fiddled with his hat, touched his vest pocket. *I am ready to transcend, Clare.* The darkness of his eyes ebbed and flowed and she sensed she would have to help him. She took another big breath and said mentally, *Hold out your hands to me. I must merge into you.*

The prospector grinned. *Always a pleasure, merging.* He stretched out his arms, his hands palm up in front of him.

She took them and shuddered. It was like holding icicles, and she moved forward, into the shadowy grays and whites of him, feeling only cold, not a single bit of flesh or substance. She trembled, shuddered, endured.

"I demand you tell me what's going on!" snapped Mr. Laurentine. Clare was just enough in the real world, hadn't been swallowed enough by J. Dawson's energy and the otherwhere she went during a transition, to hear the man. She gritted her chattering teeth and spoke between them, not bothering to try to find the man in the room and face him.

Her eyes were cold and dry and hard to blink even to see. Yet she managed to scrape up words and use her vocal chords. "Please be quiet. If . . . you . . . stop . . . me . . . we . . . might . . . have . . . to . . . do . . . this . . . all . . . over . . . again."

"But you're doing *nothing*."

"Be quiet, Dennis." That actually came from Missy Legrand. "She's shaking and sweating. Or that's condensation or something. This is very interesting. I'm sure I can use this in my acting later."

Then Clare took the tiniest step, pretty much leaned *through* J. Dawson, and the world around her faded.

For the first time she saw him in color. His black suit looked new, as did his linen shirt, his string tie, and his bowler hat. He wore the clothes he'd bought at Hawburton's Emporium with a gold nugget, the evening before he died. The incident that had led to his death. But he looked very good in them. Unlike her first major case, J. Dawson didn't carry a gun.

The rich chestnut of his hair surprised her, as did the continuing iciness of his spirit-body-self that slowed her blood. She'd forgotten how hard this was. How close she came to death herself. Surely this couldn't be good for her heart or her body. But Great-Aunt Sandra had lived a long time.

Clare shook with cold and knew she swayed. Locking her jaw, she suffered through this, watching J. Dawson walk into a huge shaft of light along a straight cobblestoned path of gold, with vibrant flowers on each side. Butterflies and birds added to the color and sound. As her otherworldly sense became sharper, she saw that he faced a gleaming gate with more fancy curlicues than she'd ever seen.

He paused at the gate, his hand on the equally elaborate latch, and looked back at her. When he touched it, the gate and J. Dawson's hand became translucent as if the gate itself wasn't there, but simply a construct of the ghost's imagination.

"What's going on?" Dennis Laurentine's voice echoed sharply in the otherwhere, snatching her back, apparently since she was being more of an observer. Wasn't *feeling* what J. Dawson did.

"I don't see anything! Nothing's happening!" the multi-millionaire whined.

And J. Dawson smiled at her, a sincere, boyish smile, and she looked into his amber eyes and *felt* the awe, the pleasure, the joy that he was finally leaving a cold, sterile world where he didn't often remember being, and passing into the next.

The place he headed for had a road of gold for him to walk and a golden gate that he *knew* would open for him. Beyond that gate were lithe forms of women beckoning to him, smiling, though he couldn't see them clearly. But he smelled the dizzying scent of flowers.

Clare became aware of a rapid thump-thump-thump in her ears. J. Dawson's heartbeat—or her own. Pure, exciting anticipation flooded her.

Still grinning, he tipped his bowler hat at her and said, *I release all my cares.* The man floated off the path and laughed. He was straight and young and had become heartbreakingly beautiful with an aura around him that even Clare could see, a pulsing rainbow.

Then he stopped laughing, his face molded into a more sober expression, though his eyes brimmed with delight. His lips didn't move, but Clare heard him anyway. *I release all things of my former life.*

White light flashed, blinding her sight to nothing . . . though the edges of her vision showed sepia. The cold dissipated but left her trembling.

There was a clatter and a quick scream that Clare thought came from Patrice Schangler and a choked cry from Dennis Laurentine.

A blanket was wrapped around her tightly, bundling her arms to her side so she couldn't move . . . and she always needed to move when helping a ghost transition. She squeezed her eyes shut to rid herself of whatever residue held her lashes down. Then she smelled Zach, sage with a trace of mint, and man.

"Hold still." He brushed at her eyes with a handkerchief. One with the odor of the perfume Great-Aunt Sandra used and Clare favored. A few seconds later she could open her lashes and see. Her eyelids fluttered as the afterimage of the light faded, then the short bout of tones of brown, then her vision settled into reality . . . a reality not as intense as what she'd seen with J. Dawson, though she was a whole lot warmer.

Zach stepped away and began to laugh. Naturally, her gaze followed him, and what he had focused on . . . a skull grinning up at Mr. Laurentine, sat on a neat pile of other bones, all of them covering Mr. Laurentine's feet. It looked as if Missy Legrand had jumped up and leapt away from the multimillionaire.

"Okay," the actress addressed the room. "The performance was great, I can use it. But I am *so over* having bones appear out of thin air. That's it. I'm leaving." She glided toward the door.

"But Missy!" Mr. Laurentine protested.

"I'm leaving. And you'll never get me back to this place again. This Colorado mountain life sucks." She opened and shut the door without another word or glance.

Clare stared at the heap of bones trapping Mr. Laurentine's feet. She breathed deeply of the early autumn air, fragrant with the scent of roses coming in from the pots on the terrace, the scent of pine and spruce and the earthier notes of grasses. The fragrance of the Colorado mountains.

Her lips hadn't quite thawed, but she said, "He . . . he . . ."

"Spit it out, Clare." Desiree lounged on a love seat and winked at her, appearing highly entertained. "What about J. Dawson?"

Patrice Schangler made a noise and Clare swung her gaze to the housekeeper, whose gaze was fixed on the bones. The woman's face was pale.

Clare laughed-coughed. "He . . . he . . . J. Dawson said he released all things from his former life."

"Guess that meant his bones," Zach said.

"He'd held on to his bones too long," she said, and knew it was right. He'd needed something to anchor him in the ghostly dimension so he stayed together enough to pass on, and had chosen his bones.

Zach gestured at the former J. Dawson Hidgepath. "You want me to take care of these for you, Mr. Laurentine . . . sir?"

Clare sent him a sharp glance. He was up to something. She flexed her stiff fingers, wiggled around, and the blanket fell from her. "I can gather and take care of the bones," she said. "I have the rest of them in a chest upstairs." She gave Mr. Laurentine a half smile. "Can we inter them fairly quickly?"

He nearly snarled, "As soon as fucking possible."

"J. Dawson wanted a grave in the Fairplay Cemetery," she reminded.

Mr. Laurentine made an irritated gesture. "You told me. I arranged for that." He stared at the skeletal remains on his feet with a curl of his lip. "It only needed this to make the whole situation beyond acceptable."

Zach went over, crouched, and carefully moved J. Dawson's skull, palming something. She wasn't sure what, but felt a spurt of pride that she'd actually seen him do it.

He began to move the larger bones, most of them broken, and that made Clare ache. He set each aside on a corner of the blanket crumpled on the floor. When he glanced at Clare, he smiled with gentleness. "The bones smell of flowers."

Clare joined him and bent over, carefully lifting J. Dawson's skull. It smelled of columbines.

Holding it in both hands, she looked at Mr. Laurentine. "I'll put these in the box for you."

"Get it done now. We'll meet at the cemetery in forty minutes." His expression was sour. "You can transfer the bones to the expensive coffin there."

Her teeth clenched until her jaw ached before she inclined her head. "Do you have a minister?"

"I'll . . . I'll . . . find someone to say some words," Ms. Schangler said.

"I'll have Dr. Burns at the gravesite to arrange the bones. I'm sure he's still interested in them," Zach stated. Clare thought about that and decided he was right.

Before she could say anything else, Dennis Laurentine stalked to the door and opened it. "Please join me, Patrice." Then he stared stonily at Rossi. "I want to speak with you, too."

Rossi strode to stand right behind him. Flushing, Ms. Schangler rose from her chair and went after him, closing the door behind her.

"Can I get the box with the other bones for you, Clare? Might be best just to bundle them all in that blanket and take them to the graveyard," offered Desiree. She patted Clare's shoulder. "Well done."

"Thanks. And it would be great if you retrieved the box." She sighed. "It's black papier mâché with dancing colored skeletons, rectangular with a domed top, and is sitting on the shelf in the closet above the clothes."

"Right," Desiree said.

Clare fumbled in her jacket pocket. "Let me give you my key—"

"Don't need it," Desiree said breezily as she exited the room.

Clare sighed. "I'm probably the only one who doesn't know how to pick a lock."

"I can teach you," Zach said. He placed a broken bone, which looked like the top of the big leg bone, the femur, on the blanket then straightened from his crouch and drew her into his arms. As usual, she welcomed his warmth.

"I'm so proud of you," he said.

"Thank you." She tilted her head and kissed his jaw. Just that simple kiss had his arms going tight around her, his mouth seeking hers, his tongue probing against her lips, exploring inside, and heat rising through her so she thought she was melting.

"Back, guys!" said Desiree.

Reluctantly, Clare stepped away as Zach did. She stooped and smoothed out the blanket, and all three of them transferred the bones to the blanket, and the other bones Clare had collected in the box to the blanket, too.

"There, all together." Desiree dusted off her hands, looked at the clock. "We're on schedule and Dennis has a car waiting to take us to Fairplay Cemetery."

"That's good," Zach said, carefully rolling the blanket up. Clare didn't flinch at the clatter of rolling bones anymore.

"By the way, Zach, what did you palm?" Desiree asked.

He lifted his brows and slid a glance to Clare.

Clare said, "You called Mr. Laurentine 'sir.' Of course I knew something was up and watched closely. What *did* you take from J. Dawson's bones?"

"You should be able to guess." Zach smiled slowly.

Clare blinked and grinned back at him. "The nugget!"

"That's right." He held it out. She just shook her head. "I don't want it."

"Cool," Desiree said. "A real gold nugget from a real mine."

"It's Clare's." Zach frowned.

Reaching out, she curved his fingers over the piece. "You keep it."

"I meant for you to have it."

"And a good decision both of you made," Desiree said. "Keep the nugget, Zach, as a token of Clare's affection and let's get out of here. I'm sure Patrice Schangler will have both your bags packed and in your truck by the time you get back."

"What!" Clare was appalled.

Zach laughed. "Here's your hat, what's your hurry?"

"What . . . what about my car? I haven't even reported it . . ."

"Later, Clare," Desiree said, taking her by the elbow and moving her toward the door.

"Just a minute." Clare still didn't like the box, but her niece did, so she picked it up to take with her. "What about my purse, and my phone, and my tablet—"

"I brought them down, too." Desiree pointed to Clare's purse on a table, jammed with the phone and the tablet in their wrong pockets. Clare organized it, then put her purse in the box. When she looked up at Zach, his lips were curved and his eyes tender.

"What?"

He came over and brushed a kiss on her lips. "You're amazing," he said louder.

"Thank you, I like you, too."

The funeral was short and sweet, just the way Zach liked. He'd offered to help Dr. Burns with the bones, but the man refused and efficiently arranged J. Dawson's skeleton, then stood back as the coffin was lowered into the ground. A minister stood and recited the Twenty-Third Psalm.

Laurentine, Rossi, Dr. Burns, and Desiree were there, and

Zach kept an arm around Clare. As the pastor finished the last prayer, the others faded back, but Clare stayed beside the graveside. The wind had picked up and rain began to spatter.

"He's gone, Clare. You sent him on yourself," Zach murmured.

A quiet bark came from beside him. He looked down and saw Enzo, who had a sad face on. *She is praying. Prayers are ALWAYS helpful.*

"Oh." Zach felt like a jerk.

Clare pulled her hand from her jacket pocket and threw a handful of silver coins on the coffin, then turned. Zach stared.

"Old Romani custom," she said huskily, "to help buy J. Dawson's way into heaven, though I know he went to a happier place."

"You do?"

She hunched a little. "Yes, if what he saw when he transitioned was true."

It was true for him, Clare. It was pretty, Zach. And pretty ladies were waiting for him, too!

"Nice to know, I guess," Zach said.

A short honk came from a low-slung, glossy red sports car. The window rolled down and Rossi waved to Zach. He tugged on Clare, but she resisted, gave his hand a squeeze. "Go ahead. I want to walk around the cemetery."

He raised his brows.

Clare needs to see a couple of graves, Enzo said.

"Why?" Zach asked.

Because she may need to come back someday to deal with the ghosts and she should learn about them, Enzo replied. He yipped. *Nothing bad, Zach! And they are close. You can keep your eyes on us.*

"All right."

Clare followed the ghost dog and Zach went over to Rossi.

THIRTY-THREE

"I'M DONE," THE bodyguard said cheerfully.

"You got fired? Sorry. I distracted you too much, having you help me protect Clare, didn't I?"

Rossi just shrugged. "I'm heading back to Denver. My girl will be glad to see me."

"You have a girl?" Zach had never seen the man call or text her. Had never heard him speak of one.

"I always have a girl. But you, Zach, surprise me."

"Me?"

"Yeah. I've known a guy or two like you. Cops. Loners." Rossi slid sunglasses on, said, "See you later, Slade," rolled up the window, and zoomed away, heading back to the big city of Denver.

The man's comment arrowed straight through Zach. He *had* been a loner, pretty much as long as he could remember. He'd had a couple of live-in lovers, but he'd always wanted to move on in a few months. Their choice as much as his.

Clare was different. A long-term woman, and serious. Not just her, but their relationship, too. Serious and intense enough to scare him. It chilled him as if he could feel one of her ghosts. All right, he could admit that. He could feel the cold of Enzo when the ghost dog was around. He could see Enzo. And there was the crow thing. Lately every time he'd counted crows, whatever their number indicated according to the rhyme had come true. He'd reluctantly decided that wasn't just his imagination.

But he'd even rather think about his relationship with Clare than the crow business. Yeah, his loner status seemed "former" now. He'd missed Clare outrageously when he'd been in Montana, thinking of her in quiet moments during the days and suffering during the nights.

She touched his arm and he didn't jolt; some part of him had known she'd come up on him from behind. The hint of that perfume maybe.

Enzo wasn't with her. Zach blinked and found the dog sitting on top of the Mercedes-Benz that had brought them. Why the phantom dog would do that, Zach didn't know, but the Lab sat with his tongue hanging out.

The deputy sheriff, Julie Wilson, walked to them, looking tired but determined. "We've already collected a lot of evidence against Baxter Hawburton. The search of his home picked up a couple of gold nuggets along with his accounting books." Clare quivered beside Zach like a tracking dog on the scent. "His ranch manager and a couple of his hands noticed him coming and going Thursday night. Zach, your information about the gold sales is coming in." She sighed. "And I called Brody, his son. After I laid it all out for Brody, he admitted that he knew where the mine was, said he'd moved to California to get away from his dad, and never took a dime from him." She shook her head. "Baxter's a broken man, doesn't look like the case will go to trial. Which is good, because the deputy district attorney is not happy at contemplating talking about psychic abilities in a public trial. He'll get in touch with you, Ms. Cermak."

"Sure. I'm not especially thrilled at the thought of testifying at a trial myself," Clare said. Not as a psychic investigator, someone who talked to the dead. She'd be mobbed by people wanting to reach their loved ones and that was just heartbreaking.

Julie looked relieved. "Baxter *will* be put away. He won't bother you again."

Zach put his arm around her. "Better him broken than Clare. He deserves it."

"Yes, well . . ." Julie took a card from her pocket and handed it to Clare. "Feel free to contact me if you have any questions about the case."

"Thank you, Deputy, I will." Clare tucked the card in her purse. She watched as the woman walked away, got in her car, and left . . . following the limousine that carried Laurentine and Desiree.

As Desiree had predicted, their bags were stowed in Zach's truck and it was gassed up and ready to roll them right home to Denver.

Jaw set, Clare insisted on going up to their room and checking it out anyway, and when they did, it was pristine and looked as if no one had been there for a week. Clare examined everywhere, even the small safe, which Zach didn't think she had used. With a last nod and a quiet "Thank you," she walked past a disapproving Patrice Schangler, who'd accompanied them up and watched the whole deal. Clare patted her purse, but her fingers didn't dip into it to offer the housekeeper any gratuity. Which was good, because Zach thought there might have been bloodshed if she had.

He hadn't known the front doors could slam, but Schangler did a good job of it after they'd taken a step past the threshold.

"The only thing worse I could have done to her is sleep with Laurentine," Clare said. "I hope Rickman is prompt and determined in receiving payment for my work . . . and Laurentine probably stopped the clock the minute those bones landed on his feet," she grumbled.

"Probably."

"Other than my helping J. Dawson, the rest of this project did not proceed satisfactorily."

Zach laughed and opened the passenger side door for her. "I guess not. But you survived, I survived, J. Dawson moved on, and we got justice done. That's a win in my book. I'm not sad to be seeing the last of Laurentine."

As Zach drove, Clare stared out the window at the beauty

of South Park but didn't say anything until they were descending Kenosha Pass. Then she sighed and leaned back, her mouth flexing down. "You really think this is done for us?"

"I . . ." Crows cawed. Two glided across the road. The back of his neck heated with a surge of tingling. He pushed on the brakes. "Damn crows!"

Clare craned, looking. "Crows?"

Zach's turn to swallow. Yeah, he was shaken. "Never mind."

But there was a bubble of lightness in his chest. "About your concerns regarding Baxter Hawburton? I don't think you should worry about it. I think you're—we're—going to be fine."

Two crows for luck.

Clare was looking at him, too intently. His gut squeezed.

"Is that your premonition kicking in, Zach?"

"I don't want to talk about it."

"You haven't and we haven't. But we should *soon*. I can help."

The lift in his spirits flattened. He glanced at her from the corner of his eye. She appeared serene, sat as if none of her bruises pained her.

"What we should do is hit your house and make love all night long."

Her lips curved and she flirted a glance at him from under her lashes. He loved that look from her. "Absolutely."

Clare had never been so glad to see a place in her life as she'd been to see the wide entry hallway of her own new-to-her historic home. Her eyes blurred with tears, which was a shame since she missed some of the details of seeing Zach naked.

They barely made it to the couch.

The next morning Enzo did not appear. Since she'd accepted her psychic gift, Enzo was less likely to stay with her every minute. He trusted her to do what she had to, and though his doggy presence chilled her body, the thought of the trust warmed her heart.

Zach drove them downtown to a parking lot near Rickman's office and Clare reminded him to turn in the receipt for payment to Rickman as an expense. Zach shrugged. Rickman had asked to meet with him at 10 a.m. before Clare came in at ten thirty.

She'd agreed to spend time in the building coffee shop before her appointment.

Zach gave her a really good kiss that weakened her knees so she sank down at an empty table before she got her latte, and at that moment, Desiree Rickman strolled in.

She smiled at Clare. "Hey, Clare. You're here for the debriefing?"

"Yes," Clare said.

"Me, too. Want coffee?"

Clare stood. "I'll get it." She'd missed having her mocha latte grande.

"Okay," Desire said. "I'll have a tall, black coffee, house blend." She ambled to the counter after Clare.

"I'm going up," Desiree said a few minutes later.

Clare glanced at her watch. "It's only ten minutes after ten."

Desiree shrugged, tossed her cup across the aisle into the trash. Naturally, the paper container arced exactly into the can.

"Clare, don't let the guys call all the shots." With a wink, she left. Clare took a last sip of her drink, threw away the rest with a little regret, and followed.

When Zach walked in at 10 a.m., Rickman and Rossi stood by the windows looking out at the mountains.

"Slade," they said in near unison.

"Rickman," Zach nodded. "Rossi."

"Good job," Rickman said to Zach. He didn't move behind his desk. The underlying tension that Rossi had carried on the job had dissipated.

"Thank you," Zach said.

"I've assigned another one of my operatives as bodyguard to Dennis Laurentine," Rickman said.

"Good to change things up," Zach agreed.

Rossi smiled at him. "I got tired of the sucker."

"The very best reason to change things up," Zach said.

Rickman cleared his throat. "Yeah. Well." Zach heard the man's breath exit his nose. "The women will be showing up shortly." He glanced at the clock. "I told them ten thirty."

"I caught that," Zach said. "Clare will be exactly on time."

"Figured," Rickman said. "Thanks for amusing Desiree at Laurentine's ranch," he added dryly.

"Your Desiree seems to be easily amused." Zach looked out the window; lowering gray clouds showed behind the Front Range. A storm in the mountains might or might not hit the city. If he and Rickman had been alone, Zach would have asked the man if his wife drove him crazy. No, he wouldn't have, but if they were ever alone and the guy loosened up, Zach might.

"Desiree drives us crazy," Rossi said with twinkling eyes. "All of us. I think it's her mission in life. But she seems to have bonded or something with Clare." Rossi shrugged his big shoulders. "Or taken her under her wing or something. Women."

The electronic door buzzed and unlatched and Desiree sauntered in. Rickman scowled. "It's not ten thirty."

"I'm here anyway."

"You're rarely on time unless it's for a job, and you weren't on the job at Laurentine's, and you've already told me every minute detail of what you did there," Rickman said. "I wanted to formally speak with Slade and Rossi."

Zach thought the guy should have been faster with that.

"Clare is here, too, since she's an early type," Desiree said.

"Desiree," called Clare.

Desiree hitched her hip on Rickman's desk. Since she was short, it was more of a hop and a slide. "I'm one of his operatives." She offered the men a stunning smile.

Clare marched in, closed her hand around Desiree's wrist, pulled her off the desk. "You told me you weren't, not on this case. You told me that you already told Mr. Rickman everything. You told me you were to show up at ten thirty a.m., like me. There's such a thing as proper procedure. Meetings with paid operatives involved in the case, then consultants or everyone involved. *I* don't know Mr. Rickman's process, but you do, and you're interfering with it."

"Probably everything they're talking about concerns us," Desiree said.

"Are you sure of that?" Clare asked.

"Well . . ." Desiree protested.

"Come along." Clare's smile was apologetic. "We'll be in at ten thirty."

Desiree let Clare rush her from the room.

Zach noticed with humor that Rickman's glance followed the women, his eyes a little glazed.

Rossi's mouth had dropped open.

The thick steel door closed behind the women.

"Boss, we've been saved," Rossi said. His stare switched to Zach and he angled his head. "You gotta keep that woman."

Zach didn't shift his stance, but he wanted to; his fingers tightened on his cane. "Clare works for Rickman."

But that man shook his head. "No. She signed one consulting agreement because we chivvied her into it, and she was planning on doing the work anyway and she's a practical woman."

"Yeah," Rossi said. "If we're going to do a debriefing, let's get on with it. Try to be charming, boss, keep her with us." He turned to Zach. "You try to be charming, too." Then Rossi shook his head. "No, you just continue with the dark and brooding and intense. Seems to work for you with her."

Zach laughed.

Rickman went and sat behind his desk, Rossi moved away from the windows and leaned against the wall, and Zach leaned against one of the barrel client chairs.

Rickman shook his head. "I suppose there's nothing we'll be talking about that can't include the ladies." He touched the intercom. "Please let the ladies in, Samantha."

Once again the door buzzed and Desiree glided in, swept the room with a look, and sat in the chair across the space to the right of Zach. Clare came in and Zach offered his hand. After glancing around the room and with a little disapproving twitch of her lips at the casual business atmosphere, she linked fingers with Zach and sat in the chair he was leaning on.

Rickman had stood and inclined his head. "Thank you for agreeing to this debriefing."

Clare said, "You're welcome." She paused. "You're paying me."

No change of expression crossed his serious face. "We're glad you took the consulting job, and are sorry that it placed you in danger."

"Are you talking in the royal we for the company, Tony, or for me, too?" asked Desiree. She leaned forward a little to connect gazes with Clare. "We are sorry that you were targeted by that nincompoop, Hawburton." She shook her head. "Really, the man was a cowardly asshole, Tony. First wanting to scare her away, or make her injuries look like an accident, then just being inept." She sniffed. "He gives tough ranchers a bad name."

"Uh-huh," Tony Rickman said, then sat down and stared at his wife. "Do you want to do this debriefing or let me?"

Desiree sighed heavily, waved a hand. "We've already talked. And everyone in this room has given you a report. Just ask us what you want to know."

Rickman pinched the skin between his eyebrows, rubbed his temples with his hand. Then his gray eyes locked on Clare again. "I wanted to express my regret that Ms. Cermak was placed in a dangerous situation while working for Rickman Security and Investigations."

"Thank you," Clare said.

"I also want to say you did an exemplary job and well represented my firm."

"Thank you."

"No one could have anticipated you'd run into a man guarding a secret gold mine on federal land who used it as his own personal savings plan," Desiree said.

"I know," Clare said.

"It's been my experience with both of Clare's cases that just the nature of her . . . profession . . . attracts the odd," Zach said.

Clare's mouth turned down. "I hope not. I don't want to go through getting hit over the head and poisoned and shot at during each of my cases." She put a hand on her still-healing ribs.

Rickman said, "There's another matter I wished to discuss. I would like to keep you, Ms. Cermak, on the roster of my consultants."

THIRTY-FOUR

"FOR OCCASIONAL JOBS . . . that fit the parameters of your expertise," Rickman ended.

Desiree chuckled.

"I'm not sure," Clare said, her teeth worrying her bottom lip.

"Mr. Laurentine was quite grateful you stopped the appearance of bones in his home and in a timely manner."

"He didn't seem so yesterday," Clare said.

"I reminded him, and one of my men escorted an early arrival of his hunting party to his ranch this morning."

"Which also put pressure on the guy . . . and reminded him he was free of any embarrassing bones and could entertain at his equinox party in peace," Zach said.

"He gave you a bonus," Rickman said. He held out a check to her.

Clare stood and took the couple of paces toward the desk. Her eyes rounded as she scanned the check. Was the size so great? She set it back down on Rickman's desk. Her lips compressed and she folded her hands. "In the papers I signed, I gave you the information for an electronic transfer of funds. Use it."

Desiree snickered.

Rickman's face froze, and Zach was pushed by his reading of the man, and Clare, to say something. "Hard to impress an accountant who's inherited a lot of money with a check, but I'd say you did, Rickman. What, Clare, you earned for this job something like a third of your regular yearly salary at your previous firm?"

Her golden cheeks took on a little color. "A quarter."

"Ah. Nice to know that you can get compensated by someone other than 'the universe' for your work, isn't it?"

She let out a small sigh and relaxed her stiff back just slightly to rest against the chair. "It's nice to know that I will have regular forms for income other than investment income to send to the IRS, like a normal person."

Desiree laughed. Rickman's nonexpression eased.

"To each their own comfort," Zach said.

"Ms. Cermak, about future cases . . ."

"Yes, I will consider projects you send to me. But I'd prefer the accounting type."

"Thank you," Rickman said. "Since I have all your reports, is there anything else that needs to be covered at this time?"

Clare sat straight again, brows down. "We missed the arrival of our vests. I would like to pay for ours."

"Yours," Zach said. "I'll pay for mine."

"And I think I'd like to purchase some body armor including the deflecting knives type or whatever"—she waved her hand—"for myself as a precautionary measure. Perhaps you can recommend some?"

Zach sensed she'd surprised Rickman.

He nodded. "We can order you some through the company for a discount."

Clare nodded. "Agreed."

Zach stood and glanced around the room. "I don't think anyone has any additional information with regard to the J. Dawson Hidgepath case, and I'd like to take Clare out to lunch."

"Um," said Rossi.

"Rossi?" asked Rickman.

The bodyguard cleared his throat. "I was just wondering.

At one time you said something about the universe payment thing for the case. Did it, ah, come through?"

"No." Clare stood, straight.

"Not yet," Zach said, taking Clare's hand and picking up his cane.

Desiree hopped from her seat and tilted her head. Zach tensed. Would she say something about the gold nugget? Maybe no other payment would be forthcoming since he'd snagged that.

"Has the universe come through before?" asked Desiree.

Clare had stiffened even more, no doubt not wanting to relate the story about the gold coin and the pocket watch.

Zach grinned at Desiree, who nearly throbbed with curiosity. "Yes." He lifted his cane. "Later, all."

Rickman stood. "Zach, you're an asset with your local police contacts, and I've heard your good rep is getting around. I should have another couple of jobs for you this week. And I have this for you." He held out an envelope.

Zach kissed Clare on the cheek before he dropped her hand, then crossed to Rickman's desk, felt the envelope. "This isn't just a check."

"The check from Laurentine for solving J. Dawson's murder." Rickman smiled. "Not nearly as substantial as Clare's. No bonus."

"I didn't fall down stairs, get poisoned, and have my car totaled in an explosion," he said. He heard a gasping gurgle from Clare. "And I'm probably not the one he'll call on if he has any more trouble. He may need Clare in the future for more ghosts." Zach opened the envelope with his thumb, looked at the check. Reasonable and in line with the work he'd put in. "What's the key card for?" he asked.

"Your key to the building. You have a space in the underground parking garage. The entrance near the gym," Rickman said. "As you know, this is a twenty-four hours, seven days a week building."

"Good deal, Zach," Rossi said.

"Thanks." Zach nodded to them all once more. "Later." He took Clare's hand. She appeared a little pale. "Let's get a really good meal in you." She'd been nervous about her first debriefing that morning and had picked at a bowl of cereal.

He was rewarded with a smile. "I'd like that."

After an early lunch, Zach had left Clare in her "ghost layer" office at her home, studying her great-aunt Sandra's journals and her own notes, which seemed to combine writing on paper and sketchy little drawings as well as clicking away at a formal report on the keyboard. It looked like she was setting up a table of contents and an index.

Shaking his head, he gave her a good kiss to tide them over until night, then he returned to his own apartment in Mrs. Flinton's mansion. The women welcomed him with more food and excellent coffee, and he spent some time entertaining them with talking about the nonconfidential parts of the case—about J. Dawson Hidgepath, the one whom his landlady was most interested in anyway. He did note she wasn't as chipper as usual, showing more her age, but though he left space open for her to unload on him, she didn't.

He did regular stuff in his own place—his laundry, put his clothes away, repacked his go duffel with different stuff, checked and cleaned his guns. When he came to the gold nugget, he put it with the pocket watch in the safe.

He watched some sports, glad to let the atmosphere of his own place soak into him, but as the sun sank toward the mountains and dusk, he got restless and returned to Clare's house.

A knock on the door, and she stood before him, and he breathed in her scent, spicy Clare.

She wore her hair long and loose, the way he liked it, and it sprang around her head, framing her face, and he caught his breath at her beauty. Whatever she'd been doing to keep it sleek, she'd stopped.

And she wore gypsy garb, full skirt, low gathered blouse. Fascinating. Tempting.

But her expression held a hint of shadow that started a ticking alarm in the back of his mind.

Still, he reached out and held her . . . heard pulsing music in the living room. For a minute he thought he'd dance her in there, then the simple flex of his fingers on his cane reminded him he was crippled. Realization crashed down, nearly flattening him. Again. He gulped, straightened his shoulders, took her hand, and led her to the room. She hadn't turned on a light and that made everything more intimate.

The music throbbed around them, low, smoky jazz with a beat. He couldn't dance well anymore, but he could step and sway.

With a sigh, he propped his cane against the couch arm, drew her close. She stiffened and that little alarm tick in the back of his mind got louder. He ignored it.

They swayed, he rubbed his face against her hair, and she became more flexible. Then the song ended and some soprano's voice rose in wordless purity that just made his heart ache, it was so close to what he felt for Clare . . . special. Not that other word that had come to mind, *necessary*.

"We fit well together," he murmured, and that did it—something. She stepped away from him, more than a pace.

She stared at him with dark eyes, and the cloudy evening sunlight in the room vanished and her face was lost in shadows. He heard a quiet sigh, a quick intake of breath, and she said, "You know, Zach, the reason that we fit so well together is because you have a psychic gift, too."

"I don't want to talk about this."

"That's the third time you've said that to me. I'm pushing, I know. So I want you to listen." Her mouth set and she ran her fingers through her hair and it fluffed out even more. She inhaled deeply, never a good sign.

"Zach, you confronted me about my problem at the ranch, about my commitment to Rickman and Laurentine. And you helped me through that." She paused. "You have a gift, like me." She moved and a last wavery shaft of sunlight painted her face luminously. Her tongue flicked over her lips, and even though his mind denied her words, his emotions seemed to close down, and a low ache began to spread throughout his body. And maybe his heart, since he was looking at some sort of doom barreling his way.

"I'm listening," he said.

"I don't exactly know what it is, or what you do, but you have some . . . insight."

His mouth dried. Flashes of crows across a gray sky haunted his mind's eye.

"That we have gifts and complement each other is part of our attraction. I think you should accept your psychic gift. You believe in it . . . on a deeper level."

"I've . . . been getting there." Letting the sucky knowledge seep through him, but not really looking at it, because it was a puzzle and he'd have to investigate it and that meant looking at his whole damn life. Looking at what happened to him and Jim.

"But you haven't wanted to talk about it."

"No."

"It's affecting you, Zach, and affecting us. I don't know when your gift is kicking in and I wonder when that might be happening. What I can do to help." The ends of her mouth flicked up in a bitter smile. "I believe I know what you're going through, Zach. Let me help."

"Why are you pushing me on this right now?"

"Because it seems to me that you will help me, in every way—"

"Sure."

"Then let me help you."

He didn't say anything.

"So. You can help me, but I'm not allowed to help you. What kind of relationship do we have if you help me, but won't let me help you?"

"I . . . can't." His mind, his emotions, flashed back to the day Jim died. It hurt and he couldn't bear to touch the hurt even with thought, let alone shape it in words and expose it to another.

"And if I can't help you, I'll feel like the weak one in this . . . I can't become dependent on you." She paused. "We have to be equal, Zach. You've seen my vulnerabilities and problems, and helped me. Let me help you."

He hadn't really . . . *leaned* . . . on anyone since he'd become an adult. Of course he'd let doctors help him, accepted help professionally. Sat through torture sessions with psychologists after the two shootings that had changed his life.

Rustily, he said, "You have helped me. Helped me get my head straight about my disability. Last month."

She put a hand between her full breasts, tightening the loose fabric over them, said softly, "Yet it feels unequal."

He watched her, but his throat had just closed and he couldn't—something in *him* wouldn't let him speak. So he waited for her to throw him out.

Staring back at him with big eyes, she ran her hands through the mass of her hair. They stood for eternal minutes. Finally she said, "All right." Her lips thinned, then she asked, "Are you hungry?"

"Only for you."

Her lashes lowered, hiding her gaze; when they came up, her eyes looked liquid. She offered her hand. "Let's go to bed."

He took her hand.

Zach's hand clasped hers firmly, and as they walked slowly up the stairs, she let the hurt drain at his refusal to discuss his psychic power. She wanted to share and help. He didn't or couldn't.

Didn't the man deserve time? And secrets? Was she asking too much? Pushing too much? Or was she making excuses for him and being dependent? She didn't know, was so confused.

And she wasn't sure that making love would help or harm . . . but they *did* connect then. She wanted his skin against hers, him inside her, an affirmation.

The sun hadn't quite set, and pink and gold light shifted through the leaves of the tree beyond her balcony to pattern her carpet.

Zach stopped her beside the bed. "Clare," he whispered.

She didn't want to hear any words at all, so she lifted her hand to his lips. He kissed her fingers, and his own hands went to the shoulders of her low-draped white blouse and pushed it down, released her bra, and caressed her breasts.

So good, his gentle touch, the stroking of his thumbs on her nipples, beading them. Yearning spiraled high. Soon, soon, her mind would click off and there would be joining, and peace.

Then he took her silencing hand, kissed the palm, and set it aside . . . so he could undress her.

He didn't speak, and the dim light didn't reveal any emotions in his gaze, but his hands, his touch, were tender. He drew her blouse and bra from her, dropped them to the ground, and held and kissed her breasts, laving her nipples until her mind fuzzed and she shifted from foot to foot with desire. His hands feathered over her torso. He stroked lightly, not pressing on her bruises, but acknowledging them, traced her ribs, then he slipped her skirt and petticoat down, returned to discard her panties.

Holding her hands, he stepped back to look at her, then moved in to kiss her lips, and she let his tongue probe her mouth. She savored his taste, and pulled his T-shirt up and off. His right hand reached to his back and he leaned and set his gun on the bedside table, and took a packet from the little drawer, dropped his own pants and boxers to reveal a thrusting erection, and sheathed himself with a condom.

Only the sound of their ragged breathing broke the quiet as they stood naked and facing each other.

They moved onto the bed at the same time, in tune like they'd been during the dance, her on the bottom and him between her open and welcoming thighs.

"I need," he whispered. He locked hands with her, and entered her slowly, and she savored the feel of his body sliding into hers, fulfilling her . . . body.

And they glided together, skin caressing skin, slow to fast to perfect release as they cried out together.

He rolled and took her with him and they lay in the fading light together and she fell asleep.

His mind had turned off when he'd made love to her, but came right back on line when she went limp with sleep.

He'd let Clare down. Let himself down, dammit. And maybe he couldn't talk about how his burgeoning psychic powers scared him. Maybe he couldn't ask her to help. Not here, not now. But maybe he had a shot of figuring it out himself, if he worked at it . . . or followed his instincts.

Right now his gut said to go, because if he stayed, he'd

hurt them both more, because she would press again and he'd remain tongue-tied. So beautiful, Clare. With luck, she should sleep through the night.

If he left, he might be able to clear this up fast, tonight. That wasn't letting Clare help him, which would also hurt her. But he wanted this faced and done. He moved silently away from her and out of the house.

A bird cried and he flinched. But this time he stopped and deliberately looked around. And saw nothing. Not a bird, and no crows.

He opened the gate and went through, descended the three steps, and walked to his truck, ready for a lonely journey, because something twisted inside him couldn't share.

He'd had no idea he was crippled inside, too. *That* he might be able to straighten.

Zach went to the place he'd be most comfortable, where strong people would surround him—a cop bar where a friend of his on the DPD hung out. Nobody would care if he talked or not, and would expect him to keep mum about hurt, his past, his lost brother, and especially his strange psychic powers.

He was welcomed . . . with reservations. Some conversations stopped and some young police officers didn't look at him because his disability stirred fears of the same in them. His friend was there, but preoccupied with a case he couldn't talk about.

Though the atmosphere untangled a thread in Zach since he was among his tribe, it also emphasized his differences. He was more like an honorary member of the tribe, shoved to the side. Maybe consulted now and then about a piece of knowledge he might have that the warriors of the tribe didn't, but he was no longer a warrior.

And this evening, some of these men and women were here in the bar because the alternative was an echoing empty apartment.

A cop's life wasn't easy, and often dangerous, and Zach hadn't been ready to settle . . . before. Especially for a woman who didn't understand the difficulty and danger. A woman who wasn't strong enough to manage the wait while he was on duty and the dread of a knock at the door giving her terrible news.

He'd been in that situation of waiting for terrible news with his brother, Jim. He'd never forget that knock on the door.

He was no longer a warrior of this tribe.

Yet as he drove through the city bright and dark, he felt that despite their different pasts, Rickman and his men were accepting him into a different tribe. As a warrior, an integral part, not a man on the fringe.

He and Clare had taken turns in growing in fits and starts; occasionally he was ahead of her in the acceptance of their new lives category.

He'd dealt with the lack of respect others would give him in his new job first. He'd had no good opinion of private investigators in all of his career. And his cop friends pitied him because he had to step down into private investigations since he couldn't cut it as a deputy sheriff anymore.

But in the depths of his heart, being disabled had always been a possibility in his career, and he'd known that.

Yeah, he and Clare had talked the "respect" thing out and he'd helped her there.

This evening, he wasn't, quite, ready to let her help him.

Because if he did have some sort of gift in the past, it had failed him in his deepest need.

He didn't want another one if it would fail him when he needed it . . . to protect Clare.

THIRTY-FIVE

A DOOR CLOSING woke her. The front door. Zach had
left. She caught her breath on a sob, moved her legs up so she
could rest her head on her knees, and let the tears wet the
sheet as she heard his truck start up and drive away.

Would he come back?

Had she backed off of her core belief, that they should be
equal partners, and compromised for nothing?

She let out a low moan, so different from the sounds they'd
made a few minutes before. Finally she got up and put on a
robe, stripped the bed, bundled up the sheets, took them down
to the laundry room, and started a wash.

Then she braced herself for the bathroom—and the
shower. She and Zach had made a practice of amazing shower
sex.

She stepped into the glass enclosure with crossing sprays,
readjusted them. She couldn't avoid this just because it reminded her so much of Zach . . . but she'd never liked the
bathroom in gray tints—who did that? Perhaps she'd consider
replacing it sooner rather than later, done in cheerful yellow
and colorful hand-painted tiles.

Enzo stuck half of his torso through the door.

"*Eek!*" she squealed, slipped, and nearly fell. He'd been hard to see because he, too, was gray-verging-on-invisible.

Hi, Clare! He gave a little sniff. *I like this water. I like the shower.*

"Enzo! You scared me!" She stopped herself from demanding where he'd been.

His tail went from wag to droop. *I'm sorry, Clare.* His head swiveled. *Where's Zach?*

"Not here." This time she said the words aloud, and they bounced harshly against all the walls in the room.

His forehead wrinkled. *You are fighting AGAIN?*

"Yes. No. I don't know," she muttered, turning the spigots off.

Leaving the shower, with her legs passing through Enzo and chilling them so that the droplets froze and clinked in tiny tones on the floor as she moved, Clare toweled herself dry, then used the squeegee on the glass doors.

"I'm done talking about my relationship with Zach. You've been prodding me about learning." She wrapped her plush robe around herself tightly and pulled the belt. "You once indicated that you could tell me which volumes of Great-Aunt Sandra's journals would be the best to learn from." She lifted her chin. "So let's go do that now."

Did she see a darkening of the mist in his eyes?

The Other answered her. *Look for the blue journals. The spirit who was Dillinger influenced her to put most of the information you—and Dora after you—need in blue journals.*

Clare gulped, thought of the rainbow-colored bindings of all the journals she'd inherited from her formerly "weird great-aunt Sandra." Only three or four were blue, weren't they?

"Maybe you'd like to point me to a page . . ."

But Enzo was drooling on her foot. *I'm sorry Zach isn't here with you, Clare.*

Another swallow. "I am, too."

Enzo licked her from ankle to shin in one long swipe. He stood and trotted toward the bathroom door, looked over his shoulder, and his eyes glittered with excitement. *But I have something for you, Clare! Yes, I do! It will cheer you up! Come look, on your dresser! You will LOVE it.* He jogged out of sight and Clare followed.

278 ROBIN D. OWENS

When she stepped on the thick carpeting instead of the cool, gray tile, her toes curled into it and she stood to savor the feeling that reminded her to live in the moment, not plan the future.

Enzo danced back to her, and around her. *Come ON, Clare. J. Dawson wanted something special from the in-between, and he made me promise to look and look and look and finally, I FOUND!*

"Oh," she said quietly, and now that Enzo was a dog once more and she could be vulnerable, she let tears trickle out. She hurried to her dresser more for the box of tissues than whatever gift J. Dawson had left her . . . and it was the ghosts who gave her gifts, not the universe rewarding her? Or maybe both . . . she'd received a coin as well as the watch the last time.

If the ghost has something he wants to leave you, he will. Enzo sat by her dresser, panting. *J. Dawson's things were all gone except for the nugget and Zach has that. But J. Dawson wanted me to give you something special.*

"So it's you who 'rewards' me?"

Enzo's eyes shifted. *Maybe.*

Another noncommittal answer. This time she wouldn't press. She caught the gleam of gold and jewels in the low light and gasped. Turning on the small lamp, she stared at the brooch. The nearly three-dimensional, full-blown rose was layered in diamonds. Down the stem, the two buds set in gold had to be cabochon rubies, and the third was another diamond. The leaves of the small floral spray were enameled green with gold edges around them, framing the rose and buds, just gorgeous. Three long stems were also gold and tied with a diamond bow. Clare touched it with her fingertips. "It's fabulous."

Yay, yay, yay, we pleased you! Enzo hopped around in circles. *J. Dawson saw a pretty flower like this on a rich lady's dress and he wanted you to have it!*

"It is very, very beautiful," she replied solemnly, looking the phantom dog in his eyes. "Thank you."

You're welcome, Clare. Enzo came and rubbed against her legs, and she decided she'd need a floor-length robe.

We appreciate you, Clare. And that you use your gift to help.

"Thank you, and thank J. Dawson for me, too."

But Enzo shook his head. *I can't. He's gone to where I can't go.*

"All right." Clare patted Enzo's head and rubbed his ears. "It's pretty early, but from the way I feel, definitely time for bed." She hesitated, wanted to ask if she'd be presented with another case very soon or not, then decided she wasn't in the mood to find out.

Maybe he could sweat the fear out of him, yank another strand or two of the twisted mess inside him straight enough that he could talk to Clare.

The gym for Rickman's agents was downtown, always a pain to drive in, but the best option. He found his designated parking spot near the door was a handicapped one. His stomach tightened, but that would help with his aching foot and leg.

Fifteen minutes later he'd changed into workout clothes and limped into the gym, cane in hand. He had to leave the leg brace on, but guys wore braces, soft and hard, when they worked out. No big deal.

Yeah, it was, but he'd get over it.

And the man grunting on the weight bench wouldn't care, not Tony Rickman. He must have caught the shadow of movement in the door because he looked at Zach and didn't settle the weight in the rests, which seemed to have been his first instinct.

"Zach," he said.

"Tony," Zach replied, moving to a strength trainer, but feeling better about the brace. Rickman wore a tank that showed a couple of tats and more bullet and knife scars than Zach had.

Man had gone through some serious pain and hospital time. No wonder he got Zach. And as Zach grunted through the last training program his physical therapist had set up, he figured that many, if not most, of Rickman's agents would be as battered as the two of them. Zach had been unlucky enough to draw the disability card, is all. Yeah, he liked Rickman. He liked Rossi. Zach could accept them as his tribe.

By the time he'd sweated through an hour of workout, he knew what he'd do about Clare.

Zach strode up to Clare's door. The pattern of lights left on was different. Clare'd awakened, and he hadn't left a note before he'd gone to untwist himself. Women hated that. He hadn't spared her, them, trouble.

He used the doorbell, and when she didn't answer, his gut did a loop and a squeeze that she was ignoring him, had already given up on him.

A worse idea was that she wasn't home. Stupid to think an independent woman like Clare would stay where he left her. The neighborhood was safe and close enough to bustling Cherry Creek that she could walk to a club if she wanted.

So he used the fancy brass knocker. No answer.

Maybe she'd gone from sad to mad. That was okay; he could deal with her anger. It even excited him, his uptight Clare coming unraveled.

He was just about to go around the fence and to the backyard—he didn't think she'd forgive him, yet, if he broke into her house . . . and had she already changed the alarm code on him? That was a question, a real indicator of where he might stand. His fingers shifted to the keypad, flicked in the air, ready to tap.

The door opened and Clare stood, hipshot and frowning, wearing a robe. He couldn't tell whether she was naked under it or not. She crossed her arms over her breasts, looking magnificent, her hair wild, her skin with a glow that he had to resist kissing.

Instead he pried one of her hands away from her opposite elbow and stuck the key fob in it, spoke first since she deserved that he did so. "It's hard for me to talk about some stuff," he said.

"I don't think partnerships, relationships should be easy." She took a breath. "How can I help?"

They stared at each other under the light. He straightened

his spine, met her dark gaze. "You can go with me to see my mother to puzzle out my psychic gift. She's up and waiting for us. We'll take your new Jeep. You can drive."

That brought shock to her face, and her gaze went beyond him to the red Wrangler parked at the curb. He'd liked the one with the granite gray metallic paint job, but Clare now spent a lot of time in a world of grays, so he'd gotten the fire-engine red. "My. New. Jeep."

Irritated, he hunched a shoulder. "Yeah. I bought it for you. Great for off-roading in the mountains . . . mountains without ghosts, even." He tried a smile. She didn't seem to notice as she stared at the vehicle.

"It's pretty," she murmured.

He winced. Looked tough and muscular to him, a nice vehicle for a guy or a gal.

Her stare arrowed back to him, her expression a little softer, and he relaxed.

Her brows went up. "You bought it?"

He expanded the explanation. "For you. I bought it for you. Your new Jeep. I have a good, black truck." He wouldn't mention that he'd gotten the option of "easy passenger access."

She blinked. "You can't give me a car, Zach. It's too expensive a gift."

But she was damn well weakening, wasn't she? Her grip on the fob was solid.

He snorted, put his free hand up against the jamb, and leaned toward her. He wanted more than a slight whiff of her, wanted a real good sniff. Yeah, she'd showered him and the scent of their sex off. "I may not have the resources you do, but I've got enough money to buy a damn vehicle for the woman I'm involved with, *exclusively*, when she doesn't have wheels." He kept leaning and leaning and leaning in until he could see tiny gold flecks in her hazel eyes, until his lips hovered close to hers.

"The woman you're involved with?" she asked in a breathy way that went straight to his dick.

"Yeah."

She sighed out, shook her head. Her hand planted against his chest and pushed. "No kiss." She met his eyes, all serious Clare. "Seen any crows today?"

He flinched, didn't pull back. She'd figured that much out about his gift, either before and hadn't said, or in the couple of hours since he'd left. "Nope. Not today, Clare." His shoulders had risen high, but he kept his stare matched with hers. "I want to . . . talk to you." More, she needed more and deserved it from him. "I want your help," he managed to mumble without wincing. True enough.

Again her gaze went past him to the Jeep.

"My mother's waiting for us."

Tilting her head, she stared into his eyes. He could have fallen deep into her gaze, lost himself.

"So, Zach, will you tell me the next time you see crows?"

He nodded slowly. "I will."

"And what the crows mean?"

He glanced aside.

"They are your 'touch of the sight' that Mrs. Flinton talked about once?"

So he moved his cane and made it soldier-straight, too. "My maternal grandmother knew a rhyme she taught to me."

Clare nodded as if she weren't surprised that whatever gift he had, touch of the sight or not, came through his mother.

He recited:

> "One for sorrow,
> Two for luck;
> Three for a wedding,
> Four for death;
> Five for silver,
> Six for gold;
> Seven for a secret,
> Not to be told;
> Eight for heaven,
> Nine for hell,
> And ten for the devil's own sell—self."

He stared at her. "Is that sufficient to show I'm accepting my gift?"

She gave him a slow nod. "For now. If you'll let me know . . . occasionally . . . when you see them."

He returned a half smile. "Occasionally, huh?"

"Yes, and I'm pleased to help you, Zach."

The exit for his mother's facility was coming up, and Zach hadn't spoken to Clare except to say he wanted her help in tracking down the source of his . . . gift.

Clare had driven silently, giving him room.

He flexed his fingers, moved his left foot, still in the braces that he was getting really tired of wearing today.

"This isn't going to be easy either. Talking to Mama about her family. My family." He grimaced. "I must've gotten whatever I have from Mama's side." He gave Clare a quick glance. "From Gran Aislinn Warren, my Scots grandmother. She supposedly had the sight."

"She *did* have the sight," Clare corrected, keeping her eyes on the road.

Zach wouldn't go that far, but kept his mouth shut.

"Tell me about her," Clare said.

Zach cleared his throat. "Gran was wealthy in her own right, and married a man who had money and 'breeding,' too. Jim and I loved her . . . and I gotta tell you about Jim and . . . and my previous gift, that failed me, failed *us*. But, but not now." He paused and Clare glanced at him, that hurting, haunted expression on her face, though he sensed it was for him, not because of him. Improvement.

Change the subject. "I barely recall my grandfather, who'd died in an experimental aircraft."

"I like your mother very much," Clare said softly.

"Yes, she's always been soft and cheerful and a little fey." He paused. "I can say now, Clare, that I . . . seem to have a psychic gift. That my mother is a little fey and her mother, Gran Aislinn, had a gift, too."

"You've made great strides," Clare said solemnly.

He found his mouth curving. "Are you teasing me?"

"Maybe. We tend to be serious people, Zach."

"Yeah, yeah, yeah." Automatically, he had her stop at a supermarket and he picked up the best-of-a-mediocre-lot bouquet for his mom.

"Good idea," Clare said. "You're sure she's up?"

"She's more of a night bird. The General's up-at-dawn habits were hard on her." Not that Zach's father had cared. Zach didn't think he'd been back to see his wife for at least three years . . . since Zach had moved to Montana, and was closer.

Close in the West was a relative thing.

They signed in at the care facility and received smiles from the staff at the front desk.

A couple of minutes later, the nurse knocked and opened the door when his mother called, "Come in!"

His mother sat in her big chair angled toward the windows, only the soft light from the table lamp illuminating the room. To his surprise and pleasure, she was reading on the tablet he'd given her for her birthday. He didn't think she'd gone beyond reading yet, but this was a serious first step. Maybe Clare could help her—

His mother placed the tablet on the table, rose with the grace that he loved, and came toward him, her hands out. He'd stood near another chair where he could prop his cane and enveloped her in his arms, held her tight. She was almost too thin.

Then she withdrew and he let his arms drop, though he'd wanted to hold her more, drink in the scent of her—mother—for longer.

She smiled at the bouquet, a lovely smile of pure gratitude, and his heart tightened, as ever, but he could have still used Enzo pulling a trinket out of thin air for him, something special to please her more.

"Hello, Mama."

"Hello, Zach." In the quiet light, her smile widened. "My beautiful son." She looked at Clare. "Hello, Clare."

She'd remembered Clare's name. Zach stilled. His mother often just lived in her own world, reality and other people barely impinging upon it.

Clare stepped forward and took the hand his mother offered and squeezed it. "Hello, Mrs. Slade."

"Geneva, please." Head tilted, staring at them, she said, "There seems to be some . . . constraint . . . between you two."

Was it that obvious? Or obvious because she knew her

son? Or was that part of *her* gift? And here he was, becoming even more accustomed to accepting the idea of a familial gift.

"Uh," he said. "Maybe." He shouldn't. He knew he shouldn't. But he reverted to childhood and shifted his feet.

"Ahhh, Zach." She shook her head.

And Clare came to him, slipped her arm through his right one. "We're working things out." She shrugged. "You know how it is, always bumps in a relationship, especially a new one when you're figuring out the balance." She gave him a look that said she remained unhappy at what she believed the current balance of the relationship to be.

His mother nodded. "That's true." She gestured to the chairs around the table by the window and returned to hers.

He took the one next to his mother and indicated Clare should move hers out of the arrangement to sit closer to him.

Then he fiddled with setting his cane against the low table just where he could reach it best. Faster. Though there was no threat. And the back of his neck tingled. Several moments of conversation had passed and his mother hadn't mentioned Jim. Nearly unheard of.

Zach couldn't bring up the topic of the "sight." Just. Couldn't. Instead he lounged back in the chair and angled his feet under the low table, smiled with warmth and love at his mother, felt Clare's steady support.

"Oh, that smile," his mother said. "That smile is what attracted me to your fath—and Jim—" She stopped and tears filled her eyes and she looked away.

Something was changing between them and Zach didn't know why and didn't understand what, but dreadful hope that she might be accepting a little reality into her life fluttered tiny wings inside him, and wonder brushed his heart. "Tell me of Gran Aislinn."

His mother's shoulders relaxed. "She was a wonderful mother, always there." His own mother's glance slid by his. "Though my father was a . . . hard man. A businessman." Her lips curved as if she tried to minimize the lack of love from there, even as Zach thought again that she'd repeated the pattern. Then she stared at him coolly. "It was more of a marriage of financial interests than affection . . . or love." She paused, stared at him. "Love is important, Zach." Her gaze scanned him, then went to Clare. "And I like the emotions flowing between you and Clare."

Clare dipped her head. "Thank you."

So his mother had intimated that she'd loved her husband. For an instant, Zach thought he caught a glimpse into her heart and the feeling she and the young military man had shared between them when they'd met. His mother had married for affection and love. Who had changed? What had changed?

"Your grandmother was always there for me . . . until . . ."

Nope, no more of his mama thinking of death. "She was great. A wonderful grandmother. She told fabulous stories."

Laughter rippled from his mother as her mind slid back to comfortable things. "Yes, she did. Fabulous and fantastic. Of voices that whispered in the wind to her . . . the spring breeze or the howling nor'wester or the fitful summer draft." Zach's mama's voice went dreamy. He hadn't known about those voices.

"My father made a great deal of money, was interested in new things." She paused. "And knew which ones to invest in," she ended lightly.

Zach got it. In a blinding of insight that literally flashed his vision white. His grandfather had known of his wife's "gift" and used it. He stared at his mother, at a loss for words. Since she seemed to be enjoying good memories, he had a little time to cover his shock.

Clare reached out and took his right hand and they linked fingers and it was great.

Suppressing an urge to clear his throat, he said in as gentle and musing a tone as he could manage, "Yes, she told wonderful stories. Stories that were passed down in her family."

His mother nodded, still calm and enveloped in memories. "That's true. We had some good family stories."

"Yes, of Thomas the Rhymer and his poetry and prophecies. And other folklore rhymes." He swallowed, kept his voice low and smooth. "Like the 'Counting Crows Rhyme.'"

His mother's brow showed lines. "I don't recall that one, especially."

Zach wished desperately for something to drink, a beer, a glass of water even. "She recited it to me at bedtime." And to

Jim, as they lay in their twin beds in their room at their grand-parents' house.

Gran's dark eyes had been piercing under old and droopy lids. Zach squelched irritation. Like all the women in his family, she'd been saying something without actually putting it into words, hinting that he, or Jim, or both of them would see crows nobody else did? Have that little touch of the "sight"?

She'd sat in the middle of the room and held their hands, as if she were a bridge and they were all connected.

An undeniably *solid* connection Zach had thought that he'd shared with Jim, a whispery tingle in his head near his spine that indicated Jim's direction from him.

Goddamn crap.

Yeah, Gran had danced around the subject of the "sight." He much preferred Clare's steady hazel eyes, her direct confrontations instead of tippy-toeing around an issue.

"Zach?" His mother looked at him quizzically.

"Sorry." He let out the sigh trapped in his body.

But his mother was shaking her head, and she picked up the bouquet she'd laid on the square coffee table and sniffed the flowers. "I'm glad you came to see me, but you and Clare should spend more time together."

He pulled in his feet, shoved up, his fingers tightening around Clare's as she stood, too. She winked at him.

His mama rose. "Jackson Zachary Taylor, you know you should." She sent a sparkling smile to Clare. "It's obvious that Clare's a special person, so you treat her right."

"Thank you, Geneva," Clare said.

"I s'pose," he grumbled as he'd always done when scolded, for show, and bent and kissed his mother's cheek, took her in another, sweeter, hug before he picked up his cane. "I'll see you later."

"Of course you will, and Clare, too. I'm glad you found a woman who unsettled you. It's good for you." A shadow came into her eyes and the past and her broken marriage, broken mind, touched them again.

"You'll always be in my heart," he said, then blinked, had to think where that had come from. His gran Aislinn.

His mother's smile was radiant, as if she recalled, too. "You'll always be in my heart, dearest Zach."

He nodded. Clare hugged his mother. The sight made his heart ache.

When they were back in Clare's Jeep, Zach said, "You mind if we drive by the family house?"

"I'd love to."

He gave her directions and she didn't just drive by, but parked across the street from the large and well-lit Victorian home. The prof tended it well. Nice paint if a little girly in peach with beige trim.

A home he'd spent some time in now and again, but not enough that he'd felt the room his parents had given him was his own. He wasn't sure he'd ever felt the places he'd stayed in were home. Not since Jim had died. Jim had had a way of making their rooms on the Marine bases seem like home, just because he was Jim. Jim and Zach together was home, and Mama. Mama had been home when he was very little.

It unsettled him to think that he considered being with a person more important and more a home than a brick and mortar building. Because then he'd be looking for a person as a home maybe. Like Clare.

She hadn't said a word while he stared at the house. And she wasn't looking at the place, but at him.

"This is my father's and his father's home," Zach said.

Clare nodded. "And it's your mother's blood that carries the 'sight.' Like my own."

"Well, I'm pretty damn sure it isn't any mystical Native American stuff in that strain from my dad. Not that we know much about that. No, it's from Gran Aislinn and her 'voices.'"

Softly, Clare said, "The voices gave her the 'sight.' A little precognition like yours?"

He hunched a shoulder. "Maybe. She never actually discussed it." His lips curled. "And it sounds like she was priming Jim and me to use the crow rhyme as interpretation for our 'gift.'" He nearly spat out the word.

Reaching over, Clare took his left hand in both of hers. "I know how it is to dislike that word."

"Can't depend on a psychic gift. Not at all."

The streetlight showed her raised brows. "Really?"

"You're always looking for rules with your own, because you don't know what you can or can't do. But it might be . . .

capricious. Ever thought of that?" Yeah, he sounded extremely bitter. He was.

Clare's expression turned to horror. "No. There must be rules!"

"Yeah, right."

She unbuckled her seat belt and turned to face him. "Tell me, Zach."

So he grated out the story of the day Jim died. Zach had told it to her before, but he hadn't put in the connection-thing between them because he'd forgotten about it. Or blocked it out. Or it had scarred him inside forever when it had failed and Jim's life had been forfeit.

He'd sweated, so he wiped his head against the shoulder of his shirt until Clare gave him a tissue.

"I can see why you'd deny your gift," she said thoughtfully. Her lips lifted in not-really-a-smile. "I'll still hold you to telling me about the crows when you see them."

"Occasionally."

She sent him a rueful smile. "I did say 'occasionally,' though I'd prefer 'always.'"

"I'm sure you would."

"I'll point out that you'll probably be seeing, hearing, and interacting with my sidekick ghost dog, and will know of every phantom I need to help move on."

"Balance, equality, and partnership," Zach said. More than he'd given any woman.

"That's right."

Not looking at her, he said, "You seem to have forgiven me."

"You listened to me." She took his hand and put it between her breasts, as she had done with her own hand when explaining how he hurt her.

He paid more attention to the softness of her flesh, her warmth, than her words. "And asked me to help."

Something he hadn't recalled actually saying out loud to anyone for a long time.

"You're special."

"Thank you." She sighed and her breasts moved beneath his hand.

"Time to leave," he said.

She smiled, put his hand on his own knee, turned, and buckled up.

They were even quieter on the trip back to Denver, until he said, "Turn here."

"That's not the way to my place."

"No, but it's the way to mine." Clare had never been in his rooms. "I'd like you to spend the night in my bed."

Her tongue came out and swept over her lips, and the low heat of desire flickered into heavy flames.

"I'd like that," she said.

Soon they were pulling into the quiet circle drive in front of Mrs. Flinton's mansion, where he rented an apartment.

As he got out, two crows cawed and strutted on the wall separating the front yard from the back. He smiled and pointed in their direction, visible from the security light over the side door of the house that led to his apartment.

"See them?" he asked.

"What?" She craned, then said, "No."

All right, he accepted that. Just simply accepted. He saw crows that no one else did. "Crows," he said.

"Oh? How many?"

"Two." He curved his right arm around her waist.

"Two for . . . what?"

"Luck, two for luck. I'm gonna get lucky tonight."

"I think I am," she said.

He opened the doors to his apartment to her and turned on the light, disarmed the security. The space wasn't as impressive as her home, but it was comfortable. Like hers.

"Nice," she said with a hint of laughter in her voice, "A man cave."

When he stepped to the bar to drop his keys in the bowl under the night-light, he paused. There, in the bowl, were two shiny keys attached to a rectangular metallic tag enameled in cream with flowers around the name *Clare*.

Then she was right by him, staring down at the same thing. He swept them up and turned to her, offered them. "Here."

Her gaze met his, held. "Are you sure?"

"Yes. We're together."

Together said a voice in his head, and he and Clare turned to see Enzo, the ghost dog, grinning at them from the couch.

Zach looked back at Clare and jingled the keys. She took them and he reached out and closed her fingers over them.

"Together," she agreed.

Author's Note and Acknowledgments

The town of Curly Wolf was based on the original town of Buckskin Joe, which was a mining town near Alma, Colorado, from 1859 to 1866. The town pumped about $16 million from mining into the Colorado (and national) economy.

Unlike my Curly Wolf, most of Buckskin Joe fell apart and a few buildings were disassembled and moved from its first location in South Park (a geological high-altitude basin of 1,000 square miles) to an area near Cañon City, Colorado.

Buildings were added and the *new* Buckskin Joe became a movie set where twenty-one films including *Cat Ballou*, *True Grit*, and *Conagher* were made. After that, the town became an amusement park and recreation area, then was sold to a real billionaire, who moved it to his ranch.

My multimillionaire, Mr. Laurentine, is a completely fictional character with fictional characteristics and backstory, as are my characters in the Park County Sheriff's Department, including the sheriffs, past and present, though from what I know of the real sheriff of J. Dawson's time period, my hero, Zach, would approve of him.

I spent some time researching J. Dawson Hidgepath (a ghost associated with Buckskin Joe) and found no contemporary sources that he was a real person though the legend of his bones is all over the Net . . . so I felt able to take liberties with the standard story.

According to that legend, his death was ruled *accidental* due to a fall near Mount Bross in 1865.

Soon after his death and burial, his body was supposed to have been found by a couple of women in their beds and reinterred each time. Legend also has it that the bones continued to appear during the 1870s and throughout Colorado until someone was disgusted enough to throw them into an outhouse cesspool.

So, with the town being moved and the bones appearing and disappearing, I couldn't really resist merging the two ideas and weaving a story.

Thanks, as always, to the librarians at History Colorado Center and the Denver Public Library, particularly the Western History and Genealogical Division. Also many thanks to Christie Wright of the Park County Archives, who helped me with the facts of Buckskin Joe and the truth that I bent and broke (like a sheriff's journal surviving in the archives) for my imaginary Curly Wolf. If you want to donate to the Park County Archives, you can do so here: P.O. Box 99, Fairplay, CO 80440.

Ms. Wright has written a book on the cemetery of Buckskin Joe and other works you can see here: southparkperils. com.

I also visited South Park City, an open-air museum Western town in Fairplay in Park County. South Park City has only a few buildings that are original to the site. As usual, I have pictures on my Pinterest page here: http://www.pinterest.com/robindowens/ghost-layer-settings/, and I have no doubt that I will be using it, and the buildings, again and again, as long as this series is going. Currently the original brewery needs help in being restored. To donate to this cause, please see this website: fairy-lamp.com/SPCMuseum/South_Park_City_Brewery_Donate.html.

Also thanks to the Law Enforcement Training Network for the paper "Tire Tread and Tire Track Evidence."

Next up, Clare and Zach are going to confront a very evil ghost born of a great deal of murderous and otherwise negative energy in Creede, Colorado.

TURN THE PAGE FOR A PREVIEW OF THE NEXT

BOOK IN ROBIN D. OWENS'S GHOST SEER SERIES

GHOST KILLER

COMING IN FEBRUARY 2015

FROM BERKLEY SENSATION!

DANGER COMES, ENZO howled, running through the bedroom door. Not the doorway, the door. Even a ghost Labrador should not have all the hair of his body standing out.

Clare Cermak's heartbeat kicked fast and she shuddered in the bed of her lover. She pulled the sheet high, even though the room was—had been—warm.

Enzo leapt for the bed and landed on her, in her, sending the coldness of his being into her legs. His dark doggy eyes showed fear. Before she could say anything, those "eyes" began to morph into bottomless black mist with jagged white streaks . . . signifying that the Other spirit who took over her happy companion would be speaking to her.

She didn't like that. When the Other came, she felt like an expendable pawn in an unknown chess game.

You are not, quite, expendable, the Other "said." The words reverberated in her head, but more, seemed to knock molecules of heavy soundless explosions through the room. Her lover, facedown beside her, began to stir and she wasn't sure whether she wanted him to hear what the Other said or not.

Judgmental eyes fixed upon her. *Not, quite, expendable,*

the Other repeated. *Your work has been . . . acceptable . . . for your first two projects. Your successor is young to inherit the gift.*

Clare had heard her psychic ability to help ghosts pass on called a gift, but she'd always considered it a curse.

We have paid you well for your gift, the Other, still standing face-to-face with her, said.

Yes, she'd inherited millions, and for each major revenant she'd aided, had gotten income. But she'd also lost her previous life as an accountant, which she'd loved.

The Other pulled the skin of his muzzle back and showed the teeth she knew were bigger than what she saw.

Beside her, Zach groaned and rolled over, opened his eyes. The Other stepped to put a paw square in his chest and Zach grunted.

It is well you are together, the Other said dispassionately. *One of you might survive, should you walk into this danger.* The faux dog's head swung toward Zach and another wave of chill and heavy air moved through the room. *You should be able to see me now, Jackson Zachary Slade.*

"I see you," Zach rasped, eyes wide open, fingers twitching as if he wanted his gun on the table next to him. That was Zach, while Clare's mind whirled in fear and dread, he *acted,* or at least confronted the thing.

I consign the girl child, Dora Cermak, to your care to protect should Clare fail and fall to this evil ghost, Jackson Zachary Slade, the Other said.

A rapping came on the door between Zach's apartment and the rest of the mansion. The Other vanished and Zach sat up, put his warm, muscular and *solid* arm around Clare. He looked down at her. "That's *not* going to happen."

Clare realized she trembled. Mostly with cold, she assured herself.

"What did the bastard say?"

She shook her head in denial of the fear spearing through her, swallowed so she found more spit in her dry mouth to speak. "Danger comes."

Zach grunted, rolled off the bed and pulled on some sweatpants, yelled to the person still pounding on the door, "Just a damn— Just a minute!"

"Probably Mrs. Flinton," Clare said, speaking of his land-lady, the very wealthy owner of the mansion, of which this had been the housekeeper's suite. She dragged on her bra, turned yesterday's panties inside out for now and put them on, slipped into her sundress.

Zach had already snagged his cane and left the bedroom. He'd gone to the door, and Clare heard him open it a little. "Mrs. Flinton?"

"I'm so sorry to disturb you. So, sorry," her voice quavered. Usually the woman exuded vim and vigor.

"Well, that's a first," Zach teased. "Come on in. Clare will be right here. You need Clare?" he said in a casual tone that amazed Clare. She was still having trouble breathing steadily. But he'd been a deputy sheriff and used to adrenaline dumps, she supposed. That didn't happen often when you were a certified public accountant at a nice, safe, job for a prestigious, maybe stodgy, firm.

"Yes. There's trouble." A drawn in breath. "An evil ghost."

Just the last three words had Clare stopping in her tracks to take a breath. Her ghost dog had dropped hints about evil ghosts during the seventeen days of her Ghost Seer career.

Good grief, it hadn't even been a month since she'd started seeing the wretched shades. No wonder the Other warned her of danger.

But Mrs. Flinton continued to talk in a whispery, uncertain voice. "I have tea and pastries in the breakfast room."

If Clare had to talk of big, evil ghosts over tea in a pretty room, she'd scream. She stomped her fear into the carpet as she joined them.

Zach slanted a look at her, then opened the door wide for Mrs. Flinton, who, for the first time Clare had met her, actually looked and acted her age, face sagging with worry, mouth quivering.

"The tea–," Mrs. Flinton.

"I have food. I'm a P.I. and I take cases in my apartment. We can talk here in the living room."

A manly room for speaking of danger as opposed to a room decorated in cheerful yellow chintz.

The woman pushed a roller walker into the room, leaning on it. She crossed to one of the big brown leather chairs, leaving the sofa or the other chair on this side of the room for Zach and Clare.

Clare felt too nervy to sit. "I'll put coffee on, why don't I?"

Mrs. Flinton, who'd unaccustomedly slumped, perked up, her pink lipsticked mouth smiling. "Coffee!"

From that, Clare figured out that she wasn't supposed to have any. Too bad. Clare needed some and thought Zach did, too. She sent Mrs. Flinton a stern look. "You'll be having herbal tea."

Mrs. Flinton pouted, then sighed. "I suppose you're right. Though what I really need is a martini."

Zach chuckled. "Not going to have that, either."

"Bloody Mary?" Mrs. Flinton raised penciled on brows.

"Nope. No alcohol here."

Sniffing, Mrs. Flinton said, "You are wrong. We stocked your liquor cabinet, and don't think I don't know that my housekeeper has given you wine from my cellar." Another sniff. "Wine that I can't have."

The return of her character and the dripping of the coffee as it filled the pot soothed Clare enough for her to slide into the living room with a pleasant expression on her face and sit next to Zach.

But Mrs. Flinton's face crumpled when she saw Clare and tears began to roll down her cheeks. There was nothing for it, Clare rose and moved over to the arm of the woman's chair, patted her on the shoulder.

"Maybe you'd better tell us what's wrong, Mrs. Flinton," Clare said.

"Please. Please call me Barbara, especially since I'll be imposing on you so much." She whisked out a lace-edged hanky and dabbed her eyes and her cheeks.

Zach snorted. "Just spit it out, Mrs. Flinton."

Straightening to ramrod stiff, not looking at Clare, Mrs. Flinton said, "Yes, I suppose I must. It's about another Ghost Seer."

Clare drew in a small breath. Maybe she'd have help. Any help would be great. "Another Ghost Seer?"

Mrs. Flinton continued, "Yes, I have a little bit of several psychic gifts, but Caden has just one, like you, and we're thinking that it must be Ghost Seeing." Her fingers crushed the handkerchief until the delicate linen disappeared into her fist.

Clare's gaze met Zach's. He nodded, as if confirming he was in this with her. As he always had been. She was lucky.

"Caden?" she asked, her voice a little higher than usual. "And who is 'we'?"

"We are me, his great grandmother, and my daughter, Caden's grandmother, who believe in psychic gifts, but not his parents."

"Parents," said Zach neutrally.

"Caden is seven." A quivery sigh followed by a rush of words. "It seems his gift is coming too fast and too soon."

"Oh my God," Clare said. No, she could not refuse to help.

"Yes, dear." Mrs. Flinton cleared her throat. She sniffed wetly, raised big, blue eyes to Clare. "There's a big, bad ghost ready to eat him."

Clare flinched. The tea kettle shrieked. Avoiding Zach's gaze, she crossed to the teapot and fussed with the loose leaf tea of twigs and blossoms in a little basket.

"Pour your coffees first, dear," Mrs. Flinton instructed. "Otherwise the water will be too hot for the herbs and ruin their efficacy."

Waiting until her hands were steady, Clare poured mugs of coffee for Zach and herself. He always took black. She was discreetly leaning against his refrigerator so she didn't check it for milk or cream or whatever. Just the smell of rich, dark caffeine strengthened her so she could lift her chin and take a mug to Zach.

He looked at her straight, all acceptance of dangerous trouble. Seeing if she faced that up-front? She didn't know. But she firmed her lips and dipped her head. As much as she'd bobbed and ducked in the past, tried to evade her gift, now was not the time to drag her feet.

The bottom line of an endangered child wouldn't let her ignore her power to move ghosts on. Hopefully she had enough mojo-whatever to kick an evil one out of this world.

Giving them all time to think about what should be said next, what plans had to be made, Clare put her own mug on a magazine on the coffee table, went back for Mrs. Flinton's tea.

"Thank you, dear," Mrs. Flinton said, and cradled the delicate china cup in both hands.

Clare sat down next to Zach and even leaned against him a little. He was much nicer than the fridge, and knew about trouble and danger. Leaning against him, accepting his expertise, didn't mean she was dependent on him.

Putting down his mug, he took the lead, as she'd expected. "Trouble," Zach prompted.

Mrs. Flinton's hand holding the teacup shook and she put it down. "Yes. I know Caden's in trouble and my granddaughter and her husband *don't* believe that. They are good, solid–"

"Unimaginative—" Zach said.

"Rational—" Clare began herself.

"Yes. Both of those." Mrs. Flinton blinked rapidly as if to keep more tears from falling. Her eyes appeared even bluer and she whispered. "I think . . . though I don't know personally or for sure, I think I've heard . . . that an evil ghost can *eat* someone." She stared, turning so pale that her carefully blended makeup stood out on her face.

Clare shivered. Zach slid his arm from the sofa behind her to wrap it around her shoulders.

"I've heard of ghosts eating people," she said. She sucked in a breath, and since Mrs. Flinton already knew about Enzo, Clare called him. "Enzo?"

The ghost Labrador simply appeared sitting between Mrs. Flinton and Clare, angled to watch them both.

Oh, no! Enzo whimpered. *This is bad. This is very bad.*

"Bad ghosts eat people," Zach said in a flat tone.

Not their bodies, Enzo said. *Their spirits, souls, essences . . .*

"Uh-oh," Zach said, but he didn't sound too alarmed and rubbed Clare's shoulder.

Clare *was* alarmed. Enzo had spoken of evil ghosts. She knew she wasn't experienced enough to fight one.

Mrs. Flinton began to hiccup in distress. Clare stood and walked around the coffee table to pick up her teacup and hand it back to her. "Drink it down, Mrs. Flinton," Clare said, her voice not betraying her inside qualms.

Nodding, Mrs. Flinton sipped, then gestured to the elegant

Hèrmes bag attached to her walker. "Please retrieve my phone from there. I have something I want you to view."

The phone in a sparkly lavender case was easy to find. "I recorded a call from Caden on SeeAndTalk. You take the phone over to Zach so you can both watch."

Clare did, sitting thigh-to-thigh with Zach. She thumbed on the app and held it so they could both see.

"Hi, Great Gram," a blond-haired boy with Mrs. Flinton's eyes whispered.

"Hello, Caden," Mrs. Flinton's voice came.

The boy glanced around. "I gotta be fast." Then he blinked rapidly, his features pinched. "They don't believe me, Gram! I tell them, and tell them, but they *won't* believe. They say I'm making it up." He gulped. "I'm not, Gram."

"What's wrong, Caden?"

"There's a ghost here in town. A real bad one. I think it was lurking or . . . you know that scary spot near where both Willow Creeks join? The place where that guy killed his wife and himself last month–"

"Caden?"

"I know I wasn't s'posed to hear, but all the kids did. That scary spot isn't sitting there no more. I think it got stirred up and now it's like dust in the wind or something." He began hyperventilating.

"Calm down a little, Caden, and tell me."

"I'm sorry, Gram. There's a ghost! A big, bad ghost and it's out to get me!"

"Get you how?"

The thin boy shuddered. "Suck my soul out of my body and *eat* it."

A harsh breath from Mrs. Flinton. "Caden, love?"

His lower lip thrust out, his brows came down. "I can *too* see ghosts. I told you. And you said you believed me!"

"I said that, and I meant it," the woman said.

"Well. I *do* see ghosts, though usually not old, old ones like this one. And I don't see this one as much as feel it, and it feels really awful. As if it has teeth, crunch, crunch, crunch, and wants to eat me. My bones, crunch, crunch, crunch. And my, my . . . the rest of me."

"All right, Caden–" Mrs. Flinton began to soothe.

304 ROBIN D. OWENS

"Caden?" called a young woman's voice.

"Gram, Mommy and Daddy don't believe me." Tears began to trickle down his face. "It comes most at night. I'm afraid to sleep. Come help me, Gram."

"Caden, where are you and what are you doing?" called the younger woman.

The screen went black. Clare glanced up to see Mrs. Flinton's shoulders hunched and shaking as she wept into her handkerchief.

Zach cleared his throat. "When did this come in?"

Mrs. Flinton wiped her eyes and blew her nose and straightened. "This morning. I checked with my granddaughter, Caden's fine and at school." Her breath rasped in and out. "I knew I could count on you, Zach, and on Clare," Mrs. Flinton sent her a look of appeal, "to help me. So I waited for you. As long as I could. I have a favor to ask you—" Mrs. Flinton began in a shaky voice.

The door to the mansion was kicked open and Tony Rickman, Zach's boss at Rickman Security and Investigations, walked in carrying a large tray holding covered dishes. Clare smelled bacon and eggs.

"I'll take care of this, Godmama Barbara," Mr. Rickman said, striding the few paces to the coffee table and lowering the tray. "I have a case for you, Zach and Clare," Tony said.

"What are you doing here mid-morning on Monday?" Mrs. Flinton questioned with starch in her tone.

Mr. Rickman went over and kissed her cheek. "Taking care of my Godmama." His mouth flattened. "And young Caden. We don't know all the particulars," Mr. Rickman stated flatly. "This case could include physical danger as well as . . . ah . . . non-physical."

Zach raised his brows at Clare. She'd always been wishy-washy about "consulting" for Rickman Security and Investigations. "Yes?" he mouthed.

She shrugged, then said, "You don't have to pay us—me—Mrs. Flinton," Clare said. "You saved my life . . . or at least my sanity."

"I agree," Zach said.

"You work for me, you get paid," Mr. Rickman said. "And you will both work for me on this."

Zach leaned down to whisper to Clare, "He's a control freak."

"We need you to go to Creede, Colorado, today," Mr. Rickman said.

"Is that where Caden is?" Clare asked.

"Yes," both Mrs. Flinton and Mr. Rickman said in unison. Mrs. Flinton sniffled.

Mr. Rickman pulled out a big, square handkerchief from his trousers pocket and handed it to her, shot a glance at Clare and Zach. "Eat," he said.

Zach leaned over and took off the silver domes. Sure enough thick bacon, soft scrambled cheesy eggs, and buttered English muffins filled the plates. Zach lifted a plate and began shoveling in eggs.

That was a man of action for you, ready to fuel up at a moment's notice while her throat was still dry and closed from dread. Clare savored her coffee.

Tony Rickman arranged his big body in the chair near them.

Mrs. Flinton said, "My daughter, Patricia, has no special gift, but she grew up with me. She *believes*." Mrs. Flinton sighed. "Patricia is out of the country." The older woman's lips pursed, showing fine lines. "I told her to stay away. I called my granddaughter and asked if Caden could spend some time with me, get him out of the town, and was politely told to keep my nose out of their business." She swallowed more tea. "And they wouldn't welcome me." Her lips pressed together and she shook her head as she gazed at Clare. "I'm not strong enough in that one power to help."

Tony Rickman grunted, "Good."

Placing her teacup on the side table, Mrs. Flinton said, "Caden is right." She sighed. "His parents won't believe him. I do. Do you?"

"Yes," Clare and Zach said at the same time.

Yes! Enzo hopped to his feet, paced and circled the room, tail thwapping the air, sending a chilly draft through the room. Mrs. Flinton and Clare watched him, Zach ate, and Tony Rickman crossed his arms over his chest and studiously avoided looking at the spectral Labrador.

Enzo came back and sat near Clare's feet, mostly in the

coffee table, looked sorrowfully at the food, then back at her. *This is dangerous, Clare. Every spirit the bad ghost eats makes it bigger and eviler. I don't want it to eat a boy.*

"I don't want it to eat a boy, either," Clare said.

Zach crunched down his bacon. "We won't let that happen," he said with complete assurance.

"Creede is a four and a half hour drive. If you leave now, you could reach it before dark." Mrs. Flinton's chin set. "That's important. I want Caden protected, and they won't let me take him, and they won't come visit me as a family. My granddaughter and grandson-in-law have a motel outside town, and they live on the premises. This is a busy time of year for them."

"Hunting season," Zach said.

"Yes. And Michael also has a business for processing game. They make a good bit of money this time of year."

"And not so much during the winter," Clare said.

"No. They are stubborn about self-sufficiency, among other things."

"Self-sufficiency is important. Even for those who have family money or trust funds."

"They love their life," Mrs. Flinton said.

Lucky them.

Rickman stretched his big body and stood and Zach rose a millisecond after his boss, still holding his coffee mug. "We'll get right on this," Zach said.

Clare got to her feet, too. "I need to go home and pack."

Mrs. Flinton pressed her hands together. "How long do you think it will take for you to . . . move this thing on?"

Destroy it, Enzo said.

"Destroy it," Clare muttered, tensing all over again. "I don't know. You know I have very limited experience."

"This is probably affecting the whole town, Clare. Horrible," Mrs. Flinton said.

Mr. Rickman rolled his hand. "Give me a shot at a time period, Clare."

"It shouldn't take more than," she looked at Enzo, "two weeks."

The dog's forehead wrinkled but he didn't contradict her.

Clearing his throat, and looking out a window, Mr. Rickman said, "There's a big tourist event, car show—Cruisin' the Canyon—Saturday and Sunday in Creede." He rolled a shoulder. "I have a classic car, thought about attending."

All the blood drained from Clare's face, she felt it going, along with her knees that wobbled, then gave out so she plunked back down on the couch.

Zach lowered his coffee mug. "If a supernatural murderer is anything like a regular one and looking for a big score–" He shrugged.

"A lot of deaths to feed him," Clare whispered.

This is SO not good. Enzo hopped up and down.

"How soon can you leave?" Rickman repeated. "Or do you want us to charter a flight, arrange a car?"

"I can do that," Mrs. Flinton's chin lifted. "Money can't buy everything, but it can make things a whole lot easier. And it sounds like every hour might count."

Mr. Rickman grunted, looked at his highly engineered watch. "It will take a little time to set everything up, make all your travel arrangements."

"Creede has an airport?" Zach asked.

"Yeah," Mr. Rickman said.

Zach narrowed his eyes. "How populous is the town?"

"About four hundred full time residents," Mrs. Flinton said.

Angling his head at his boss, Zach said, "A private charter arriving and the people on it would be news for a small town." He looked at Mrs. Flinton, "Would reach the ears of your granddaughter and grandson-in-law. Would let them know we're coming and piss them off. Better if we went undercover, at least at first while we get the lay of the land."

"You're right," Tony Rickman said. His jaw muscles flexed. "Alamosa is about an hour and a half drive from Creede. We can fly you into Alamosa and rent you a car there."

"Sounds good," Zach said.

Mr. Rickman turned on his heel. "I'll have my secretary set it up: the flight, the car, the stay at the motel. Hopefully they aren't booked for the weekend."

"I must finish this by the weekend," Clare said through cold lips. All of her was cold. Again. As usual. She'd had eight days to help her first ghost transition . . . on. Then had helped her second in five days. Yes. She'd kept track. Four full days to destroy a ghost-seer-eating ghost. The process of which, the whys and wherefores, the *hows* she knew nothing about.

"Clare, how soon can you leave?" Mr. Rickman asked.

Clare jerked from her dread-filled thoughts. She blinked and shrugged, looked at Zach. "An hour?"

He conveyed negative in a quick flick of his eyes that she thought Mr. Rickman and Mrs. Flinton missed. Since he didn't want to speak up, she trusted him and amended her answer. "Sorry, more like two."

"Right. We'll send a car to pick you up at your place in, say, two and a half hours."

"All right."

Mr. Rickman's hand went to his inside suit jacket pocket and he pulled out a wallet and a platinum credit card, offered it to Zach.

Who put both of his hands on the curved handle of his old-fashioned wooden cane. "Sorry, can't take that."

"It's a business card for you and your expenses," Rickman bit off.

"So it has 'Rickman Security and Investigations' on it," Zach pointed out. "Which the family—what's their names?— would recognize. All the locals might."

"All right." The card went back into wallet and pocket. "The family is—"

"Jessica and Michael Velick," Mrs. Flinton said as she rose, and moved toward them with her walker. Now she appeared calmer, close to her old sprightliness. She angled her head at Tony for a kiss on the cheek. He bent and complied, put an arm around her thin shoulders and squeezed. "We'll handle this," he said in a grim tone, meeting Zach's gaze.

It occurred to Clare that that male look might mean sending out his security force. Zach had told her most of Rickman's employees were ex-military special operations kind of men. She wondered what they thought they could do about a soul-eating ghost. She had no illusions whatsoever that *she* would be on the front line of this battle. She took her tepid coffee and drank it down.

Mrs. Flinton said, "Thank you, Clare. I have full faith that you can . . . destroy this evil revenant."

Great. Clare put her empty cup on the coffee table, stood and kissed the woman's cheek. "I will do my best." She said it quietly, but it was a vow. Zach moved around her and kissed Mrs. Flinton, too. "We'll do our best and we'll save Caden."

"And Creede," Tony Rickman said, putting on his sunglasses. "My take on evil is that it doesn't like to limit itself to one person or one town or one valley, even."

Zach smiled and put his arm around Clare's shoulders. "Clare saves the world." He sounded completely confident she could do it.

She thought she'd be eaten by a ghost.

There's just something about Clare.
Apart from the ghosts…

FROM AWARD-WINNING AUTHOR
ROBIN D. OWENS

GHOST
SEER

A GHOST SEER NOVEL

In Denver, a young woman learns she can see ghosts. And
when the ghost of a Wild West gunman needs her help, she
finds herself getting close to a sexy private investigator.

PRAISE FOR THE NOVELS OF ROBIN D. OWENS

"Engaging…sizzling…almost impossible to put down."
—*The Romance Reader*

"With every book [Owens] amazes and surprises me!"
—*The Best Reviews*

robindowens.com
facebook.com/ProjectParanormalBooks
penguin.com